About the Author

Lexie Winston has been an astronaut, rock star, princess and time traveller. In her dreams. But none of the dreams have lived up to what becoming an author has been like. She gets to live in a world of pure imagination, and her heroines get to do the things she's always wished she could.

When not writing books, Lexie is a mother of two gorgeous teenagers and the wife to a patient and understanding man. They live in Western Australia and are lorded over by a black toy poodle. She loves camping, reading and if her iPad was stolen, her world would explode. (It has the kindle app on.)

And check out my website at lexiewinston.com

The Collectors Division

(Reverse Harem Series)

Guardian

Guardian's Blood

Guardian Ascending

Collectors Division Omnibus

Arbor Vitae Coven

(Paranormal Romance Series)

Candy Conniptions

Dreamy Delights

Fangtastic Fireworks

Neighpalm Industries Collective

(Adult Bully Reverse Harem)

Abandoned Girl

Broken Girl

Tormented Girl

Wanted Girl

Cherished Girl

Superficial Girl - Jacinta's Story

Seductive Sins Collection

(Reverse Harem Series)

Glorious Gluttony

Gangs, Guns, and Glory

Galaxy Circus

(Sci-Fi Reverse Harem Series)

Apprentice

Stagehand

Broken Promises

(Dark Poly Romance Series)

Secrets Kept

WANTED GIRL

LEXIE WINSTON

First published by Neighpalm Publishing in 2021

Wanted Girl: Neighpalm Industries Collective

Mobi : 978-0-6489412-8-6
Print: 978-0-6489412-9-3

Cover design by Infinity Cover Designs
Edited by Inked Imagination

Prologue

Thomas

"Dead! What do you mean dead!?" I'm still trying to catch up on what my friend from the agency is telling me, and I can't help but feel like there's some punchline I'm just not understanding.

"You asked me to look into the PI Declan was using, so when our scanners picked up some police chatter about being called out to the address you gave me, I decided to check it out. Uniforms found him dead, sitting in his chair with his throat slashed. Someone must have snuck up on him from behind without him noticing or putting up a fight since there were no signs of struggle." Jake sounds weary, and I feel a little guilty about adding to his plate, but that quickly disappears because this is Harlow and my family's welfare that's on the line.

My cell starts to ring, and when I look at the screen it's Jaxon. A groan unconsciously escapes my mouth, but I seriously can't help it. It's not that I don't want to talk to my brother… right now, there's obviously just a lot on my mind. For now, I send him to voicemail, so I can keep talking to Jake. Scrubbing a hand across my face, I lean back in my office chair and spin, looking out over the LA skyline.

"Were there any signs of who may have done it?" I ask him, and he grunts.

"No, but it just so happened to be your family's file on his desk when it happened. It looks like it's been rifled through, with bloody prints all over it. The perp must have been wearing gloves because there are no distinctive patterns to the prints, and the blood has been identified as the victim's. I couldn't tell you if anything was missing or not, but it does look like he was looking into your sister's mother and her family. A business card was dropped on the floor, though there's nothing to say whether the PI had gotten the card or if the perp dropped it. It was for a biker bar out east in the town that your sister is from."

"*Not* my sister," I growl a little defensively. Though I probably should be trying to think of her like that, I just can't shake the feeling that I'm making a big mistake by not joining my brothers in the quest to woo her. I roll my eyes at that. *Woo her?* Bloody Jacinta in my head.

My phone rings again, but I reject Jaxon's call once more. He can wait. He's probably just ringing to gloat about what a good time he and Kai are having in Hawaii with Harlow. I know they'd planned on going snorkeling and to the zoo before coming home this afternoon even though they'd had that accident. I wanted to demand they bring her home immediately, but Dad told me to let it go. To let them have one more day before they get back here and Harlow gets a security detail. Not to mention, there's the little fact of them being in *Hawaii*. It's not like I can force my brothers to do anything, regardless of how much more sensible my plan is than theirs.

"Yeah, okay, sorry. Your dad's daughter, then?" he questions, and I grunt my approval. "Look, there is some kind of connection between there and here, but we're missing something. I'm just not sure what it is or how we can put it all together. But once we find that missing link, I have a gut feeling it will all fall into place. It'll just take a little more time since I'm doing this as under the radar as possible." We're not supposed to use government resources for our own gain, and I really don't want to involve the agency with something like this. It's small potatoes compared to the things that they deal with daily, so as frustrated as I am by the situation, I need to let Jake do this in the time he can sneak in.

"Okay, well, keep me in the loop. We're heading to Europe at the end of the week, but I'll be available by phone if needed. Dad and I have some business we need to attend to, and the rest of the family is accompanying us. I'm going to tuck them away somewhere safe that no one knows about while we do it. When we come back, I'll fly to the East Coast and sniff around myself. I'm sure either Jaxon or Oliver can come with me for cover. Both need to check out their businesses over there."

"Will do. Let me know if you need anything, and don't forget to reach out to our operatives in Europe if you need back up. Better to have them step in before someone else gets hurt."

We hang up, and I'm left looking out my window, not really focusing on anything, as I try to process the information. Why would the PI be killed? Unless he was getting too close to whoever is responsible for all this... I need to call Jake back and ask him if he got a copy of whatever was left in the file.

Before I can pick up the phone on my desk, my cell starts to ring once more. Grabbing it, I slam my finger onto the screen.

"What is it, Jaxon? I don't need to hear all the details about your holiday in paradise," I growl at him.

"Tom, it's Harlow. She's been attacked again." Jaxon's words have me stopping mid-rant.

"Is she okay?" I ask carefully, not sure I want to know the answer. The silence on the other end of the line is deafening as I wait for him to respond, my heart practically seizing in my chest.

I'm not sure if I believe in a higher power, but my birth family certainly did. For the first time in over a decade, I say a quick prayer to the big man in the hope that he might listen to a wicked boy's pleas.

Kai

The water is a cool, refreshing relief on my sore muscles as I slip into the water for our snorkeling adventure. Harlow hovered around us for a little while until she got the hang of it, and then she was off, chasing turtles and fish like a natural. She barely startles when a little reef shark darts away. A broad grin tries to stretch around my snorkel as I watch her, but it's a little tricky. When I'm finally reassured she's good, I put my head down and start enjoying the scenery. I've been watching her more than I am the reef, which probably isn't a surprise. I don't really want to stop looking at her at all. She's become some kind of obsession to me, and this trip has only made that fascination grow stronger.

Jaxon's not far from me on my left, but he keeps

stopping to check on our girl too. *Our* girl… Who would have thought? I get a deep feeling of satisfaction at that, and it will be even better once all of my brothers have significantly groveled and we have Thomas on board. He'll be a hard nut to crack, but I have faith that Harlow will eventually break through his defensive shell. If anyone can get through to the loving, devoted partner he can be, it's her.

Even underwater, I hear a motor start up, but I figure it's not the tour boat, so I don't worry too much. As I keep paddling, the noise becomes louder, so I pop my head up to check, my heart skipping a beat when I look for Harlow but can't find her. Doing a circle on the spot, I see her, but she's too far out of the safe area of the tour.

Fuck my life. There's a jet ski heading right toward her.

"Harlow!" I scream as I start to swim toward her, kicking my flippers as fast as I can to propel myself through the water. Her head comes up, and I can see her eyes pop in panic under her mask. She swings around and pulls the pool noodle out from under her belly, waving it around in the hope that the jet ski rider sees her. Unfortunately, it keeps coming because that's just the fucking luck this family has had lately. I kick harder, and my heart practically stops when the jet ski clips her, not bothering to slow down in the slightest. With a muffled shout, she goes under, and the first fissures of a break form in my heart. What am I supposed to do if something happens to her?

The jet ski makes a hard turn and takes off in the opposite direction, but all I can do is keep racing toward where I saw Harlow go down. The driver is covered head to toe in a wetsuit, so I can't even get an idea of what he looks like, and even if I could see his face, my eyes are really all for Harlow right now. As I get to the spot that's practically branded in my brain, I stop, and thankfully she hasn't gone far. I reach down, grab hold of her hair, and yank her to the surface. I'll apologize for that later since I think it's more important that I make sure she's alive.

She comes up spluttering and holding her head which thankfully has only a bump and a small open wound. There's a slight trickle of blood sliding down and around the mask on her face, but it looks like the cold water has already made it slow.

"God, Harlow, are you okay?" Jaxon's already swimming over, and he grabs Harlow's noodle on the way. When he reaches us, he helps me get it under her before the three of us swim back to the tour boat, the two of us supporting her on either side with the noodle helping us keep her afloat. For the first few strokes, her head is lolling a bit, like she can't quite make sure it stays steady and straight.

"Ouch," she eventually whispers. After that, she coughs and splutters some more, but at least some of her initial grogginess has faded. "Yeah, he definitely hit me. If Kai hadn't gotten to me and yanked me up by my hair, I would have been a goner." After that, she seems to struggle to swallow, her face screwing up in pain at the action. "I felt myself black out, but the sting of him grabbing my hair jolted me. I think I swallowed a bit of water though. My throat and lungs are burning, and I'm a little dizzy."

"I can't believe that asshole didn't even stop to check if you were okay. What the fuck did he think he hit? There's no way he didn't see you!" While Jaxon is ranting, I'm studying our girl. I can tell by the look on Harlow's face that she doesn't believe it was an accident any more than I do, but we both keep quiet for now. No need to amp up Jaxon's panic before we get her back to the boat.

When we get back to the boat, the tour operators are all quick to help us back onto the boat. They're almost as panicked as Jaxon, firing off worried questions at us, which I'm sure has as much to do with keeping their jobs as it does for Harlow's well being. Thankfully, they realize pretty quickly that we need more than an interrogation. One of the more helpful guys starts handing the three of us towels while someone else takes care of our snorkeling equipment.

Jaxon and I quickly get rid of our wetsuits before helping Harlow out of hers. Jaxon bundles her up in a large towel, swaddling her like some kind of baby, not that I can blame him, and shuffles her directly into the cabin of the boat. I catch a glimpse of him snuggling her onto a comfy chair before I realize one of the tour guides is still standing next to me. I tear my eyes away from Harlow and my brother to see what he wants. "Would you like us to call for a boat to come get you and return you back to shore?"

I don't even ask the other two what they would like to do; I just want to get us back home. "Yes, that would be great, thanks."

After handing me an ice pack, the guy hurries away. I wrap a towel around my waist before joining Jaxon and Harlow in the cabin, sitting next to her on the chair. "Are you cold, or is this shock?" I ask, realizing there's a persistent tremble in her body. Jaxon gets up to grab the rest of our gear while I do my best impersonation of a space heater, rubbing my hands up and down Harlow's arms. When he gets back, he grabs the hoodie he had on earlier and pulls it over her head, taking care not to jostle her too much.

"Thank you." Her teeth chatter, and she tries to smile at us both, but it's a half-hearted attempt. She's a trooper, that's for damn sure, but there's just no hiding her current discomfort. I hand her the ice pack, realizing that was a stupid decision when her trembling makes her nearly smash it into her head. Okay, I can totally handle this. I'm no expert in taking care of other people, but I can sure as hell hold the ice pack for her. With a gentle pressure, I press it to the bump on her head, feeling myself warm with the grateful smile she gives me in return.

The tour operator returns. "The boat is on its way. Would you like some hot drinks to warm you while you're waiting?" Jaxon and I both shake our heads, but when Harlow goes to do the same, I stop her.

"You need something hot and sweet. It should help with the cold and the shock," I tell her.

With her reluctant agreement, her face screwing up into a little grimace like that's the last thing she wants right now, I send the man away with a request for hot chocolate. Both Jaxon and I huddle in close, hoping to warm her with our own body temp, but I'm not sure we're much help because our skin is just as cold as hers. In the rush of the moment, trying to get her to safety and now being faced with this instinct to just stay within reach of her, neither of us changed into dry clothes.

Before long, he returns with the hot chocolate in a takeout mug. "The wait shouldn't be too much longer. Please let us know if we can do anything else. We've arranged for a medic to be on hand to check you over when the speedboat docks," he informs us before leaving us be. Harlow wraps both hands around the cup before taking a sip, her quiet sigh of pleasure making me feel a little warmth inside. I couldn't keep her safe in the first place, but hopefully this is at least one little decision that can help take care of her now.

"Not too sore on your throat?" I check, a little worried because she said it hurt.

"No, actually, it feels good, soothing," she assures me with a smile, and I feel the first bit of tension leave my body.

On her other side, Jaxon has dug his phone out of our bag and has it up to his ear, probably calling one of our family members to give them the update. I should get mine out too and call James to tell him we're on our way, but instead I sit back in the chair next to Harlow, put my arm around her, and pull her close. It doesn't take much encouragement before she snuggles into me, slowly sipping her drink.

My gaze travels around the room, stopping on Jaxon when I realize he's got that frustrated look on his face. "Who are you calling?" I ask him, and he looks up with a frown.

"Tom, but he's sent me to voicemail twice," he growls before trying once more. He must have luck on the next try because I hear him growl, "Tom, it's Harlow. She's been attacked again."

So Harlow and I aren't the only ones who had thought about it. I feel her stiffen underneath me at his words.

"She's okay, got a lump on her head and swallowed a bit of water. I'll tell you about it when we get home. We're leaving the tour early." Tom must be saying something because Jaxon is quiet again.

"Good, I was going to ask you if you could do

that." Through the window on the side of the cabin, I can see a speedboat pull up next to the larger tour boat, so I stand and pull Harlow to her feet.

"Yeah, okay, I've got to go. I'll let you know when we're in the air."

Jaxon hangs up and grabs all our gear while I keep my arm around Harlow. He leads the way to the side of the boat where there's a little door that opens. The staff have grabbed a line from the smaller speedboat. He chucks our gear on board before jumping on himself.

"Are you going to be okay until we get to the plane? You can have a hot shower after we've taken off, and we can sleep the rest of the way home," I offer to Harlow as Jaxon holds out a hand to help her.

"God, that sounds amazing. Yes, please," she says as she takes his hand. Once she's on the speed-boat and out of the way, I join them, waving off the offers of help.

The three of us get settled on a bench seat, and before long we're back at the marina, where the waiting medic hovers over Harlow the second we all climb off the boat.

"The cut on her head is superficial and has already stopped bleeding. Head wounds always bleed badly, but it will heal fine with no scar. She may have a slight concussion but should be fine to fly. Just rest for a few days, and if headaches persist, see a doctor."

Preliminary medical check-up taken care of, we make our way to our car in the secure parking. On the way, Jaxon stops to speak to the guard at the entry while Harlow and I keep walking, but he catches up before long.

"The guard said nobody came near our car. Should we call the police and report the jet skier?" he suggests as he throws our stuff into the back of the Jeep. I unlock the car and help Harlow up into the backseat.

"No!" she says rather loudly before taking a breath and continuing at a lower volume. "No, I just want to go home, please." The two of us exchange a glance, and I can't help but feel that there's the same emotion in my brother's eyes: helplessness. We couldn't stop this, but like the hot chocolate or just snuggling with her on the chair, if we can at least get her home, we can help her feel a little bit better now. With the jet skier long gone and no way to prove the incident was connected to our car accident, what could the police do? We'd just be prolonging Harlow's discomfort by staying here.

"Of course, let's go home, but we'll need to tell Detective James about both incidents," I warn her.

"Yes, anything," she agrees gratefully. "All I want to do is go home, curl up on the bed next to Holden, and spend a couple of days resting with him. I want to be back to normal when we go to

Europe at the end of the week. I don't want anyone leaving me behind."

"Even if you weren't back to a hundred percent, I don't think that would be a problem. Both Dad and Tom would insist on you coming, I'm sure. If you hadn't noticed, Harlow, we're growing to be a bit attached to you and your safety," Jaxon says wryly as he climbs into the back with her and wraps his arm around her shoulders, gently shifting her body so that she's leaning against him.

"Just get comfortable. The drive won't be long," he tells her as I climb into the driver's seat. Before I get us out of there, I peek into the rearview mirror, selfishly needing just one more glimpse to see that she's okay. Her head is on Jaxon's shoulder, and my brother's got his phone out again, tapping away, probably letting James know to expect us.

He's right; the drive isn't long, and although I'm concentrating on the road and where we're going, I've also got so many other things running through my head. The deal with the Blaze twins, Holden, our upcoming trip to Europe, but mostly Harlow and my worry about what the fuck is going on. I'm hoping Tom might have more of an idea by the time we get back. Hopefully, they got ahold of Declan's PI and he's made some inroads into Harlow's mom's background. I know they were talking about looking into the people around us every day, like drivers, staff at our businesses, and all that, but I feel like this is going to be somehow connected to her instead. Maybe we need to look into Harlow's friends from college? I'm almost a hundred percent sure that Maxine and her family have nothing to do with the stalker, but what about someone in their friend circle? We really need to sit down and talk this through logically. So far we've all been reacting to what's going on, and no one has even bothered to sit down with Harlow and really talk through it.

When that realization hits, I suddenly feel like we're all idiots. Yeah, it makes sense that we wanted to go straight to protecting her, but you don't ignore the most valuable member of any team. Harlow could have the answers even if she doesn't realize it. I'm sure Tom would already have thought of that if he wasn't so thrown off by her being here and what she could potentially mean to all of us.

I pull up to the private part of the Honolulu airfield, parking the car in a spare bay. Jaxon helps Harlow out and walks her across to where the plane is ready for takeoff, meeting Chris at the bottom of the stairs. After a quick conversation, they both climb up while Chris jogs over to me.

"Hey, man, can I give you a hand with the luggage?" he says, reaching for Harlow's bag. Once he has it, he starts walking back to the plane with me a step behind, carefully considering the man in front of me. Both Chris and James have been on the island the whole time we have. The person on the jet ski was fully covered in a wetsuit, and he likely would have had enough time to get back here after he hit Harlow. But what would be his motivation?

"Listen, James had a mechanic go over the plane this morning, just to make sure it hadn't been tampered with while we were at the hotel," Chris says over his shoulder to me. "After Jaxon called us last night, we both got here early this morning to supervise him. Neither of us wants to take any risks with your or our lives. It seems like this stalker can follow you anywhere."

Chris' words have a quiet sigh of relief escaping my mouth before I can help it, and I can feel some of the tension drain out of my shoulders. I hadn't realized I'd prepared myself for a fight until just this moment. So it couldn't have been either of them. Fuck, this is making me think things that I shouldn't have even considered.

I follow Chris up the stairs and stow our luggage in the right place. "Thanks for that. Let's get airborne as soon as possible please," I tell him, slapping him on the shoulder before moving into the cabin and taking a seat. Jaxon already has Harlow settled with a blanket over her lap. I hear Chris close the stairs and feel the cabin pressurize.

"Once we get airborne, take a shower to warm up and get out of your swimsuit, and then you can have a nap," I say to her as I buckle my seatbelt. We're sitting in a group of four chairs that are two sets of two facing each other.

"Shall I grab you some clothes out of your bag?" Jaxon asks as the plane starts to taxi out to the runway.

"Yeah, that would be great, thanks." Harlow is still looking a little pale, but she gives my brother a small smile.

"Are you going to be alright in the shower, or do you need a hand?" I wiggle my eyebrows suggestively in the hope it brings a bigger smile to her face. I'm definitely not pressuring her for any real intimacy, though I don't know if I have the willpower to turn her down if she shows that she's interested in that.

She chuckles, the slight sound making my own smile more genuine this time. "I've got a feeling that the shower isn't going to be big enough for the both of us, but thank you."

I stop wiggling my eyebrows. "All joking aside, I think it would be better if I at least came in so I could keep an eye on you. We're not sure if the bump has had an impact. I'll just come in and stand around to make sure you're okay. I wouldn't want you slipping while in there."

Her smile drops as she nods. "Yeah, you have a point. Okay then."

"Hey, guys, we're about to take off. Weather looks clear between here and LA. We have a meal prepared which will be served as soon as we get to cruising altitude, and then you can all nap until we get home."

Jaxon pulls up a phone in the arm of his chair, replying to James. "Yeah, hey, can you give us an hour before serving the meal? We're all going to take showers and wash off the salt water." After a quick thanks, he hangs up. We're all silent as the plane finishes its taxing and the engines rev for takeoff.

"Thank you both so much for this," Harlow says, suddenly breaking the silence. "Despite the two incidents, I have had an amazing time, and I would love to come back with you one day."

Jaxon grabs her hands and squeezes it as I lean forward and do the same thing to her knee. "It was our pleasure, believe me, and I can't wait until the next time we can do this."

Jaxon echoes my sentiments as the plane starts to hurtle down the runway. Harlow grabs hold of the armrest with her empty hand and clenches hard to Jaxon's in the other.

"Don't worry, Harlow. By the time we get back from Europe, you will be an expert at this."

While I know he's talking about the flying part, the wary part of my brain, the part that still can't shut down the niggling worry for Harlow, takes it in a more sinister light, thinking about how many times she's had to pull herself back together after an attack. Jaxon didn't hurt her, I know this, but someone else is trying their hardest to put her through everything they can. God, I hope Tom figured something out.

Chapter Two

Harlow

My head is throbbing and my body is a mess of aches and pains both inside and out. My lungs and throat are sore from the small bit of water I swallowed before Kai managed to haul me up, and my body is still aching from the car accident. I'm so disappointed that what had been such an amazing trip was ruined by two separate incidents.

Were we delusional in thinking we could do this without the stalker following us? I mean seriously, what do they want with me? Do they want me to go home? Or do they want me to die? What would anyone benefit from me dying? I have nothing. Mom left nothing behind but a bunch of junk, and I can't think of anything I might have done to anyone for them to want me dead.

A hand on my arm startles me, and I realize I must have been drifting. I'm still on the plane, with Jaxon's hand shaking me, and when my eyes meet his, they're heavy with worry. Such a different look to the one of pure loathing he gave me that day I had first arrived in California. Which had also been super different to the one clouded with lust that very first night in the club. There's one thing you can say about Jaxon; he's most certainly not one-dimensional. I've got to say I prefer the lust and the worry to the hatred.

"Come on, honey, let's get you showered and warmed up." He unclips my belt and helps me to my feet. When we get to the bathroom, Kai is already there with the shower running. "I'll leave Kai to help you while I grab you something to wear." He carefully passes me to Kai, and a small smile graces my lips. These two are treating me like I'm made of crystal, and I don't think anyone has ever shown so much care over a few bumps and bruises. I think I need to remind them that I train stunt horses and regularly get banged around. At some point, anyway. Maybe I'll just enjoy the attention for a little bit first?

"No, Harlow, don't laugh at us. I know you're tough and strong and whatever, but you almost died on my watch… *twice*," Kai scolds as Jaxon closes the door behind him. "It was terrifying, and you're going to have to excuse us if we're both a little over-protective for a little while." He's quiet for a moment before he mutters something, almost too low for me to clearly make out the words, but it sounds like, "And just wait until the rest of those assholes get their hands on you."

I've still got the towel wrapped around my waist and Jaxon's hoodie on, so Kai helps me out of both before stripping me of my bikini. He must be concerned because not even my naked body is distracting him from the task of helping me into the shower. A groan leaves my mouth as the hot water hits my cold body, and the sting quickly disappears once I start to warm up. I put my head under the stream of water, letting it cascade down to drown out everything around me. God, that feels good.

A pair of hands on my hips has me jumping slightly before a naked Kai hops in behind me. "Huh, wouldn't have thought there was enough room in here for the two of us." I chuckle as I step back a bit to let him in, a yelp escaping when my body touches the cold walls.

He quickly pulls me closer until my front is flush with his, and he looks down at me, the concern in his eyes now replaced by a sparkle of something that's refreshing and alluring and just so inherently Kai. "Well, I wasn't going to hop in, but you looked so lonely, and what would happen if the hot water made you dizzy and you fell? I thought it was my civic duty to get in and protect you from any more damage."

I grin up at him, sliding my body along his as I

rise up on my toes to kiss him quickly, a rush of, dare I say *love*, flowing through me. I won't look too closely at that just yet though. "My hero, what would I do without you?" I shift to pull away, but he deepens the kiss, his hands sliding down to cup my ass and bring us closer together. His rapidly hardening dick presses between us as my skin prickles with goosebumps from something other than the cold.

He pulls back and leans his forehead against mine, the rushing water making it seem so much more intimate for some reason. Maybe that's all the romance movie industry's programming kicking in. How many times have people dramatically made out in the rain? "God, my heart almost stopped when I saw it hit you and you went under."

His golden brown eyes are filled with worry, and his hold on my ass tightens. "I want this done, Harlow. I want whoever it is that's doing this to pay, and I want our lives to go back to the way they were with the added bonus of having you in them. I want you to be happy here with us, for you to choose to stay, and I want to support you in any choices you make regarding your career."

I shiver for an entirely different reason now. It's not from the building desire or the reminder of what could have happened, but from the pure need I feel in his voice and the fact that I want it too. All of it. I really want to see what will become of us. I know that when knowledge of our poly relationship hits the media, it will make my chances of getting an internship at a world-class zoo practically zero. If my reputation was damaged by a libelous billboard that was barely up for even an hour, it's surely going to take a hit from being in this unconventional relationship.

I hadn't wanted to think about it before because at first all I had was attraction. Intense, melt your panties kind of attraction, but no more than that magnetic pull. But when Oliver and Holden started to let me in, then Kai, and now even Jaxon is making moves to create a connection between us, well, now it's turning into something a whole lot more than just the melted panties. The kind of comments Kai's making, that more than one of these men are making, speak to a desire to establish something concrete, something that isn't just based off of a mutual desire to fuck like rabbits until either of us finds something more intriguing. I had told Declan that I wanted to be with someone who knew for sure that I was what they wanted, and some of these Summers men are going out of their way to show and tell me that I'm the girl in their sights.

Now, I find myself wanting this, almost needing it. It's like my life has been missing something, but these men and this family fill that void. Once upon a time, I never would have considered giving up my dream for someone else, but I don't see this as giving it up. I may just have to put it on hold. I'm sure someone out there will take a chance on me eventually, and as much as I didn't want to use my dad's name, I'm not really as opposed to it now as I was before. Maybe that will help open some doors so that I at least get a chance to prove I can earn my keep. In any case, I'll worry about that once the whole stalker issue has been resolved, which hopefully will be soon. For the moment, I have a beautiful man standing in front of me, and he's just bared a part of his soul that I can't ignore.

"I like the sound of that." The smile he gives me is blinding. He's just leaned in to give me another kiss when the door opens and Jaxon comes back in. The glass surrounding the shower is frosted, but he can obviously see our silhouettes.

"Hey!" he exclaims. "I thought this was about getting Harlow warmed up. If I'd known getting naked with her was an option, I would have offered to stay."

"You snooze, you lose," Kai taunts, and I give him a little shove, but he just holds me tight.

"Next time I almost drown or something happens, you can be the one that helps me shower," I joke back, but the silence that fills the bathroom tells me it falls a little flat. Noticing the way Kai has stiffened ever so slightly, I groan. *Smooth, Harlow. Freak them both out, why don't you?* "Sorry, I didn't mean it."

"I know, Harlow. It's just a little too soon," Jaxon replies. "I'm going to check out what James and Chris have got us to eat. I've left some clothes here for you."

"Hey, what about me?" Kai complains, and I hear Jaxon snort.

"Nope, you're on your own." The door clicks as he exits, and my stomach rumbles at the same time. Kai looks down in shock, and I blush, still feeling that heating of my cheeks despite the warmth of the water.

"I'm starving," I grumble, and he lets go of me to grab the shower gel and sponge.

"Let's get you washed and dried then, so we can feed the monster that is currently residing in your stomach because it sounds ferocious." I can hear the laughter in his voice, but I'm too distracted by his hands all over me to respond. But he doesn't start anything. Like a perfect gentleman, he washes my body, following with my hair. Once done, he leans over and shuts the water off, quickly jumping out and grabbing the towels. He wraps one around me before drying himself off.

Giving me a soft kiss, he opens the door. "I've got to dig out some clothes since Jaxon didn't, so I'll meet you out there." Before I can even respond, he closes the door, leaving me disappointed. I'm really happy that he's got some kind of feelings for me and is taking care of me like that. It's sweet, but damn it, I could have done with a little more sugar in the form of kisses.

Sighing, I step forward and wipe the condensation off the mirror with my hand. My reflection is a little shocking. I'm paler than normal, with a big egg just next to my temple above my right eye. There's a small cut, but it's not bleeding. I guess it probably washed away in the ocean, and now that I think about it, I do remember the medic commenting something about head wounds and blood. The rest of me still aches from the crash, but all in all, I could be worse. I've gotten hurt just as much after a bad fall off one of the horses in the past.

Looking down at the pile of clothes Jaxon left, I realize I don't recognize any of them. Where did these come from? When I grab the t-shirt and shake it out to get a better look, I smile with delight. Jaxon has given me one of his to put on, and since no one is watching... I bring it close to my face, burying my nose in the fabric in the hope that it might smell like him, but all I get is some generic detergent. I'm a little disappointed, but I pull the shirt on anyway. I'm not bothering with underwear, nor does it look like he provided me with any anyway. Sneaky man.

I pick up the next item, expecting it to be a pair of my yoga pants, but it turns out he's feeling a little territorial. I could get used to this. He's given me a pair of his sweatpants as well. I put them on, but they're way too big, so I pull the drawstring as tightly as it goes, wanting to take advantage of this little gesture of his. Like Kai sneaking into the shower with me, I have a feeling Jaxon just wanted to be close to me in some way. I smile at myself in the mirror. Though I look like a little girl playing dress up, I'm fucking comfy. Using my towel, I dry my hair, careful to avoid the lump on my head. My arms get sore from holding them up though, so I throw the towel on the sink, grab a brush and my scrunchie, and head out of the bathroom. They have a sister. One of them can definitely help me deal with this situation.

Out in the cabin, the boys have set a little table up between the four seats. I'm not sure where it came from, but I don't care because there are platters of subs and cans of soda, and my stomach growls once more. I head over to them and squeeze past the table, sitting myself down in Jaxon's lap before passing him my brush and scrunchie.

"My arms are sore. Can you braid my hair for me?" He takes the brush and begins to gently pull it through my hair as Kai snorts.

"How did you know he was the one to ask to do that?" He grabs one of the subs and puts it on a plate in front of him before popping the top of the can of soda.

"Because I know he's a good brother, and I'm sure he learned to do Jacinta's hair at a very young age." Jaxon's hand stills in my hair, and I feel him grow tense underneath me, so I turn and drop a kiss on his cheek before settling back in. Ignoring the growing tension, I reach for a sub of my own.

"Damn, these look amazing." I put one on my

plate as he continues to brush my hair before I feel him start to twist it into a braid. "I'm freaking starving. Even though my throat hurts, I really need to eat."

Once Jaxon finishes, he puts the brush down on the table, but there's still the slightest bit of tension in his body. If I weren't sitting on his lap, I might not notice it, but it's hard for him to hide it with us being so close right now. I reposition my body so I'm now sideways across his lap and wrap my arms around his neck. When his eyes meet mine, they're still a little cloudy with memories, but I place a gentle kiss on his lips. I know that the comment about him helping Jacinta probably brought back memories of why he had to be the one to do it, but I don't want to shy away from parts of who he is. Jaxon is a man, a temperamental, sometimes clever, and altogether too cheeky man, but being a brother is also a huge part of his identity. I don't want him to hide from that fact and the baggage that might accompany it. Hopefully the kiss shows him that. As I try to pull away from him, his arms come up and wrap around me, holding me in place as he swipes his tongue across my lips, asking for entrance. I let him, and although the kiss deepens, he pulls away before it gets too far. When his eyes meet mine again, they're now clear.

"Thank you," I tell him as I get up and sit in my own chair.

"You're welcome." He squeezes my knee and

then switches his focus to the food in front of us while I grab my sub and take a huge bite. When I look up at Kai, he's watching the two of us with warmth. He mouths 'thank you' to me, so he definitely saw Jaxon's reaction to me referencing their childhood.

"Oh my god, these are freaking amazing!" I say around a very unladylike mouthful of food, but I don't care. Fuck me, my tastebuds are singing. "Where did they get these from?"

Kai and Jaxon both chuckle. "Our chef at the hotel would have made them. Our hotels always cater our flights if we're in a city that has them," Jaxon explains, grabbing his own.

"Well, sign me up for that. I had always heard that airline food was horrible." For whatever reason, this earns another round of laughter.

"It is—if you fly commercial. We're just spoiled, and soon you will be as well." We quietly sit and eat as I contemplate his words. I know he was only joking, but I don't think I'll ever get used to this level of wealth. Don't get me wrong, they all work very hard for their money. Even though we were away for a mini vacay, they both worked while we were there. Same as when Declan helped me with the horses. He managed to squeeze in work in the short time we were there. Now that I've peeked into the insides of their lives, I can see that they are nothing like the spoiled playboy manwhores the tabloids have made them out to be. In fact, I wonder when was the last time any of them just kicked back and relaxed.

We're all fairly lost in our own thoughts as we eat, or just so damn hungry that we're unwilling to let talking take up time we could be chewing. Kai gets up to make tea and coffee, but I refuse, my soda being enough for me. While he does that, Jaxon cleans away the crumbs and empty platter because that's all that's left.

"I'm going to grab a quick shower," he tells me once that's done, disappearing into the bathroom.

When Kai comes back with his mug of coffee, he folds the table back into the wall of the plane, handing it off to me while he nudges me to the side and changes the seats into their bed form. With all of our seats laid out, we basically have a double bed. Kai takes his coffee over to the couch that runs along the opposite wall.

I'm debating whether to join him or not when Jaxon comes back out in a fresh set of clothes.

"Do you want me to drop the other side for you, or are you going to sleep there?" Jaxon asks Kai as he grabs pillows and blankets for the two of us.

"No, I'll nap here, just throw me some bedding. I want to do some more research on that hockey team I was looking at on the way over, and I need to make sure those contracts were sent to the brothers." Just like that, he proves the point I was figuring out for myself. Although he looks like an adrenaline junkie with too much money, the reality is so different.

"Okay, but don't forget you were in an accident yesterday too," Jaxon cautions as he hands him the bedding. "Your body needs to recover too."

Kai smiles at his brother, a teasing glint in his eye. "I'll sleep, *Dad*. I promise this won't take long. Why don't you worry about making sure our girl gets a good night's sleep?"

He says this a little suggestively, and I start to hope that Jaxon might make up for Kai's earlier lack of attention. But he helps me into bed then climbs in on his side, pulling the fluffy blanket over the both of us. He gathers me in his arms and spoons me from behind, the two of us fitting together in a way that's perfect—ridiculously comfortable, much too close for my self-control, and utterly safe. I can smell him, that freshly washed scent that makes me want to sink my nose against his skin and just breathe him in. I wiggle a little, trying to get comfortable.

"Sleep, Harlow. There's plenty of time for us to play once you're back to full health," Jaxon whispers in my ear, his breath tickling across it.

I take him at his word, and as the lights in the cabin dim and Kai switches on a lamp above him, I feel my eyes get heavy. With the warmth and comfort of Jaxon behind me, I drift off.

Chapter Three

Harlow

When we get home, we're met at the airport by a very concerned-looking Thomas. While he helps Jaxon and Kai put our gear in the trunk of the big blacked-out SUV, I thank James and Chris, giving them both a kiss and a hug, along with an apology that I hadn't had a chance to catch up with them.

The guys are waiting for me, so after I promise that I'll hang out with them in the cockpit at some point on our Europe flight, I slowly make my way down the steps and head for the backseat. Thomas has had his hand on his gun, eyes darting back and forth, on alert the entire time. Before I can get in, he stops me with a hand on the arm. "I'm really glad you're all okay."

Things are still a little strained between me and

Thomas. I'd really like to get to know him better, and god knows his brothers want me to give him a shot, but he keeps this wall up around himself at all times. The only time I've ever seen him let it down was that day when I first arrived and they were skeet shooting off the patio. Since then, he's had his emotions locked down tight. Even now, it kind of feels like he's saying it because it's the right thing to do. But maybe, just maybe, his tight grip on my arm might be saying something all on its own.

"Thank you, so am I," I reply lightly before climbing into the car while he gets settled behind the wheel.

"What's with the personal chauffeur?" Jaxon jokes from the passenger seat. Kai quickly claimed the back with me, jokingly telling Jaxon that he'd gotten to hog me on the plane. "I thought Dad would send the limo."

I can see Thomas frowning in the rearview mirror. "I called Dad and let him know what happened as soon as you told me, and he decided that we wouldn't be trusting anyone but family members and Hope until after this stalker situation has been resolved." Thomas' voice is rumbly and tinged with that elusive accent as he navigates his way out into the traffic leaving the airport. That, if nothing else, tells me he's definitely unsettled.

"That sounds fair," Kai says from next to me, reaching out to take hold of my hand. "Has there been any movement on the case? Has anyone been able to track down Declan's PI? What about you, Thomas? Have you been able to make any progress on this?" Kai sounds as frustrated as I feel about the whole situation.

Thomas glares at Kai in the rearview mirror while Jaxon waves a hand at him. "Stop it with the 007 shit. We told her about your side gig. It's not like we could have hidden it forever now that she's a part of the family." He twists around to look at me, his face solemn. "Even if she goes back to the East Coast eventually, she'll still be a part of this family, and we all know that secrets are what break us apart, not hold us together."

He's not wrong. Most of our problems would have been avoided if Mom had told Dad about me in the first place. But then again, I would have grown up with these guys as my brothers, and I would have missed out on whatever it is we're building here.

I watch Thomas in the mirror, noting the way his eyes soften slightly as he concentrates on the road in front of us. "Yes, I guess you're right. There have been some developments, and I know that all you probably want to do is go to bed and forget about today, but I'm afraid Dad has called a family meeting. We need to bring each other up to speed. Like you said, no more secrets."

"We napped on the plane, so I'm good for a little while." Jaxon mumbles something, agreeing with Kai's statement.

"What about you, Harlow? How are you feel-ing? Dad wants to know if you want to see a doctor? He'll get one to come out to the house and look you over. We've just got to call him and let him know." Traffic is getting heavier the farther we drive from the airport, so Thomas' eyes stay fixed on the road, but there's something calming about that voice of his.

"Damn, should have brought the heli," Kai complains as the car starts to crawl.

"We used it for the office this morning, so the others are using it to return home. Harlow?" he prompts after answering Kai.

"I'm okay. Nothing is broken, and the bump on my head isn't bad. It was probably more shocking that I went under than anything else. Kai got to me before I breathed in too much water. And I think I can manage another meeting. I may need Mrs. Hayton to make me a coffee, but I'll be fine." This time, he does take his eyes off the road briefly, but after an assessing gaze at me—damn, I feel like he's seeing everything about me right now—he doesn't push it.

"Mrs. Hayton has gone home to visit her sister in Germany. I'm afraid we're a self-sufficient house-hold at the moment, but somehow I don't think that will bother you at all." *Right, I completely forgot about that.*

"Did Josh and the horses get to the East Coast

okay?" I ask him, remembering the other things that were going to happen.

"Yup, they're all settled in with Melinda and Chuck, and Josh and Chuck get along famously." Relief flows through me at that, but it's followed up by a hit of guilt.

"Fuck, I've been so distracted this weekend that I never called Jacinta to see how Prada and Coco are doing."

"Don't worry about it, Harlow. I don't think she's upset at all. You saved Prada. Seriously, Jacinta thinks you walk on water now. She's even been complaining about the boys monopolizing your time and how it will be her turn when you get back. You probably need to prepare yourself for living out all of the sister moments she never got to have."

Thomas is laughing, and the other two quickly echo it. I feel my cheeks heat, but I don't know if it's because of the words or the fact that his chuckle is deep and hearing it does things to my lady parts. *Damn it, you can't be happy with the brothers you've got? You've got to play Pokémon and collect them all.*

I shake the lust away. "Well, I guess that's got to be better than being on her bad side." They laugh even harder at that.

"Don't be so sure. She'll be all up in your life now, interfering and sticking her nose in, and you won't be able to get rid of her," Jaxon says affectionately, if not a little exasperatedly.

"Yup, you've been warned," Kai adds in.

"When we were in college and lived on our own, Jacinta and Jaxon would come and stay occasionally. We threw a big party one night, but Jacinta was as territorial back then as she is now, and, well, there was this girl I really liked... She had a few drinks, got naked, and climbed into my bed, which normally I'd be pretty stoked about. Unfortunately, Jacinta had been doing rounds of our bedrooms to make sure that they weren't being used for hook-ups."

Jaxon chuckles. "Yeah, she thought that was the grossest thing ever. Someone else having sex in your bed."

"Eww, she's not wrong," I add in.

"Anyway, she grabbed this girl by the ear and dragged her downstairs, still naked, and tossed her out the door with her clothes behind her, shouting that I wasn't so desperate I needed naked chicks throwing themselves at me. The girl never spoke to me again, but I figured if Jacinta was enough to scare her off, she wouldn't survive our family." His eyes burn with affection when he looks at me. "Unlike you, who not only stood up to her, but flipped her upside down. It was amazing."

The rest of the trip home is quiet and relatively uneventful. The guys talk a little about random things, but nothing that I care to be involved in, so I just watch the scenery go by. As we pull into the road that our estate is on, I try to get a look at the abandoned mansion across the road, but with the sun dipping below the trees, it's already shrouded in shadows. Even with that barest of peeks, my brain is already hooked and whirling. Stalker be damned, I need to ask Dad for Emma's number so I can organize a time to see inside. I'll take an entire battalion of bodyguards if it means I can have this little adventure for myself.

I huff out a breath of frustration and have turned back to face the front when I see Jaxon looking at me over his shoulder. He's got a smile a mile wide.

"What are you laughing at?" I ask a little shortly, and he shakes his head.

"Nothing, really. I just think it's cute how much that house fascinates you. You know, when I had some spare time over the weekend, I did some research and found a couple more abandoned places that I thought you might like to explore while you're here." A little frown appears between his eyes. "That's if you'd want to spend the day with me sometime." He sounds a little unsure, so unlike the confident, assertive man I know him to be.

I keep getting glimpses of vulnerable Jaxon, which is almost as appealing as his other side, but it's still sad to know that it stems from the same kind of upbringing as mine. I know he was young when he came to live with the Summers, but that just shows that sometimes those early experiences create the deepest wounds. Children aren't meant to carry the weight of trauma, and I'm not surprised these marks have been left within him. So much like the ones that I hide from the world too.

But if there's one thing I can't do, it's let my reactions to him be overwhelmed by the sympathy or the empathy that I feel. I like a good cuddle and some comforting words as much as the next person, but I don't want to be defined by my trauma or treated with kid gloves. He needs to know and feel that I see him as someone worthy of spending time with, someone who's attractive, exciting, and whole —despite the pieces of himself that someone else tried to break or take away—and that's what I'm going to focus on right now.

My heart races at his words, thrilled that he went out of his way to find something I might be interested in doing. "Wow, yeah, that would be awesome! Thanks, Jaxon. What did you find?"

The frown disappears, and his face lights up with that cocky grin I definitely do recognize. "Now, I can't be telling you all my secrets. A man has to keep some things a mystery," he teases as Thomas pulls the car into the open garage.

We're all getting out of the car when the door connecting the garage to the house flies open. "You're finally home. I've been waiting for ages!" Jacinta's voice echoes through the large space as she comes barreling toward me, completely bypassing her brothers, including Jaxon.

I don't get a chance to brace myself before she flings her arms around me. I stumble backward, lucky enough that Jaxon is able to catch us, and find myself sandwiched between the twins.

"What the fuck, Harlow? It's like you don't want to be in this family. One might think you're almost *trying* to do anything you can to escape," Jacinta growls at me as she pulls away and puts a hand up to the bump on my head. "Stop it. It's enough. You're stuck with us now. You can run, but we will be able to find you wherever you go." Her whole demeanor is full of concern, and it's almost enough to concern *me*. God, the guys weren't kidding when they said Jacinta was all in now.

Jaxon chuckles from behind me, the sound sending a delicious little rumble through the parts of me that are pressed all too closely against him. "Whoa there, Jazzy. That's sounding a little stalkerish."

"Yeah, you just need the Irish accent and the whole 'I will find you, and I will kill you' thing, and you'd be pretty bloody scary, sis." Kai squeezes past us, carrying some of the bags, and Thomas follows quickly behind with the rest.

Jazzy? Thomas has a point, but I'm still stuck on that little name drop. That's the first time I'm hearing that nickname, and I raise a questioning brow at the new sister of mine who's currently all up in my face. Jacinta shrugs, looking a little sheepish. "Jazzy is what the family calls me in private, but it's not anything I like sharing with the rest of the world. Can you imagine what it would be like, trying to get people to take *Jazzy* seriously? But, well, now that you and I are besties and are going to be sisters for real, I gave them the go ahead to call me it again."

Well, that's a bit sweet and awfully thorough of her. I suppose if someone would go through the trouble of concealing a nickname from their supposed enemy, it'd be Jacinta. I don't know whether to be impressed or frightened by the depth of her strategizing. I can't even begin to process any of that, so I let it go and accept that I really am part of the family now if I'm being allowed this coveted nickname.

Jacinta lets me go and flips Kai off before yanking me out of Jaxon's arms. "Go away, Jax. You've had all weekend, so it's my turn. She didn't even call me, and I'm feeling neglected." She tucks her arm under mine, and we follow the guys into the house, my new bestie/sister/abductor practically dragging me along.

Huh, this is a whole new side of Jacinta that I'm seeing, the fun, slightly needy sister that the brothers have repeatedly told me she can be.

"I cannot fucking believe Cecelia pulled that stunt on you. We need to come up with a way of making that bitch pay."

And there it is. Phew, for a moment I thought she had been replaced by a changeling or a pod person or something.

"I can't understand why Dad keeps that woman

around. I can't wait to see what excuse she has this time. Thank god she won't be allowed to just come and go from here whenever she pleases anymore!"

I can't get a word in edgewise as Jacinta continues her rant, but I'm okay with that. I don't have the same kind of history with Cecelia that the siblings do, but I guess our couple of interactions really haven't gone well. I think back to her threatening me before the premiere and then my retaliation at the hospital, which she obviously volleyed back with the luggage fiasco. I can't imagine what perceived insult or offense I have done to her, but I can't believe she thought I would just roll over and take it.

The current state of silence makes me realize Jacinta has stopped talking, seemingly expecting an answer from me to something I've obviously missed.

"Huh?"

Jacinta huffs in frustration. "Were you not listening to what I said?"

"Ah, no?" I wait for the explosion, but her eyes soften with sympathy.

"Of course not. You were attacked again and gravely injured." I roll my eyes at her dramatics. "You're probably not feeling up to planning revenge right now. We'll have a solid day tomorrow to work out our best action," she says as she leads me into the formal dining room. I haven't been back in here since our horrifying meal on that first day, and the noise is what draws my attention first. Everyone is here, and they're busy welcoming Kai and Jaxon back home when they all catch sight of me.

"Harlow!" A chorus of voices greets me, and my head pounds, causing me to wince as they swarm toward me. Jacinta automatically steps in front of me, guard dog sister powers fully activated.

"Stop it, all of you. Have you forgotten she almost died a few hours ago? Give her some space." A small chuckle leaves my mouth, but it seems to do the job since everyone but Dad backs off. He gently but surely moves his other daughter out of the way after quickly whispering in her ear, though not so quietly that I can't hear it.

"I'm so proud of you for looking out for your sister like that. It's great to see it."

Jacinta flushes with pleasure and moves aside for Dad, but she doesn't leave more than a few steps between us.

My eyes prickle with tears and a lump the size of a melon appears in my throat as my dad gathers me into his arms. His hug is this solid wall of reassurance that finally breaks my emotional dams, and I start to quietly sob into his shirt.

"Harlow, god... Over the years, I have spent many sleepless nights worrying about my children, but I think you are going to be the worst of them." I can hear the humor behind the words, but that doesn't help. I just start to shake with everything pouring out of me at once—shock, exhaustion, frustration, disappointment. How in the world is it possible to feel all of these things at once? "My girl, my sweet girl, I'm so sorry this is happening. I don't know if we're the cause or if this psycho followed you from home, but I promise we are going to do everything we can to protect you." Dad's vow to me is fierce, and I don't doubt its truth.

Finally, the quiet murmurs behind him have me trying to push everything back down. A hand with a tissue comes into view as Dad steps back, then Nana takes his place.

"Here, my darling. Wipe your tears and come join the meeting of minds." Nana gives me a quick kiss on the cheek, and I'm grateful that she doesn't push for more. I think if she did, that would be my complete undoing. Emotional overload and useless for the rest of the night.

She shows me to a seat in between Oliver and Holden. Neither of them say anything, but the moment I sit down, warm, comforting hands grip my legs on either side. It's just what I need to pull myself together. I wait, expecting Dad to lead the meeting, but it's Thomas who clears his throat and starts us off.

"I think everyone is aware that Harlow wasn't as safe in Hawaii as we thought she was going to be. After speaking with the police there, we've confirmed that the car situation was no accident. The brake lines had been cut, not all the way through but enough for the brake fluid to leak out. By the time you got back to the hotel, it was gone, causing your brakes to fail." No one looks surprised at the information. "And as for the jet ski, although we don't know for sure, we are going to assume the accident was another attack. Thankfully, not as successful as they'd hoped if they were trying to get rid of her. I know it scared all of us though, so if that was their intent, they succeeded. It could have been a fatal situation just as easily, so we have no way of knowing."

"But to what end?" Declan growls, his frustration obvious. "What do they hope to achieve? With both the car accident and the jet ski, she could've died. How does this person benefit from her death? Not to mention, that car accident could've taken Kai, Jaxon, or both with her. Is that a sign that they've just been warming up by targeting Harlow?"

Clearing his throat, Thomas captures our attention again. "At this stage, we still don't know, but I do have a development which I haven't shared with any of you yet. I was going to, but then Jaxon called, and I got busy making arrangements for Harlow's security. In the end, I knew we'd have a family meeting so I could tell you all at once."

"Well, don't leave us hanging boy," Poppy demands. "Get on with it."

"Declan asked me to investigate his PI. He hasn't been able to get a hold of him since he tasked him to look deeper into Harlow's family. We've all been a bit... distracted lately, which is the only excuse I can give for not pushing this to happen sooner. I'm sorry for that, but at least I know something now." He pauses and takes a sip of the water in front of him, leaving us all hanging. I can hear Declan practically growling across the table, and Oliver snorts quietly next to me.

"My friend at the agency, Jake, called me. Turns out the PI was found dead, his throat slashed. The file he was looking through was missing all the papers inside, and, of course, that file was labeled Summers. It looks like he might have been going in the right direction, but someone wasn't too happy about it. I may be able to dig up more based on any contents of the office or the file, but it'll take time for Jake to trickle that information to me."

The table erupts into noise as everyone tries to talk over one another, but my stomach just sinks. Another death that I'm semi-responsible for. It wasn't enough for me to feel guilty about my mom's death; now I have another to feel guilty about too. I look to Holden next to me and thank a higher power that he's still with us. Whoever is doing this is obviously not afraid to kill. How many more people are going to die before this is over?

Oliver

My family erupts into chatter at Thomas' announcement, and Harlow's body stiffens under my hand. My eyes meet Holden's on the other side of her, and he gives me a slight nod; he can feel it too. If I'm guessing correctly, Harlow is going to feel guilty about what has happened, but she really has no need to. She didn't hold the knife that killed the PI, and she is most certainly not responsible for the one that did. She's just someone who feels a little too deeply, and unfortunately, those deep feelings tend to take her in the direction of assuming responsibility for others' decisions.

Dad manages to quiet everyone. "Look, in light of the situation, I have put off the trip to Europe. It will give both Holden and Harlow enough time to recover further from their incidents and allow Thomas to lay down some smoke screens regarding where we're going. Only the people at this table and Hope will know the exact whereabouts of our accommodations when we go away. I'm asking all of you to not go anywhere alone, and as of today, you have a bodyguard, Harlow."

Up until that last sentence, Harlow had been looking agreeable, but the bodyguard proclamation makes her stiffen even more.

"What? No way. I don't want some stranger following me around all the time. How safe will that be? We won't know whether they could be bribed, or they may already be a plant, or the stalker themselves," she bursts out, sounding disgruntled, but Dad holds up his hand.

"I thought you'd feel that way, so while the house and the rest of us will be guarded by the company I hired, Tom is taking a leave of absence as CEO of Neighpalm Airlines, and I'll be stepping in to help out. Because he has the appropriate training, he will be the one to shadow you."

Her mouth drops open in horror. "Fuck no," she whispers, but I don't think she meant for the words to slip out. She's got that look on her face that people get when they admit something awkward. Tom's eyes harden at her reaction, and his mouth pulls into a straight line. It's the resting bitch face that he's perfected so well, mind you, Jacinta calls it his resting cunt face. He only turns that on when people are hurting his feelings, making unwanted advances, or he's on the scent of a great business deal.

"I can assure you, I am perfectly capable of protecting you." She does a double take and starts waving her hand in panic.

"That's not what I was worried about. I don't want you getting hurt if he decides to take another shot at us or something," she says, scrambling to explain herself.

I watch Nana try to hide a small smile, but she sees me smirking at her and gives me a wink. Oh, I bet it was her idea or she at least pushed the brainstorming in that direction. The meddling woman, getting the two of them to spend so much time together. She's an evil genius, not to mention he is perfect for the job.

Tom's frown smooths out when he realizes that Harlow was worried for his safety. In fact, you wouldn't know it if you didn't know him as well as I do, but I'd say he looks kind of pleased even though he's desperately trying to hide it.

"Harlow, do this for us," Dad cajoles her. "Tom is aware of the danger. Although he doesn't use it on a day-to-day basis, he is well trained to be able to deal with anything that arises."

She throws her hands up in defeat. "Fine, but how about a compromise? I really don't plan on going anywhere. I'm kind of glad that the trip to Europe got pushed back. I feel like I haven't stopped since I got here. Spending some time just getting to know you guys will be awesome. That's why I came here after all. It's not about trips to Hawaii or Europe; it's about family." My whole family practically melts into puddles of goo at her words, and I'm feeling my own warm fuzzies too. Seriously, Harlow has made their year with that one comment alone. "How about if Thomas just comes with me if I leave the house? I'll let him know with plenty of advance warning. That way his life doesn't have to be put completely on hold for me. I'm sure he's got things he'd rather be doing than hanging out with me twenty-four-seven."

Dad and Poppy are frowning, but Tom nods. "Fine, but that means you can't even go over to the stables without me. I'll leave you be at home, but the minute you want to step out that door, I need to be notified."

She screws her nose up at that, so I guess she thought that she'd still be able to visit Prada and Coco or go for a walk. The meeting winds down after that, with the rest of us surrendering to whatever security measures Dad wants to put in place. We know the value of having it since we've lived through threats before. Security was pretty tight for a while after Jax and Jazzy's mom broke in, so we're not likely to really argue with him anytime soon.

The meeting officially breaks up, and while no one leaves, a couple of individual conversations start up. Harlow turns to look at Holden as she takes my hand off her thigh and holds it in hers. "You are looking so much better than when I last saw you," she tells him, and I can't tear my eyes away from the bright smile that transforms his face for only a moment. It drops all too soon, his response to her telling me exactly why.

"I wish I could say the same for you."

Holden has spent the last few days taking it easy. His arm is still in a sling, of course, but his aches and pains ease more and more every day. He's been using the hot tub a few times a day, and it's really helped. Plus, it's done wonders to give us some more time to reconnect and get closer to one another again. Tomorrow, I'll be heading into the office for the first time. The thought of leaving him has been hard to stomach, but now that I know Harlow will be here to keep him company, I think I can do it without having a panic attack in the process.

"Ouch, man, that's a bit harsh," I tease him, leaning in to whisper in her ear. "I think she's as beautiful as ever."

She doesn't get a chance to respond because Kai and Jaxon interrupt to say goodnight to her. She stands up and hugs them both, giving each a lingering kiss on the cheek and thanking them for such an amazing weekend. Her cheeks blush a pretty pink when they tell her that it was their plea-sure, and I start to feel even happier.

The last few days have been amazing. Holden

and I have reconnected on a level that I never would have dreamed we ever would again. We talked and cuddled and just indulged in spending time with one another. The relief I feel from giving myself permission to love him again is immense. For years, we had been comfortable around one another but not to the level the rest of our family was. Never were we ever going to have the kind of relationship that I have with the others. They are family, but he is my lover. I once thought he would be my only love, that I was doomed to live out the rest of my life without the kind of connection we once shared. Yes, we were teenagers, and yes, we needed to grow and mature, but I now hope that that immature love will develop into something deep and forever.

While we worked on ourselves, we also talked about what we can do to make Harlow realize the six of us are what she needs. Jax and Kai's goodbyes to Harlow imply my brothers made good headway on wooing our girl over the weekend. Even Jax, who Jacinta declared to be in last place, must have made some progress. Now Den and I have to just make sure that we stay somewhat in the lead.

The two of them disappear, probably heading off to their rooms. Tom has already retreated, and I overhear Nana, Poppy, Jacinta, and Dad discussing Jacinta's arm of the business. Tomorrow, she's going back full-time, but all I can make out are snippets about future plans and easing back into the swing of things. Which leaves only Declan, still seated and watching us from across the table. As she continues to ask Holden about his recovery, my oldest brother gets up and stalks around to her side of the table. The man who usually holds everything so close to his chest steps up to her chair, a look on his face that I'm not really certain I've ever seen before. He has her attention now, dropping the hand that was in mine. She smiles carefully at him, not quite sure what he is doing, and I'm not entirely certain that he knows either. He doesn't say anything, and it looks to me like he's warring with himself. I hide the smile that wants to cross my lips because my big brother is always so steady and sure. It's actually kind of nice to see him ruffled, and lord only knows Harlow has kept him ruffled from day one.

"Hi, Declan. How are Princess and the kittens doing?" Damn, that is an arrow straight to his heart. He grabs her by the arm, and I jump up, ready to stop him from manhandling her, but he very gently encourages her to stand. Stepping into her body, he brings his arms around her, ignoring that everyone has stopped to watch him. Nana and Jacinta are grinning with glee.

Without any hesitation now, he places a gentle kiss on her lips before stepping away. "Welcome home, Harlow." He turns and walks away, leaving Harlow speechless, her eyes studying him in a way that promises they'll be following up on that in some way later.

"Well, shit. Big brother's got game." Holden chuckles next to us, and I give him a fist bump. Once Harlow comes to her senses, she smacks our hands down.

"Did he just…? What was that?" Harlow, still standing, looks shell shocked. The others stand up, drawing my eyes over to them, their conversation appearing to be finished.

"Well, if you don't know what that was, he's obviously not doing it right." Nana walks over to Harlow. "Come on, dear, let's get you some painkillers to help ease the aches and then maybe a hot chocolate to help you to sleep. I think an early night is probably much needed for all of us. Too much excitement over the last few days has got us all on edge."

"Actually, Nana, that sounds awesome. I'll make them," Jacinta volunteers.

"No!" Harlow jumps when the rest of us enthusiastically respond to Jacinta's offer.

"No, let me do it, and we can just pretend you did," Dad adds in, wrapping his arm around her shoulder and leading her out to the kitchen. Nana and Poppy follow, talking quietly, while Harlow looks between me and Holden, raising a questioning eyebrow.

"Jacinta is a *horrible* cook and has been known to burn milk in the microwave," Holden explains, getting up to offer her his good arm before escorting her into the living area. I leave them sitting on the sofa and make my way to the kitchen. Nana and Poppy are nowhere in sight, so I'm assuming they've gone to their own wing for some peace and quiet. Dad and Jacinta are talking quietly.

"It's a three-month contract, Jazzy," Dad says as he pulls some mugs out of the cupboard while she grabs the milk from the fridge. "If you don't like them by the end of that timeframe, you can get rid of them. Both, one, or neither, it's all up to you, but give them a chance. Having a little healthy competition might help with your creativity. But when it comes down to it, you're still the CEO of the company and their boss."

I know Jacinta has been worrying about her return to work this week. Every time I've seen her over the weekend, she's either been muttering to herself or has her sketchbook in hand, pencil moving furiously across the pages. I've been a little worried about her, hoping that maybe Harlow can have a chat with her now that the two of them are getting along better. Because I swear, even though we are still adults, Jazzy is always going to be my little sister, and all I want to do is punch whoever is upsetting her. Last time I checked, HR frowns upon that sort of thing.

She was briefly distracted when she had heard about the stunt that Cecelia had pulled. My gaze goes from my sister to my dad as I think about his PA. Why on earth does he keep that woman around? I think us telling him how we felt before the others flew to Hawaii went a long way in making him see how bad the situation with her has gotten, but no immediate steps have been made to get rid of her.

I'm shaken out of my thoughts as Jacinta heads to the microwave carrying two mugs, but Dad heads her off. "Stop it, Dad. I can do this."

He takes the mugs out of her hands, places them in the microwave, and closes the door. "I know you can, sweetheart, but we all know that your talents lie in fashion and not food. Just go see how Harlow is and let me do this. Grab her that tylenol so Nana doesn't have to. After all their worrying, you know your grandparents could use some rest too." She huffs, stomping out of the kitchen without an argument, though she does flip me off on the way past when I unsuccessfully try to smother my smile.

He sets the timer and presses start before turning to face me, leaning back on the bench. Dressed in jeans and a casual shirt, my dad looks young enough to be our older brother, with only a tinge of gray in his blond hair. I can understand what a young woman may see in him.

He crosses his arms and stares me down before a smile breaks out over his face. "I'm really happy to see that you and Holden are working things out. It's nice to see something going right at the moment." He runs a hand through his hair, something he's always done when he's frustrated. "What does this asshole want, Oli? How are we going to keep Harlow safe when we don't know that?"

I can see the torment in Dad's eyes, but I think it's time for some hard truths. Jaxon had called me while Kai and Harlow were checking out the new surfers he's been looking to sponsor, and he told me about their theories of Cecelia holding something over his head. What other reason could the brilliant businessman have for keeping such a horrid woman on his staff... unless he was sleeping with her. A shudder wracks my body at the thought. Although she's tried it on with all of us, there's just something about her. Something predatory, but not in a good way, like a black widow, ready-to-devour kind of way. But from the look on his face when we suggested that option, I think he's telling the truth about not sleeping with her. So what could it be?

"Dad, is Cecelia blackmailing you?"

The frustration turns to panic as my dad's whole body stiffens. "Why would you think that?" He avoids the question with a question of his own, and then the microwave beeps, giving him an excuse to turn away from me. I grab the other two from the bench and put them in while he grabs the chocolate powder and mixes it into the first two mugs, avoiding looking at me.

Huh, that's not like Dad at all. The one thing I admire about him the most is he always looks you in the eye no matter what he has to tell you. It was one of the reasons Holden and I started to trust him.

"Dad," I push, and he sighs, his shoulders sort of hunching in. When he turns to look at me, he's devastated. Devastated in a way that I have never seen before, not even when Holden was shot. Holy fuck, were we right?

"Can you give me a week? Give me a week to sort a few things out, and then I will tell you all everything. I need you to keep this between you and me for the moment. Can you do that for me? I'd appreciate it." With that, he takes the two mugs of hot chocolate out to the girls, leaving me reeling. The sound of the microwave echoes through the silent kitchen, only the pounding of my heart giving it some competition.

Fuck. I have to keep this a secret from everyone, even Holden and Harlow? God, I hope Dad gets this shit figured out so they'll forgive me.

Chapter Five

Harlow

Dad brings out our hot chocolate, Oliver following not far behind, but instead of joining us on the couch, he says he's going to take his up to his room. There's an obvious tension between them that doesn't do much to calm the lingering nerves that I'm dealing with. Oliver gives both Holden and me a kiss on the cheek then quickly disappears without a backward glance.

"Is everything okay?" Jacinta pries, not willing to leave the awkwardness alone.

Dad sighs. "It will be." He also gives me and Jacinta a kiss on the cheek and Holden a squeeze on the good shoulder before he leaves too.

"Huh. I wonder what that was about?" She merely looks curious, but Holden is wearing a look that mirrors how I feel, his brow creased with worry.

"Do you think it has to do with us?" He's voicing exactly what I'm thinking, though I don't know if that's a comfort or not. If more than one person is thinking it, doesn't that somehow make it feel all the more valid?

"God no." Jacinta waves her hand. "Dad has always been supportive of you two, even when there wasn't a 'you two.' Not to mention he's keeping an open mind about Harlow and you guys too. Seriously, Dad is amazing when it comes to all of us. It's got to be about something else."

We fall into a contemplative silence as the three of us drink our hot chocolate. My mind races, thinking about what could be wrong between Dad and Oliver.

"Back to work tomorrow, Jazzy? I bet you're looking forward to that." Holden breaks the silence, and I'm grateful for it because my mind was stuck. What if he was lying when he told me he was okay with all of this? It wouldn't be the first time a parent lied to me, but I just don't want to disappoint him or taint the relationship between us.

Jacinta chews on her lip, and a little line appears between her eyes. "I'm excited about going back to work, but I'm nervous about the new designers." She looks at me, and instead of even a hint of the ice princess that she was when we first met, there's a softness in her eyes, a vulnerability that makes her seem much more approachable and dare I say more delicate than she ever has. "You know them. Shit, you helped pick them. What are they like?"

I think carefully before I answer. She's trusting me, so I'm going to be honest rather than taking what could be a chance to mess with her a bit. "Both are extremely talented, and Jace is awesome. He's going to be living with Shane and Alex for the duration of his contract and then reassess if you decide to keep him on." Her frown disappears at the mention of Shane and Alex, and I see the interest lighting up her eyes. I smother a smile but make a note to manipulate some interaction between Jacinta and my new friends. Something that doesn't involve her being their boss or them needing to impress her. "They all seem to get on like a house on fire—actually more like a raging wildfire—but that's not going to affect him at work." She looks a little confused for a moment, but Holden gets it right away if his snort is any indication. Her eyebrows jump in surprise when she finally gets what I'm alluding to, but that interest is still there.

"I'm looking forward to meeting him. Nana showed me his portfolio, and his designs are divine. I want to plan an evening dress line since we haven't done one in a while. Maybe a separate line that only does elegant ball gowns." She's so excited about the idea that she's practically bouncing on the sofa, and I really like seeing this side of Jacinta.

She's so enthusiastic she reminds me of Max. I can now see how the two of them were friends years ago. Knowing her history now, I completely understand that ice princess defense mechanism. I wish I hadn't had to find out firsthand how she lashes out when unsure, but I also get why she did what she did.

Holden smiles at her indulgently, making it all the more clear just how much her brothers love her. But then he turns to me, narrowing his eyes. "What about the other designer, the female one who actually turned up the next day and started work? Nana said something about it while you were away. That she was eager to learn everything she could."

Fucking hell, Holden. I shoot him a death stare, but he smirks, not intimidated in the least. I had told him and Oliver how I was sure that Jacinta and Rowena were going to clash. I was hoping she would stay distracted with Jace so I could skip over Rowena.

Jacinta must see the look I give Holden because she stops bouncing. "Harlow," she purrs dangerously, "what aren't you telling me?"

"Well, would you look at the time?" I make a show of looking at my bare wrist before getting up. "Looks like it's time for bed. My head is *really* starting to pound again." I'm hoping bringing up my injury is enough to distract her, but her vise grip over my invisible watch keeps me right where I am.

"Harlow," she growls.

A big sigh of defeat wooshes out of me. I know I'm going to have to face the music, so I sit back down. "To be honest, I thought she was talented but a stuck-up bitch. She's trained through some exclusive design school, and her designs are beautiful, but the girl just rubbed me the wrong way. I also think part of the reason Nana hired her was to keep you on your toes, but I have this gut feeling that she's going to cause problems. I already overheard your assistant and her talking smack while Hope and I were there. Like, what the hell is up with that? I swear Hope and Lindy almost came to blows." Jacinta rolls her eyes, and Holden just snorts again in amusement. Damn man.

"Please, those bitches won't know what hit them. I'm not worried in the least. They better watch their backs *and* their jobs. As my assistant, Lindy has been lulled into a false sense of security about her worth to me and the company. She's been getting a little too big for her boots." She releases the hold on my hand and smiles at me, giving off a slightly serial killer kind of vibe. "I do love a challenge." She stands up, giving Holden and I both kisses on the cheeks. "Right, I'm going to order some Chinese to be delivered and curl up in our wing to read a book. Do you want me to get you guys anything?"

My stomach rumbles once more, and both Jacinta and Holden's eyebrows jump at the sound.

"I would go with yes." Holden chuckles as he

gets to his feet. The sweatpants he's wearing sit low on his hips, and now that they're within my direct line of sight, I can tell he's not actually wearing any underwear beneath. I'm distracted, my eyes lingering before I can shake my head and look up. Both Holden and Jacinta are watching me with enough amusement that I flip them off. "Food would be good, please."

With a clap of her hands, she decides, "I'll order a heap, and we can eat family style in our wing." She moves away, pulling her phone out of her pocket. "I'll message the others and see if they want any too." She disappears, and when I stand up, Holden refuses to move an inch so that I find my body pressed up against him.

His good hand comes to my hips, and he's watching me when I look up. "Like what you see?" Without waiting for me to answer, he kisses me. It doesn't last long, but when he pulls away, he leaves me breathless. "I missed you, Mistress." A smile crosses my lips at his words, but his hand tightens on my hip. "Fuck, you've got to stop worrying us." The smile slips, and I frown at his comment.

"Damn it, Den, it's not like I'm going out of my way to get hurt." I shift to pull away, but he only grips tighter.

"Don't go, babe. I know. It's just killing us not being able to fix it for you." He rests his forehead against mine, and I wrap my arms around his neck, careful not to jostle his arm between us. This is nice, this feeling of being wanted and missed.

He pulls away. "Come on, let's get a good spot on the couch while we wait for everyone to join us for food. Maybe we can watch a little tv or a movie and just chill," he suggests as he moves away.

"That sounds amazing, actually," I tell him as he takes my hand. Together, we walk toward our wing of the house.

We're eventually joined by the rest of the siblings once the food arrives. The meal is delicious, and the company is really good as we chat, talking about nothing and everything, all while avoiding the subjects of the stalker, Cecelia, and Jacinta starting back at work. I learn more about everyone's interests and hobbies, and they actually ask me about mine and what it was like growing up with Chuck, Melinda, and Max. Jacinta gets a little self-righteous when I talk about Max and her tendency to ignore me when her high-society friends are around, promising me that will never happen with her. Oh, the turn-around in attitude, but I won't point it out.

Eventually, I just can't stay awake, so I wish everyone a good night and make my way back upstairs. Holden comes with me, just as ready for bed as I am, and as he stops at his door, he leans in to give me a kiss, but I grab hold of his hand. "Do you want to sleep with me tonight? Or is it still too much for your arm?"

A blinding smile brightens his face, and he shakes his head. "No, my arm is okay, and I'd love to, thanks. I'll just brush my teeth, then I'll be there."

He steps into his bedroom as I continue on to mine. With Kai still downstairs, chatting and hanging out with the others, it's quiet up here.

As I step into my room, I let out the deep breath that I've been needing to release. I had fully expected to find it trashed like the other one had been, but it looks like it hasn't been touched since I left. Looking down at my outfit, I decide to just leave Jaxon's shirt on, simply replacing the sweatpants with a pair of panties. I've never been able to sleep with any kind of pants on; I always end up uncomfortable.

Once done, I brush my teeth and climb into my bed, shivering when the cold sheets touch my skin. Just as I snuggle down, my door opens and Holden enters the room. He's wearing only a tight pair of boxer briefs, his arm still in a sling, so the rest of his delicious body is on display, his nipple rings calling for my mouth.

He hurries across the room and slides into the bed on the opposite side. "Shit, it's cold. Come here." He uses his good arm to drag me toward him then settles down with me tucked against his side.

"How did you get your shirt off without any help?" I ask him as he nuzzles into my neck, causing goosebumps to appear on my skin.

"I think I can manage to remove my clothes all on my own, Harlow," he grumbles, sounding a little bit put out, but he doesn't stop snuggling. Well, isn't he being a little adorable and bratty at the same time? Hmm, I think maybe it's time for a little play.

"Oh really? Did I give you permission to remove your clothes?" He freezes, and I pull away to look at him. I can see a hundred things running through his mind as his eyes heat before he lowers his gaze.

"No, Mistress, you didn't." His body is practically vibrating in anticipation, and this time the tension in the air is promising all good things.

"Well, I guess you need to be punished then." I hide my smile even though he's not looking up at me.

"I am yours to do with as you wish," he replies, his voice dropping all seductively. How do men do that? I wind up sounding like James Earl Jones when I try to do that.

But all I do is snuggle up to his chest and place a kiss over his heart. "Good night, Den. Sleep well." I throw my leg over him, definitely not missing out on the brush of his hard cock through the thin fabric of his briefs.

The rest of him stiffens underneath me in disbelief. "But, Mistress, don't you wish to punish me?" he pushes.

"Oh, I believe I am." I rub my body against him in a pretend attempt to get myself comfortable before settling down and closing my eyes. He starts muttering about cock-teasing Mistresses before he pulls me closer and kisses me on the head, and I just might not resist the urge to smile. He's still muttering about getting me back soon, but it's easy enough to tune it out. The sound of Holden's heartbeat under my ear is a reassuring balm to my soul, and before I know it, I drift off to sleep.

Chapter Six

Harlow

I spend the next week relaxing at home. Everyone has been going into work every day, leaving Holden, Thomas, and me on our own. My bodyguard has held true to his word; Dad made the arrangements for him to take a leave, so he fully intends to stick around in case I go anywhere—or at least that's what I was assured when I tried to convince him to go to work.

After a couple of days of doing nothing, I'm starting to go out of my mind. Alex and Shane are both on jobs, so I can't call them. Holden and Thomas spend a lot of time in Dad's office, working, and Max's filming schedule is so brutal I give up after a few short phone calls. I'll catch up with her once filming slows down a little bit. I ordered a whole heap of new clothes and had them sent to the house, but unwrapping and putting them all away only took a little while. Finally, I have no choice but to ask Thomas to come with me so I can have a look at Prada and Coco. Anything to get out of the house. Even a walk around the gardens would be nice at this stage of the game.

"Come in," is the response after I knock on the door to the office. When I enter, I can see they've set up laptops on each side of the desk, sharing the space with one another. Sure, they're sharing space, but they couldn't be any more different. Holden's on a call, but he doesn't miss the chance to flash me a bright smile, while Thomas is already frowning, looking up at me with some kind of expectation in his eyes. I've really tried to pull him out of his shell a little bit the past few days, but he's hanging on to his defenses like his life depends on it.

"Um, I was wondering if I could go out to the stables and check on Prada and Coco. I think it's time that Coco actually got some exercise. I know Jacinta has been scared that something is going to happen to him and hasn't taken him out into one of the day paddocks yet, but it's time. And I also thought maybe I could do that then get some fresh air, maybe walk around the gardens." God, I'd even take a swim even though the temperature's dropping.

I just want to be out of this house so badly that I don't care about how I'm rambling at Thomas right now. Let him see that I'm on the verge of losing my mind. It's fine. Everything's fine. Yep, I'm picturing that meme right now.

To my surprise, Thomas stands up, slamming his laptop closed. "Yeah, actually, that sounds like a good idea. I need to stretch my legs too, and maybe the fresh air will help me think clearer."

We both wave to Holden then make our way outside. I'd already put on a pair of jeans and boots in the hope that he would say yes, so I only need to stop at the side door and grab a light jacket while Thomas grabs what he needs. Because we went out the side door, we bypass the deck and recreation area and head straight to the stables across the back expanse of lawn that gets used as the helipad. Shoving my hands deep into my pockets, I peek at him out of the corner of my eye, studying the change of his expression as he gets lost in thought. He has his hands shoved in his pockets too, and he's sort of hunched in on himself.

"Want to talk about it?" I ask him, and he kind of jumps like he forgot I was there. That's not like him. He's always on the ball, alert and watchful.

"I just can't figure out this stalker thing. It's almost like there are two separate people doing this. Up until Hawaii, there was no real attempt on your life—just malicious damage plus threatening the others, which can be chalked up to whoever being obsessed with you being pissed at them for Jacinta's stunt. So, what changed? What made them escalate to trying to kill you? I really think there are two people involved in this. There's just one big question: are they linked, or is it a coincidence?"

His words floor me. Two different people having a problem with me? Fuck my life. One potentially murderous stalker was more than enough for me. I had been avoiding thinking about it all week, typical me behavior, but I can't ignore it anymore when he lays it all out like that.

"But what about the saddle, pushing me into the pool, and the photo of DS?" I add in.

He growls, "I'm pretty sure that's the same one who did all the damage to your room and Oliver's car. Just another way to frighten you."

"But why? Why frighten me? What did they hope to achieve with it?"

"Maybe trying to get you to run home to Connecticut?" Thomas speculates.

"Okay, that sounds fair, but what about the two attempts in Hawaii? It was sheer luck that we weren't seriously injured during the car accident, and had Kai not gotten to me as quickly as he did, the snorkeling accident would have been a whole other story. Why is one trying to scare me and one trying to kill me?"

"Yeah, but that's where the theory of a second person comes in. Otherwise, we're missing out on something big that would have pushed the initial attacks, which were more aimed at harming us, to changing them to being about harming *you*. Fuck! This is so frustrating."

We're at the stable doors by now, so I pull them open. A quiet nickering greets us, a huge smile fills my face at the sound.

"Come on, help me get these two into a day paddock. I'm sure not thinking about it for a while will help. Then we can walk up to the gate and see if the mail has been delivered. I'm still waiting on a couple of packages from Amazon, and our brains deserve a break from this stress."

We quietly work together, getting the mare and her foal into halters and then clipping on the leads to take them out. Coco is skittish, but I know Jacinta has been working with him, so I throw my arm over his neck and give him a pat. As we walk, I keep talking to him calmly, the two of us following Thomas and his mother out into the fresh air. The colt's ears prick up, his nose lifting like he's scenting the air, and he starts to prance a little bit. Prada picks up her pace, almost towing Thomas along behind her in her impatience to get outside. Thankfully, they don't have to wait too long before we're unlatching the gate, pushing it open, and letting them enter.

After we join them inside, we let them both loose, knowing they're ready to enjoy this taste of freedom that they've been missing. They both spin on their hocks and take off along the fence line. Coco's gangly legs kick up as he bucks a couple of times in joy. Thomas and I climb back through the fence and rest against it, watching the two run together. It doesn't take long for Prada to start munching on the grass instead, but Coco is curious. He sniffs along the fence line toward us before turning and racing back to his mom.

There is something purely joyful about watching a foal explore new surroundings for the first time. Eventually, he gets bored and sidles up to his mom for a drink.

"Come on. Let's go get the mail." I tug on Thomas' shirt and pull him toward the front of the house. "Did you know this is the longest I've gone without riding since I was given my first pony," I tell him conversationally, trying to keep his mind away from his worries. Maybe trying to keep my mind away from them too. "I think I'm starting to get withdrawals. It's weird because it hasn't been all that long since Holden's accident, but it feels like a lifetime ago at the same time. So... distract me from the withdrawal, Thomas. Tell me something about you that I don't know."

I can see him thinking about it, but I can't read the emotion behind those thoughts. *Did I push him too far?* He seems to be determined to keep me at arm's length, but I'm just as determined to get to the heart of what makes him tick.

"Like Kai and Declan, I have my pilot's license for both planes and helicopters," he starts, and it's something, but I want to know more.

"What about hobbies? What does Thomas Summers like to do on his days off?"

"Going off grid, fishing and hunting. Dad has a cabin at Lake Superior, and we always take two weeks off every year and head up there. But I use it on my own as well. In the summer, I like to do some camping too. There's a great camping spot we like to use at South Lake Tahoe. We'll take the kayaks and do some hiking and fishing there too." When he turns and meets my eyes, the shadow is gone, replaced with happy memories of the past with his family.

"That sounds fun. What else do you do as a family? Any other traditions I have to look forward to?"

"Aunt Merideth and Dad alternate between themselves each year for Christmas, so some years we head to London and have a cold Christmas at her place, and sometimes she comes here for the sun. Despite it being winter, she says it's more sun than London gets in summer."

"She owns the Sugar and Spice empire, doesn't she? Sex toys and strippers, porn and prostitutes. I believe those were the headlines I saw once."

He laughs and smiles ruefully. "That she does, and if you think the press came up with that byline, you'd be mistaken. She has the final say in everything, and she's just as ruthless if not more so than Dad. She spends quite a bit of time flying between here and the UK because Sugar and Spice has a gentlemen's club and burlesque show in Vegas. She likes to be hands-on with everything, and with such a delicate operation, it requires immense trust in your board or you do it all yourself."

"Well, I can't wait to meet her," I tell him as we get closer to the front gate.

"She should be here for the fundraiser in a couple of weeks, and I know she's going to be thrilled to meet you too."

A temporary guard house has been put at the front gate so the poor guys don't have to stand in the open all day. As we approach, Vic steps out with a couple of packages in his hand.

"Oh hey, Harlow, Mr. Summers. I was just about to head up to the house to drop these off." He smiles as he hands over three packages before disappearing back into the hut.

"I'm just going to see if they've spotted anything noteworthy today." With that, Thomas leaves me leaning against a tree with my packages in hand. I'm still in sight of him, so he's dutifully fulfilling his guard dog requirements. Looking down at my packages, I can see that two of them are from Amazon like I'd expected, but the third has no label on it except for our address. While a surprise package might have been exciting at any other time, I'm immediately wary of what this might contain.

I drop the other two on the ground and tug at the tape holding the mystery one closed. Pulling it off, I peel back the flaps to reveal what's inside, my heart racing just enough to tell me that this could be a mistake. When I see its contents, I just know I should have been smarter about the whole thing. Nestled in a bed of tissue paper are two Ken dolls.

One has shaggy dark hair and is dressed in swim shorts and holding a surfboard with tattoos painted on—tribal swirls over one shoulder and across the chest. *Kai.* The other is wearing a suit and has shorter dark hair. There's a drink in one hand and a vibrator in the other. *Jaxon.* They both have bullet holes in the middle of their forehead. Under them, there's a note. Not wanting to disturb the dolls, I carefully list the box and try to read it, but all I can make out is the word *whore.*

"Tom," I call out, and there's no hiding the shock and nerves that have already crept into my entire body. He quickly comes out of the guard house, concern written on his face.

"What is it?" His eye drops to the box. "Fuck. Vic, can you call the detectives on this case? They'll want to take it away and dust for prints."

Vic does what he's asked as Tom gently pries it from my fingers. "Leave it here, Harlow. I'll walk you back to the house before I come back to wait for Detective James."

He puts it in the guard house with instructions not to touch it any further. "The outside of the box will be useless because it's been through the mail, but they might get lucky with something on the inside."

He walks me back to the house, and when we get there, he shouts for Holden who comes running.

I must zone out, getting lost in the daze that's trying to protect my mind from this new shock. The next thing I know, I'm on my bed with Holden pressed up against my side, stroking my hair and telling me everything is going to be okay. I realize my cheeks are wet from tears, but I'm just too tired to care, so I settle down, close my eyes, say a small prayer to the big beyond that this all stops soon.

Chapter Seven

Harlow

The police retrieved the package, and a few days later, they called and informed Thomas that they'd managed to lift a partial fingerprint off one of the dolls. While that could be good news, our relief was short lived. At this stage, there was no match in the system, leaving us no options but to stay on guard and wait until the next opportunity to find something out about him or her… or them.

Thomas, on the other hand, was thrilled. He claims it means the stalker is getting sloppy, and he says it's just a matter of time before he fucks up again. So I try to put it out of my head by sending out a couple more job applications, playing dress up in Jacinta's wardrobe, getting yelled at by Jacinta for playing dress up without her, and having cuddle time with Princess and the kittens. By the time Friday rolls around, I'm about ready to go insane.

When I wake that morning, the other side of my bed is empty and the sheets cold. Kai had told me the night before that he needed to get going early and would try not to wake me when he got up, so he must have been successful. I haven't spent a night alone since I got back, with Kai, Holden, and Oliver all taking turns to keep me company. Unfortunately, despite the nightly presence of these gorgeous men, I've been cockblocked on all sides, and I'm starting to get annoyed. You would think I'd be getting sexed up all the time, right? What else happens when you've got five guys wanting to commit to you and at least four who are ready to give out some orgasms? But no, I've barely seen any of them during the day.

Kai and Oliver have been going into the office or whatever else they do as part of their jobs, and Holden has kept himself busy in Dad's office. I've managed to coax him out a couple of times for a movie but not very often, and Thomas is just as bad. For a man who's supposed to be on a break, he's been working awfully hard. As for Jaxon and Declan, they've been too busy, coming home late at night. I really need to make an effort to track them down this weekend.

Rolling out of bed, I shower and get ready for the day. The bump on my head is only a bruise now, and my aches and pains from the crash are basically nonexistent. I'm ready to do something. I make a quick plan and grab my laptop, figuring I can get some stuff done while I eat breakfast. I'm going to apply for my California veterinarian license so that when I decide for sure that I'm sticking around, I can find myself a job, or at least some work as a relief vet.

When I get downstairs, the living area is empty, but I can hear murmuring voices. I put my laptop down on the coffee table and go in search of company, discovering Holden and Thomas in the kitchen. Holden, his arm still in the sling, is sitting at the island, and Thomas is at the stove, cooking what smells like bacon.

"Good morning." I give Holden a kiss on the cheek and round the island to get to the coffee machine, smacking Thomas on the ass on the way past. He whirls in my direction, tongs in hand, mouth agape. "I do like my men barefoot and smelling like bacon." I look down at his shoeless feet beneath his sweatpants, realizing this is the most casual I've seen him all week. It's like it's taken him a few days to get into the swing of not going to the office every morning—must be a creature of habit. When I look back up, he's still gaping at me, so I wink before turning my attention to the coffee machine while Holden chuckles behind me.

"You do make a good house husband, Tom. You always were the best cook out of all of us," Holden says conversationally as I pour myself a cup, adding some milk and sugar before joining him at the island. Thomas has tracked my movements, but I can't tell what look is in his eye. There's definitely still some surprise, but there might also be some wariness and, dare I hope for it, some interest? "Dude, you're going to ruin your streak if you don't pay attention to the bacon. If I wanted it burned, I would have asked Jazzy to cook it."

Thomas whirls back to his bacon and manages to save it. I watch as he puts it out on a couple of plates that already have toast on them. He then cracks a few eggs into a bowl before adding salt and pepper and cream, whisking them, then pouring them into a pan. It doesn't take him long to cook those either, and before I know it, he's placing bacon and scrambled eggs with toast in front of me and Holden before taking a seat in front of his own plate.

"Thanks, Tom," Holden says, his mouth already half full of toast. My eyes meet Thomas' for a moment, and I smile.

"Yes, thank you, what a lovely surprise." We'd been having toast and cereal all week, so this makes a nice change. "What are everyone's plans for the day?" I ask a little sarcastically, seeing as none of us have been anywhere all week.

"Well, actually, I have a meeting at the office with one of the bands I represent, and I need to have my dressing looked at and possibly removed, then see the PT. I've pushed it back as far as I can, but I need to meet with them today. So I'm heading into town, which means you're on your own for the day."

My mouth drops open in horror as I look between the two men. Holden doesn't seem to notice, but Thomas does, of course. I doubt he misses much.

"Is everything okay, Harlow?" Thomas asks.

"Please don't leave me here on my own. If I have to be confined to the house for one more day, I'm going to go insane," I beg, causing Holden to look up.

"You can come with me to the office if you want, sit in on my meeting. It won't hurt for you to get a feel for the music side of the business. You helped Nana with Couture last week, and it won't be much different to that," he says, taking a sip of his coffee.

I look to Thomas, and he shrugs. "I don't care. You can arrange to meet up with your friends Alex and Shane too if you want to, so long as we can go to their place. We're fairly sure they have nothing to do with your stalker. They've both got alibis for the incidents, and security is tight in their building. I've already checked into it, and we'd need a special code to access their apartment, which only they and Jace currently know. As far as your options go, I'd much rather you're there or in Neighpalm HQ if you need some time out of the house."

Now it's my turn to gape in surprise. "You had

them investigated?" I don't know how I feel about that.

Thomas simply shrugs again, letting out a deep breath when I stare at him, waiting for a response that uses actual words. "I asked them outright, and they were happy to answer my questions and provide their whereabouts for the occasions. Look, Harlow, it would have been negligent of me not to look into any new people in your life here in LA. Plus, they're a part of Jacinta's life too—or they will be. I can't let my sister spend time with people who could be psychotic."

After receiving a ridiculous amount of text messages from Alex accusing me of being a bad friend, I'd finally given in and FaceTimed them. There was no avoiding the bump on my head, so I explained what had happened while I was away. There was plenty of teasing about what went on between me, Jaxon, and Kai, and possibly some teasing back on my parts about a certain not-so-icy queen wanting to get in the middle of them, but neither of them mentioned being a part of the Summers Inquisition.

"Harlow?" Must have gotten lost in my thoughts since Thomas looks like this isn't the first time he said my name.

"Yeah, you're right. It would have been silly not to at least make some inquiries. I'm glad that they were cleared. Listen, maybe it would be easier if I asked them to meet me for lunch at the office. We can have it in the garden like when Dad had lunch with me."

Thomas looks impressed with my maturity, but Holden has a small frown on his face like he's wondering what I'm up to. I mean, he's not wrong. If I *accidentally* double book with Jacinta as well, and the four of us, and I guess Thomas if he's now my shadow, have lunch together... Well, wouldn't that be something?

"That works. Holden's doctor and PT are coming to the office as well. We'll drive into the city, and you guys will have your meeting with Holden's band. While you're having lunch with your friends, Holden can have his PT. We can head home with everyone in the heli tonight, maybe push for everyone to have an early finish since it's Friday." As he lays all this out, he begins cleaning up because he apparently has to be efficient at all times. I can't say that I mind a man who's willing to do the dirty work, but it's also another hint that Thomas has some serious relaxation issues.

"Oh yeah. What about a game night?" Holden asks. "We haven't had a family game night in ages! I'll send everyone a message about it so they can start getting ready to lose."

"Game night?" I ask, and Thomas snorts.

"More like Battle Royale," he says sarcastically, but Holden's shaking his head.

"No, Harlow, it's awesome. Sometimes it's

poker, or pictionary, or even Cards Against Humanity. We have drinks and snacks; it's a blast."

"Be prepared," Thomas warns me, raising his voice a bit to be heard over the running sink. "Nobody cheats and lies at games as well as the Summers."

I chuckle as I jump up. "Here, let me do that. You cooked, after all, and I'm sure you've got to get ready. And don't be so sure you Summers will have it in the bag. The Bostons are no slouches in the cheating and lying department either." It's nice to be able to joke around with them. God knows I never would have gotten away with a comment like that when we first met.

"Thanks, but don't say I didn't warn you. You guys have half an hour, and then we need to go if we're making that meeting on time," Thomas tells Holden before backing away and waving a vague goodbye as he hurries out of the kitchen.

Holden's phone starts to ping as I quickly finish the rest of the dishes. "Aw, Nana and Poppy are out. They have some charity function tonight and won't be home, but Dad's in, and he's inviting Emma and her girlfriend." He looks up at me, then down at his sling, a calculating glint entering his eyes. "Might need you to sit on my lap and help me. Ya know, since I'm so damaged and all."

I empty the water into the sink and wipe down the counter before grabbing his empty plate and putting it in the dishwasher as well.

"Fat chance. It's every man and woman for themselves." Regardless, I walk over to him, stepping in between his legs when he opens them to make room for me. "Maybe I need you at my feet, taking care of my every desire."

I wrap my arms around his neck, minding his sore shoulder. Our relationship has just gotten better this week, and the thought of having him at my feet makes my panties damp. I kiss him, putting in all my pent-up desire, until we're both breathing heavily when we pull apart.

"There would be no place I'd rather be than at your feet or between your thighs, but Dad being there might make that a little awkward."

I step away and pull him up as I go. "Yeah, that's certainly one way to cool the desire."

We both head back upstairs to shower and change. "Holden, what do I need to wear to this meeting? I mean, is it formal?" My mind runs through what clothes I have left over from my trip to Hawaii. When I had ordered clothes from Amazon, I hadn't thought about ordering office-appropriate attire. Hopefully, one of the dresses that I picked out will do because apart from that, all I have is casual shorts and tops. I've been living in the guys' sweats all week like a bit of a slob, and I'm pretty sure no matter how casual Holden thinks it is, that really won't cut it.

"Wear what you're comfortable in. A nice pair

of jeans and a top or one of those dresses like you were wearing last week."

"What is this meeting about?" I ask just as we get to his room.

He blows out a sigh of breath. "One of my bands is on the verge of collapse, and this is a crisis talk to see if we can figure out how we can go ahead." He just sounds tired when he talks about it; there's none of that energy or enthusiasm that I've seen before when he talks about music. "I really don't know where we go from here if we can't come to some kind of resolution. We may have to drop them altogether, which I don't want to do because I really like them. They're the band that won the first season of Dec's reality show *American Superstar,* and they've been a huge hit for us."

"Which band is it?" I ask, my curiosity getting the better of me. I remember the show, but I don't think I caught more than one or two audition episodes.

"Ninja Starfish," he replies, and I just about swallow my tongue. Holy crap, they are *huge,* with a legion of fans. They were the next boy band that came along not long after One Direction went their separate ways. Could the same thing be happening to them?

I shake off the sudden nerves at meeting such a huge band. I mean, I met Cayden Storm and Jarred Reed last week, so this can't be too hard. I'll sit in the background and listen in.

"Are we going to be the only ones in the meeting?" I gesture between the two of us, and he shakes his head.

"No, Hope will be joining us and a couple of our legal and publicity team members." *Awesome. That'll make my plan to camouflage with the wall even easier.*

"Do you need help getting dressed?" I ask him, and his worried face relaxes with a cheeky grin.

"Oh, I am never going to say no to you helping me in the shower, Harlow."

I do a double take, but of course he can't really wash himself with one arm. Do I want to start anything in the shower with him? Am I finally getting a bit of action? Hell yeah, I am.

I hurry after Holden, following him into his bathroom where he's already got the water running. He's struggling to wrestle down his sweats and boxer briefs one-handed, so what does a good samaritan like myself do? I take pity on him and drop to my knees, pulling them down his legs until they pool on the floor at his feet. His long, gorgeous cock juts out, now at eye level with me, and I swear, when the piercing in the end catches the light, my mouth practically starts to water. Looking up, the heat in his eyes is combustible. There's no way this isn't happening. I lean forward and run my tongue along the underside of his thick length from base to tip, and a deep groan rumbles from his chest, his good hand resting on top of my head with just a little bit more pressure.

"Fuck, Harlow," he moans as I pull back.

"How much time did Thomas say we had?" I tease, grinning at him.

"Screw Tom," he mutters, trying to pull my head back to his dick, but I stand up instead.

"No," he complains, looking devastated, but I just smirk.

"How about we take this into the shower, so we can kill two birds with one stone?" That gets a more enthusiastic reaction, his eyes lighting up and his cock bobbing in anticipation.

"God, I love how you think." We remove the sling before I carefully help him peel off his wife beater, my eyes drawn to the piercing glinting in his nipple. When I get my hormones under control for about two seconds, which at this point is quite the achievement, I help him put the sling back on, but then something occurs to me.

"What about that?" I ask, pointing to it, and he shrugs as he steps into the shower.

"I've got another. I'll change it when we get out. I have to keep it on until I see the doctor and PT today."

I shuck off my pajama shorts and the tank I was wearing and suddenly realize this is the first time I've been naked in front of Holden. His eyes practically devour me as they run the length of my body, and I can see his breathing increase. If his eyes linger for a moment on that Oli merman, well, it doesn't bother me.

"God, you're gorgeous," he rasps as I step into the large shower, pulling the door behind me. His hand goes to my hip, and our lips meet in a clash of passion, his cock hard against my stomach as our bodies press together. The warm water beats down over the top of us. Conscious of how little time we have, I pull away and drop to my knees again. I take his length with my hand and lower my mouth to the flared head, flicking my tongue over the piercing in the end to draw another groan from his mouth. The small slit in the end starts to leak fluid, the taste salty and sharp as I lap at it before my mouth engulfs the fat end, hollowing my cheeks and sucking. His hips flex forward, sending him deeper, and he moans again, his hands gripping my hair to the point of being tight but not painful. His arousal throbs under my hand as I continue slow and steady motions, sliding my mouth up and down his engorged flesh.

"Fuck, Harlow," he mutters as I speed up my movements. "I'm going to come."

Using my spare hand, I roll his balls as they tighten up with his impending orgasm. He tries to pull me away, but I shake my head, and his leg muscles lock up as cum floods my mouth. Finally, he holds still, a long groan echoing through the bathroom as I swallow him down.

Holden tries to help me up, but I wave him

away. He won't be much help with his arm in a sling anyway. I slowly make my way to my feet, washing the cum down with a swallow of water from the shower. He kisses me hard on the mouth before trying to drop to his own knees, but I stop him with a shake of my head.

"Another time, we have to get ready. Thomas will be waiting for us," I tell him, and he agrees reluctantly.

"Fine, but I'm holding you to that." He kisses me hard again before reaching for the soap.

Chapter Eight

Harlow

After I help Holden wash, dry, and replace his wet sling with a new one, I'm about to help him with his clothes when Thomas knocks on the door.

"Hey, I told you half an hour. What's taking so long?" he asks as he walks into the room, stopping suddenly when he finds a naked Holden and me wearing only a towel.

"Oh hey, great. Can you help Holden with his clothes? I'll just run and get dressed." I quickly escape, not even contemplating answering the question of why we took so long. Snickering, I picture Thomas helping Holden into his briefs. God, do I have time to sneak back with my phone and take a picture?

Deciding there's probably not enough time, I run to my room and straight into the closet to search through the dresses. Thankfully, there's one that is more suitable for the office than all of the rest, a maxi-style dress with capped sleeves and a lowish neckline that won't have everyone staring at my cleavage. The top half molds to my body, but the skirt flares out from my waist to the floor.

Not bothering with a bra due to the built-in shelf of the dress, I quickly pull it over my head, then tug on a pair of underwear. A denim jacket and a pair of sandals complete the outfit for now. There's no time to dry my hair, so I give it a quick brush before twisting it into a bun and pinning it to the back of my head. A quick coat of mascara on the lashes, a dash of lip gloss, and I'm ready.

Grabbing my trusty backpack, I hurry downstairs. As I pass Holden's room, there's no sound of the guys, so I guess they're already downstairs. How could they have beaten me? Thomas must have slam dunked Holden into his clothes. I chuckle at the mental image of that as I run down to the living area to grab my laptop and shove it in my backpack before racing to the garage.

Thomas and Holden are sitting in the same SUV that he'd had at the airport the other day. Oliver had told me during the week that it was bulletproof, along with some other special modifications. I quickly climb into the backseat, and before I even have my seatbelt on, Thomas is driving out of the garage and down the driveway.

"Wow, you guys were quick."

"Well, you were a little longer than the thirty minutes I told you," Thomas grumbles, avoiding my eyes in the rearview mirror.

I smile, remembering why we were longer than the allotted time. *Absolutely zero regrets about that one.*

"Trust me, bro, you would have taken longer too if you had a sexy, wet woman at your feet." My eyes widen, and I can feel my cheeks turning a little pink at Holden's words. Is this a normal thing for brothers to be so open about? I mean, it's not like Kai and Jaxon seemed to hide much from each other, but they've both been up close and personal with my vagina. I guess Thomas' possible brother-husband status, or whatever the fuck you call it, makes Holden feel a little less shy about being open with him. Not that I'm thinking about marrying them, I'm just super happy with getting to know them. If that leads to me being sexed up, that's enough of a bonus for now.

"Harlow?" Holden's voice has me jumping, and I realize I'd zoned out for a moment.

"Sorry, what did you say?" I ask. "I was thinking about something and wasn't paying attention." Holden turns so that he can see me, and from the look on his face, he's got a pretty solid idea of what I was thinking so hard about.

"Did you get a hold of Alex or Shane?" Holden

asks, sounding amused that he caught me daydreaming.

"Shit no, I got distracted by the shower, and then General Hardass was rushing us." General Hardass is right for more than one reason. When I slapped him on said ass this morning, my hand hurt. The boy doesn't miss squat days, not that I plan to explain that reason for why the name fits him.

Grabbing my phone out of my jacket pocket, I shoot off a quick text to Shane and Alex about lunch. While I wait for a reply, I message Max. I really need to get in some phone time with her, so hopefully she'll be free for a call later. All those rushed phone calls over the last week of my "rest time" were definitely not adequate girl time.

My phone pings with a reply, and it's Alex with a very enthusiastic yes. He and Shane are at a shoot this morning that should be wrapped up by one. It's not far away, so they'll meet me at one thirty for a late lunch. Even though they try to insist on taking care of the food, I convince them I've already got it covered. Which is a total lie, but if I'm going to surprise them with Jacinta, I need to make sure there's enough food for everyone, not to mention my shadow, Thomas.

The timing of their shoot will give me enough time to go to the meeting with Holden and maybe even some spare time to fill out my license paperwork and do the open book law test that's required, if that gets done early. I may need to call Melinda and ask for her to scan my certificates and things for me. Not to mention I probably should call her anyway. God, I'm a terrible sort-of daughter.

They've been on my mind a lot, but sometimes thinking about someone and loving them doesn't mean that it's easy to just pick up a phone and talk to them. It seems like there's always some kind of distraction or fucked up mystery doll package… or jet ski accident… or shooting that just takes over. Regardless, I need to do better. I want to reassure them, and I guess myself, that I still love them. Even if I'm here, it doesn't mean I'm going to forget about them or anything. I think maybe my insecurities are playing havoc, and I need reassurance just as much from them.

The long drive to the office seems to go by quickly. With music playing on the radio, the ride has been fairly quiet, apart from a few conversations between Holden and Thomas, but I don't really pay attention to them. I finally got a chance to finish the book I was reading this week, and when I needed something new, I raided Jacinta's well-stocked bookshelf in our wing's living area and found a new one. The book I picked is about seven deadly sins and how they need redemption. There's also some kind of bet between God and Lucifer. I'm loving it so far, and Lucifer is my favorite character. But while I was browsing through her shelves, I found the most ridiculous collection of books by a male author named Chuck Tingle.

The one that left me gaping was called *Handsome Sentient Food Pounds My Butt And Turns Me Gay: Eight Tales Of Hot Food.* Seriously, there was a story about getting fucked by a corncob. When I asked her about it, she rolled her eyes and huffed. Apparently, it's her brother's idea of a joke. She lost a bet, so she had to order every one of his books and put them on display on her shelf. In any case, I wasn't ready to have gay food porn in my life, so I went with the seven deadly sins instead.

I'm deep into my book when the car rolls to a stop, and I realize we've parked underground at the Neighpalm building. Thomas stops the engine and quickly hops out, the movement of his suit jacket revealing a peek at the bulge that can't be anything but a gun. I wish he was wearing a bulletproof vest as well, but that would look strange in an office building and draw more attention than I want.

"Stay there a moment while I have a look around," he orders before slamming the door closed on the two of us.

I'm drumming my fingers on the door of the car, my nerves going crazy now that I'm back in public for the first time since I got back from Hawaii. The reality of the situation, that I have a bodyguard, is rearing its ugly head, and I start to panic about what might be out there, waiting for us. Shit, I've always been fairly brave, at least on the surface. When you're semi-raised by a mother who feeds off of weakness, you figure out how to hide your fear. I learned very quickly to adopt a resting bitch face, showing no emotion whenever I was with her and her cronies. Well, okay, maybe it's more of a resting blank face. I'm not that great at the whole bitch part, but maybe Jacinta can give me lessons now.

Holden undoes his seatbelt and turns in his seat, looking at me with a patient but small smile.

"Don't worry, Harlow. Thomas is going to make sure everything is okay. Trust him," he tries to reassure me, but when I don't stop drumming my fingers, he goes for a distraction. "Hope's going to meet us in my office, and we'll go to the conference room from there."

"Have we got time to stop and see Jacinta? I want to invite her to lunch, and I kind of want to snoop and see how things are going."

Holden glances down at the watch on his wrist, some expensive-looking piece that has what I think is the red and green Tag symbol on it. "Yeah, we've got about half an hour before we're expected. I'll just text Hope and let her know what we're doing so she doesn't worry."

I smile at his thoughtfulness just as Thomas comes back and opens my door for me.

"It's all clear. Let's get moving." He holds out his hand and helps me out of the car. He has me walk in front of him while he covers my back, his arm wrapped around my waist as we move quickly to the nearby elevator. I can feel the warmth of his body through the thin fabric of my dress. Thomas is taller than I am, and more broad, and it feels nice to have him at my back for protection. If I wasn't so nervous right now, I might be paying more attention to the part of my brain that says we'd like to have him behind us for a whole other slew of reasons. Good to know I can still be horny as fuck while also fearing for my life. Not sure if Darwin would approve of *that* survival instinct.

The elevator door opens as we get to it, and we walk straight in. Before anyone can join us, not that the parking garage is overly populated right now, Holden hits the button for the Couture floor.

As we slowly start to rise, Thomas removes his hand from my back, and I do my best to shake off the pang of disappointment that hits me. They are not Pokémon, and I need to keep reminding myself of that. But even though the better part of my nature wants me to stop objectifying them, I really do want to collect them all. Although I don't know much about him, and he is still fairly closed off toward me, watching him with his siblings the night we got back from Hawaii was a real eye opener. He was warm and open, and wow, he has a killer smile. I wish I could see it aimed in my direction.

"Why are we going to Couture?" he asks, putting a bit of space between us.

"I'm just going to ask Jacinta if she would like to

have lunch with me," I explain, not meeting his eyes, but I can hear Holden snort quietly on the other side of me.

"Harlow is doing her own little bit of match-making." I finally get up the nerve to take a peek at Thomas, and he's looking at me like I knew he would be, with this penetrating stare that I swear can see into my soul. But I guess whatever he sees doesn't upset him because he nods, the hint of a smirk on his face. Holy shit, I just about stumble in surprise. I guess Holden is shocked too because he waves his good hand at him.

"What? What's all this about? Why are you smirking?" The smirk disappears, quickly replaced by General Hardass again.

"If Jacinta ends up with a harem of her own, then she is no longer our problem."

Holden is speechless for all of five seconds before he's laughing and raising his hand for a high five which Thomas enthusiastically returns. "God, I love the way you think. Your mind is so devious."

I roll my eyes at them as the elevator comes to a stop on the right floor, stepping out while the two of them follow me, soft chuckles still escaping. The girl at the reception desk smiles warmly as I approach. Unlike others in the building, she's been pleasant and kind to me from day one, even before Nana introduced us.

"Good morning, Harlow. How was your trip to Hawaii?"

"It was great. Thanks for asking, Lucy. Is Jacinta in, and has she got a minute?"

Lucy's smile wobbles before she straightens it once more. "Ah... yes, she is in the Wardrobe with Lindy and the two new designers. Or that's where I heard the last bit of yelling coming from."

Oh dear, that sounds ominous.

"Okay, thanks. We'll see if we can sort that out, don't worry," I reassure her and take off in the direction of the Wardrobe. I can hear Holden and Thomas wishing her good morning on their way past.

As I move down the corridor, I can hear loud voices, so it looks like that's still an ongoing problem. I start to walk a little faster after I hear something crashing.

"Jesus, what is going on in there?" Holden asks as I push open the door and walk in.

The noise comes to an abrupt stop at my appearance, and as I look around the room, I can't decide whether to laugh or cry.

There's a ladder wobbling precariously, and next to it, Jacinta is lying on top of Jace, cradled carefully in his arms, though it looks like her knee got him directly in the balls if his red face is anything to go by. There are colorful feathers fluttering all around the room, some still slowly falling from an open cupboard above the ladder. Lindy and Rowena are also present, but they're nowhere near the ladder, so I'm guessing neither of them were involved in that. Both have faces like thunder-clouds though, so I'm guessing they were involved in the argument part of the yelling.

Thomas is the first person to recover. "What the fuck is going on in here?"

Rowena and Lindy both start to talk, one over the other, but I tune them out as I watch Jacinta and Jace on the ground. She's asking him if he's okay, patting him all over to check for injuries, and he's reassuring her he's fine while trying to make sure she's okay. It's so freaking cute seeing them both flustered. I'm even more excited with my idea now that I can see how attracted they are to one another.

"Stop! One at a time," Thomas yells, needing the extra volume to be heard over the two women. "Lindy, go."

"Jacinta insisted on climbing the ladder to get that box of feathers down, and Jace tried to stop her, especially because she's wearing those heels, but she didn't listen. The ladder started to wobble, and she tipped over, but thank god he caught her." *Some loyalty. Bitch throws Jacinta right under the bus.*

"I tried to stop her!" Rowena chimes in. *And there's the new girl to pop it into reverse and do a second run over.*

"Who are you?" Thomas demands, looking her up and down. Holden snorts once more behind me in amusement. That guy needs to learn to keep his reactions to himself.

"I'm Rowena, the new designer for Neighpalm Couture." She simpers, fluttering her eyelashes at him.

"One of them," Jacinta says from between gritted teeth. She and Jace have managed to get to their feet, but both are still covered in feathers.

"Holy crap, Jazzy. It looks like a chicken farm exploded in here," Holden says, not holding back his laughter at all. She flips him off.

"Yeah, yeah, I should have let Jace climb up to get it. But I knew exactly which box it was." She shrugs, sending feathers floating down to the ground.

"Tom, Holden, these are my new designers, Jace and Rowena. These are my brothers Holden and Thomas." She does the introductions before shaking herself down. The others exchange pleasantries while I go over to Jacinta and start to brush her down.

"Hey," I say to her, and she leans in to give me a hug, transferring some of the feathers to me.

"Hi, what are you doing here?" she asks, laughing and plucking them off my dress.

"I needed to get out of the house. Staying in one place was driving me nuts. What are you doing for lunch? You want to meet me in the conservatory?"

Her eyes shine as she gives me a big smile that I never thought would be directed at me. "I'd love to! That would be awesome."

A sound has me turning to where Lindy is looking at the two of us incredulously. Oh, I guess she didn't get the 'Harlow and Jacinta are BFFs' memo.

The silence is a little awkward until Holden steps in. "Well, okay then. That's done, so we will leave you to it. Got places to be and big bands to rip a new one." He turns and disappears out the door with Thomas following behind. Jace approaches me before I go anywhere, giving me a feathery hug before I can leave. The two of them laugh when they catch my eye roll, and my god, even their laughs sound adorable together. I don't know what I need to do to make this happen, but I've decided it's inevitable.

"Hi, Alex and Shane say I keep missing your calls. They told me your trip was a mess. Are you okay?" he asks, looking worried.

My eyes go to Lindy and Rowena who aren't hiding their interest in the conversation. Noticing their obvious interest, Jacinta growls at them, "Well, don't just stand there! Clean this mess up! We've got shit to do today."

"I thought you said they hated each other," I hear Rowena mutter to Lindy not so quietly.

"They did," Lindy hisses back.

I pull Jace and Jacinta away from flapping ears. "How about you come to lunch today too, and I'll give you all the messy details."

With his agreement, I wave them off and hurry

after the guys. Jacinta's raised voice follows me down the corridor, bringing a smile to my lips.

She's got a lovely voice when I'm not the one she's yelling at. I can totally get behind this sister gig.

Chapter Nine

Holden

Leaving Harlow to talk to Jacinta, I escape the disaster that is the Wardrobe, still chuckling when I get to the elevator. Thomas is directly behind me, but I can't get a read on what he's feeling.

"Should we be leaving Harlow alone?" I ask him.

"I had both the new designers checked out, and they were cleared. Lindy hasn't been checked yet, but she'd have to be a fucking stealth assassin to get at Harlow with the rest of them in that room, so I think it's okay. Plus, Lindy has been with Jacinta for what, two years now? There really is no reason to suspect her."

I shrug, leaving it to the expert, and the elevator doors open to Oliver already standing inside. My skin prickles at the sight of my old—hopefully not for long— lover. He's reading some paperwork and doesn't look up as Thomas steps in. When the doors begin to close, I stop them with my good arm which has him looking up in annoyance. With just a wink, the frown disappears, his face lighting up with a grin.

"Hey! I didn't know you were coming in today." Before I can answer, approaching footsteps broadcast Harlow's arrival, and his grin grows even bigger when she gives me a kiss on the cheek as she steps in. "Oh, another surprise, my two favorite people together. How did I get so lucky?" Harlow gives him a quick kiss, so I follow her example. His mouth curves under mine before I pull away, and I've got to admit that it's hard to put distance between us. He looks a little dazed at our surprise kiss attack, and he's not the only one. As the doors finally close, I see the receptionist's eyes widen while her mouth drops open in surprise. Whoops, I guess rumors will be flying around the office in no time. We may need to discuss that with the family before game night begins.

"Did you get that sorted then?" Thomas asks Harlow, nodding back in the direction she came from.

"Yup, Jacinta and Jace are both joining me for lunch, and as I walked away, Jacinta was yelling at Rowena and Lindy to clean the mess up. Fun times." The sarcasm isn't hard to miss, but she's smiling.

Oliver widens his eyes and starts to open his mouth, but Tom stops him. "Don't ask. It's not worth it," he mutters.

"I'll tell you later," I assure him. "I've got that meeting with Ninja Starfish today. I've put it off as long as I could, but things are about to implode, so I couldn't delay it any longer. Gotta worry about that first. Harlow is going to join me in the meeting. She's been going crazy, and we were worried she was going to do something silly."

Harlow's eyes widen at my words. *Whoops, didn't mean to say that out loud.* Tom and I had been talking about it in the kitchen this morning before she'd arrived. He had been watching for signs of cabin fever and knew she was coming to her limit yesterday, hence the outing today and him offering to take her to Alex and Jace's. Contrary to popular belief, we're not stupid men. We weren't willing to risk her getting hurt again if she took matters into her own hands. Jaxon has also made plans with Emma for Harlow, Thomas, and him to tour the house across the road tomorrow, but he wants to be the one to tell her.

The elevator stops again, and when the door opens, our oldest brother is waiting. His eyebrows raise as he takes in the four of us, but we shuffle over and make room for him. He steps in, facing

Harlow, but instead of turning around like the rest of us, he stops there.

"Well, isn't this a nice surprise," he purrs, and while Harlow's focused on my fool of a brother, I roll my eyes. When Declan turns on the charm, he's practically a heat-seeking weapon, and no matter what he might say, I think he's had Harlow's coordinates pinned since she helped with his beloved Princess. He reaches up and pushes a lock of Harlow's hair behind her ear. "It's been so long since I've seen you, beautiful. First, those assholes drag you off to Hawaii with them, and now work is kicking my ass. I miss you. Say you'll have dinner with me tomorrow night?" He's backed her up against the wall so that his body is pressed against hers. I can see her breathing increase, and her arms come up to his hips so automatically, it just feels like she *needs* the contact with him. He's overwhelming her in the hope she won't say no. Well, coming on strong is certainly one way to try to make this happen.

"Nope, not unless I get to tag along as well," Thomas butts in, and the look that Declan shoots him would shrivel a lesser man's balls. Oliver and I snicker like schoolboys, both of us gleeful at the showdown of wills between our two most serious brothers.

"I've got ten on Tom," Oliver whispers in my ear, his teeth dragging on the lobe after. A shiver shudders down my spine.

"I say Declan will win, and then you need to blow me."

"Done!" he shouts, and the other three look at us in surprise. "Sorry, carry on." He waves his hand at them, and they go back to arguing once they realize we're both fine.

"Come on, man. I'll book a private room at Capo, and we'll drive there in the armored tank you bought, then come straight home afterward," Declan cajoles, but Thomas stands firm.

"No, it's not happening. Set something up at home. Why don't you have a picnic in the conservatory? You can order in, and then you can both have a drink without having to worry about getting home. I won't have to chaperone, which is what *will* happen if you take her anywhere else." Declan starts to argue, but Tom holds up his hand as the doors open to my floor. Harlow steps around Declan, who stops her and kisses her gently before going back to his argument with Tom. She looks a little overwhelmed as she joins my side, and as the door closes, with Tom, Dec, and Oli still inside, the fucker mouths *I win.*

"Damn it," I growl, startling Harlow out of her daze.

"You two weren't making bets, were you?"

"Who? Us? No, of course not! We learned our lesson when Oli had to get a tattoo of your choice." Her hand goes up to where I know the merman that looks like Oli is, and a small smile twitches her lips before she raises an eyebrow in suspicion.

"Somehow I very much doubt that." I push her up against the closed elevator doors and nuzzle into her neck, my back to the reception area.

"I'm sure you can show us the errors of our ways, Mistress," I whisper quietly into her ear. I can feel her nipples pebble into hard rocks as I slide my leg between her thighs, but just as I'm about to kiss her, a throat clears behind us, making us both freeze. Fuck! I forgot we were at work. Maybe I should be embarrassed, but I'm not. It's been so long since I've felt so excited and lost in someone else, not since Oliver and I first got together, and I won't be embarrassed about wanting to grab that feeling every chance I get. Stepping away from her, I turn around and face Hope, a sly smile on her lips, instead of my very frosty-looking receptionist standing behind her desk.

"I just got word that Ninja Starfish are on their way up, so you may want to move away from the doors. Though I doubt Harlow will complain if she winds up falling into one of those very delicious boy's arms," Hope says dryly.

"Welcome back, Holden. Thank god you're okay. I was so worried when I heard you had been hurt in a horse riding accident," Missy coos from behind Hope.

"Thank you, Missy," I tell her politely. Her comment proves that Dad's story, minus the gunshot, of course, has made the rounds of the building, which is good, but I've always felt uncomfortable around her. Never have I made any inappropriate remarks or showed any interest other than professional, but she still flirts with me. I probably shouldn't have insisted she call me Holden, but Mr. Summers is Dad or Poppy.

"Come on, no time for pleasantries! Let's get to the conference room, and Missy can bring them there when they get here. The lawyers and publicity people won't be joining us until after we've had a private chat with them. I thought it would be better to get to the bottom of the problem first without too many people around."

"Good thinking," I tell my best friend as she leads us in the direction of our conference room. She's tucked her arm through Harlow's, the two of them talking quietly on the way.

Just barely able to make out the words, I chuckle. While Hope is glad Harlow is okay, she's also giving her a gentle reaming for not getting in touch with her. Trust Hope to smoothly blend in that scolding. She was freaked out when I told her what had happened, but I had managed to hold her off this week while Harlow recovered. I guess all bets are off now. I'm not sure if it's the best or scariest thing in the world for all the important women in my life to be getting along. God forbid Hope, Harlow, and Jacinta team up. We'd all be fucked.

"What are you doing for lunch?" I hear her ask.

"Oh, I'm having lunch with Alex, Shane, Jacinta, and Jace," Harlow answers, and Hope stops dead, her hand on her hips.

"And I wasn't fucking invited?" Harlow is blinking in what could be shock, surprise, or fear, no idea, and before she can react, I grab my friend and nudge her down the hallway ahead of us, wrapping a reassuring arm around my girl.

"Settle, Rocky. Harlow is playing matchmaker." The amount of surprise on Harlow's face is adorable. "Babe, it was practically written all over your face."

She shrugs, not denying it. "Actually, Hope, you can help if you want." That wipes the disgruntled look off Hope's face, and I squeeze Harlow's waist in approval. Of course inviting her to be a part of the shenanigans is enough to appease her.

"Yes, I'm in! Just tell me what to do."

"Well, if you come find me, maybe ten minutes into the meal, and tell me that there is an emergency with something, I can give my excuse to leave so they have to have lunch on their own. Together. All that sexual tension those three guys put out will be enough to drive Jacinta wild, or that's what I'm hoping."

Most guys wouldn't want to hear anything involving their sister going wild, but Tom made a good point. It would be amazing for Jacinta to make some connections outside the family, and if those connections happen to be with men who will treat her right, I'm all for it.

Hope nods enthusiastically, so excited by her conversation with Harlow that she would've walked into the door had I not opened it for her. "I've got you, babe, then you and I can sneak to my office up here and have lunch."

"Hey, that's *my* office," I complain. I'd like to say that she looks contrite, even apologetic about displacing me, but all I can see is a twitch of her lips that dares me to continue. Yep, between her, my sister, Nana, and Harlow joining the ranks, my life is run by women. I don't hate it even though I might fear it.

"The second desk that's been placed in there tells me it's mine as well." I feel my eyes widen in surprise.

"Second desk?"

"Yup." She pops the p smugly. "Nana had one brought in for me at the beginning of the week. She says if I'm going to be your right hand woman now, I need my own space."

Of course Nana would do that. She's so thoughtful, and she loves Hope like one of her own. She'll take off running with any opportunity to tie Hope more tightly to the company and our family. "Well, good then. Does this mean you're going to take the position of VP of Neighpalm Records?"

"Yes, but I'm not giving up being head of Public Relations. I've got a really great team, and my second in command is going to get a promotion, but I'll still give approval on the big things."

A thrill runs through me at my bestie's words, and I grab her and spin her around with my good arm before giving her a big kiss on the cheek. "Awesome, I knew you'd eventually cave. Alright, if I know you, you'll have a game plan for this meeting. How about we sit down so you can give us a quick overview?"

Harlow is watching us with a delighted smile on her face. There's no hint of jealousy, which I'm happy with. Hope has been my friend for a long time now, and I couldn't stand it if there was tension between the two.

"Well, I have a feeling the two of you will be unstoppable. Ninja Starfish better watch out if they're going to cause problems," Harlow says happily as she takes a chair and pulls it away from the table. She doesn't sit down until it's tucked in a corner, out of the way.

My smile drops, a frown taking its place. Hope's face mirrors mine as she looks at Harlow.

"What are you doing?" she asks before I can.

"I'm sitting out of the way," Harlow says, like it's obvious.

"But why?" I ask cautiously, not wanting to upset her because I have no idea what she's thinking at the moment.

She stammers a little. "Because... I'm not part of the business?"

"Bullshit, you're a Summers! They're all your businesses." Again, Hope hits the nail on the head. "You sitting in is no different to Brad or Poppy and Nana or any one of the siblings sitting in. Get your ass over here."

I kiss my friend on the head and whisper thank you to her. If we want Harlow to make a home here with us, we need her to know that she fits with us in all respects—as part of the family, as a lover/partner, and as part of the businesses. Every little sign that we want her here with us is hopefully undoing an ounce of the pain and discomfort that we inflicted on her in the first place. Going over to Harlow, I help her to her feet before moving her chair back to the table, right between Hope and me. "Hope hit it on the head, babe. You're one of us and deserve a place here. Plus, I wouldn't mind an unbiased view of today; you might have some insight that we don't."

A knock on the door has her nodding and quickly taking a seat. There's no time for her to argue, thank goodness, because it looked like she was revving up for one. A moment later, Missy shows in the five guys from Ninja Starfish, their manager, and someone I don't know, but he's holding a briefcase and has the slimy lawyer look.

Well, it looks like they came to play hardball. I look around the group as they all take seats, noticing there is a very visible divide. What the fuck is going on here?

"Hey, guys, Giselle. Welcome and thanks for allowing me to reschedule this meeting." I start off with pleasantries because there's no need to go straight for the jugular. Gotta lull them into a little sense of comfort before you do what needs to be done.

"Yeah, man, no problems. I'm just glad you're okay," Jessie replies, pushing a hand back through his shoulder-length hair. Jessie, Sacha, Tristan, and Kyan are on one side of the table, with Cash, Giselle, and the stranger on the other. Fuck, this really does not bode well.

I glance toward the lawyer-looking dude with raised eyebrows. "Who are you, and why are you in this meeting?" He pulls out a card and hands it to me. *Howard Jonson, Attorney.* Yeah, that tells me fuck all. I throw the card on the table and cross my arms. "Okay, so that's who you are, but why the fuck are you here?"

Before he can answer, Giselle interrupts. "How about you introduce us to the other stranger in the room? I thought this would be a private meeting."

The table is an oval shape, so I don't miss the look that comes across Hope's face at the audacity this woman has to speak to me like that. Giselle isn't employed by the band. She's employed by *me* for them, so where does she get off talking to me like that?

I swallow down my annoyance, letting her think she's okay for the moment. "Sure. This is Harlow, my father's biological daughter, but I'm sure you know that." I can tell by the look on her face that she does.

"So why is she in this meeting?"

For a second, I'm worried. Not about Giselle or whatever nonsense is running through her head, but that Harlow is going to get up and leave. Thank fuck, when I look at her, she's amused. There she is, that beautiful fiery girl who refused to let us chase her away. I thought the stalker had taken some of the spark out of her, but I can see the woman who stood up to us all has returned.

"None of your fucking business to be honest," she tells her, and Giselle looks like she's swallowed a rotten grape. "But maybe I'm here for your job." Giselle frowns, but then she smiles smugly like she knows something we don't, like she's not worried she just had her job threatened. Ahh, now we're getting somewhere.

"Okay, enough of this. What the hell is going on? You guys got into a brawl in a club, and now you've asked for this meeting."

It's like I've opened the floodgates, and the words come pouring out. I try to listen to what everyone is saying, but I can't make heads or tails of it. I hold up my good hand and stand up to get their attention. "Alright, let's do this one at a time."

Chapter Ten

Harlow

What comes out of Jessie's mouth is nothing short of Jerry-Springer-worthy drama. Apparently, the manager, Giselle, wasn't all that professional with her clients. She started a relationship with both Jessie and Cash and played them off one another. Jessie caught on and dumped her like a hot potato, but Cash, well, he believed the web she wove, and it turns out that she convinced him he had more talent than the other four have in their little toes and should go solo.

Then the lawyer dude speaks up, demanding that Cash be let out of the contract and that there needs to be a division of royalties and such.

By the end of the story, Holden looks so gobsmacked I can't help but feel sorry for him. I'm sure that's not his usual reaction, he seems to be cool under pressure, but I guess this blindsided him. Hope and I exchange a glance.

"Okay, if you would just give us a moment, we will have our lawyers join the meeting." With that direction, Hope stands up, with me ready to follow suit, but Holden's still struggling to process all the drama. I kick him in the shin before I get to my feet, and that seems to snap him out of his disbelief. Now he just looks pissed. He storms out, and Hope follows him.

I look to Jessie, who is just as good looking in real life as he is in his music videos. "I'll send Missy in to take your drinks order. This shouldn't take us long."

He smiles at me, but I can see the strain on his and the other guys' faces. Cash, Giselle, and the lawyer just look smug. Assholes.

I hurry after Holden and Hope, and sure enough, I find Holden swearing up a storm in his office while Hope tries to calm him down.

"What the fuck are we going to do? She's fucking Yoko Ono'd them." He's tugging at his hair with his good arm, so I hurry over and wrap my arms around him, holding him tight. The last thing we need is for him to get so worked up that he opens his healing wound. He shudders in my arms, all the built-up emotions easing, before he takes a big breath and steps away to sit down on one of the couches in his office.

"Thanks, I needed that. Okay, quick brainstorm. Harlow, I want your fresh eyes. Tell me what you thought."

I think back to what I had observed in that room. There were some serious issues that are not just going to heal overnight. "You seriously want to know what I think?"

Both Hope and Holden nod. "Let him go. If he wants a solo career, let him go." They both frown.

"That would be giving in to his arrogance though," Hope points out, and while I understand why she might think that, I have to shake my head.

"No, it wouldn't be. I didn't say offer him a solo contract. I said let him go. I mean, check with the rest of the band first, but I think they would be okay with it. None of them looked happy at all. And sack that bitch's ass. Isn't there something in her contract that says no fraternizing with the clients?"

Holden looks to Hope for advice. "What is the exact wording of the contract they signed? Are they entitled to any royalties or rights as far as the music goes? And yes, good idea, let's check Giselle's as well. No matter what happens with the band, she is out of any Neighpalm-related business."

"I'm just looking now." Her fingers fly across the screen of her tablet as she scans the band's contract. "According to this, only the writers of the music and/or lyrics are entitled to continue receiving royalties if the band ever decides to stop performing. They've also far exceeded the advance we gave them on signing with Neighpalm Records, so as far as I can tell, we could let him go and not owe him anything. We would have to check with the rest of the band to confirm whether he was involved with the writing of the songs."

"Okay, let's get the other four members in here and have a private chat with them," Holden agrees. Hope starts to stand up, but I stop her.

"I'll get them for you. That way you can wait for the lawyers and the other members of the PR and brief them before you're back in the others' sights," I suggest, and I know it's a good idea when their shoulders release a tiny bit of that tension. I can't imagine how stressful this is for them. Thank goodness that I don't have to deal with this on a day-to-day basis. I would have an ulcer. I appreciate Dad's intentions with having me observe the different aspects of the Neighpalm empire, but so far, I'm perfectly happy to avoid any long-term involvement in these companies. Dealing with humans sucks. God, I miss working with animals. I need to give Princess and those adorable kittens a cuddle tonight.

When I get back to the conference room, the band members are shouting at one another, hurling insults across the table, but it all comes to an abrupt stop when they see me. "Hi, Holden would just like a quick private meeting with you guys. If you don't mind, I'll show you to his office." The four non-assholes quickly get up, looking glad to be leaving the room.

"Hang on a minute. Why is it private? What is he talking to them about that he can't say in front of us?" The lawyer sneers, probably thinking he's intimidating me if the way he puffs up his chest is any indication.

"How about you sit your ass down? We should have an answer for you shortly, but there is more than one person involved in this decision, so it's only fair that they get a chance to talk about what they want too." I eye Cash, noting that he has this whole arrogant demeanor to him, like his shit doesn't stink and he thinks the whole thing is a joke. I cannot wait to see him get booted out on his ass.

"But, but, but," Giselle stammers oh so elegantly. "Shouldn't I be in the meeting because I'm their manager?" I laugh out loud at the comment.

"Oh honey, looks to me like you've already picked a side. Doesn't seem to me that you have all of their best interests at heart. Don't worry, you'll get a chance to speak to Holden too. Probably. Maybe."

Giselle sits back down, and Cash takes her hand, whispering to her. I'm not sure what he said to her since it was too quiet, but the reappearance of her smug smile makes it seem like they have something up their sleeves.

Leaving them in the conference room, I lead the

rest of the band members back to the office. My heart goes out to the guys, seeing a sad and subdued demeanor that's so different from anything I've ever seen on tv or in videos of them. It can't be easy to have a member of what should be your family decide they want to leave you behind. Actually, I know that's not easy. Story of my fucking life.

"Hey, guys, come in and take a seat." Holden smiles at them reassuringly and gestures to the couches. He pulls over the two chairs that were in front of his desk, sitting in one while Hope settles in the other. I awkwardly stand to the side before he waves me over and plonks me down on his lap. What the fuck? I struggle, trying to get up, but he holds me still.

"Guys, have you met my girlfriend Harlow?" he starts off. "This is Jessie, Sacha, Tristan, and Kyan." He points to one after the other, and although they smile politely, Kyan looks confused.

"Didn't you say she was your sister?" I stiffen up, but Hope and Holden both laugh.

He squeezes me, returning some of the calm I helped him find a few minutes earlier. "Don't panic. We're going to get this question a lot."

"The rest of my siblings and I are adopted and were raised by Brad Summers. Harlow is Brad's biological daughter, but they only just found each other recently. So there's no blood relation. If we're being technical, I guess you could call us her adopted siblings, but we're only just getting to know each other. And, well, what I feel for her is nothing like what I feel for most of my siblings."

Kyan's confusion clears from his face.

"But we're not here to talk about us. I just wanted to touch base with the four of you and ask how you feel about all this."

They exchange glances, and I get the feeling they really don't want to rock any boats.

I climb off of Holden's lap, get his chair from behind his desk, and pull it over. He pouts, which makes the guys laugh, but I just don't feel comfortable there while we're discussing something business related.

"Look, did you just want to talk to me about it? Holden and Hope are your bosses, and I get that you may be worried that you're jeopardizing your careers even though I can assure you you're not."

Holden and Hope look at me with surprise, but right at the end they exchange some kind of smirk. Idiots. I just know how it feels to be the underdog, and at the moment these guys are most definitely that. I bet they think their bandmate is fucking everything up for them all, and they're worried about whether they're going to have careers once this meeting is finished.

Jessie, who seems to be the spokesman for the four of them, shakes his head. "No, it's alright. What we need to say can be said to all of you."

"Okay then, great. So tell us."

"It's no secret that Cash has never been that

easy to get along with. When you put us together, we were all strangers, but the four of us were stoked just to be given the chance. Cash has always been a little bitter. He thought he was good enough for a solo career," Jessie explains, and I can see this is news to Holden and Hope. "He's good at appearing as a team player, but the reality of that is far from the truth."

"Yeah, and although he has a great voice, he hasn't got a single bit of musical creativity in his bones. He hasn't once been involved in writing any of the songs. He's happy to sit back, letting the four of us do that, then reap the rewards once it's done," Tristan chimes in angrily, and I watch as Sacha reaches out and grabs his hand, squeezing it. They're pretty quick to drop their hold when they realize I saw, but I don't care what they do or how close they are. I try to convey all of that with a wink, but with the tense topic of discussion, I can't tell if it makes them feel any better.

"He and Jessie have always clashed, and Giselle didn't help things either. We tried to warn both of them not to get involved with her, but they didn't listen. Thankfully, this dickhead came to his senses quickly, but Cash keeps throwing it in his face that he won the girl." Sacha sounds defeated, and my heart goes out to him.

"So I get the feeling none of you would be sad to see him go?" Hope asks, and they all shake their heads.

"To be honest, it would be a relief, but we also don't want to give up the group. We love what we do." There's an earnestness in Kyan's voice that borders right on the edge of desperation. He means every word he's saying, and he doesn't have his pride getting in the way of showing that.

"Okay, so what I'm hearing from you is that it would be a relief to get rid of him. Well, I guess that's what we'll do." They look shocked at hearing him say that and worried as well. What kind of reputation does Holden have? So far, he's seemed nothing but kind and understanding. How in the world has their manager tortured them to make them so afraid of speaking up for themselves and what they want?

"Don't worry, Holden has no plans to get rid of all of you, do you?" I turn to him, raising my eyebrows in that universal 'dude, say something' face that hopefully jolts him into action.

He emphatically shakes his head. "Fuck no. We'll happily get rid of the baggage, aka Giselle and Cash, and I have a feeling they'll regret their newfound freedom pretty fast. He had no part in writing the songs, so he has no claim to any of them. We'll give him some kind of settlement and make him sign a non-disclosure so he can't talk about the circumstances of him leaving the band. If he does, we'll sue. That manager of yours might have convinced him that he's the top dog, but he's fighting against Neighpalm Records, not just you guys. He'll learn his place soon enough. Speaking of managers, we'll be getting you a new one. In fact..." He stops and looks at Hope, the two of them communicating without words. They've been friends for so long they can do that. After her nod, he continues. "Now that Hope has decided to become my right hand woman, I might personally take on the management of the band."

"So you're not going to offer him a solo contract?" Tristan sounds both curious and hopeful, but I can't blame him. If my bandmate had treated me like shit then tried to launch his own career, I'd be a little salty about his future success too.

"Fuck no!" Holden exclaims once again, and everyone laughs, breaking the tension in the room. "He's proven he has no loyalty to you guys, and he's difficult to deal with. No one at Neighpalm will touch him with a ten-foot pole."

"But because we won't be able to talk about what happened either, we're going to have to do something to appease the masses," he says thoughtfully, pausing like he's trying to run scenarios through his mind as we speak.

"How about we run another competition to replace him?" The four guys start to shake their heads, but I hold up my hand. "Hear me out. We could get Declan involved in the production. You could have auditions, but you guys would have full say in who is in or out until you narrow the selection down to like 20. Once some of them are weeded out, we move you all into a house and you get to know each other. That way, not only do you get a new member, but it's someone you've chosen and spent time with. We could even film some of it so the fans think that they're along for the journey too. Allow them to vote for their favorites, but of course you guys get the final decision. Maybe someone can get removed each week or something. I'm sure Declan's production company can come up with something that keeps you all happy and gives you an appropriate time to make the best decision and protect your team dynamic."

Hope and Holden are looking at me like I just provided the answer to their prayers, but the band still seems super wary. Oh well, sometimes you've gotta really push to sell something. I forge on, wanting this to work. There's not much that I can do for Holden—the man is a Summers after all—but I *could* potentially fix this for him.

"Of course, we could set you up in a large house for the duration so they're not in your personal space. That would also give us enough room for them, and everyone would sign a non-disclosure form so that they couldn't talk about what happened once they left unless it was pre-approved by you guys and Neighpalm." There's a little light starting to spark in their eyes, so maybe my enthusiasm is contagious.

"Harlow's right. This is going to be huge news, and we need to do something to distract the media so they don't go looking for dirt. Luckily, we'll be able to gag both Cash and Giselle, but it won't stop rumors, especially once they realize Giselle was fired at the same time. But you guys are our priority. If you want us to come up with another solution, we can still think about it, but Harlow's idea is really good. It's a win-win for all of us, a little bit of publicity sleight of hand."

"As long as we get final say—even if our decision is that we don't want any of them—I don't mind," Sacha says, sounding tired. "I just want Cash gone. He's a real asshole." The others chime in with their agreement.

A knock on the door has us all looking toward it as Declan comes in.

"Hey, you wanted to see me?" he says to Holden. My eyebrows jump in surprise. I hadn't even seen Holden text him.

"Yeah, Dec, thanks for coming. You know the guys from Ninja Starfish." Holden gestures to the guys, and they all exchange pleasantries.

"Yeah, I do, but you seem to be down a member," Declan comments as he comes over to me. He leans in and gives me a kiss too, which is unexpected but not unwelcome.

"Hello, trouble, what mischief are you getting up to today?" God, this new version of Declan is delicious, and I can't help but melt on the spot.

"What the fuck? I thought she was your girl-friend," Jessie blurts, rocking back in his chair, and I can see how this may look to him, especially considering why we're all here.

"Easy, man." Holden holds his hands up. "I share my girlfriend with my brothers. She's not another Yoko, don't worry."

"Huh?" I swear, the look on Jessie's face is one I've only seen in those gifs where the adorable puppy tilts his head. Ya know, the one where he looks completely confused, but he's just so cute that you want to squish his cheeks and rub his belly. Not that I'm going to do that. They already think the' situation is fucking weird.

"Look, it's a long story, but it seems to be working for us. I also have a relationship with Oliver, which existed before we even were adopted by Brad. So I'm sure that we're probably going to end up in the tabloids once everyone finds out, but I'm hoping you'll keep things quiet for the moment. I also hope that you know we won't judge you for any relationships you choose to pursue." I can see him looking at Sacha and Tristan when he says that, so I guess he saw what I did.

He leaves that for the guys to think about as he explains the situation to Declan. By the end, Declan is excited about the idea. "I'm all in. We can get a team together and start working on it as soon as possible if you want. Then we can do a press release at the same time that you announce Cash's departure from the group. Make sure you put in the contract that he gives us a week before he tells anyone."

"Are you guys in?" Holden asks. The band had been talking quietly amongst themselves while he was running through the basics with Declan, but I know what their answer will be. For the first time since I saw them enter the other meeting room, they look like they have some life back in them. They're not looking like kicked dogs anymore, and although their worries are far from over, they're starting to show a little hunger and eagerness to move forward.

"We're in. We just want Cash and Giselle gone. If we can manage that without him taking any rights to our music, then we'll do anything you want us to," Jessie says, speaking for the group.

"Yeah, he kept trying to tell us he was going to stop us from ever performing those songs again," Kyan tells us. "It's been so stressful. It would be like having to start all over again even though we wrote most of them."

"Okay, do you want to head back to the conference room? I'll get the lawyers to draw us up some contracts." Hope stands up, and the guys follow her back to the room, leaving me with the two brothers. My pulse starts to race when I realize that I've got not one but two Summers' full attention. If the guys from Ninja Starfish were just starting to look hungry, then Declan and Holden are absolutely ravenous.

Harlow

I stand up and start to edge away, feeling like I'm being stalked.

"Harlow, was that all your idea?" Declan purrs, his hand reaching out to stop me. He crowds into my front as Holden closes in behind, holding me in place.

"Ah, yeah?"

"It's so very sexy the way your mind works. We couldn't have come up with a better idea ourselves," Holden says next to my ear, making goosebumps appear all over my arms. Declan's big hands come up to my waist. If it was just him and me, I might be a little more nervous because we haven't had too many moments together. But somehow, having this interaction with both Declan and Holden eases something inside me even as it sparks and stokes a flame.

"How did you come up with the idea?" Declan looks down at me from his height, an eyebrow raised in question.

"I just thought about how I'd feel if my favorite band broke up. Even if it's not the original line-up, I'd prefer to see them with another member than go their separate ways. And who knows? They might even be better now."

"Well, the guys seemed happy with the idea, and letting them choose was a stroke of genius, so we don't run into the same problem again. I guess it's been a long few years for them if Cash has been a douche from the beginning." Holden gives me a kiss on the neck then pulls away, sighing. "As much as I'd like to stay and play, I need to do a few things before we go back into that meeting."

"Oh, Sharon from legal was out in the waiting area when I came in," Declan tells Holden, not looking away from me.

"I'll go and speak to her about what we need. We'll reconvene in ten minutes, Harlow," Holden says, but I can't look away from Declan's stare.

"Right. Well then, I'll leave you to it," Holden mutters before he leaves, but the echo of his chuckle tells me he's not actually upset.

"Hi." The word comes out sounding breathy, and I want to kick myself. When did I turn into a simpering mess around this guy? Probably right around the time he decided to pull his head out of his ass and bring his A game to the party.

"Hi." His lips turn up in a little smile as he backs me up against the wall. "Did I tell you how beautiful you look today?" he asks as my back hits the wall, his body pressing into mine.

I shake my head. "No, you didn't say much at all. You were too busy arguing with Thomas about our date. Who won?"

His smile disappears, the growl that escapes his mouth telling me the answer. "I'd love to have a stay-at-home date with you in the conservatory," I tell him, and the frown smooths out. "I'd be happy to have a picnic in my pajamas if it meant I was getting to spend time with you." In my head, I was saying it to appease his ego, but as the words actually come out, I realize it's the truth. I really don't care where we are or what we do. Spending time together is what counts, and I want that. I honestly want to spend time with Declan.

His smile returns. "A picnic in your pajamas? Does that mean we'll be in your bed as well? Because I won't say no to that." Before I can answer, he swoops down and kisses me.

Unlike all the kisses we've had just recently, this one is full of fire and a promise of something more. A tantalizing taste of what sex with Declan would be like. A raw carnality that I've never experienced before is creating an ache deep within me. There's no gentle caress, no whisper of heat, just a fierce dance, savage and raw and all consuming. My body becomes pliant against his, and his mouth curves up under mine.

He pulls away, and I chase after his mouth, throwing away any pride I might have clung to. Damn the arrogant man. Both our chests are heaving, and my panties are damp. I was on the brink of an orgasm from rubbing against his thigh, and now I'm feeling pathetically cranky.

"Damn it, I want to bend you over Holden's desk and see how your pussy feels around my cock." His dirty words have me moaning quietly. "But I also want to prove to you that this isn't just about sex, so I'm going to back away and let you go to your meeting with my brother."

He does as he says, but I can't miss it when he stops to adjust the thick length that's pushing against his pants. He winces, and I almost do the same in sympathy. That cannot be comfortable. "I'm just going to sit at Holden's desk for a moment before leaving. I don't like the way Missy looks at me... makes me feel like I'm a gazelle and she's a starving lioness." I straighten out my clothes and smooth back the flyaway bits of my hair, ignoring the urge that says I should go out there and establish some kind of old-school safari dominance in the form of hair pulling and a chokehold. I'm pretty sure I've got the worst of the urges under control, but I can't stop the claws from peeking out.

"From what I can see, she's not a particularly

fussy lioness. In fact, she seems like a thirsty bitch to me. Unless she's got some tic that makes her flutter her eyelashes at all the pretty men."

"You think I'm pretty?" The question is meant to be teasing, but the man is so smug that I know he needs a little ego control.

"Yeah, but I also think the band is pretty too, so maybe I'm not the best judge either." His cockiness drops as I wave goodbye and walk out with the last word. Of course, I don't tell him that I'm currently too happy with him and his brothers to truly look anywhere else. I'll let him stew on it for a little while, arrogant asshole.

I'm smiling when I walk back into the conference room. The tension is high, and I can tell that Giselle has been kicking up a fuss despite the new guests to her tantrum.

"How come they got a private meeting but we didn't?" She points at me. "She said we would get our turn." Holden and Hope look at me, and I shrug.

"I lied. The three of you made it very clear where you stand on the situation." I move around the table and take my seat next to Hope and Holden, no longer feeling like I should sit out. Although I know this business isn't for me, I am super happy that I can give my input and support my family in any capacity they require, even ways they weren't expecting.

"Okay, this is what's going to happen. Sharon

here is drawing up the contract as we speak." Holden points to the older lady in the room who has a laptop sitting in front of her. Cash and Giselle look excited, which honestly almost makes me laugh. They are going to be shocked when they discover what the contract is for. "But first, we'll have you all sign a non-disclosure form before we go any further." A young man, who I'm assuming is Sharon's assistant, hands forms to all of the band members, the lawyer, and Giselle.

I'm shocked that they all sign the form without even questioning what's in it, though Hope and Holden are pleased. I guess they're pretty common when you work in the entertainment industry

"Okay then," Holden continues once they've all finished. "Cash, you are getting what you want. As of today, you will no longer be a member of Ninja Starfish, and according to the original contract you signed, you have no rights to any of the band's lyrics or music since you were not involved in writing any of it. I'm sorry that you weren't happy, and we wish you the best in your future endeavors."

The room is quiet as everyone digests what Holden just said. I watch Cash carefully as he takes in everything, waiting for the moment he finally realizes what just happened. His mouth drops open in shock, and he turns to Giselle. "You said—" He breaks off as she shushes him.

"I will be taking on the role of Cash's manager as well as managing Ninja Starfish, and we'd like to negotiate for a solo contract for him," she states confidently even though the shadow in her eyes tells us she's worried. Good, she should be.

Holden snorts, but this time it's not from amusement. "Actually no, you're fired. Effective immediately. There is a no-fraternization clause in your contract, and you well and truly broke that. Not to mention even if there wasn't, I wouldn't trust you as far as I could throw you. You've proven to be sly and manipulative—not someone we want working for Neighpalm. You tried to play with the sharks, but you're just a guppy out of your depth."

It's her turn for her mouth to drop open. I really don't think she considered she would be fired. She blinks a couple of times before looking at the lawyer. He's been reading over the already signed non-disclosure contract, but what's the saying? No point closing the barn door once the horse has already left the stable. Something like that anyway. She stammers, "You-you can't do that."

"You bet I can," Holden replies.

"I'll destroy you in the media," she threatens, but Holden only points at the form in the lawyer's hand.

"Maybe you could have tried, but you signed the form. Anything that is said to the media from here on out will be considered breaking this contract, and we *will* sue you. Think about whether it's worth it."

She stands up and slams her hands down on the

table. "It doesn't matter. I've got other companies that have shown interest in Cash. We'll get him a contract somewhere else." She's angry now, and there's no missing the vindictive glint in her eyes. "I'll also go to the media and tell them all about what goes on in the inner workings of Ninja Starfish. I think they would be interested to know what the boys get up to in their private lives."

The lawyer clears his throat, and the flush to his cheeks tells me he's come to the realization that they signed away all their rights without even reading them. "Yeah, no, that's covered too. It says here that you signed one when you became their manager, so anything you say will be liable as well."

Her face pales as the reality of the situation finally hits her, and she looks at Cash. "Come on, let's get out of here. I'm going to reach out to my other contacts. We'll be fine." But when they all start to leave, Cash looks back, eyes narrowed at his ex-bandmates.

"You'll pay for this," he threatens before he disappears.

"Well, how fucked is that?" Hope says after a moment of shocked silence. "He started everything then blamed you guys. What an asshole! And they didn't even stick around to hear what's going to happen next. Damn it, I wanted to see his face when he realized he was being replaced like that." She accompanies the last word with a snap of her fingers, a dramatic little move but certainly fitting. I have zero doubts that it will be easy to replace that dickhead. Ninja Starfish is hot right now; people would kill for the chance to get the publicity of being part of their band.

The tension breaks with her blunt words, and relieved laughter fills the room. Phew, that was full on.

We spend the remainder of the meeting hashing out the details of their new contract, and then it's finally time for me to leave.

"Sorry, but I have to run. I've got another appointment." Holden stands up with me as I say my goodbyes and walks me to the door while the band waves me off.

"Thanks for your help, babe. Have fun playing matchmaker."

He gives me a kiss, and Hope shouts out behind me, "I'll be up in twenty minutes, okay? Oh, and I ordered food for everyone because I know you forgot about it. It should be delivered soon." A moment of panic hits me, but it eases with her words.

"Thank fuck, you might just be right about the forgetting thing." She winks at me in return. "I'll come find you later," I tell Holden. I don't trust him to be honest about whether he has to wear his sling or not since I know he's fed up with it. For my peace of mind, and Oli's, I want to hear exactly what his PT has to say.

I give him another kiss and head toward the

elevator, happy with my morning and even happier about the task in front of me. I've never played matchmaker before, and I'm excited about it.

When I get to the conservatory, I realize I've been so busy that I left my laptop in Holden's office and haven't applied for my license like I had planned. So after I've had lunch with Hope, I'll have to do that.

I stop at the reception desk before going forward. "Hey, Lucy, did things get better or worse as the day progressed?" I ask quietly, and she giggles.

"Um, I'm not sure it got better, but it didn't get any worse," she says diplomatically, and I cringe again. "If it's any consolation, Lindy and Rowena just left to get lunch."

A sigh of relief leaves me. I wasn't sure what I was going to do if they crashed our party. "Thank goodness for that. I've got food coming up, and Alex Winters and Shane Silver are both joining me for lunch. Could you send them to the garden room when they get up here?"

"Of course, Harlow, and I just got a call saying your food was on its way up. I'll be happy to show them to the garden room."

"Thanks, Lucy, you're awesome." With that, I make my way toward the garden room. When I get there, the humid air rushes out of the entrance as soon as I push the door open. I can hear murmured voices but can't see anything yet, so I follow the path through the plants until I get to the little clearing where there's a table and chairs. A memory of me having one of my first meals with Dad flashes into my brain, bringing a smile along with it. The last time I was in here I didn't really get to explore, but now that I have a spare couple of minutes, I decide to have a little look around. Behind the clearing is another area which has actual trees planted in it—hibiscus and frangipani and big leafy foliage. So I continue to follow the path through, searching for the voices, until I reach a T-junction and need to pick a direction. Choosing to go right, I follow the path until I get to a little man-made waterfall. It's not very high, maybe to my waist, but it's flowing over some rocks and into a pond.

All of sudden, I'm grabbed and shoved up against the wall, a hand over my mouth stopping me from screaming. I thrash my body about, trying to dislodge the person who has their weight pressed against me.

"Stop moving, Harlow, and I'll remove my hand." Thomas' voice is harsh and low, but I still my body as he demanded.

Once he's sure I've stopped, he removes his hand, but his body stays pressed against mine. And although I'm still breathing heavily from fright and just about ready to knee him in the balls, my body is also responding to the weight and heat of him.

I look up at him, and he's scowling at me. "What the hell?" I try to move him off of me, but he doesn't budge.

"What were you thinking? I could have been anybody," he growls. "Are you not taking your safety seriously?"

I take a deep breath and let it out, trying to calm my rapidly beating heart and traitorous body.

"I wasn't thinking. I just assumed I'd be all right." Our eyes meet, and I'm surprised to see that anger is not the only thing in them. In fact, the rapidly hardening length in his pants tells me that he may not be as indifferent as he pretends to be. I adjust myself so that it pushes against my throbbing core, but his eyes widen and he rips himself away from me when he realizes.

"Do better," he snaps before stalking back down the path in the opposite direction. I guess he wants to continue this aloof facade. Well, that's his problem.

Letting out a huge breath, I follow after him and head back to the table. With Thomas' warning in my head, I probably shouldn't search out the voices I heard since they may not be friendly. But then I bet the few dollars in my purse that Thomas already knows who it is and has deemed them safe. He's too extra to not have beat me here and checked out the place before I even got into the elevator.

When I get back to the T-junction, I find Jace and Jacinta coming from the other direction. Jace has a smile on his face, but Jacinta is quite frazzled. In fact, for a woman who is usually stylish and put together, she looks… wrinkled. I try to peek around them to see where they came from, but Jacinta grabs me by the arm and propels me forward.

"What were you…" I try to ask, but she cuts me off.

"Oh, Harlow, you're here! Great. I'm starving." She quickly changes the subject, and Jace chuckles. When I turn back to him, he winks.

By the time we get back to the table, Alex and Shane are chatting with Thomas and there's a mountain of food on the table.

Jacinta stops shortly, a little gasp escaping her mouth, and her breath stutters once more when Jace passes us to greet both Shane and Alex with a kiss. Holy wow. I fan my face then stop and look at the woman next to me, my eyes widening when a growl slips out of her mouth.

"Did you…" Again, I try to ask a question, but she cuts me off. Stepping forward, she puts on a bright smile that I can tell is slightly forced.

"Alex, Shane, what a surprise! Harlow didn't say you guys were joining us for lunch." She greets them, and they both go to her and give her a lingering kiss on the cheek, Shane winking at me over her shoulder. Yes, full-court press from the guys. Jacinta is not going to know what hit her.

"Oh, it was a last-minute thing. I'm sure she just didn't get a chance to tell you." Alex covers for me before they both approach and hug me, Alex giving me an extra-tight squeeze because neither of them knew about Jacinta and Jace either. Everyone is surprised today. "Apart from a couple of phone calls, we haven't had a chance to catch up since we did the trip to Louisiana with Jace. And now that her warden has allowed her to leave the house..." He winks at Thomas, who raises an eyebrow in amusement. "We thought we'd take full advantage of it."

"Come on, let's eat. I'm starving," I announce, heading for the table. I just need to get the rest of them eating so they can't run away once Hope comes over with my alibi.

Chapter Twelve

Harlow

Sure enough, just as everyone has dished up plates of the yummy food, Hope arrives and announces that I'm needed elsewhere. I can see the questioning look on Jacinta's face, but before she says anything, I jump to my feet.

"Damn it, and I had just started lunch!" I'm not sure my acting is all that great because Thomas raises that enigmatic eyebrow once more, but the other guys don't miss a beat. I'm pretty sure they're all picking up what I'm putting down. "Come on, Tom." I slip up and call him by his family nickname, but quickly go on, hoping no one notices. "You better escort me to make sure no one kidnaps me or makes an attempt on my life again."

That goes over well... not. The room falls into awkward silence, and Jacinta's face looks haunted at the reminder. Alex, the sweetie, reaches over and grabs her hand, giving it a squeeze before scolding me. "Harlow, that's not funny. How can you joke about such things?"

"Yeah, sorry, you're right. But if I don't joke about them, there's a good chance I'll fall to pieces," I quietly apologize, and their faces all turn sympathetic. Not wanting to see the pity, I quickly wave goodbye and pick up my full plate. "I'm just going to take mine with me. Hope, you should help yourself. There's plenty of food. You should bring yours too," I instruct Thomas. "I'm not sure if we'll get back in time to eat." Hope makes herself a plate as everyone else at the table starts to eat, and Thomas slowly stands up and grabs his own.

"I'm so sorry about this," I repeat to Alex and Shane. "I'll call you tomorrow, so we can make plans. We're not going to Europe until next weekend now, so I'm sure we can fit something in before we go."

"Sounds good," Shane assures me as Alex winks and Jace waves a hand. Jacinta starts to say something again, but I cut her off.

"I'll see you tonight at game night!" As master of the smooth exit strategy, I hurry Hope and Thomas out of the room before she can question us. The three of us make our way to the elevator before silently stepping in.

"So what's so important that you needed

Harlow for?" Thomas asks dryly as the elevator heads for Neighpalm Records once more.

Hope looks at me, and I shrug. "It's all part of my matchmaking scheme, and I know you know that." I poke him in the chest with my fork.

"Just checking. So where are we going now?" he asks, looking between the two of us.

"Our office. Holden's still chatting with Ninja Starfish in the conference room, and I thought we could have lunch before the doctor and PT get here."

Thomas nods his head. "Okay, I'm going to my office, then I have to talk to Dad about something. Let me know if you plan to go anywhere else."

I gape at him. "Just *okay*? You made a huge fuss in the garden room, practically manhandling me in your anger, and now you're just going to leave us?" The elevator doors open in front, and Hope steps out, leaving me with the stone-faced Thomas.

"Get off the elevator, Harlow," he deadpans. I step out, but as I watch the doors close, I think I see one side of his mouth curl up the smallest amount. Nah, I must have imagined things. Otherwise, I think I'd just have to fall over in shock. Shaking my head, I follow Hope to Holden's office.

"Hey, what was that about him manhandling you?" she asks as we enter his empty office and take a seat on the couches.

I put my plate on the coffee table in front of us and breathe out a tired sigh. "Wow, it's been a busy morning." I try to stall, pushing away the escaped tendrils of hair around my face.

"Harlow, don't avoid my question." I look up at my friend; her brown eyes are sparkling with amusement as she shovels a forkful of food into her mouth.

"Ugh, freaking Thomas cornered me when I got lost in the garden room, demanding to know why I wasn't being more careful. Scared the crap out of me by putting his hand across my mouth and pushing me against the wall. What is it with men pushing me up against hard surfaces?"

She wiggles her eyebrows and gets up, going over to a mini fridge and pulling out two bottles of water. "I don't know, sounds like fun to me." She hands me one of the bottles before unscrewing the lid of hers and taking a drink. "You're getting to him, Harlow. Before you know it, your harem of five will be a harem of six, and women around the world will mourn the loss of the eligible Summers men."

I roll my eyes at her. "Please. Thomas has made it clear to me that I'm only a job." I know I'm trying to deny it, but I secretly wonder if she's right. He didn't feel uninterested. In fact, he felt extremely interested until he ripped his body away from me. "Anyway, it's not all it's cracked up to be, trust me. I have five boyfriends, and do you think I can get any of them to put out? Seriously, until this morning, they've been treating me like fragile glass. Well,

Holden, Oliver, and Kai have been. I've barely seen Jaxon or Declan this week, and we're certainly not at the sharing a bed stage. I swear I'm so frustrated that I'm likely to jump the next one I see no matter where we are."

"Well, I guess that makes me the luckiest one of all." Looking up, Oliver is standing at the door I hadn't even noticed had opened. Though from the look on Hope's face, she had.

I feel a blush creep over my cheeks as he joins me on the couch, throwing himself next to me. "Here I am, now proceed with the ravishing." He reclines with his arms wide, causing Hope to giggle with laughter.

"Settle, loverboy. Let me eat some lunch and build up my energy first." I pat his leg, and he pouts playfully before sitting back up.

"I saw Thomas in the elevator, and he told me about your matchmaking schemes." He tries to pinch something off my plate, but I pretend to stab him with my fork. "I guess once Jacinta is all tucked away, it will be your turn," Oliver says to Hope, who instantly stops giggling and shakes her head.

"Oh no you don't, Oliver Summers. Just because you're blissfully happy and getting every-thing you've always wanted, don't you go sticking your nose into my business. I am perfectly happy being single and ready to mingle."

He looks at her, all signs of joking gone from his face. "Hope, you're an honorary Summers. It would be remiss of us not to make sure you weren't blissfully happy like the rest of us."

Bam! Heart melted. Jesus freaking Christ, these Summers boys are lethal. Sweet, kind, and caring, not to mention smoking hot, they are the whole package, and now I want Hope to have the same thing. But I will need to involve Holden in my matchmaking schemes this time; he knows my new friend better and should be able to help me.

I change the subject to lift the light tension in the room. There's a story there, but now is not the time. "So what are you doing here?" I ask my heavily tattooed honey as he tries once more to steal food off my plate. Rolling my eyes, I give in and hand him the rest, receiving a kiss on my cheek in trade.

"Thanks, you're the best. I wanted to be here when the PT and doctor came. I don't trust Holden to be honest because he's had enough of wearing the sling."

"Yes, I had the same thought," I tell him, going over to where I'd stored my backpack and pulling out my laptop. Now that I've finished eating, I might as well get started on my license and test.

Hope's phone beeps with a message, and when she looks at the screen, she groans. "Well, that was short and sweet. I've got to go. The PR department is having drama and needs me to weigh in on something." She stands up, taking her plate with her. "Can one of you let me know what they say about

Holden?" Our cooperation assured, she takes her leave.

"And then there were two." Oliver wiggles his eyebrows at me. "Shall we do that aforementioned ravishing now?" he asks, grinning at me with delight.

"Fuck, you're never going to let me live that down, are you?" I roll my eyes at him as my laptop loads the right page.

"Probably not," he agrees. "I would be negligent in my role of boyfriend if I wasn't making sure your needs were met."

"Well, keep it in your pants. I've got to do this, and I'm sure the doctor will be here soon."

I forget about him sitting there as my fingers fly across the keyboard, taking care of my application for the California vet license and shooting off some more applications for intern positions. I'm happy here with my new family, so I might as well try to find myself a job. If anything is successful, then I'll know staying will be the right decision.

When I look up at one stage, I find Oliver has stretched himself out along the couch, and his eyes are closed, face relaxed in sleep. It has been a stressful few weeks for us all, and sleep hasn't been our friend. Oliver especially has been showing signs of strain because of what happened to Holden. I don't want him to be stressed out, but I'm so pleased for them that they're back on track and openly showing the depth of their feelings for one another. And once their relationship is firmly back on the sexy train, I'd love to climb aboard. Or in the middle. Or watch it leave the station. Fuck, I just want to be involved somehow.

Another half an hour goes by before I'm finished, and I'm just leaning back in the chair when his office door opens. Holden walks in followed by two people wearing medical scrubs. One is a male, wearing blue scrubs, and he's looking at Holden like he'd like to jump him instead of checking over his wounds. The other one is a woman with a friendly smile on her face and green scrubs, featuring a logo on the left hand side of her chest. I can't make it out from here.

All three of them stop suddenly when they take me in. The nurse's eyes narrow as he spies me, but Holden's face lights up in a grin. "Oh hey, babe, is this where you got to?"

I hold a finger up to my mouth to shush him, but movement on the couch tells me that Oliver is already awake. I smile, one that matches Holden's, as we watch him sit up and rub his eyes, his now pale blue hair sticking up at all angles. He blinks owlishly before standing up and stretching. His top rides up, exposing the washboard stomach covered in tattoos, and I just about swallow my tongue.

"Babe… Babe… Harlow!" Holden's chuckling as I startle when he calls my name. "You've got a bit of drool there." He points to my mouth, and I totally buy into it, wiping the back of my hand across it before I realize he's joking. Oliver chuckles too, the smug asshole, and they both receive the pleasure of being flipped off.

"Okay, where shall we do this?" Holden claps his hands and looks at the two medical professionals for input.

"Well, did you want to do this in private?" the male asks, raising an eyebrow, but Holden shakes his head.

"Nope, I've got nothing to hide. They've both been playing nursemaid, so they've already seen everything I've got going on." I didn't think anyone could purse their lips enough to make it look like a cat's asshole, but this guy manages to do that while conveying all his disdain at the same time.

Is this the nurse who flirted so blatantly with Holden the day he was released from the hospital? Oliver had told me about throwing his card out the window. From the annoyed look on Oliver's face, I would say it is.

Oliver narrows his eyes at the nurse, and I can see the cogs practically spinning in his head. I need to jump in before he says something.

"Hi, I'm Harlow," I say to the two newcomers, "and that's Oliver. Are you the doctor?"

The woman in the scrubs steps forward, a friendly smile on her face. "Hi, I'm Kelly. I'm Holden's physical therapist, and this is Sam. He's the nurse who's come to look at Holden's wound to make sure it's healing up nicely so we can start working on the rest."

"So what happened? I thought a doctor was coming out to look at him," Oliver blurts out, unable to just be quiet.

"Well, our doctors are quite busy and really don't have time to be making house calls," Sam says shortly to him, and Kelly's eyes just about bulge out of her head. I don't blame her. I don't think there are many people who would call out the Summers family for requesting a house or office call.

Kelly jumps in for damage control. "Doctor Evans sends his apologies. He was all ready to come, but they had an emergency, and he wasn't able to leave. He said that it should be healing well and that Sam would be able to check over it for you. As long as there's no sign of infection, I think we will be good."

"Okay, let's just set up over there and get this done, shall we? We've got places to be tonight, and I don't want to hold you two up if we can avoid it." Holden's blatant dig at Sam is well hidden behind a friendly smile, but from the look on Kelly's face, she doesn't miss it at all.

The session is awkward for all involved since Sam blatantly flirts with Holden through the whole thing. I had to hold Oliver back a couple of times, but like I whispered in his ear, the sooner they're done, the sooner they can leave.

Holden's wound has healed well, with no signs

of infection, so Sam gives the okay for him to leave the dressings off now. Then Kelly goes over some exercise to help him get full mobility back into his shoulder and gives him permission to leave the sling off too.

We have a very happy Holden once they finish up, and he ushers them out of the room with a polite thank you. When he closes the door behind them, I hear the lock click. He grins at Oliver and me with a gleam in his eye, drinking in the way I'm snuggled into our boyfriend's lap. I can feel him stiffen beneath me as Holden stalks across the room to us, flexing the hand of his newly freed arm. I shift to stand up and move away, but Oliver's grip tightens, causing my heartrate to speed up as the thrill of excitement flows through me. What are they up to now?

Harlow

"Holden, what are you doing?" I ask as he continues to prowl closer, a man firmly set on a target. Again, I try to escape Oliver's grasp, but he holds me still, forcing my legs over the top of his and then widening them so I'm spread eagle and unable to get away.

Holden comes around to our side of the desk where he gets down on his knees and shuffles over, his hands resting on my thighs and his eyes full of heated promise.

"I do believe I owe you for this morning," he says as his hands start to push my dress up, raising an eyebrow as if to ask permission to keep going. The grin that lights his face when I nod is full of heat and promise.

"Oh, and what did I miss this morning?" Oliver

grumbles teasingly in my ear. His hands start to roam, skimming over my hips then up to my waist and stomach as he presses little kisses into my neck.

"Well, Miss Harlow here made our brother yell at me because we were late after she decided to help me in the shower."

"I'm sure it was completely worth it." Oliver sucks on my pulse points before using his teeth to scrape along my neck. My nipples pebble and my core throbs as I wiggle on his lap. I can feel him growing harder underneath me as Holden pushes my dress up to my waist, placing little kisses along the inside of my thighs before hooking his fingers underneath my panties.

"Last chance to say no, Harlow," he warns me, but I shake my head.

"Fuck no, don't you dare stop." The words roll out of my mouth before I can stop them, and the guys chuckle. Oliver's big hands cup my breasts as Holden pulls my panties down my legs, leaving me bare to both of them, before tossing them onto his desk. They both suck in a deep breath, and Oliver pulls down the front of my dress to expose my naked breasts.

"I've been trying to figure out all day if you were wearing a bra or not," he whispers in my ear. "Sneaky girl, teasing me while we're at work."

"Have you been feeling neglected, Mistress?" Holden rumbles as he blows a hot breath of air across my lips, teasing me just inches from where I really want his mouth. "I would have thought Kai was taking care of your needs."

"No, that asshole wouldn't put out either. It was like you guys had some secret discussion to clam jam me until I fully recovered from my accidents," I growl, and he looks up at me, his hazel eyes smoldering with unspoken lust.

"Well, it's best that I take care of my Mistress' needs, now isn't it?" And with that, he runs his tongue through my soaked folds as Oliver pinches at my nipples, the two sensations causing a loud moan to leave my mouth. My hands claw at the chair as the boys work my body into a frenzy of built-up need. Holden teases my clit with lazy flicks before devouring me with his mouth and teeth, fucking me with his tongue. Not to be forgotten, Oliver cups my breasts, kneading them, and plucks at my nipples. My breath is ragged, and I can feel a trickle of sweat running down the back of my neck as my head thrashes back and forth with the intensity of this fire they're stoking.

"More, I need more," I gasp out in the hope that Holden will put me out of my misery, but all I can do is practically sob with disappointment when he pulls his mouth away.

"Shh. Mistress, we'll take care of you." Beneath his words comes the whisper of a zipper lowering. My eyes, which had been squeezed tight against the onslaught of sensation, fly open, but it's not Holden's pants that are coming off. Instead, he's unzipping Oliver's.

"Lift her up a little," he rumbles, and Oliver's hands leave my breasts to slide under my thighs, lifting me up as he also lifts his own hips. Holden quickly pulls Oliver's jeans down before he settles himself back on the chair, his bare cock now lying against my throbbing wet folds, his piercings glinting in the light.

I can't tear my eyes away when Holden takes Oliver's cock in hand before his mouth engulfs it, taking him down to the base. Behind me, Oliver grunts and his chest heaves.

"Holy fuck," he groans, and together we watch Holden's head bob up and down before pulling away, his eyes blazing with heat.

"Condom?" he rasps, and I shake my head.

"I'm on birth control and clean," I tell them, the words almost strained by my excitement.

"So am I. I get tested for work all the time," Oliver says, nuzzling into my ear.

Holden doesn't wait any longer. Oliver lifts me just enough while Holden lines his cock up, then with one smooth move, he thrusts, letting me slide down until I'm impaled on his thick cock.

I throw my head back and moan, but Oliver grabs me by the hair and turns my head, covering my mouth with his as my pussy quivers around his hard length.

"That's right. You keep her quiet. It wouldn't

surprise me if Missy was listening at the door," Holden grumbles before dipping his head. *What is he…?*

Holy fuck. As Oliver starts to thrust in and out, Holden flicks his tongue against my clit again. I can feel his mouth traveling up and down, and I know he's not leaving Oliver out of the delicious torture because our boyfriend's moaning into my mouth nearly as loudly as I am.

With hard and steady thrusts, Oliver and Holden take me to a high I have never experienced before, making my body throb like one big overexposed nerve. My cries of pleasure are muffled by the mouth over mine until Holden latches on to my clit and gives one strong suck. There's no stopping it now. Arching my back, I scream, not caring about the nosy secretary, as Oliver buries himself as deep as he can, grunting his own pleasure. I can feel myself clenching around his hard cock while neverending waves of pleasure wash over me. Oliver's head burrows into the hollow where my neck meets my collarbone, whispering little snippets of praise that barely make sense to me in the euphoria of the moment. Holden delivers a couple of gentle licks as the pleasure waves start to peter out before sitting back on his heels, a self-satisfied look on his face that's wet with my release. My head spins from the intensity and the overwhelming wave of emotions that rush me in the aftermath of such an intimate encounter.

"God, you two look beautiful," he says with quiet reverence as he watches us come down from our blissful sexual high. "I am such a lucky man." He gets to his feet and leans over, gently kissing me before moving to Oliver and kissing him as well.

When he steps back, he turns away, adjusting himself before heading for the bathroom. Oliver nuzzles my neck, and once again, I turn my head to kiss him, but this time it's less fire and heat and more—oh fuck, I'm in deep—love. As our tongues tangle with one another, I feel more than see Holden return. In his hand he has a wet cloth, and when Oliver and I finally manage to tear ourselves away from one another, he helps me to my feet. A little moan escapes my mouth as Oliver's semi-hard length leaves my body.

"Feeling a little tender? He really knows how to use that cock, doesn't he?" Holden teases while he cleans me up. As soon as I'm ready, he moves on to Oliver, running the cloth over his dick that's glistening with my release.

"So, have you two.." I break off, kind of feeling awkward about bringing up the subject of them being intimate, but I guess this is the adult thing to do. I mean, I'm barely proficient at managing a relationship with one other person, let alone five different relationships while also being in the middle of two of my boyfriends who are also boyfriends. Wow, yep, that sounds a little confusing even to me.

They exchange a glance and shake their heads.

"No, not yet. We weren't sure where we all stood, even after our conversation. We both have feelings for you, and neither of us wanted to alienate you by letting ourselves get lost in each other. We've experienced life without our relationship, and while we agree that we love each other and are extremely happy to have a second chance, we equally agree that this relationship with you is important enough that we want to get it right."

"Guys, I'm going to be honest." I grab one of each of their hands and squeeze. "One of the things that scares me about this relationship with all of you is not being able to sexually meet your needs. If you two are taking care of each other, my vagina will probably weep with gratitude." They both gape at me before they start chuckling, which lightens the atmosphere. "Seriously, have at it. I'd love a front row seat but don't think that you need to invite me. I will not be upset at all if you guys want to have some moments that are just for yourselves. I love you…" I break off as I realize what words just slipped out of my mouth. Shit! Panic starts racing through my veins, wondering if they heard what I said, and from the stunned looks on their faces, I guess they did. But as I stand there worrying about it, I come to the realization that it's true. I *do* love them, and damn it, if all the near misses I've had recently have taught me anything, it's that you need to embrace life while you can.

Even outside of that, I think that there's something about each of them that I just want to fall into. Like the tip of an iceberg, what I've seen so far is only a small percentage of who they really are. Even though some of what I saw was a bit ugly, I'm also realizing that what lies beneath that has the potential to be big enough to take my breath away.

Lifting my head, I smile at them. "I love you both, and I want you to be happy. If you want to fuck like rabbits even when I'm not there, well, go for it." I try to keep it casual in case neither of them feel the same way, but before I can take another breath, they exchange a glance and yank me into a three-way hug, their arms wrapping around all of us while they press kisses into my hair.

"I love you too, Harlow," Oliver says, shuddering with emotion. Holden doesn't say anything, but as he pulls away I can see a tear running down his face before he takes my mouth with his, the force of his emotions showing in the kiss.

He pulls away and rests his head against mine. "You're everything we could have hoped for."

Our moment of joy is interrupted by a sharp knock on the door. "Shit!" I step away from him, trying to straighten myself. My hair had come undone from its braid when Oliver was using it to direct my head, and I'm sure I'm flushed.

"Holden, Mrs. Summers was looking for you," Missy calls through the door, causing me to frown.

"She couldn't pick up the phone and call?"

growls Oliver, expressing exactly what I was thinking.

Feeling a little territorial, I march over to the door and fling it open wide enough that she can see the two guys behind me. All three of us clearly look rumpled, not to mention my panties are still lying on Holden's desk, and if that wasn't enough to tell you what we were up to, her nose wrinkles as the smell of sex reaches it.

"Hi, could you call Nana and let her know we will meet her at Thomas' office? Holden is done for the day, so we'll be heading out." She looks past me to Holden, and I growl, "Don't look at him. Look at me. Now, go and do what you were told." I channel a little of my inner Jacinta, and when I close the door on her, the guys are gaping at me.

"Harlow, I don't know whether to be turned on or off right now. You just sounded like Jacinta." Oliver's nose is screwed up in confusion, but Holden just chuckles again.

"I'm so turned on it's ridiculous. Can you come and run interference every day?"

I roll my eyes and go over to the desk to grab my panties and pack up my laptop. "That's what you've got Hope for," I tell him as he makes a lunge for my underwear, snatching them up before I can. He shoves them into the pocket of his pants, and all I can do is shake my head.

"Isn't that a bit cliché?" I ask him, putting my

laptop into my backpack. The cheeky brat shakes his head, completely smug.

"Don't care if it is or not. I can't wait to see the look on Thomas' face when they fall out of my pocket at his feet."

"God, what are you, twelve?"

"Harlow, when are you going to realize that at the heart of all men is a twelve-year-old boy snickering with laughter?" Oliver teases as he leads us out of the office, holding the door open for Holden and me. The three of us head to the elevator, Holden stopping to give Missy some instructions, but neither Oliver nor I deem to show her politeness.

"She needs to go," I mutter out the side of my mouth, and he gives a small nod.

"I'll get Hope on it. I don't think she'll be able to put up with her for long either." He side eyes the desk as he shares the simple plan, and I really hope he's right. Missy's blatantly flirting with him even though she knows exactly what the three of us were doing in there.

That settled, another subject pops into my mind. Might as well ask while I've got him here. "Oli, why do you get tested for work?" I ask him, a little unsure how I'm feeling. Does it mean he's been sleeping with his clients? I'm fine—more than fine, actually—with him and Holden, but I think that's about my limit. They had something together that predates me even knowing of their existence; I have no right to control that. I *do*, however, have a firm right to shove my foot up the ass of any man or woman who tries to become an overly friendly part of their lives now. Or up Holden or Oliver's if they make any new "friends" without talking to me about the situation.

"We made it a policy at Neighpalm Ink to look after the health of our artists, and being that we deal with blood all the time, I like everyone to get checked every couple of months to make sure they're okay." Oh, well, that's ridiculously sensible and totally not worth getting upset about. Gosh, these guys really are something. It's amazing that he looks after his staff like that, not to mention a relief to know it's for that reason. As always, I think my face betrays my thoughts because there's a heat across my cheeks that says I'm probably blushing right about now, paying for jumping to the quick conclusion.

"I promise you, Harlow, when I tattoo someone, it's usually nothing like it was the day you came in. I'm professional and friendly, but that's where it stops. I don't want to shit where I eat, as the saying goes." He leans in and whispers in my ear as the elevator doors open, "Though you should take another trip to the shop with me. I wouldn't mind getting you back on my table... or bent over it."

Now the heat is still there, but I'm flushed for an entirely different reason by the time Holden finally catches up to us, letting the elevator close behind him.

"Hey, babe, what did you say to Harlow that has her flushed again?" Holden backs me up against the wall of the elevator, his eyes on Oliver the entire time.

Oli just shrugs, what's likely supposed to be an innocent smile on his face. "Just telling Harlow that I'd love to give her another tattoo."

"I'm not sure I believe that. Something like that wouldn't have her blushing like a nun at a porn convention." Holden runs a finger over my warm cheeks as I push him away.

"That..." I poke a finger against his chest. "Was weirdly specific, and stay back, you're not starting anything in the short ride it takes to get to the right floor."

Oliver holds out a hand toward the emergency stop button, just about to push.

"No, don't!" I shout, and he freezes, looking disappointed. "Look, it's not that I don't want to, but the next time I want it to be the three of us, and a quickie in the elevator isn't what I want for that first time. Later, sure, ravish me as much as you want, but I just want it to be special."

I smile as my words melt the exteriors of the two men in front of me.

"That sounds perfect." Oliver steps up and gives me a kiss, followed by Holden, but before we can say anything else, the elevator stops and the door opens.

"Okay, let's go see what Nana wants. Maybe we can get the rest of the family moving, too. I'm ready to kick ass and take names in this family game night." Holden strides out, and we follow behind him, bypassing the secretary who simply smiles and waves as we walk past.

"Oh, Harlow, you have no idea what you are in for," Oliver mutters out the side of his mouth, but I just grin with anticipation. I love being part of this family now that they've laid the weapons down.

Chapter Fourteen

Thomas

When my office door opens without a knock, I know it's going to be one of my siblings on the other side. So it's no surprise to me when Holden, Oliver, and Harlow walk in. Nor is it any surprise that the three of them look a little rumpled and smell like they've been messing around. My brothers have made it no secret how much they're into Harlow, and I'm happy for them... even if there is a *tiny* ball of envy sitting deep in my soul. Once upon a time, I probably would have been the first one of us to pursue Harlow. She's sexy, intelligent, interesting, and has all the makings of what I would call the perfect woman. But that was before I became jaded with the world, before I had my heart ripped out and stomped on by the woman I had planned to make my wife. After that mess, I no longer see things through rose-colored glasses and will never make the same mistake again.

Though the memory of Harlow's sexy body pushed up against mine in the garden room and the scent of her hair in my nose may very well haunt me for a long time to come. What was I thinking, getting so close to her like that? I should have known better, but I was so angry at her for taking more risks. Who knows who could have been around; it wouldn't have taken much for someone to hide somewhere and try for her again. Although the building is fairly secure, it's still a big building and people can walk in off the street.

Watching her from under my eyelashes, I really am envious of the easy way she interacts with Holden and Oliver, the gentle touches and small smiles as they carry on the conversation they had been having as they walked in.

Steeling my spine and banishing those thoughts to the recesses of my mind, I clear my throat. "And to what do I owe this pleasure?" I ask drolly. Harlow stops suddenly at my question like she only just realized I'm in the room, her eyes shuttering with uncertainty. I feel like kicking myself for putting it there, but maybe it's for the best. I would not be good for her, and my brothers certainly need her too badly for me to fumble into a relationship with her and chase her away. All too interested, I watch as she shakes it off and puts another smile back on her face as my two brothers continue into my office. I can't help but admire the strength this woman has, especially after facing off against my blazing anger earlier. Most people would be cowering in the corner, but not Harlow. She just picks herself up and keeps going. Now, what she had to go through in order to instill that strength in her... I can't think about that right now; it only makes me angry to remember that her childhood has some things in common with my siblings' and even my own.

Soon enough, Oliver distracts me by throwing himself into one of the chairs in front of my desk, a lazy sprawl to his body that only he seems to have perfected. It's been a long time since I had that kind of peaceful ease in me. I'm almost as envious of that as I am their camaraderie with Harlow. Holden comes around and stands next to me, clapping me on the shoulder before leaning his ass against my desk, hands in his pockets.

"Are you just about ready to get out of here? Do you know what anyone else is doing, if they're ready too?" He sounds all chirpy and has a gleam of mischief in his eye even though he's behaving himself at this point. I need to be on alert though because you just never know with my brothers.

I snort as I think about his question. "How would I know? When did I become everyone's keeper?"

"Oh, Tom, don't be like that. You pretend to be a grumpy asshole, but we know the truth. We know how you really are inside. Buried deep, *deep* down, you're a teddy bear waiting for his honeypot," Holden coos, and I narrow my eyes at him.

"Have you been smoking weed at work?" Both Harlow and Oliver crack up at my question, but Holden simply smiles before removing his hands from his pockets and clapping me on the shoulder again.

"Nope! Can't I just be happy? I've been given the mostly all clear, and I'm feeling much love for the world at the moment."

Of course, he's not wearing his sling anymore. Fuck, I really must be tired not to have noticed it. Sleep has been elusive all week since I've been doing background checks on every person I could think of from Harlow's life. It all came back with nothing, which is driving me halfway mad. The only lead we have is the mother's possible murder, but fuck, she was into some shady shit, so it could have been completely unrelated. I need to figure out the identity of the woman who visited her the day of her death, but the trailer park had no form of security cameras nor did any of the surrounding trailers. I couldn't even find a working security camera anywhere around the entrance, so there is no record of anyone coming or going either.

The business card is a solid clue, but I want to take a trip out to CT and investigate it personally. No more trusting others to get the job done or risking another life. Whoever killed the PI is obviously determined to keep things secret. I've basically exhausted all avenues here, so I just need to find a time to head out to the East Coast. I really don't want to leave Harlow on her own, but would I be risking her life by putting her closer to where this all may have originated from? If the theory I shared with her about two different stalkers—not to mention two different motives—is correct, then there might be someone coming for her on *both* coasts. They were followed in Hawaii, and both our home and Neighpalm headquarters have been tainted by these "gifts" from the fucking creep, or creeps, so really nowhere seems wholly safe.

I shake it off and plaster a smile on my face for the sake of my brother. "Hey, that's great, man. I'm happy for you. Just don't overdo it too quickly, or you'll find yourself back in the sling," I warn him, and he grins, this one a touch softer. It's the smile that says he thinks his big brother is being silly and overprotective.

"Don't worry, man. I'm being careful, but it's nice to know you care." He moves back around to Oliver and Harlow who have been watching our interaction with amused smiles on their faces. I'm sure Holden and Oliver are up to something, but I just can't work out what.

A knock on the door has me calling out enter before I can accuse them of anything, and in walks Nana.

"Ah, there you all are!" she exclaims as she

deposits kisses on those three before coming around to gently place one on my cheek. Her violet fragrance teases my senses, bringing me the comfort I always feel when I'm around this woman. If there was anyone who was going to restore my faith in women, it would be Grace Summers. Ever since I first arrived in their lives, she has been a shining beacon of love and warmth, things that were so sorely missing from my life up until then. She was the reason I had wanted to marry Clarissa and create a family and life with her. I wanted to give my children exactly what Dad, Nana, and Poppy have given all of us. Even now, I still can't believe that I got it so wrong. I was completely blindsided when Clarissa sold us out. I thought for sure my biological family had been right in thinking that I deserved nothing but to be tormented.

"What a shame they couldn't have all shared her." Nana's tone has me looking up and rolling my eyes. I'm guessing that they're talking about what happened with Ninja Starfish. Declan had given me the rundown earlier. He was all excited to begin planning the new reality tv show that they're going to use to choose a new member.

Harlow rolls her eyes. "No, Nana, I am a hundred percent sure they all dodged a bullet there. He was a selfish asshole, and she was a manipulative bitch. Good riddance to them both."

Nana sighs. "Oh well, maybe they will keep it in mind when they choose their next member." I can practically see her scheming. I swear the woman puts more effort into trying to fix people's love lives than she does her businesses, and considering she's a damn good businesswoman, that's a terrifying thought. "Maybe I should have a word with them. Such nice boys, always so polite whenever I've seen them."

Harlow, Oliver, and Holden are smiling at her antics, but of course they are because they're all sexed up and have those good endorphins flowing. What happens when jealousy and envy come into the mix? I'm sure the smiles won't be so free then. That's when they'll be glad that I kept myself apart from this. I'll be around and ready to pick up the pieces.

"Thomas Summers, don't you snort at your nana. Just because you're all jaded and bitter doesn't mean there aren't others out there who would be happy to have love." Like a child, I instantly feel bad when Nana scolds me, that is until I remember why I am like I am.

"No offense, Nana, but I have the right to be jaded and bitter. My fiancée sold me and our company out for money. And to be honest, I think a poly relationship sounds good in theory, but the reality is very different. You wait until the media gets hold of the news that Harlow is dating five of her adopted brothers. They're going to crucify them all, but especially her. Let's see how everyone stands up to *that* scrutiny."

The room is quiet so I look up from my desk to find three furious faces and one who looks like I stabbed a knife directly into her heart.

"Fuck you, man," Oliver growls, but despite the anger permeating the rest of the room, Nana just shakes her head.

"Wow, Thomas, I cannot believe you just said that." Her disappointment stings more than anything else, and I drop my head into my hands and rub my face again, trying to clear the feeling of utter weariness that has just swamped me.

"Fuck, I'm sorry. That wasn't fair of me. I haven't been getting any sleep, and I'm afraid my filter may be broken."

"You think?" Sarcasm from Holden is nothing new, but there's also a layer of scorn that my brother doesn't usually direct toward me.

"Maybe we need to find someone else to be Harlow's bodyguard if you're so run down. You surely can't protect her if you aren't at your best," Nana muses, her eyes narrowing in concern.

"No!" I jump out of my chair, the damn thing dramatically falling back behind me. "No. It's okay. I'll do better and get some sleep this weekend. I've been burning the midnight oil with these background checks, but they're all done now. We don't have anything else planned at this stage, so I will be fine once Monday comes around again." My chest is heaving after all of that rushes out, and the concerned gleam in Nana's eye changes to something else. A small smile graces her lips before she nods in assent. Damn that woman's perception.

She stands up. "Fine, but I think you owe the others an apology. What you said was incredibly hurtful, and I know that's not the real you. I was coming to tell you that the helicopter is ready, and everyone will be finished for the day in about twenty minutes. Have a good night, and we will see you when we get home tomorrow." With that, she kisses Harlow on the cheek, whispering something just for her ears, then waves to the rest of us before she takes her leave.

The tension in the room returns as Oliver reaches out and grabs Harlow's hand, squeezing it reassuringly. Another sigh leaves my mouth. "Fuck, I'm sorry. Really, I'm happy for you all and hope things work out. Just ignore my tired, grumpy ass."

"Yeah, well, how about you think before you open your fucking mouth?" Holden growls at me as he helps Harlow out of her chair and leads her to the door.

Oliver stands but doesn't follow them. As the door closes behind the other two, he looks at me. "Tom, you know I love you, but if you don't get your head out of your ass and see what is directly in front of you, you are going to make a big mistake, one you're going to regret for the rest of your life. Stop choosing misery over the possibility of happiness. Even at the chance that something goes wrong. That's no way to live a life." My normally fun-loving brother is completely serious for a change, and it's hard not to pay attention. "At least open your mind to the possibility. You're going to be spending a lot of time in Harlow's pocket since she's not happy while confined to the house. Take the time to get to know her because once you do, you're going to realize she's nothing like that vapid viper that you were engaged to. In fact, they couldn't be any more polar opposites. You need something to live for besides this path for revenge. I understand why you set off on that road when everything first went down, but it's time to walk along a different one." Oliver walks toward the door and pulls it open. "I miss you, my brother. Please come back to us. Give up the agency before you lose any more of your soul than you already have."

I lean both hands against my desk as my head drops in disappointment. God, I'm such an asshole. That broken look on Harlow's face was exactly the way she looked the day Jacinta unveiled her billboard. How could I have stooped so low? Vowing to do better, I'll take some of Oliver's advice and at least make an effort to get to know her. Especially since she does seem to be happy with my brothers, and what's more important is that they seem to be happy sharing her. Even Declan and Jaxon, who haven't been around much this week, seem happy with the situation.

Pushing off the desk, I'm bending down to pick up my chair when I spy something just in the footwell. Setting the chair right, I lean down and pick it up, mouth dropping open in surprise when I realize what it is. Hanging off my finger is a pair of damp pink lace panties. Now, I know they weren't there before, so that can only mean one thing. Holden dropped them there, and Harlow was sitting in my office with no underwear on. No wonder he had that mischievous look on his face when he was leaning on my desk.

Unable to control myself, I rub them between two fingers, feeling the slickness left behind on them. It's all I can do to not bring them to my nose and breathe deeply. Fucking Holden! Blood rushes to my dick at the thought of Harlow spread out over my desk, but I adjust myself, willing those thoughts away. Fuck.

I shove them deep into my jacket pocket despite the fact that he's going to know I kept them if I don't return them to him or Harlow; I don't want to embarrass her. Not that I think it would, otherwise she wouldn't have let him take them in the first place. But I bet she didn't realize he was going to taunt me with them.

I make the decision just in time, too, because seconds after I pocket them, Dad walks in. Like the others, he doesn't bother knocking, and the serious look on his face has me on red alert.

"What's going on, Dad?" He doesn't sit; instead, he paces back and forth with a restless, frustrated energy that's not usually like him.

"Those assholes at NW European Airlines have decided to shop around for a buyer," he growls.

"Shit! We knew it was a possibility when we had to push back the merger for Harlow's sake, but I was hoping that wouldn't be the case." He scrubs a hand through his short blond hair. Poor Dad. As thrilled as he is to have Harlow in our lives, the threat of the stalker is taking its toll even though he hides it well.

"Yes, well, now we need to 'woo' them. They're holding a dinner in Prague next weekend, and if we aren't there, we'll lose our opportunity. I want this, Tom. We need a win." Dad stops his pacing and looks at me imploringly.

"Okay, okay. Let James and Chris know to have the big plane ready. We'll leave on Wednesday, which will give us all plenty of time to get packed and ready. We'll drop Harlow and the rest at my house in Ireland before continuing on to the Czech Republic. Nobody knows I own it, and with one way in or out, it's practically a fortress, so they should be safe there. Don't worry, Dad. We've got this."

His eyes become sympathetic, and I brace myself for what he has to say. No one ever gives me good news when that look is in their eyes. "Listen, Tom, I think it would be better for Harlow to attend with us."

"Why?"

"Because the company we're competing against

is RAE." Fuck, it feels like a lead block just landed in my heart. Russian Avionics Executive is the company that Clarissa took our plans to. It's a Russian-based aeronautical company, and the CEO is a slimy bastard who we were never able to catch because he had some kind of diplomatic immunity. I'm not sure if I will be able to stop myself from punching the smug asshole in the face.

"Think about it. Harlow can be your emotional protection while you continue to protect her."

"I don't need 'emotional' protection," I sneer, unable to keep my disdain from my voice. It's a sensitive topic for me, and sometimes I lash out as a reflex. Being aware of it doesn't make me any better able to fight the knee-jerk reaction. I shake my head and try for a gentler tone. "And even if I did, why would I use Harlow?"

"Well, the only other female would be Jacinta, and attending with her won't show you've moved on. That Clarissa's betrayal didn't affect you. He'll think he's won if he sees how badly it hurt you." I mull over his words, starting to see he has a point, especially from a business perspective. "Think about it. I'm heading upstairs to the helicopter. Don't be long."

Dad leaves, and as soon as the door closes behind him, I pick up a letter opener and throw it. Despite the sense in his idea, I'm still more riled up than I'd like to admit. "Fuck!" The knife lodges in the door and shudders back and forward. What I wouldn't have given for that to be Urie Sokolov's heart. God, I can just imagine his gloating smile if he wins this contract. I'd probably shoot him between the eyes. Having Harlow there as a buffer might not be a bad idea. Though I think I'll ask everyone how they feel about it. I don't want to put my brothers' girlfriend through any of that if they don't approve of it.

Just as I'm turning my computer off, my door opens, with Declan peering around the corner, looking between me and the letter opener lodged in the door. "Thank fuck Dad told me to give you a minute. When I didn't hear any destruction, I thought it would be safe." He steps out from the safety of the door and yanks the offending weapon out of the hardwood. "Come on, you look like you could do with a beer."

He places it on the bookshelf not far from the door and waves me forward with no questions asked. It's one of the things I love most about Declan. He doesn't push. I mean, he will eventually, but he'll give me a chance to get my head straight first, and for that I'm grateful. Grabbing my jacket from the back of my chair, I put it on over my gun holster and follow my brother to the elevator.

Chapter Fifteen

Harlow

When we arrive at the helicopter, Kai and Jaxon are already standing outside, chatting, big grins appearing on both of their faces as we approach. I just can't believe how lucky I am, though the warm feeling filling my heart is definitely reminding me. I'm sure I'm going to wake up at any moment and realize this was all a dream, so I'm going to make the most of it while I can. Bouncing over to them, I brush off the somber mood Thomas had caused and wrap my arms around Kai's neck to give him a big kiss before moving to Jaxon. My movements are still a little hesitant, but he steps into me and wraps his arms around my waist, not pushing for anything more than a simple hug as I melt against him.

"Hey, gorgeous, you look like you've had a good

day." He looks from me to Holden and Oliver, and his lip turns up in amusement. "A very, *very* good day. I've got to say, I'm a little jealous." I feel my smile drop in worry. Is he joking? Is jealousy going to become a problem already? He quickly shakes his head, eyes widening like he realizes he might have just said the wrong thing. "I mean, I'm just jealous that I wasn't there too," he assures me.

Oliver claps him on the shoulder. "Yup, you missed out." I groan at the matching smirks on Oliver and Holden's faces as they climb into the cabin. Assholes.

"Soon," he tells me, his eyes heating with a promise of things to come, before climbing in after the other two.

I wink at him. "I look forward to it."

"So how was your day?" I ask Kai as the other three start a conversation, and he groans before pulling me into his body again.

"I would have much rather stayed in bed with you."

I chuckle, finding an easy moment of happiness in his answer. "But then you would have been all by yourself when I had to come in with Holden."

"I think I still would have preferred that," he grumbles before kissing my cheek. "Climb in. I'm flying this bird home tonight, and I've got to finish my checks." He helps me up the steps before going around to the pilot's side and climbing in.

Jaxon grabs me when I get close and pulls me

down on his lap, not allowing me to pass him. A giggle leaves my lips, and he nuzzles into my neck, telling me how much he has missed me, before letting me slide off his lap and onto the seat next to him. Out of nowhere, my ninja of a new sister flings herself into the seat on my other side, throwing words at me before I can even try to talk to Jaxon.

"What the fuck, Harlow? I thought we were friends now." Jacinta is frowning at me, her eyes clouded with hurt.

Shit, what did I do? I look around the cabin, hoping someone can help me out, but Jaxon shrugs at me. Holden and Oliver, my only other lifelines, are busy talking to Kai. After a moment of frantic thinking, it occurs to me what she might be upset about, so I raise my eyebrow at her.

"So the fact that I arranged for you to have lunch with three very delicious men who may be as interested in you as you are in them isn't something a very *best* friend would do?" I cross my arms and stare her down, but I can't keep up any playful fierceness. I'm realizing that the hurt in her eyes is actually a glimpse of Jacinta's insecurity. Trust is a hard thing for her, thanks to both her mother and the slimy women that have been in and out of her brothers' lives, so I guess it makes sense that a part of her might honestly be unsure about whether I had her best interests at heart. Maybe she thinks I could be trying to embarrass her or manipulate her through her connection to them, but that couldn't be further from the truth.

"Jacinta, if I wasn't a hundred percent sure of Alex and Shane's interest in you, I wouldn't have set anything up. And from the looks of things in the Wardrobe, it seems you and Jace may be just a little smitten with each other as well. I want you to be happy, and I want them to be happy too. From what I know so far, they're all really good guys, and who wouldn't want their friend to have someone… some*ones* who will be good to them?"

She blushes and won't meet my eyes as she grumbles, "Who says *smitten*?"

"Look, it seems the three of them have got something going on. Whether that becomes a permanent thing or not, that's for all of you to navigate, but I know Alex and Shane were interested even before Jace was in the picture. Now, take it from me, life is too short to pine away for someone or to not take a chance just because it's scary." Jaxon grabs the hand that isn't in Jacinta's and squeezes tight. "Don't be that person, Jazzy. Carpe diem. Seize the day, or cock… cocks, or whatever." Next to me, her brother gags, the teasing dramatics making me chuckle. "But be happy. I'm pretty sure you gave me similar advice not that long ago." When she meets my eyes next, there's determination in them, and she gives me a quick nod just before Dad enters the helicopter.

He leans in and gives both Jacinta and me a kiss

on the cheek. "There are my pretty girls." He slaps the boys on the knee before sitting down across from us. "Declan and Thomas are on their way up. Let's get this bird running." Kai flicks a couple of switches, and the turbine starts to whine as the helicopter blades slowly turn above us. The noise builds as the rotor gets faster and faster, and all of us pop on headphones to help block out the sound as we watch Thomas and Declan run over, bent slightly to keep balance. Dec climbs into the co-pilot's seat as Thomas joins us in the cabin and shuts the door behind him. Once he's seated and belted in, the helicopter shudders, lifting into the air.

The trip home is relaxed even though Dad gives us strict instructions the moment we land. "Ok, I'll order the food to be delivered to the front gate in an hour. That should give you plenty of time to shower and change, and I'll message Emma to let her know that we're home and ready for her to come on over."

"Dad, wait," Thomas calls after him and quickly jumps out, following him. The rest of us are not far behind, but as we get to the house, Thomas pulls out his gun while two security guards appear out of the shadows. "Just let us check things over. Security said nobody has approached the place, but it's a big house. There are some spots where the camera angle isn't great. It won't take long with the three of us looking." Dad starts to argue, but Declan stops him.

"Let him go, Dad. He's trained for this, and it will give us all peace of mind." With a sigh, Dad agrees, and the three men disappear into the house. It's a long and drawn-out wait as Jacinta moves closer, leaning on me for comfort. It's nice to have her, which is something I never would have expected to feel. Actually, it's nice to have all of them.

Thomas returns, the two security guards having gone out the front once they deemed the house safe. "Come on," he says with a smile. "I'm ready to kick your asses at poker." At that taunt, the Summers come to life again.

"Nope, not poker tonight. It's Cards Against Humanity," Jaxon tells him. "There are too many of us for that."

"I'll leave you lot to sort that out while I message Emma and grab a quick shower." Dad hurries off without even looking back.

"I can't believe the first woman Dad has been interested in ages, who isn't horrible anyway, has a girlfriend," Jacinta moans as we follow along more sedately. "He had lunch with them while you were in Hawaii and couldn't say enough nice things when he got back."

"It's nice just to see him having a social life. Cecilia always kept him so busy with work that I haven't seen him have any fun for a long time. The three of them also played a round of golf at Dad's club with Nana and Poppy last week too," Jaxon adds in, throwing an arm over his sister's shoulder as we all hit the stairs.

"Ugh, Cecelia. Let's not mention the witch. She might hear her name on the wind and appear." Jacinta screws up her nose, and the rest of us chuckle.

We all split up and go in our separate directions, Kai walking me to my door. "I'm going to give Max a call after I finish my shower. Come get me if you end up waiting for me."

"Sure thing, babe." He gives me a kiss and goes to his room.

My heartbeat automatically speeds up as I open my door, that reflex taking longer to go away than I would have hoped. But it soon settles when the door reveals my room in perfect condition. Placing my backpack on my bed, I strip off and take a quick shower. Throwing on a comfy pair of yoga pants and an off-the-shoulder sweatshirt, I make myself comfy on the bed and pull my phone out of my backpack to call my bestie. Let's hope she answers and isn't mad at me.

"Hey, I was wondering when you were finally going to remember your original family," she answers, but I can't tell if she's serious or joking. Fuck.

"Umm. Well, I *have* tried, but every time I called you, it went to voicemail. That, or you barely had five minutes to speak to me," I stammer, not quite sure how to respond.

She chuckles, and although it lightens the tension a little bit, I can tell she's still upset about something. "Relax, Harlow. I've been so busy on the set I've hardly had time to breathe. The actress rides this time, but I've had to fill in for a few shots that they deemed too dangerous for her."

"Did it all go okay? You sound funny," I push, not wanting to let go of what's bothering her.

"Yeah, yeah. I'm okay. They were hard, and I took a tumble off Sampson. I've got a bit of a concussion." She mumbles the last part, probably a little embarrassed to admit she sustained an injury. Max and I both have a lot of pride in what we do and faith in our skills. I get a little grumpy when I mess up too.

"Oh, I know how that feels." I chuckle in sympathy with her, the sound dying off when I realize I haven't told her about anything that happened in Hawaii yet.

The silence between us is deafening as I wait for the response.

"What do you mean, you know how that feels? Not anything recent... right?" Max's voice is calm, but I can hear the storm building behind it.

"Ah... yeah, well, there was a reason I've been trying to get ahold of you," I bite back defensively.

"Right, like you tried real hard, Harlow. I think I had like two missed calls, and neither of the voice messages said it was important. You know I would have forced them to give me time for you if you said it was urgent." Aw shit, angry Max rears her head. Maybe she's right? I guess I could have tried harder, but to be honest her track record in putting me first hasn't been great either.

"So you only return my calls if it's important? Wow, I feel *so* special." Yes, I'm annoyed. After spending all this time with the Summers family, I realize the way Max sometimes treats me isn't what families do for one another. I deserve better, and I'm going to demand it. What's the point of making a stand that the Summers stop their bullshit if I let other people in my life keep up behavior that treats me like less? I don't really know what's gotten into me, but maybe I'm finding a little bit of the backbone that I've gone too long without using.

There's another long pause as the hurt tries to ramp itself up into my veins, telling me not to cave first. I hear her sigh over the phone. "You're right. I'm sorry. I'm tired and grumpy and sore and taking it out on you. Tell me what happened. Please."

We spend the next half hour talking about my trip to Hawaii and the things that happened, and then I ask her about the movie and if she's having fun on the set, hoping she might share with me who was in her room that morning, but she's incredibly closed off about it. It's not hard to take the hint when she keeps changing or avoiding the subject.

"I can tell something's up, Max." There's another telling silence. "I'm going to let it go for now, but when I see you next, I'm going to pin you down until you spill. God, it can't be any more dramatic than dating my five adopted brothers while fending off a psycho stalker."

She chuckles, but the sound is missing some of its usual energy. "I guess when you put it that way, no, it's not. Okay, deal."

We hang up not long after that, with Max ordering me to call Chuck and Melinda too, so it's another half hour before I can head downstairs. But I'm finally not feeling as guilty about not keeping in touch. Everyone is fully up to date, and even though Melinda wanted me to come home, Chuck convinced her it might not even matter, that I should stay where I am, being protected by Thomas.

When I get downstairs, the living room is empty. Where the fuck is everyone? I can't be the first person ready, can I? But a knock at the front door has me turning and going back out the front. It must be the food. Should I be opening the door without Thomas? Well, I'm here now.

But when I get there, it's Emma with a pretty woman standing next to her. "Oh hey, come on in." I open the door wider to let the two women in.

"Hello, Harlow, this is my partner Molly. Molly, this is Brad's daughter Harlow." Emma introduces us while I hold out my hand, receiving a firm shake in return.

"Pleasure to meet you, Harlow. Your dad has told us all about you." Molly is probably around the same age as Emma, with long, curly blonde hair and blue eyes. Her skin is golden like she spends time outside. Like Emma, she has an athletic-looking figure although she is slightly taller.

I smile warmly. "The pleasure is all mine, but I'm afraid I have no idea where anyone is." A slight blush covers my cheeks. But just as the words leave my mouth, Dad appears from the set of stairs I haven't explored yet. When he sees the ladies behind me, his eyes light up. Damn it, Dad is crushing hard, how disappointing for him, but when I turn back, both ladies appear thrilled to see him too. Hot damn, could Dad be getting a sandwich of his own? He pushes me out the way and greets them both with quick kisses on their cheeks.

"Hi, I was coming to see if you were here and where Harlow was. The games room is soundproof. Come on, I'll show you the way."

I let him and the two women go first, but as we go down the stairs, there's only enough room to walk two abreast, so Emma drops back next to me.

"How are you, Harlow? Brad told us all about what had happened. Is there anything we can do?" Wow, Dad must feel comfortable with them if he's sharing all the goings on with them. When I look her in the eye, there's no calculation or manipulation, which I'm familiar with from my mom, only genuine worry.

"Thanks, Emma, but nothing that I can think of. I just have to wait until someone finds a lead or they get bored and give up. Hopefully sooner than later." The noise traveling up the stairs has me smiling. "I hope you're ready for this. I have a feeling that the Summers take game night very seriously, " I warn her, and she tucks her arm through mine, stopping me before we get into the room. Her brow crinkles with worry as her eyes flick from me to where Dad and Molly went.

"We're nervous. We really like Brad, and him inviting us to spend time with his family is a big thing, but he's told us stories…" She breaks off, and I pat her on the arm reassuringly.

"Trust me, Emma, you'll be fine. The kids will be on their best behavior. You wouldn't have even made it through the door if they had not approved." She releases a big sigh of relief. "I'm glad to hear you guys are interested in him. I had seen his interest in you on the first day, but when I heard you already had a partner, I thought he would be friendzoned. I'm happy he wasn't even if I don't want to think about logistics." She giggles when I screw up my nose, and we continue down the stairs.

"If it's any consolation, it blindsided us too. But we're both interested in seeing where this could go."

"Okay, but don't hurt him. According to the kids, he hasn't been serious with anyone ever. I think my mom did a real number on him." She nods just as we enter the room, and I don't miss the hint of sadness in her eyes.

"Babe!" Oliver shouts, jumping out of his seat and practically running over to us. "Hi, Emma." He gives her a kiss on the cheek, leaving her looking shocked, her hand raising to the spot he kissed as he drags me away. "You can be my lucky charm. Come sit next to me."

Jeers, shouts, and kernels of popcorn are thrown at us from everyone else in the room. But as I sit down next to Oliver, there's a huge dash for the chair next to me, with Declan just edging out Jaxon as the winner. Eventually, everyone settles down after introductions, and as the cards get dealt, I feel the huge smile taking over my face.

"Hey, what's that look for? Have you got some good cards?" Jacinta asks, pointing a carrot stick in my direction, but I shake my head.

"Nope, just really, really freaking happy." The rumbling of voices drops off as everyone silently acknowledges what I said. Oliver and Declan's hands both find my knees and squeeze.

"And we're really happy to have you here." Dad beams, and the silence is broken as everyone chimes in. In that moment, I just about melt from all the love and laughter.

Chapter Sixteen

Harlow

Once I was seated and finally got a chance to look around the room, I realized it was a bigger area than I had thought. After my exposure to the Summers' lifestyle, I totally should have predicted that though. We're sitting around a large poker table, so big they must have had it custom made in order to fit the whole family plus a few guests. Behind us, there's a pool table and an air hockey table. Along one wall there's a fully stocked bar, and on the other side there are pinball machines and arcade-style shooting games as well as comfy sofas and chairs for seating.

The drinks are flowing and the food has been devoured as we settle in for another round of Cards Against Humanity. The responses have been thick with sexual innuendo, and some of them are frankly despicable, but the laughter has been loud and long. I've had to wipe my eyes a few times to chase away the tears. Declan's hand on my knee has slowly crept upward the more he's had to drink, and I've had to smack him a couple of times. He's been whispering in my ear every time a dirty response is played, telling me about how he'd like to do that to me. Like, what the freaking hell has body snatched this man? Seriously, how did he go from the serious, suited Declan to jeans and bare feet lecherous Declan. I won't deny that my panties are wet with want, my body praying he'll make good on all his promises, but this is just not the right moment, damn it.

Across from me is Dad, with Emma and Molly seated on either side of him. On the other side of Emma is Jaxon, and I've been watching the two of them carry on a private conversation that's been impossible to hear beneath everyone else's laughter and playful teasing. But finally they break off before Emma turns to me. "So, Harlow, Jaxon has asked for you to come through the house on Sunday if you want. I okayed it with the trustee, and they don't have a problem with it seeing as Grace and Howard are old friends of the count."

I gape at her, then at Jaxon, who gives me a wink. "Are you serious? That would be awesome!"

"Why don't you and Jaxon come for breakfast

with us in our cottage, let's say about nine, and we'll go after that. They're also sending over a record of the animals that were in the zoo when the count disappeared. They have noted down what was there and where they went. Jaxon said it was something you were really interested in."

He even asked about the animals?! Damn it! Did you hear that sound? That was the rest of my resentment shriveling up into a ball and going poof. When these men decide they're all in, they really pull out all the stops.

"I can't believe you thought about that," I say to him, and he just gives me this gentle smile. I remember that one from our very first encounter. God, that feels like it was so long ago now. This was the smile that hooked me that night in the club, and I'm definitely no more resistant to it now. The brightness of the moment is only dimmed the tiniest bit by Declan muttering next to me about asshole brothers not playing fair. Apparently, he said it loud enough for the others to catch it because everyone chuckles.

"I'm sorry, Emma, but I'll be tagging along if you don't mind," Thomas adds in, looking awkward as fuck.

"Of course, Thomas. You're more than welcome. Any of you can come if you want."

Dad's cell rings, and he pulls out of his pocket, frowning at the screen. "That's weird. It's the security guard at the gate." Thomas jumps up and pulls out a gun from the back of his pants, going straight into overload. He had opted not to drink, saying he wanted to make sure he was alert and capable should anything happen. The others had scoffed, but I guess he made the right choice.

"Dude! Where did you pull that from?" Kai's a little wide-eyed from the alcohol and his brother's slightly extra reaction, but he's the only one. The others don't look surprised by their brother having his James Bond moment, but they are watching Dad with a close eye, waiting to hear what's going on.

Dad holds up his hand and waves Thomas back down as he answers. "Yes?" He's silent for a moment before panic crosses his face as he looks from Jaxon to Jacinta. "Fuck, okay, thanks for letting me know. We can handle her."

He hangs up his phone. "Sit down, Thomas. It's just Cecelia. I'm pretty sure she just discovered she's been locked out of all Neighpalm systems." A heavy sigh leaves his mouth.

"Jacinta, Jaxon, I'm sorry for what I think is about to happen. I only hope you will forgive me. In the beginning, I kept it from you for real reasons, but after that I just didn't know how to bring it up when you were old enough."

Dad's cryptic apology is overshadowed by the slam of the door at the top of the stairs and Cecelia's subsequent screech. "Where are you? I warned you what would happen if you crossed me."

"Holy shit, you were right," Kai whispers, looking at me.

She appears in the doorway, fury on her face, her mouth curved in a sneer. Dad stands up, his hands slamming down on the poker table.

"Damn it, Cecelia, I've had enough of your shit. You've held this over me long enough, and I will not stand for the way you treat me or my children anymore. You went too far this time with Harlow and her clothes. What delusional part of you thought that would be overlooked?"

She blinks, shocked by his reaction, I think. What did she think he was going to do, cower? Well, to be fair, if she's actually been blackmailing him for who knows how long, I guess it makes sense that she wouldn't expect him to have a backbone.

Emma stands up, her hand on her girlfriend's shoulder. "Maybe we should go." Cecelia's attention goes to her.

"Who the fuck are you?"

"No, Emma, sit down. This concerns you in a roundabout way too. Two years ago, Cecelia applied for the position of my personal assistant. She wasn't going to get the job since she wasn't anywhere near qualified enough for what I wanted, and during the interview, she must have realized she didn't have a chance. She dropped all pretenses and basically told me that if I didn't hire her, she would go to the media and tell them that I'm guilty of child trafficking." My adopted siblings burst into loud curses and shouts of denial.

Cecelia crosses her arms, looking smug, but there's also a hint of worry on her face. "And I still will if you don't reinstate my privileges." How she can even take herself seriously, I have no idea. *Yeah, bitch, because now you don't have like a bazillion witnesses to your blackmailing.*

Dad sits back down, running a hand through his hair, and his eyes that are so much like mine are tired and sad. "No, you won't. This week, when you supposedly signed a document for a raise, it was actually a non-disclosure form. You didn't read it properly. Your arrogance convinced you that I'd never do anything to strike back at you for the lies you've held over my head for the last two years, and I suppose that's my own fault—it took much too long for me to get tired enough of your bullshit to fight back." He growls before continuing, trying to resume some kind of calm. "I have also been speaking to the relevant authorities this week to make sure that whatever possible charges might have stuck so many years ago are no longer relevant. The children I 'bought' are now adults, and the only person who would be in trouble now is the woman who sold them to me. You've got nothing."

"Fuck you, Brad. I might not have anything from a legal standpoint, but I can still do damage." She turns to Jaxon and Jacinta. "You know it's you two, don't you? I can see on your faces you've realized that your mommy made a killing off selling the two of you. The only reason she came back in your teenage years is because she'd blown through all that cash and wanted to see what else she could get out of that spineless father of yours or the two of you idiots."

Jacinta gasps, and Jaxon reaches for her hand, his eyes hard as he stares down the woman trying to cause trouble.

"It's no big news that the woman was despicable, so that isn't a surprise to either of us. I'm not sure why Dad thought he would have to keep it a secret." Jaxon's tone is nonchalant, but I can see the hurt he's trying to hide.

"Oh no, that's not the exciting part. The exciting part of it is *why* your mother sold you to him. Why did she approach your dad of all people offering him her children? It wasn't known that Brad was looking to adopt more children back then. He had only just adopted Declan."

"Cecelia, don't do this. Let me tell them, and I'll allow you to walk away with a generous severance," Dad warns her.

"No fucking way. I told you not to mess with me," she snaps at him before turning back to the twins. "The reason is because your father was one of Brad's best friends, just like Chuck is. The three of them were the three goddamn musketeers back then. Brad, Chuck... and Dragos." A gasp escapes

Emma's mouth, but I'm still feeling a little too confused to grasp the weight of this big reveal.

"Ah, I see you've put it together. You must be the lesbian caretaker from across the road." Cecelia looks down her nose at her. "That's right. Dragos is Count Bucătaru's only son, which means that Jaxon and Jacinta are the count's only grandchildren and the heirs to the giant estate across the road. Your *father* might have given you a wealthy life after he bought you, but he's also been lying to you and kept you from your true family legacy. How does that feel? Hurts, doesn't it, to know that the parent you've relied on has been completely full of shit."

The room is silent after Cecelia drops her final bombshell. Dad just looks defeated, and Molly grabs his hand, giving a little squeeze of encouragement.

Jacinta, however, is on her feet, that cold regal mask on her face. "Get out! There is no reason for you to stick around now. Consider this your notice of severance. We will have any personal belongings sent to the address that personnel has on file for you. Don't be expecting any references. When I am done with you, there won't be a single business in California that will hire you. In fact, I'm pretty sure I can have you black balled throughout the United States. Maybe try the fast food industry. They might take you on."

Cecelia shrugs, her twisted expression showing none of the worry she should rightfully feel at the moment. "My work here is done. If it causes trouble in your miserable family, I'm pretty fucking happy about that."

Jaxon stands up this time, wrapping an arm around his sister's shoulder. "That's the thing though, Cecelia. What you don't realize is that something like that isn't going to cause trouble. We are secure in the knowledge Dad loves us, and if he kept this information from us, it's for a good reason. We trust him, and I'm sure he will explain everything to us once the trash has been taken out." Dad looks up and meets the twins' eyes, relief shining in his.

While Jaxon was talking, Thomas moved to Cecelia's side, and he now takes her by the arm. She screeches and tries to pull away, but he has a firm hold. She starts to struggle, but then her eyes meet mine, and the mania clears as another smirk appears. What the fuck is that about?

"Fine, I'm out of here." Her gaze moves to Dad. "But *you* are going to regret crossing me." She yanks her arm out of Thomas' grip and storms back up the stairs with him following close behind.

The tension is fierce as we all absorb what just happened, sitting in silence until a whistle leaves Oliver's mouth. "Holy fuck, she was on a rampage. I thought she was going to turn green and Hulk Smash."

His comment breaks the tension, and everyone explodes into a cacophony of questions. But my eyes are on Jacinta and Jaxon. Although they are putting on a brave face, I can see that this has affected them. Dad must see the same thing as me because he gets up and goes over to them. He approaches them carefully, and as we watch, he reaches out. I can tell by the stiffness of his movements that he's bracing for rejection, but he had nothing to fear. Both twins melt into his hug like nothing has changed.

He pulls away from them. "Come on, I'll tell you all the story so I don't have to repeat it. Do you mind if Emma and Molly hear it too? Emma's going to need to hear it anyway so she can let the trust people know that heirs have been found."

"I'll pour some more drinks." Holden jumps up and goes behind the bar, Kai getting up to help him. Thomas returns before Dad can start.

"She left like a bat out of hell. I've told security that she's not allowed back on the premises, and I called Jake and told him to look into her deeper. I don't like all of this. How did she know all the facts? I wonder if she has a connection to the twins' mom. She disappeared off anyone's radar when they broke into this place and hasn't surfaced since." Thomas asks as he throws himself back into the chair. "Emma and Molly, I think it would be better if you stayed here tonight. You guys are vulnerable over in that cottage, and now you're on her radar. Not to mention the fact that whoever told her about the twins' dad may be interested."

"Do you really think that she would target Emma?" Molly leans over and grabs her partner's hand.

Thomas shrugs. "Probably not, but no point in stressing about it. That being said, I would recommend talking to the trust about upgrading the security for the estate." He breaks off, thinking for a moment. "Or I guess that will be your guys' responsibility now," he says, looking at Jaxon and Jacinta. They're still in Dad's arms, neither of them answering Thomas' claim.

Jaxon pulls away and helps Jacinta back into her seat before taking his, and Dad does the same. Emma and Molly drop hands, but I notice each of them giving him a squeeze of encouragement on his arms. Aww, they're so good for him. I want that to work out.

Dad rubs a hand across his face and sighs. "Cecelia isn't wrong. Dragos was my best friend, and although Mom and Dad speak fondly about the count, he wasn't a good guy. Yes, he threw flashy parties, and outside, his public face was eccentric and well loved, but the man was a demon behind closed doors. Dragos was terrified of him; it's why he spent more time here than he did over there. His fortune was not made through entirely legal means either. Don't get me wrong, the money was laundered and is now squeaky clean, but most of it was originally made through drugs, guns, and sex trafficking. Dragos didn't want anything to do with his father and had managed to avoid the family businesses until Carmen, Jax and Jazzy's mother, came along. He fell for Carmen hard, but it was a setup. Carmen was one of the count's working girls, but Dragos didn't know that at the time. He fell in love with her and thought she felt the same way. Who knows? She might have had genuine feelings in the beginning, but maybe his dad had something over her or threatened her life or to expose her role in his businesses, or I don't know..."

Dad goes over to the bar and pours himself a very large glass of whiskey, tossing half of it back. "I don't know what happened, but two weeks later, all three of them disappeared—Dragos, his father, and Carmen. The authorities searched high and low, but there was no trace of them, not until Carmen turned up a month later, pregnant and claiming amnesia. Nobody believed her, but they also couldn't charge her with anything, so they let her go. With no significant leads, the case grew cold, and she disappeared not long after that, only to resurface four years later with you." Taking advantage of Dad's pause for a breath and another gulp of his drink, Holden and Kai distribute drinks to everyone else before they both take a seat back at the table. Everyone's focus is still on Dad, but his is on the twins.

"Carmen was always a bit of a party girl. I mean, we all were when we were younger. But I could see she was headed down the same road as

Harlow's mom was, and I had tried to warn Dragos, but he didn't want to see it. I think he just wanted one good thing in his life that was just for him, and he thought Carmen was it. When she turned up on my doorstep years later, I could tell she was well and truly addicted to something. I'm not sure what. I didn't care to ask, and I was going to close the door in her face, but then the two of you peered out from behind her skirt. In that moment, she knew she had me. She dragged you both out and shoved you at me. Do you remember?" Dad asks, and both nod their heads shakily. "By then, Mom had come out to see who was at the door, and she took you away to get something to eat. You looked like you hadn't eaten in days."

"I remember. I thought she was a beautiful guardian angel coming to save us," Jaxon whispers, his eyes lost in memories. "And when I asked her, she just hugged me and told me she would do the best she could. Violets have always given me a sense of relief since that day."

"She was the first person other than Jax to tell me how pretty I was," Jacinta says quietly, "and that I was a good girl." The room is silent as we all acknowledge the fact that she was four before anyone apart from her brother said anything kind to her.

Dad clears his throat, his eyes a bit misty. "Anyway, she told me that you were Dragos' and threatened to kill you if I didn't give her money. She didn't want much, at least not to me, and I couldn't stomach the idea of letting you go anywhere else with this woman. The signs of abuse were obvious, so I made her a deal. I gave her a much larger sum in exchange for you—permanently. My lawyers drafted documents, and she signed away her parental rights. There were a couple of caveats, of course, but I just needed to get you away from her. I was told that it probably wouldn't hold up in court if she ever sobered up and came back, ready to fight for you guys, not to mention the legal issues of paying someone off in exchange for their children… The term 'child trafficking' might have been thrown out there, but I was already too far gone. I took one look at the two of you and fell in love. I wasn't letting you go, and I knew that Dragos, if he were able to have a say in it, would have wanted you with me. I needed to honor my friendship with him and do what was best for you two, no matter any of the potential costs to myself."

Tears are streaming down both Jacinta and Jaxon's faces by now, not to mention Emma and Molly's, and I can see that all the guys are feeling the emotions swirling through the room as well.

Jaxon suddenly stands up, his chair falling over in his haste, and throws himself at Dad. "Thank you," is all he says as he hugs him hard. Jacinta quickly follows after him, her arms locking around both Dad and her brother.

"Hey, Thomas, I hear you're the sharp shooter.

Why don't you show Molly and I how good you are at one of these games?" Emma stands up, dragging Molly with her to one of the arcade machines. Thomas jumps up, the gratitude for this woman shining bright in his eyes as the rest of us move away to give Dad and the twins a private moment.

Chapter Seventeen

Harlow

A little while later, Dad announces that he's done for the night and offers Emma and Molly a nightcap in his wing. They all leave, and the mood is solemn and somber once more. We did a pretty good job of rallying while they were here, not wanting Emma and Molly to feel uncomfortable or for Dad to beat himself up more than he might already be doing, but now it's just us. Well, most of us. Thomas took his leave not long after Dad, Emma, and Molly, saying he was going to have a look at the security footage to make sure that Cecelia had left with security at the front gate, and then he wanted to have a walk around the estate just to make sure nothing was out of place.

Jazzy throws herself onto the couch next to me. "Phew, I don't know about anyone else, but I think I need to get drunk." There's hurt in her eyes, and even though she's in a secure place with Dad, I think the subject of her mother was too sharp for her feelings to shield themselves.

"All right, one drunk Jazzy coming up," Kai announces, jumping up and starting to make some kind of concoction behind the bar. Before long, we're all getting messy and loud.

It's like we all make a silent agreement not to talk about the revelations of the night, so for the next hour, we keep the subjects light, the alcohol flowing, and the games playing. I play a round of pool with Declan that devolves into nothing but steamy innuendo while the others try to keep Jaxon and Jacinta's minds off of everything. The pool game is long and drawn out as neither of us are doing very well at sinking the balls in the pockets, and when there are still a few balls on the table, Holden stands up.

"Okay, I think maybe it's time we get the two of you to bed." His finger wavers as he points at Jaxon and Jacinta.

"Thanks, bro, but you're not my type," Jaxon slurs, leaning on his sister who giggles madly.

Oliver stands up. "It's okay because he's *definitely* my type, and I don't like to share."

"Hey!" I grumble, and Oliver turns to me and blows a kiss.

"Oh, but I will share with you, and I guess share

you with all of them. Shit, that means I do share." He looks so cute, all confused.

Kai rolls his eyes, smoothly standing up and actually managing to stay in place without a wobble. It looks like one of us stayed fairly sober. I guess he was pouring all the drinks. "Come on, lover boy. Let's help the babies to bed then."

Between Kai and Holden, they manage to herd Jacinta, Jaxon, and Oliver up the stairs, leaving me alone with Declan.

"Well, I guess we've still got a few more balls to go." I turn to look at him, but what I see has my heart racing. He drops his pool cue on the floor and starts to stalk toward me. I'm so stunned that I don't move, and before I know it, he's yanking mine out of my hand and throwing that away too. He grabs me by the waist and hauls my body against his, a squeak leaving my mouth as my hands come up to his chest.

"Those are not the balls I want you playing with," he growls before he slams his mouth against mine. All the built-up sexual tension between us overflows in this one kiss. Gone is the patient, teasing man from the last few days, and here is the same one who had me up against the barn wall so many weeks ago. But now there is no lingering anger or annoyance; this is pure heat and desire.

His mouth plunders mine, all teeth and tongue, nipping, sucking, licking, and biting, tasting like sin and paradise rolled into one. My fingers curl in his shirt, and it's all I can do to hang on and enjoy the ride.

He pulls away, both our chests heaving with ragged, shallow breaths as his lush lips curve up in delight. "Harlow, stop me now if you don't want this." His voice is low, husky, and enticing even though his words are giving me a chance to slow things down, but I don't want that. We've done enough dancing around each other.

"Shut up and kiss me," I demand, winding my arms around his neck and pulling his mouth back to mine, a grunt leaving his lips with the tight grip I have on his hair. His mouth slants over mine, slower this time, possessing me deeper than before, and that fire and heat is now a slow smoldering burn. Leaving my mouth, he rains kisses down my neck, causing my body to arch into him. His hands slip under my thighs, and in a flash I'm sitting on the edge of the pool table. Spreading my thighs, he steps into my body, his thick length pushing against my aching core. His mouth continues its journey downward at the same time as he pulls off my shirt. Throwing it to the side, he steps back, his eyes locked on my pebbled nipples.

"Gorgeous," he rumbles before his big hands cup my breasts, kneading and tweaking the nipples. I groan when he takes one hard peak into his mouth. The warm sucking sensation pulls me deeper into my happy place, his tongue sweeping back and forth across the needy bud. My hands leave his hair, and I lean back on them in an attempt to hold myself upright as my body starts to melt under such delicious torture.

With a popping sound, he pulls off, placing his hands between my breasts and gently pushing me backward until I'm lying against the pool table, my hips raised up on the edge. His hands trail down to the band of my yoga pants, those eyes of his sparkling. Sliding his fingers under the waistband, he pulls them and my panties down in one smooth movement so that I'm completely bare to him. Stepping back, he pulls his shirt over his head and throws it to the side before he devours me with his gaze.

"Holy fuck, you are a feast for my senses, Harlow." Declan's voice is all rumbly and delicious, causing goosebumps to pebble across my limbs with the sound of it. Stepping back into me, his fingers trail up the inside of my thighs as he closes the distance between us, his warm breath trailing across my most intimate parts. I throw my head back when his tongue rakes through my swollen folds, one smooth, slick glide that sends a searing hot bolt of pleasure screaming through my body.

"Oh god yes, Declan." I try to grab hold of something, but the smooth felt of the pool table makes it so I can't. I fist them instead, attempting not to yank his hair out of his head. My legs wrap around him, holding him in place while his mouth makes love to me again, mimicking what he did to my mouth earlier. Licking, sucking, and nipping before he thrusts his tongue deep into my center. "Fuck!" Pulling back, he slides two fingers into my pulsing channel and sucks hard on my clit until my orgasm blasts through my body in a wave of pleasure.

"Agghhhh." Again, I can't control the sound that leaves my mouth as I ride the waves, my pussy spasming around his fingers. Lost in the intoxicating sensations, I slowly start to come back to myself as he slides his fingers out and steps back, dropping his sweats and boxers until he's just as naked as me. Licking my lips in anticipation of what's to come, I can't look away when he fists his thick cock in his hand.

Putting my arms up, I reach for him, but he shakes his head. He reaches down with his empty hand and hauls me up, giving me a quick kiss before helping me stand. "I don't really want to have to explain to Dad about stains on the pool table." With that, he spins me around then gently pushes on my back so I'm now bent over the table.

"Good thinking," I pant as he runs his dick through my wet folds. Lining it up, he pushes slightly so he's just barely inside me before his hands cup my breasts. He curves his body over mine so his mouth is at my ear, but then he stops. "Shit, protection!" He goes to pull out, but I stop him.

"Are you clean?"

"I've never had sex without a condom before, so I'm assuming I am," he rumbles.

Well, that's a surprise that I'm certainly not mad about. I turn my head to look him in the eye. "I'm clean and protected if you want to try it out."

He runs a hand down my spine, and that simple gesture just feels so fucking good. "I never realized how different it would feel…" He must come to a decision because instead of pulling out, he grips my hips tight.

"You look so pretty bent over for my enjoyment," he rasps as he thrusts hard, pushing deep into my still-tight channel. Both of us grunt with the sensation when he's fully seated, and he nuzzles my ear. "Your pussy grips me so good, baby. So wet and hot and tight." He sucks a path up my neck, which I'm pretty sure is going to leave marks, but I'll worry about it later. I'm light-headed from the sensations and the alcohol still burning through my system.

"Are you ready for me to own you?"

"Yes, own me," I beg him as his hands leave my cupped breasts, one going around my neck while the other grips my hair and pulls it back.

"Tap me on the thigh if this is too much," he tells me before pulling back and thrusting hard again, setting a furious pace, as my spine arches like a puppet being controlled by her master. A long moan leaves my mouth as he works his thick cock, the bite of pain in my hair an exquisite counterforce to the pleasure he's working on my body. I feel a trickle of sweat run between my breasts and down my body as he drives himself deeper and harder with each thrust.

Running his tongue up my neck, his thrusts hit that spot deep inside that sends my body on a slow spiral toward another orgasm. Both of us are breathing hard, quiet whimpers and not-so-quiet pleas falling from my lips as I beg Declan to give me what I need.

"Please, Declan," I cry, but he chuckles darkly.

"What do you want, Harlow?" His hand tightens around my neck. "Tell me," he grumbles as he continues his punishing pace.

"I want to come," I plead, and his hand leaves my throat, drifting down to tweak a nipple on the way past.

"Good girl," he praises as he pinches my clit, and I explode. Pleasure tears through me, stronger and more intense than before, and my knees buckle at the onslaught. But Declan holds me in place as he continues to bury himself in my slick wet heat, the fluttering of my channel proving to be too much for him. With a loud groan, he tucks his head into my shoulder, biting down as he buries himself to the hilt. His cock pulses as the sharp pain in my shoulder sends ripples of pleasure through my limbs. He places kisses on the spot that he had bitten and runs his hands gently up and down my body.

"Baby, you feel so good; your pussy feels like it's made for me. I can't wait to do that again." His careful caresses and kisses, combined with his praise, make me feel all warm and tingly inside, but I pat him on the thigh, hoping he'll move since my hips are now telling me that being bent over a pool table is not all that comfortable in reality.

Pulling out, he helps me stand up before he picks me up and carries me toward the nearby bathroom. His lips caress mine as he juggles me before opening the door.

"Get the light, will you, baby?" he asks, so I feel around for a switch, squinting when I find it and the room lights up.

He puts me on my feet next to the shower and reaches in to turn on the water before focusing back on me.

"Wow," I stammer, finally able to find some words, and he chuckles.

"Yeah, wow." He sounds smug, but really he has every right to be. He can fuck like a god. Pushing my sticky hair off of my face, he slides his hand around my waist then moves closer, kissing me with a slow, seductive slide of his tongue swirling with mine before he pulls back. Reaching out, he tests the water, adjusting it to the right temp, and steps in, pulling me in behind him. He gathers me to him again, and we just stand there letting the hot water run over our bodies, my head resting against his chest. His hands continue to caress my body, and his dick starts to harden against my stomach again.

I step back, looking a little wild-eyed at him, and he shrugs. "You feel so good, and it's been a long time for me. I've been wanting this for a while now, and one time with you is not going to be enough. But first..." He reaches for a loofah and pours a generous amount of soap onto it before using it to wash every part of my body. With gentle touches, he washes and conditions my hair, taking the time to massage my scalp and make sure that I'm feeling especially taken care of in a way that I hadn't expected. Is it bad that these little moments keep surprising me? What does it say about me that these men and their gestures catch me off guard even though they made it clear that they want to... court me?

When we're finished, he lifts me up and pushes my back against the wall of the shower, our chests smashed together. A cheeky grin is on his face as he buries his cock in my throbbing core once more. I gasp, followed by giving him a matching grin as I get used to his size. The pace isn't furious this time, just a sensual shift of his hips to build us up once more. Gazes locked, unspoken emotions glistening in his eyes, his mouth mirrors what his cock is doing to my pussy, his tongue sliding against mine. That rolling glide of his thick length in my sensitive channel doesn't take long to get me back to the edge of orgasm. He leans in and takes a nipple into his mouth, sucking hard before nipping. A lump of emotions burn in my center, and tears prickle my eyes as the rush of pleasure jolts through me fierce and sizzling as he wrings one more orgasm out of me before following me over that edge.

Dried and redressed, we raid the fridge in the games room for tonight's leftovers. He and I snuggle together on one of the pull-out sofas as we talk about everything and nothing. Once we finish the food and clean up, he scrounges up some pillows and blankets, the two of us sharing the feeling that we'd rather not separate right now. Together, we make the sofa bed and climb in. There's a slight hesitation from me, not completely sure where we go from here, but Declan doesn't flinch. He gathers me into his arms, throwing one of his legs over mine. He put only his boxers back on, so the hairs on his legs tickle mine as he rubs back and forth across my skin.

"You're so soft and smooth; it feels so good," he says when I raise my eyebrow at him. A smile breaks out, and I snuggle into his chest, placing little kisses on the skin in front of me. I feel him kiss the top of my head, the gesture warm and comforting.

"What do you think will happen now?" I ask quietly, and he pulls back to look at me.

"With us or the twins?"

"Both?" I ask, not entirely sure which I meant either. I feel him shrug.

"Nothing changes. You keep looking for jobs, getting to know us all, and rating me at the top of your sexual prowess list." He stops and winks at me, waiting for the chuckle that I can't hold back. He smiles, so I think that was the response he was looking for, something to break up the seriousness of the moment.

"As for Jax and Jazzy, we'll just have to wait and see. But don't worry, they're not going anywhere, and if they do, they won't go far. At least now you won't need anyone's permission to look at the house. Hell, you could probably ask to move in, and they would both bend over backward to let you. On second thought, maybe not. I have a feeling that Jazzy's going to want the family close while they're dealing with the residual feelings from all of this. Having us together makes her feel safe."

He keeps it light, but I can tell by the grip he has on my body that he's worried about his brother and sister.

"Do you think Cecelia is going to cause problems?" I don't think I want to know this answer, but my feelings are betrayed by the tentative waver in my words.

This time, he winces. "Harlow, I have no doubt that woman will do everything in her power to cause trouble. Just what kind of trouble remains to be seen."

My heart is fast in my chest as I think of all the possible scenarios, but when Declan shifts around, I stop worrying about what ifs. I'm in the arms of a smoking hot man who really knows how to use his god-given love stick. I promised myself I would stop living in the past and letting it define me, so it's time to look forward to the future, and future Harlow is a horn dog. And by future Harlow I mean first thing in the morning Harlow, as I can't stifle the yawn that leaves my mouth. My eyes drift closed as the warm heat of Declan's body and the delicious fresh clean scent of him surrounds me, sending me into a deep and comforting slumber.

Chapter Eighteen

Declan

Being woken with Harlow's mouth on my cock is a pleasure like I've never felt before. It isn't just about the sexual heat; the emotional involvement with the woman who's doing it makes it that much better. A moan slips out of my mouth before I can help it, and I reach under the blankets to fist her hair in my hands. Her mouth slides along my length, and an electric current of intense desire rams its way into my body, causing my balls to tighten. Holy fuck, I'm going to finish quicker than a schoolboy on prom night. Pulling her up from where she is, I settle her above me, her thighs on either side of mine and her eyes sparkling.

"Good morning." The huskiness of her voice sends a shiver of need down my spine as her lips quirk up, mirroring the mischief in her eyes.

"Hmm, good morning indeed." Before she can respond, I lift her again and lower her down onto my dick, her saliva helping me slide home as a groan leaves her mouth and her eyes become hooded. She rests her hands on my chest and leans forward, her hair hanging down until a curtain of blonde surrounds us. "Now it's an even better morning," I rumble as she circles her hips.

Pushing her hair out of our faces, I watch her ride my length, a flash of lust tightening low down. "Yeah, baby, that's it. Ride my cock. You know, that's what I thought about the first time I saw you riding those horses. I was so mad at myself for imagining it was my dick you were riding instead. I could tell by the way you moved your hips that it would be amazing, so I sat there with my cock harder than a rock for this woman we knew nothing about." She smirks before biting her lip, and my heart gets a little bit more attached. Her concentration on her own pleasure is sexy as fuck. Fuck, I had been skeptical when my brothers suggested this arrangement, but I'm so fucking grateful I was open minded enough to give it a go. They're going to be smug as fuck when I tell them that I'm falling in love with her, but I think I have been from the start. That fire and passion and tenacity that she's held so fiercely despite everything that has been thrown at her are nothing short of amazing.

Grabbing her by the waist, I help her when her

movements start to falter as her pussy tightens around my dick. It clamps down around my cock, a rush of heat and warmth, as she throws her head back and shouts, "Fuck yes!" Grabbing her own breasts and tweaking her nipples, she rides out her pleasure like a wanton goddess. I feel myself drawn to look at her. My eyes can't wander, and my mind barely has the wherewithal to even come up with words at this point. Everything I am right now is wrapped up in her. As she starts to slow, I take over, thrusting once, twice, before I find my completion, her name a prayer on my lips.

A short time later, I convince her that she should probably get dressed before the games room is invaded by the rest of my family. I'm not too manly to admit that the grumble she lets out as she rolls out of bed can't be described as anything other than cute. I can't help myself; when her pert ass is in the air, I move closer and take a bite, earning an even cuter yelp as she moves quicker than I've ever seen her move before.

"Okay, okay, I'm going." She swats at me, and another chuckle leaves my mouth. I lie back, hands behind my head, watching her cover up her tight little body, and it hits me that this is the most I've laughed in a long time. In fact, last night the whole family was just happier, the atmosphere lighter. Though I'm pretty sure there won't be so many happy faces this morning. Thoughtful faces, yes. Very hungover faces, absolutely.

A shirt hitting me in the face knocks me out of my musings. "Come on, stud, hurry up. I'm going to get breakfast started. It's up to you to clean up down here." Harlow leans in and kisses me before disappearing up the stairs.

The smile on my face is wide as I climb out and find my sweats next to the pool table and pull them on. I make quick work of removing the sheets and throwing them in a pile to take upstairs before putting the sofa to rights once more. Then I survey the room. There are glasses everywhere from my siblings, so I quickly gather them and set them in the dishwasher behind the bar before adding detergent and turning it on. Grabbing a cloth, I wipe over all the sticky surfaces, leaving the edge of the pool table for last, then ditching the cloth once done.

Thankfully, there are no hard-to-explain stains, though I'm not sure it would bother any of my brothers. I'm just pushing all the chairs back into the poker table and thinking about turning on the air to disperse some of the sex smell when my phone vibrates in the pocket of my sweats. I'd put it on silent last night, not wanting to be disturbed, but I was waiting on some information from one of my production teams, so hopefully this is it.

Sure enough, it's my production team telling me the reality show for Ninja Starfish has been hashed out and is ready for me to green light it. I need to set up a meeting with Holden and the guys to go over the details, which should probably happen before we go to Europe so the team can get the ball rolling while we're away. As I send a quick response, thundering footsteps on the stairs have me looking up. Kai comes down, taking two at a time, a wild expression on his face.

"Where's Harlow?" he asks breathlessly as he looks around the room like I'm hiding her under a table. I finish up my text and shove my phone back in my pocket.

"In the kitchen. She said she was going to get started on breakfast. What's wrong?"

"Thomas said that he got a phone call from security at the front gate. A whole heap of media vans just pulled up, so I googled us. Look what that bitch did!"

He holds up his own phone, the screen showing one of the big media outlet's breaking news page. ***"Summers heirs in incestuous poly relationship with their new sister"*** is across the screen in big letters with photos of Harlow with Jaxon and separately with Kai in Hawaii, as well as her with Holden at a club.

"Holy shit." My mouth drops open, and I can't even try to hide the shock hitting me now. "Cecelia. She couldn't talk about the twins, so she gave them an even better story. Fuck, what else did she tell them? About Oli and Den, maybe? Thankfully, she doesn't know about Jacinta's prospective harem. Come on." I slap him on the shoulder and take the stairs the same way he did. I can hear him following behind me, but we don't make it past the front door before it's flying open, an enraged Thomas stepping across the threshold.

"Fuck!" he screams, then launches his cell across the room where it hits a wall and practically disintegrates. Holy shit, Thomas has become pretty unflappable since the Clarissa incident, so to see him like this now is really concerning.

"Hey, man, it will be okay. We'll call a press conference to release a statement. Everything will be fine." Kai pats Thomas on the shoulder, but he shrugs him off, pacing back and forth across the entry foyer.

"That's not it. I don't care about the fucking press. I care about the photos. How the fuck did they get those? The trip to Hawaii wasn't announced to the press, and both shots were taken using long-range telescopic lenses. The one of her and Holden leaving the club and getting into the limo is the same. There was no press around that night, so where did that shot come from? Why would a random person take those photos and then offer them just when the media outlets needed them?" He stops ranting, staring at us both until we realize what he's saying.

"They wouldn't, but Harlow's stalker might," Kai points out, appearing to be as distressed as I feel. Fuck.

"Assuming Cecelia leaked these stories, does that mean she also has a connection with Harlow's stalker? Or did the stalker leak the story as another way to distract us? Or, holy shit, what if she *is* the stalker?" My mind whirls with both possibilities.

Thomas runs a hand through his already disheveled red hair. "I don't know, but when I called Jake last night to look into her background, I also asked to make sure she went home instead of taking a side trip to Oli's shop or the office to destroy anything. He had some local connections put on it, but Cecelia never returned to her apartment. She seems to have vanished into thin air between leaving here and the time he was able to mobilize his guys. They've started searching, but as of now there's no sign of her." There's blatant guilt in his voice that's totally undeserved but totally Thomas. I might be protective of my siblings, particularly my sister, but Thomas *really* takes the idea of keeping us safe from threats to a new level. He seems to take it personally every time something slips through the cracks to hurt us. Even when there's no logical way he could've acted differently to stop it.

"Don't be too hard on yourself. You weren't to know." As usual, Kai can be counted on to read the emotions in the room. My goof of a brother is very socially literate, and even though some of us might be professional charmers, there's just something about Kai that's so good and caring. He notices people, and there was no way that Thomas' unwarranted guilt was going to slip by him either.

"I can't believe we had her right under our noses and didn't know. But if she's the stalker, she can't be acting alone. She had alibis for some of the incidents. And why? She was already fucking with all of us, so why bother complicating things by adding Harlow to her list? With her blackmailing Dad, what threat does Harlow pose? She wasn't even connected to the dirt Cecelia was holding over his head. Not to mention she always acted like she wanted in his pants or his bank account, and Harlow's no threat to either of those. Dad's got more than enough money to go around." Thomas' brow is creased in confusion as he blows out a sigh and bends down to pick up the pieces of his destroyed cell.

"Yeah, I wonder why Dad went along with that from the start instead of telling her to fuck off?" Kai bends to help him, not noticing the door to Dad's wing has opened. He's standing there with Emma and Molly behind him.

"Well, your dad's not a superhuman, and I panicked. Yes, I was probably not going to be charged with child trafficking, but the press surrounding it would have been bad enough to make our family miserable for a long while. Then there's the fact that I had no idea how the twins would react. I assured myself that I would get a handle on things and then tell them so I could get rid of her, but I guess I got comfortable. Better the devil you know and everything. If I could keep an eye on her, then maybe I could figure out where she had learned the information. But I never did, unfortunately." He sounds sad, and regret is flashing in his eyes as he twists his hands together in a nervous gesture, one I haven't seen him do for a long time. Emma eases her hands in between his and stills their motion, simply holding his hand in comfort with no words necessary. Molly reaches for his shoulder and gives him a squeeze of support. Well, hello, Dad, you dog. If it wasn't for the seriousness of the situation and the fact that I would be disrespecting his women, I might have asked to high-five him.

"So what's going on? Why the long faces? Is everyone feeling a little rough this morning?" Dad asks, trying to ease the tension with a joke and a smile, but unfortunately it falls flat. Thomas tells him about the media fallout, and Dad's face becomes thunderous.

"She did what!" he yells, and we all jump. Mild-mannered Dad just about did his own Hulk out. "Get our lawyers on the phone," he orders, and I nod, pulling my cell out of my sweats and jabbing in the number, but Kai jumps up and stops me.

"Before we get too worked up, let's have breakfast. From the smell of it, I'm pretty sure Harlow has been doing some cooking. She also needs to be told about it before she looks at any social media or anything this morning." Kai pulls out the sensible card and gets everyone calmed down and moving toward the kitchen. Molly and Emma hang back, and I can see they're about to try and make their excuses, but I just wrap an arm around each of them so they have to walk with me.

"Come on, ladies. I can see the way you look at him," I say quietly as we follow behind the other three. "You may as well see what you'll be getting into if you're involved with my dad. Being a Summers comes with a lot of perks, but it also comes with the crap. You need to decide whether you want to ride the rollercoaster or get off now," I warn them gently. I like them both, and I would hate to see them give up so early in the game, but it's better they decide now than bailing once Dad is all in. They exchange a glance, and with that weird mental telepathy long-term partners are known for, they must come to some kind of agreement because both relax under my arms as I shepherd them into the living area. The dining table is already kind of set with piles of silverware and plates. From the kitchen, I can hear the sounds of Ninja Starfish being butchered, and I wince. Well, I guess Harlow is good at so many things she can't be an amazing singer as well.

"God, what is that sound, and how do we kill it?" Holden and Oliver appear, looking a little worse for wear. Holden is glaring like he's personally offended by the noise, which I guess is well earned. For a music executive, it probably is a crime against music.

"That's your girlfriend," I tell them as I hold out a chair for Molly while Dad does it for Emma before we take our own seats.

Oliver pulls down the reflective shades he was wearing inside the house. "Are you serious? That's Harlow? No, I've heard her sing before, and she sounded nothing like that."

We all frown at each other as Jacinta walks through the kitchen door, a plate of food in her hand.

"Oh yeah, that explains it," Kai says as he takes a seat at the table. Much to her disgust, Jazzy is completely tone deaf, but she always gives it a royal try.

"Here, sweetheart, let me take that." Dad hurries over to her, taking the serving plate from her and putting it in the middle of the table. He then grabs her and holds her at arm's length to get a really good look at her. "Are you okay?"

She pats him on the cheek before kissing it. "Yes, Dad, I'm fine. Jaxon and I did some soul searching last night when we sobered up."

"Where is he?" Dad asks, the worry in his eyes clear.

"He's in the pool." She moves away from Dad and walks over to both Emma and Molly, giving them kisses on the cheek, then each of us brothers. "I'm glad you're still here; we wanted to talk to you. I'll go get him and tell him everyone is up." She moves toward the terrace doors, and I decide that Harlow probably needs some help in the kitchen. Slipping away from my family, I find Thomas in the kitchen, manning the coffee machine, while Harlow is at the stove, frying more bacon and scrambling eggs. I exchange a look with my brother behind her back, trying to ascertain if he's said anything, but he gives a little shake of his head. The radio is playing in the background, and Harlow is shaking her hips and bopping to it. She looks so cute, her pert ass shaking back and forth in time to the music, that I feel terrible that we're going to ruin this mood. Stepping up to her back, I lean my body against hers. First, she tenses up, but then she practically melts into me.

"Hey, baby. Anything I can do to help?" I whisper in her ear, unable to stop myself from nuzzling her. She swats me away with a laugh.

"You could butter a few more pieces of toast if you don't mind." She points to the toaster with another half-full serving tray next to it. "I seem to have lost my assistant. Did you see where she got to?"

"Jazzy has just gone to get Jax out of the pool,"

I tell her, and I feel a little of the warm fuzzies when she looks relieved. Instead of being bothered by sharing, it makes me feel good that she cares about and wishes well for the same people that I care about. Right now she's got so much going on, but it makes me feel better to know that regardless of her own baggage, she still wants to protect them and see them through theirs.

"Thank god. Did you hear her singing? I never would have guessed Miss Perfect Jacinta Summers can't carry a tune to save her life." She winces before turning back to the stove, and Thomas and I chuckle with laughter.

"That's a well-kept Summers secret," Tom adds as he grabs the finished coffee pot off the machine. "She has something on all of us so that we will never tell. Watch out, she'll be looking for blackmail material on you soon." He disappears through the kitchen door, leaving it swinging in his wake with Harlow looking contemplatively in his direction, a little frown wrinkling between her eyebrows and her lip clasped between her teeth.

Hmm, looks like she's not as indifferent about my stoic brother as she tries to pretend.

"You know, every now and then I see these flashes of what I'm guessing he was like before his heart was ripped in two," she says to me quietly. "I wish I could see them more often."

"You and me both, baby." I finish buttering the

last couple of pieces of toast and throw them on the tray. "Just keep doing what you're doing, and I'm sure he will return to us in no time." I kiss her cheek as she turns off the stove, putting the rest of the meal on the last serving tray, then both of us return to the living area for breakfast with our family.

Chapter Nineteen

Harlow

There's a smile on my lips as I push through the kitchen door with my hip. This new side of Declan is fun and oh so delicious. But the minute I walk into the room, it falls silent. If that's not a giveaway that something is going on, I don't know what is. Choosing not to panic, I place the tray I'm carrying on the table.

"Dig in! Don't let it get cold," I tell everyone. "'Whatever the problem is now, we can talk about it after breakfast." Everyone starts to pass plates and grab their food, and soon the only sound is the clanking of utensils. It's a sort of tense but peaceful start to the morning, with no one stopping until a noise has us looking over at Jaxon and Jacinta's entrance. Jaxon is rubbing a towel against his hair, his shirt in the other hand and a towel wrapped around his waist. Hurrying over to them, I grab Jacinta's hand.

The two of us had such a nice start to the morning, her torturous singing notwithstanding, and I just didn't want to break that moment between us by asking how she was. Now that we're with everyone, I feel like it makes more sense to check in. I can't be the only one who's wondering how she and Jaxon are doing, and at least this way she won't have to repeat herself a million times.

"Hey, how are you both this morning?" Jacinta's smile is bright, but her eyes show the truth. I'm pretty sure it's not about what Dad did, but everything they found out about their biological family. I feel a kinship to them at this moment. God knows I'm way too familiar with shitty families, or mothers at least. Their father doesn't seem like such a bad guy according to Dad.

"We're okay," she says airily as she moves past me to the table. I raise an eyebrow in disbelief, but Jaxon gives me a small shake of his head and mouths *later*. Well, okay then, all of us are in denial this morning. At least we'll all have company.

Jaxon and I join the others at the table, and for the next half hour or so, the conversation is pleasant and completely benign. I ask Jacinta about Prada and Coco, and I overhear Declan talking to Holden about the concept for the Ninja Starfish show. But the serenity can't last, and it's Emma who's clearing her throat for our attention after a quietly whispered conversation between her and Dad.

"I'm sorry, Harlow, but we're going to have to put off your tour. I had to advise the trust of the appearance of the heirs, and I'm afraid it's sent them into a tizzy." A pang of disappointment hits me, but I quickly shake it off. It's not her fault this has happened. "Look on the bright side, you'll now have direct access to the place once everything gets approved." She points at the twins, trying to lighten the moment, but they both became somber once she started talking. "I'm not sure how the both of you feel about this, and it's really none of my business, so I'm not going to probe, but the manager of the trust wanted to meet with you both today. Your dad gave his OK for him to come up this morning, but he wanted me to run it by you guys as well. If you're not okay with it, I can put them off for a day or two. There will need to be a DNA test, but I trust your dad's story, so it's merely a formality to appease the proper authorities. The lawyers can tell you more about it when they get here. After that, I'll start making arrangements to find new accommodations since I'll no longer be needed to manage the property." She breaks off, startled when the twins shout in unison.

"No!" They exchange a glance, then Jaxon continues in a quieter voice.

"We wouldn't dream of kicking you out of your home. Stay, please. Jacinta and I… Well, we really aren't ready to pick up and move or anything like that. No matter how close it is to home." His eyes are practically pleading with Emma to stay.

"Jaxon can keep it if he wants, but I don't want anything to do with that place ever." Jacinta stubbornly crosses her arms. "As far as I'm concerned, I'm a Summers. Nothing else existed before that. I'll take whatever tests they want because I know that will help make your life easier, Emma, but that's the extent of my involvement."

The room falls silent with just the sound of breathing as everyone absorbs what she had to say.

"But, Jacinta, sweetie," Dad starts, and she holds up her hand.

"No, Dad. Right now, that's how I feel, and I want you to respect it. In a few days when I've had time to absorb it, maybe I'll feel differently. For now, just leave it be."

He nods, looking devastated for her, but if I've learned anything about Dad so far, it's that he'll respect her enough to do as she asks.

Jaxon runs a hand through his damp hair, and there's no question as to whether he's uncomfortable right now. "I don't know how I feel about it. I'm still trying to absorb the information, to be honest. I'm not going to turn my back on it, but I'm going to need a couple of days. I'll do whatever tests they need to. It's not much, but it's a start, and that might be all I can handle right now."

Emma nods sympathetically while I put my

hand on his towel-wrapped thigh and give it an encouraging squeeze.

"Whatever you decide, I'll support you. Anything you need, okay?" I whisper to him, and he turns to look at me, eyes filled with surprise. "Jax, you're essentially going through what I did a few weeks ago. It's a huge upheaval in your life. Let me be there for you."

He reaches down and grabs the hand I put on his thigh, holding it like it's his lifeline, and Jacinta gives me a small grateful nod from the other side of him.

"Well, while we're discussing unpleasant things..." Thomas sits up straighter in his chair. He had been lounging, or should I say looking like he was lounging, all relaxed and casual, but I could tell by the tension in his shoulders and the shadow in his eyes that he was just biding his time. He looks at me before glancing around the table. "The threat of her NDA was not enough to deter Cecelia from talking to the media yesterday."

"What!" Oliver shouts, sitting up straighter in his own chair.

"Let's get the lawyers onto that," Holden chimes in, with Jaxon and Jacinta adding their opinions, but I can tell by the grimace on half the table's faces that none of this is news to them.

"Well, she didn't actually talk about the company or about the twins and Dad. She, and we're assuming it was her as it's too much of a coincidence not to be, leaked the details of Harlow's relationship with the five of you."

Before I can help it, I gasp, and I can practically feel the blood draining from my face. "Oh my god." My heart just about stops at the announcement. It's not that I'm embarrassed about any of it. I knew it would get out there eventually if we kept going, but I was just enjoying being *us* without any outside influence, and I was hoping when it did get out, it was because we were the ones controlling it.

"I'm calling Hope," Holden announces, jumping to his feet, phone in hand. "She needs to get here for damage control."

"Sit down, Holden. I've already sent the heli- copter for her and Mom and Dad," Dad says, running a hand through his already messy hair. *Must be where Jaxon gets the reaction from.* I would have assumed that Emma or Molly had had something to do with that earlier, but now I know he's already been stressing out this morning.

"And of course it's all nasty trash, and there are a hoard of reporters at the gate. If any of us are going to leave—not that I think that's a good idea— it would probably just be better to do it by air for the next few days," Thomas continues.

"God, this is a shitshow." Declan slams his fist down on the table as I think about the conse- quences of this.

Chuck, Melinda, and Max already know about it, so I'm not worried about that, and everyone who is important to the guys knows too, so I guess it can only be damaging in a professional capacity. But really, how bad could it actually be on that front? They're all CEOs of their own businesses, plus the board of Neighpalm Industries is everyone at this table as well as Nana, Poppy, and Poppy's sister Meredith. So the likelihood they're going to lose their business is practically nonexistent. Dec and Holden may lose a few clients, and sales for Jaxon, Kai, and Jacinta might go down. Maybe even Oliver too? But it could also benefit them all. What's the old adage? Even bad news sells, or something like that.

As far as it concerns me, I really don't care that the world now knows I'm in a relationship with these guys; people would speculate whether I was Brad's biological daughter or not. The billboard already hit my reputation, so this isn't the first time that I'm getting some kind of Summers-related backlash. Maybe that's why I'm not so freaked out about this? I've already had a little taste of judgment from the world, albeit because of something totally different, but that experience didn't kill me. It sucked, and yes, I need to be more assertive and work harder to find opportunities, but I'm okay. Either that, or I'm doing an excellent job of numbing myself until reality actually slaps me in the face. I think I already knew that any association with the Summers might come with its fair share of drama, and if I'm being honest with myself, I can't ignore the fact that a polyamorous relationship was always going to raise eyebrows. The press just turned it into something even juicier with the bullshit sibling angle.

I'm so lost in my thoughts that I haven't been listening to what's going on around the table, but of course I don't clue into that until my name is being called.

"Harlow! Are you okay?" When I look up, everyone is staring at me. Of course it was Kai who asked the question. My hand is still in Jaxon's, and it's his turn to give mine a squeeze.

"Ah yeah, I'm okay. I'm just considering the fallout and all that."

"You're not considering whether this is worth it or not?" Holden reaches his arm around Oliver and gives him a side hug at the worried tone in his voice.

"No." I shake my head, sending him a reassuring smile. "No, I'm all in. I wouldn't have started anything with any of you if I wasn't prepared to see where it went, good or bad. And I can hardly bolt now at the first sign of trouble. Actually, it's not even the first sign. Through all this stalker drama, you guys have stuck by me." I can see how relieved the five of them are at my words. It's kind of hard to be more reassuring with other people at the table, but I'll make sure to touch base with each of them today.

"Alright. Let's wait for Hope and Mom and Dad

to get here before we start considering our state-ment to the media, if we even address it at all. Sometimes I think feeding into the bullshit makes it worse. How about I do the dishes?" Dad declares, and Emma and Molly jump up too.

"We'll help," Molly says. "I don't feel like battling the media to go home just yet. Emma needs to be here when the lawyers arrive anyway."

"How about a movie marathon in the theater until then?" Holden suggests. He stands up and stretches, exposing those abs that inevitably distract me for a moment. When his shirt comes down and I look up, he's smirking at me. "I have a phone call I need to make, but after that I'm good to go."

"Yes," groans Oliver. "It's about all I can manage this morning."

"I'll pass. I want to try to find where the photos in the news outlets came from. I'm going to make some phone calls to a friend or two I have in the media, and if I can't find anything out, I'll get Jake to throw some official weight around," Thomas says, draining the coffee from his mug then heading out without glancing backward. The rest of us help Dad, Emma, and Molly clear the table.

"I'm going to grab a shower," Declan says before giving me a kiss on the head and disap-pearing.

"I think I'm going back to bed," Jacinta says quietly as we finish up. "I kind of just want to wallow." I grab her and give her a big hug, trying to pour everything I'd like to say into that one embrace. We're getting better at this sister thing now that the weapons have been lowered, but I don't want to overwhelm her so I settle for something simple.

"If you need me, just let me know. I'll bring junk food and alcohol, and we can have a pity party in your room. Just us girls."

Her eyes light up, but she shakes her head. "Maybe after the lawyers have been by. I'll probably need it then."

"Deal."

Before she walks away, she grabs my hand. "Can you make sure Jax is okay? He keeps telling me he is, but I know he still feels tremendous guilt from how Mom treated me before we got to Dad. None of that is his fault; that was all her. Just make sure he's okay for me?" I look over to where he's talking to Kai.

"Of course I will." She hurries over to him and says something I don't hear, then leans in and gives him a hug before doing the same to Kai and leaving the kitchen. Dad and the ladies are chatting quietly while they wash and dry the huge pile of dishes.

Kai gives Jaxon a hug then picks up a dish towel. "How about I give you a hand too so we can be done quicker?" he says as he joins the others at the sink, leaving me and Jaxon. I walk over to him and grab his hand.

"Come on. I need a shower, and you look like

you could do with one too." He's quiet as we walk back to our wing and bypass the empty living area before getting to the stairs.

"They'll be putting the movie on in the big theater. I don't think you've seen it yet, but it's set up like the real thing. I hope you like action movies because that's all we normally end up watching."

I bump his hip lightly with mine. "If it doesn't have robots, dinosaurs, fast cars, or a Chris, then I'm probably not going to watch it. I'm sure I will be fine." Quickly enough, we're at his door, and he drops my hand, looking up as though he's about to say goodbye for now. *Yeah, that's not how this is going to work.* I push him into the room and close the door behind me, loving that adorably confused frown. It's such a cute look. Normal Jaxon is hot and sexy and confident, which is a major turn on, but vulnerable Jaxon is a heartbreaker.

"What are you doing?" he asks as I start to shimmy my yoga pants off then step out of them.

"Saving water." I grab him by the towel and pull him toward me. The confusion leaves as his lips meet mine, and I have this absolute need to deliver a kiss right to the corner where they've curled up in a smile.

When his tongue sweeps into my mouth, a flurry of sensation erupts from my belly and spreads to between my thighs. Tugging at his shirt, I wrestle it over his head, our mouths only parting for the brief moment before he returns the favor. His hands come up to remove my bra, then he stills and steps back, eyes smoldering with desire as he takes in the sight of me wearing nothing but panties.

"Do you mean to tell me you were sitting at breakfast with no bra on and I didn't notice? I'm so ashamed of myself." He places a little kiss across the top of each rounded globe as a smile crosses my lips. "Poor neglected things, I should make up for that now." He chuckles and leans in, drawing one pebbled nipple into his mouth and sucking before flicking his tongue across it, fast, wet, and quick, causing more heat to throb deep inside me. A groan leaves my mouth before I can stop it, and my knees weaken. He feathers little bites all around the soft tissue of my breast before moving back to the nipple and rolling over it with his tongue once more. My fingers press into his arms in an attempt to hold myself upright when one of his hands slowly slides down to the band of my panties.

With great difficulty, I yank myself away from him, using the rest of my willpower to withstand that pouty lip he wields like a weapon. Pulling him by the towel, I drag him into the bathroom and turn on the shower before yanking the towel from around his waist. I had been expecting him to have his swim shorts on underneath, but instead his cock juts out, released from its confinement. My eyes on his, I reach out and wrap my hand around the hard length, stroking it a couple of times as his mouth drops open and his eyes grow hooded. Swiping my thumb across the top to catch the drop of precum that's already leaking, I bring it up to my mouth and slowly lick it off.

It proves to be his undoing. He yanks my underwear down and grabs me by the thighs, picking me up and marching into the shower. With unrelenting passion, his mouth takes mine. The only thing I know right now is that I am *so* screwed. These Summers men know how to fucking kiss.

"Fuck, your legs wrapped around my waist feels amazing," he mumbles into my neck as he bites and sucks a path back to my breasts. "Just like I'd imagined that very first night. All the things I wanted to do to you..." He's mumbling while alternating between biting, licking, and sucking both of my nipples while I grind myself against his hard length, practically writhing in his arms.

"Fuck, Jaxon, no more. Can't wait. Need you now," I beg, pulling him closer as my body burns out of control.

He pulls his mouth away from my feverish skin, the water rushing over the top of us doing nothing to cool the heat between us. Pressing his head to my entrance, his eyes meet mine, holding my gaze as he smoothly slides into my warm and wet channel. My hands grip his hair and tighten, causing him to bite his lip and release a strangled moan.

"Fuck, Harlow, you feel so good." His hands tighten where he's holding my thighs, and he bends his knee to get more leverage before pulling back and thrusting in hard.

"Yes!" I shout, not caring if anyone hears, and my hands slip from his hair to grip onto the tightly strung muscles of his shoulders. Pinning me to the wall, his forehead against mine, his mouth hovering just out of reach, he stops. Buried in me, his breathing is ragged and uneven. This frozen moment is going to kill me in either the best or worst way. Digging my heels into his ass, I encourage him to move. "More, Jaxon, give it to me."

"Give me a second. It's better than I thought it would be," he pleads, and I feel a sense of smug satisfaction. This dead sexy man is being undone by me. But then I feel him stiffen. "Shit, protection." Damn, I really need to get ahead of this conversation with each of the guys. Well, communication skills are definitely ineffective when my vagina is otherwise engaged.

"It's okay." I smooth a hand over his chest. "I'm on birth control and clean, but I did have unprotected sex with Declan last night and this morning." I feel the tension drain out of him, and he gently kisses me.

"Okay, I'm clean too, and I know Declan was tested recently too."

"So you're good to go?" I ask breathlessly, trying to get some kind of movement. He chuckles.

"Hold on tight," he whispers. His breath tickles

my ear, and I squirm some more. With the sound of the water running and our breathless moans, Jaxon moves his swollen shaft inside me, slowly gliding over that spot that makes me gasp and clench my legs tighter. Just as slowly, he withdraws inch by torturous inch until I'm begging and pleading for more.

"More," I demand, and he finally stops teasing me and begins to pump wildly, his hands gripping my thighs tightly enough to bruise. Eyes locked to mine, I watch pleasure play across his face. Faster and harder, his strokes move against my g-spot, his pelvis rubbing against my clit, and all I can do is hang on and arch my back, reveling in the building ecstasy. His mouth finds my hard nipple and bites down, striking me with a searing bolt of pleasure. Lost in the moment, I convulse in his arms as my climax rolls through me.

"Jaxon!" I scream as he buries himself deep, his body shivering with his own climax. My pussy ripples around his cock as we breathe heavily, the mist and steam from the shower surrounding us in our own private bubble.

When my eyes find his, gone is the shadow of pain; it's replaced with something that makes my heart skip a beat. He's looking at me like I'm his savior, and when he pulls free and lets me slide down the wall to gather me in his arms, I feel cherished and wanted, and it's perfect.

Chapter Twenty

Harlow

Jaxon's cute pout is back in full force when I get out of the shower and grab one of the fluffy towels he has hanging on a rail, but at least the haunted look in his eyes has eased. "Don't sulk. I haven't got any clothes here, and I need to run upstairs and get some. I also need to check my phone. I'm sure I probably have messages from Max and Chuck and Melinda that I need to respond to."

The pout gives way to a frown, and just like that, the distraction of sex is forgotten beneath the maddening roar of our real-world troubles coming back to life.

Towel securely wrapped around my body, I open the glass door and peek my head in, giving him a gentle kiss on the lips.

"See you soon," I tell him, and although he gives only a silent nod, I can tell by the cloud in his eyes that he's back to thinking about his own problems. "If you hurry, maybe we can continue with the fun on my bed."

Immediately, the cloud disappears, and he reaches for the soap with an eagerness that I've never seen before. Sex can't fix any of our problems, but, to be fair, there aren't really any easy solutions here. Whether Jaxon and Jacinta decide to move forward with their newfound inheritance or not, there's still the emotional baggage that's been stirred to life. So, sex won't fix anything, but if it helps gives Jaxon some momentary relief or comfort, well, sign me and my miracle vagina up for the task. Closing the door, I chuckle and hurry out and up the stairs to my room.

I search for something to wear, dropping the towel to the floor of my closet. Grabbing a bra and some panties, I quickly pull them on before grabbing my live, love, heal shirt. Max had bought me a whole heap of vet-themed shirts for last Christmas, and I love them all. This one had been in the wash when the stalker destroyed my room, so it was the only survivor of that mess. After tugging on the shirt and wrapping my dripping hair up in the towel, I look between the jeans and yoga pants again. Cozy and comfortable feels like it's the right way to go, so yoga pants will be my new best friend for the day. I mean, I want to be comfy while watching a movie. Shimmying them on, I head back out into my room and grab my phone from the bedside table. Sure enough, there are five missed calls from Melinda and ten from Alex, but strangely none from Max. I guess she's probably busy on set.

I shoot Melinda a text to tell her I'll call her this evening when I know more. Yes, I'm avoiding them, but what is there to say? Then I shoot the same message to Alex. By tonight, Dad will have a game plan, and I can tell them what's going on. Right now, all I will be doing is assuring them I'm fine, and that would be lying. I'm not a hundred percent fine. I hate the fact that it was taken out of my control, and I'm just not ready to talk about it when there's nothing positive to say.

Once I finish my messages and get responses from both Melinda and Alex, I open up my laptop. I had sent out a few more job applications yesterday to a couple of zoos and a nearby horse breeder, and I want to know if I have any responses to them or the ones I sent out a few days ago. It's been fun being on vacation, and we still have our trip to Europe, but I'm ready to go back to work. Helping with Prada reminded me of why I chose veterinary medicine as a career, and I'm starting to get that itch under my skin from being too idle and away from animals.

When I open up my email, I can see there are a couple of responses to some of my applications, and as I read through them one by one, my stomach drops. Each and every one of them tells me that due to the scandal surrounding me, there is no way they could consider me for any position. Then they have the nerve to wish me well in my future job search!

That's how Jaxon finds me, staring at my computer screen in horror. *This*. This is that reality slap that I was blissfully ignoring during breakfast. "Harlow, honey, what's wrong?" he asks, climbing onto the bed behind me and wrapping his arms around me.

"Cecilia got just what she wanted. She has literally ruined me. I hadn't even thought about this when they told me about her going to the media." I gesture to my laptop, pull myself out of his arms, and start pacing back and forth. Jaxon mutters as he reads through all the emails. "I'm never going to be able to get a job anywhere. Certainly no zoo will take me on for an internship; my dreams are destroyed. I mean, I might be able to find a job in a small animal clinic in some backwater town who are desperate, or I could go back to Chuck and Melinda's, but nothing here. I'm screwed."

The tears spill over and stream down my face as I start to sob, and I barely take another step before his arms are wrapped around me once more. He doesn't say anything, just holds me as I cry out my frustration, placing gentle kisses on my head and rubbing his arms up and down my back. It feels like forever ago that I was in Hawaii, thinking so optimistically about my prospects. With the hurt that I'm feeling right now, I almost can't believe that I'd been so steady and sure that someone would take a chance on me. Yeah, after the billboard, I still stood a chance. But now? Unless I let Nana, Poppy, and Dad go full Summers on this and just buy me a zoo or a non-profit or something, I'll never have a career in California. I might actually have to let them do it; I just don't think I can leave my newfound family… my boyfriends behind.

When I've finally exhausted all my tears, the anger comes back. "I hope Thomas finds out she's the stalker. Then she'll have to go away for a long time and become someone's bitch. Ha! Could you just imagine perfectly-put-together Cecelia as someone's bitch?" I wipe the tears from my face and try to pull away from Jaxon, but he stops me.

"You okay?" The frown on his face puts a cute wrinkle between his eyes.

I shake my head. "No, I'm not, but I will be," I promise. I'm about to say something, though I honestly have no idea what, when another email catches my eye. I don't recognize who it's from, but the subject line says, *Re: Bostons*. I'm starting to get that feeling, that almost nervous twitchiness that wanted to warn me not to open that goddamn mystery Barbie package, but my survival instincts have always been at war with my curiosity. Despite my dwindling common sense screaming at me, I click on it, and my stomach lurches. Pictures fill the body of the email, each one displaying Chuck, Melinda, or both, taken with what has to be a long-range lens. Beneath the sickeningly casual stalker collage is only one line of text: *I'm watching them too.* Behind me, I hear Jaxon's breath catch, letting me know he's seen this next surprise too. I slam down the laptop closed and growl in frustration.

"Fuck! Why is this happening to me? What did I do in a previous life that caused so much bad shit to happen in this one? How can I fix this? How can I make it so that my loved ones aren't in the firing line?" I can't stop the flow of panic-filled words that flow from my mouth. "You guys have already been targeted and now the Bostons. Who's next? Shane, Alex, and Jace? That's all I've got left. The sum total of the people I care about in this world." I jump to my feet as the terror is replaced with a visceral anger. One so strong I'm practically shaking.

"Fuck it. You know, I have had it with this asshole, whoever it is. I'm done with being scared! I think I'm going to start carrying a gun too. I'm going to talk to Thomas about getting me one because I will not play the victim anymore. If this guy thinks his creepy scare tactics are working, he's going to be fat out of luck. He better hope we don't come face to face because I won't hesitate to put a bullet in his head, and I will be *completely* justified."

Jaxon's mouth drops open in surprise. Okay,

that's fair. He probably wasn't prepared for his girlfriend to jump from sexytime Harlow to weepy and hopeless Harlow to murderous and unapologetic Harlow. Poor man's probably got some kind of whiplash.

"Sorry," I apologize, "I hate feeling vulnerable. It reminds me of every time I was ever around Diane. Come on, let's go watch that movie. I need something to distract me from everything."

"Well, we could always stay up here. We could continue what we started in the shower." He wiggles his eyebrows suggestively, leering at me, and I chuckle, which I think is the response he was looking for.

"How long do you think it would be before Oli or Den came looking for us?" I ask, and he grumbles.

"Yeah, I'm not sharing you with them. Before we go, just let me shoot Tom a message about the email. He can come grab it, and maybe he'll even be able to trace where the emails came from."

"Okay, good thinking." Putting my laptop under my arm, I pull out my cell and call Melinda, leaving a message about the newest shit we need to be careful of. I'll try again later, but at least for now I've warned them. Tucking it back into my pocket, I let him take me by the hand and lead me downstairs, but I stop him at the bottom.

"Jaxon, can we maybe not mention what

happened to anyone else? I'm not ready to talk about the rejections, and I don't want to worry the others about the emails. I know I shouldn't keep secrets from my boyfriends, let alone family, but I just need a little bit of time." I don't meet his eyes when I ask, knowing that would somehow make it more real again, but he squeezes my hand without pushing for more.

"I'm the last person who's going to force you to talk about something that you don't want to," he assures me before leading me to the theater.

I'd expected it to look like a standard movie theater, but what I hadn't expected were the rows to be filled with sofas, making it possible to snuggle with the person you're sitting next to. In one of those comfy seats is where we find Oliver and Holden. They're snuggled up together with a blanket over their laps, looking as cute as can be. I'm so glad they're mending their relationship. Kai is sitting on his own, and Declan hasn't arrived, so I guess he must be still making phone calls. Jaxon leads me past the snuggle twins, but they sneak attack and haul me into their cuddle pile. I struggle to get away, but before I know it, they've manhandled me into a spot between them and wrapped the blanket back over us to very effectively trap me in place.

Jaxon reaches for me, but Oliver swats his hand away. "Away with you. You've had some time today, so it's our turn."

Grumbling, Jaxon moves down the row to a free seat while Kai chuckles at everyone.

Warm hands find my thighs on either side, and Holden sighs, a contented sound. "Much better." He then closes his eyes, a serene look on his face. Movement on the other side has me turning to look at what Oliver is doing. He reaches down the side of his seat, and a leg rest suddenly comes up as the back of the seat reclines, putting all three of us into an even more comfortable position.

"What are we watching?" Jaxon sounds amused, and when I take a look at the screen, I find the *Tiger King* on it in full cinematic glory. I groan, but Oliver waves his hand in excitement.

"This is reality tv at its finest! Declan only wishes he produced something like this; it's fucking riveting." He sounds excited, but I just roll my eyes. "This guy breeds tigers and rescues them from people who think that having a tiger would be a good pet. He has an arch nemesis who also does the same thing, but she killed her husband or something, and they're fighting over who has the best zoo."

"Really?" Kai somehow sounds genuinely interested, so Oliver keeps going.

"Yes, and he's in a poly relationship with two other men, *and* one of his employees got their arm ripped off by a tiger."

"Stop, just stop," I beg Oliver. "This guy is an idiot. He wasn't trying to save tigers; he was trying to make a quick buck. It could have been a good idea if he actually kept them in good conditions, but most of them were half starved in horrid little cages, and as for the babies, he just bred them so he could go around to shopping centers and make money. There was no real conservation involved. He wasn't educating people on the stupidity of having an animal like a tiger for a pet. Or how so many breeds of tigers have become extinct due to poachers and the illegal animal trade. Not to mention, he was putting bullets in them when they had outgrown their cuteness, thus their usefulness. As for the woman, she wasn't much better! She could have ignored his idiotic claims, but no, she had to be as much of an idiot as he was."

When I finish my rant, I realize everyone is looking at me with varying degrees of shock.

"Sorry," I mutter, "it's a sore spot. He lived out this perverted version of what I want to do, and it pisses me off." Three of them laugh, but there's a more somber emotion in Jaxon's eyes. It doesn't slip by me that he's probably thinking about those emails, but I just don't want to get into that with the others right now.

"I'm sure you'll be saving all the animals before you know it," Holden assures me before throwing an arm over his face. "Can you wake me when it's lunch time?" he asks as Oliver tucks me into his side. Unfortunately for me, we continue to watch the ridiculous program until Declan arrives.

"Jax, Dad's lawyers and the lawyers for the trust have all arrived. Plus, the helicopter just landed with Nana, Poppy, and Hope. Dad asked for you to come meet with them." Right as Declan's delivering that message, Kai's phone pings.

Jaxon reluctantly stands up, and we can all see the hesitation. "Come on, I'll come with you for moral support if you want," Declan offers, giving me an apologetic look, but I just shake my head. I think it's awesome he's offering his brother support.

"Shit, I have to go too. One of my athletes has been injured. I need to make some phone calls, see what kind of help he needs." Kai hurries off without a backward look, and Jaxon moves to stand in front of me, leaning in to give me a kiss, but Oliver shoves him away.

"No, my lips, not yours," he growls, bringing a smile to Jaxon.

"Don't be so greedy, Oliver." Jaxon smacks him on the shoulder. "Share your toys." Declan and Jaxon leave, closing the door behind them, while Oliver nuzzles into my shoulder.

"Finally just the two of us. How are you doing with that wicked bitch outing us?" His words quiet into a whisper as the sound of Holden's heavy breathing reaches us. I guess he really is hungover if he's asleep.

"Did you keep Holden up all night?" I ask Oliver teasingly, avoiding the question he just asked. What am I supposed to say? I'm not going to lie, but I really don't want to talk about it at the moment.

Oliver shakes his head. "No, unfortunately, he passed out not long after we went to bed. We were making out, and things were getting heated, but then he was snoring." I snort, completely amused by him being so disgruntled. It's almost enough to rival Jaxon's pout, which is both impressive and effective in reinforcing how deep I'm in with these men.

"Well, I'm sure the combination of alcohol and healing from a gunshot wound was the reason for that, nothing to do with you," I assure him, running my hand over his nicely defined pecs. The tight shirt he's wearing is a gift and a tease, working away at my self-control. Granted, Jaxon just topped up my love tank, but what can I say? I guess they just make me insatiable.

He's still pouting, but I can see the insecurity in his eyes, so I let my hand drift lower, sneaking under the blanket until it's stroking the rapidly hardening length in his pants.

"It just feels like we can't get back to where we were. I don't want to force him to have sex with me, but I really don't know how to talk about it with him yet. I'm pretty sure he wants it too, but there's so much baggage between us that it feels like an insurmountable barrier."

I turn to look at him, my hand drifting off his cock, but he quickly shoves it back. Despite his less-than-serious action, when I look up into his eyes, the fear shining there is obvious. He always seems so confident and sexually aware, but this situation with Holden has him shaken.

"Would it help if I was there?" He shrugs, so I decide to take the matter into my own hands. Getting up, I lock the door to the theater and then turn the blasted *Tiger King* to something else. When I get back to Oli, I pull the blanket off and climb onto his lap, straddling him. I kiss him without a second thought, rubbing myself against his thick length, savoring the fact that there's barely more than a layer of sweatpants in my way. For a little while, the two of us make out, removing our tops so that our hands can wander up and down each other's bodies until we're both panting.

Oliver unclips my bra and cups my heavy breasts in his hands, his calluses rubbing deliciously across my nipples. Moving closer, he drags his soft lips across the skin before taking one of my nipples into his mouth and sucking. A bolt of pleasure hits me from that simple action, stoking the flame that's always lit around these men. I arch my back, the two of us pausing when we hear what sounds like a groan. We find our previously sleeping partner watching us, eyes blazing with need. Reaching out a hand, I gesture for him to close the distance between us, so he shuffles toward us until he's side by side with Oliver. Impatient, I grab his shirt, pulling him the last few inches toward me. I want him too, and I won't hesitate to show it. I lick across his lips until he opens them so I can plunge my tongue into his mouth while still grinding on Oliver. He groans and throws his head back as I reach my hand toward the bulge in Holden's pants, stroking my hand along the hard length. The moan he lets loose is music to my ears, only hastening my decision of what to do next. Breaking away from them, I point to each of the men in turn.

"Your turn. I want to watch the two of you," I order them, and Holden's eyes become hooded. Sitting back on my heels, I hungrily watch as they reach for one another. Oliver tentatively brushes his lips across Holden's like he's testing the waters before he nibbles on his plump bottom lip. The groan that escapes Holden's mouth sounds tortured, and he reaches in and palms Oliver's head, fusing their mouths together. I can't bear to look away while their tongues penetrate one another's mouths, stroking and swirling and tormenting each other and me. Holy shit. I grind down harder on Oliver's cock, and he thrusts back, moaning into Holden's mouth.

Now breathing heavily, Holden pulls away and looks at me. "What do you want, Mistress?" he asks breathily, his hand still tight in Oliver's blue hair. I look to Oliver and see the need in his eyes. Like the weight on Jaxon's shoulders, I can't fix all of this for them, but maybe I can nudge them along to lighten the pressure a little bit.

"I want to watch Oliver fuck your ass while you

fuck me," I tell him boldly, reveling in my role of mistress. I just hope I haven't overstepped. It would be a disaster if he backed off now, but from the way that Holden licks his lips before biting down, I think I'm fine.

"Naughty Mistress, but I'd hate to disappoint you and leave you wanting. I guess we better do as she asks. Roll off, Oli." I scramble to the side, allowing Oliver to move before lying back in his spot. He strips off his sweats, and I ogle his tight, lean tattoo-clad form before it's his turn to crawl up my body. His hands caress my legs then peel my pants and panties down my thighs before spreading them wide. Without any prompting, he licks a long line up my sopping wet folds, eliciting a deep groan from my mouth.

"Fuck, Oli," I grunt, and he grins up at me.

"Harlow, you taste so good." The words are barely out of his mouth before Holden leans in and turns his head, kissing him hard then pulling away. Lost in the moment, Oli's body tries to follow, wanting every moment of contact with our boyfriend.

"You're right; she tastes delicious." Holden grins at me too, and I start to squirm impatiently. He dribbles something cold and wet onto my pussy before pushing Oli back on his heels and dribbling a little something on his cock too. "I know how much sex you're having, and I don't want you to end up with a rash or chafing," he says before gripping

Oli's cock and massaging the lube in. Oli's eyes roll back into his head, but he soon recovers and uses a finger to spread the lube around my lips before plunging it deep inside me.

"Oh." I sigh at the feeling of being filled, and when he pulls back and adds another finger, the second gasp is undeniably louder. My eyes lock on to where Holden is caressing Oliver's thick length, the laddered piercings glistening with the light. Holden's hand disappears underneath Oliver, causing him to groan and do a sort of wiggle before Holden's hand reappears. This time, he shuffles forward on the couch so that his dick is in line with my mouth. "Will my mistress please assist with lubrication?" he asks politely, staying in character, but I don't think he's taking no for an answer. As soon as I open my mouth, he surges in, and I gag the slightest bit. He winks at me when he pulls back, his cock glistening, before dribbling a little more of the little packet onto his palm and coating his cock even more. He shuffles Oliver out of the way and positions himself between my thighs, hovering over me. Leaning in, he kisses me, then his mouth drifts lower, taking one of my pebbled nippples. He nibbles lightly before laving it with his tongue, then suctioning. I groan again, all of my focus narrowed down to that single point of contact, but I'm soon distracted by the fact that he's lining himself up with me.

"Ready, baby?" he asks, and I nod. I try to bring

up my heels to encourage him, but Oliver slides in behind Holden and holds my thighs, his hands running up and down my legs. Just as Holden slams himself home, Oliver gently nibbles on my calf.

"Holy fuck!" I shout in surprise, and I feel Holden's piercing slide along that pleasure spot deep inside creating all sorts of sensations. Still giving my leg some affection, Oli's teasing nibbles harden into more of a stinging bite, giving me an edge of pain that I hadn't expected to like so much. My core throbs, and I throw my head back as I ride the feelings out.

He slowly slides in and out a couple of times, building up the beautiful friction, but just when I start to pant, he holds himself still.

"Are you watching?" Oliver growls, and I lock my eyes on both of them. Oli must have been stretching Holden while he was moving inside me. Holden's mouth drops open, and his eyes glaze over as Oliver pushes his way into his tight channel.

"Yeah, that's it. Take my fat dick into your ass." *Whoa, Oliver has some dirty talk game.* "Oh god, Holden, you're so tight. Fuck, I've missed your tight ass." He rains kisses down Holden's spine while they both breathe in and out.

"Holy fuck, you have no idea what this feels like. Harlow's cunt is so tight, and with you in my ass, and that piercing… God, I'm about to explode." Holden whimpers like he's trying hard not to come too soon, and there's this irresistible edge of desperation to the sound that does ridiculous things for the pleasure taking me over.

All that dirty talk has me right on the edge of an orgasm. I can feel my pussy fluttering around Holden's thick length.

"Move, please, just move," I beg, and Oli draws out of Holden, which draws him out of me before slamming back in, forcing Holden to echo the movement. That's how it continues for a few more strokes, with Holden and Oliver being incredibly vocal about everything.

"Fuck, I've missed you. Never again am I letting you go," Oliver growls at Holden, biting him on the shoulder as if that's how he'll seal the truth of his promise. Holden shouts before bending closer to take one of my nipples back into his mouth.

"You try anything like that again, and *I* will paddle your hot ass until it's a pretty red color. Once the tears are streaming down your face, I will fuck it until you can't walk," he threatens, and Holden's whole body shivers with excitement. I had thought the submissive thing had been all an act for me, but maybe he really does enjoy being it.

A few more thrusts is all it takes, and my nerve endings overload from both the sensations and the sight of the two of them moving together. My orgasm detonates, a wave of pleasure flooding my body, and I cry out, clamping my thighs around Holden to hold him in place. I must set off a chain reaction because he's coming as well, and after a couple more rough thrusts, Oliver buries himself deep into Holden's ass, shouting incoherently.

The smell of sex permeates the room, and the sound of our breathing is louder than whatever is playing on the screen in front of us. Holden is a dead weight on me, and it looks like Oliver may have collapsed on top of him too. Though that doesn't stop him from peppering kisses across Holden's shoulder blades, praising and caressing him. Holden shudders on top of me as I run my own hands up and down his sides, and when Oliver's eyes meet mine over his shoulder, they're filled with such soul-wrenching relief I feel tears welling up in mine.

Thank you, he mouths, and I sit up, as much as I can anyway, and press my mouth to his before pulling away.

"As sexy as that all was and as cute as I think you are, can you please get the fuck off of us?" I grumble toward the end, not sure I can still feel my pelvis. Actually, that's not true because my pussy is still joyously fluttering around Holden's cock. He groans as Oliver pulls out and disappears somewhere. It's my turn to run my hands up and down his spine, getting a good grope of his ass before I'm tapping him out too.

Oliver returns as Holden extracts himself, handing around a bunch of damp napkins for us to clean up with. Once we have taken care of that, he tosses them in the trash before turning the extraction fan on. The two of us tug on clothes, almost stumbling from the mix of endorphins and our recent workout, before Oli comes back.

"I've got it to suck for the next twenty minutes, then it will switch over to blow," he says as he rejoins us.

Holden and I giggle a little deliriously, and he rolls his eyes at the two of us before pulling his own clothes back on and climbing onto the couch. I'm snuggled between the two of them, and I'm feeling good, comfortable, and relaxed. So much so that I feel my eyes become heavier until I know no more.

Jaxon

My heart rate speeds up to a million miles an hour as Declan walks with me to Dad's office. Meeting up with the lawyers makes everything we found out last night all too real. Jacinta and I are the only heirs to Count Bucătaru's estate, or the only ones that they can find. Knowing that I possibly have a father out there, one who could may even want us, if Dad was telling the truth anyway, is a hard fact to swallow. For so long, both Jacinta and I have lived with the shadow of our mother's rejection. Jacinta more so than me.

Last night, Holden and Oliver put us both to sleep in my bed, much like when we were younger and had had a nightmare. Usually, it was Jacinta crawling into my bed, but I would never turn her away. So when I woke up in the middle of the night, my mouth feeling like the Sahara, I got myself a drink, and when I got back to bed, I found my sister wide awake, a haunted look in her eyes that are identical to mine.

"I don't want it, Jax. I want nothing to do with anything that's been tainted by her." She shudders, lost in her memories of our mother. Grabbing her hand, I squeeze it, a little trick that usually helps bring her back to the present.

"It has nothing to do with our mom, Jazzy. This is from our father's side." Despite the attempt at reassurance, she shudders again. My heart just about cracks with each shiver of her body. I hate seeing my sister like this. I would go through this turmoil for both of us if I could. Since I was a child, I'd been ready to sacrifice anything necessary to give my sister even just a few moments of peace.

"No, from the way Dad tells it, the count was as crooked as Mother. If she was his whore, who's to say that he's not our father instead of his son? Or any other man he might have directed her to sleep with," she spits out, and I can't argue her point. Mother certainly wasn't turning men away; there was a forever revolving door in our house.

"We will do the DNA tests, or whatever it is they want from us, and we'll go from there. If you really want nothing to do with it, I'm sure we can come up with some kind of arrangement. We can even sell the damn estate. I don't want you to be unhappy."

Murmured voices tell me we have arrived at Dad's office, and Declan gives me a squeeze on the shoulder before nudging me into the room. The office has been rearranged, with additional chairs that I recognize from the formal dining room, so that everyone can have a seat. Apart from Dad, Jacinta, Emma, and Dad's lawyer Forrest, there are three other people—two older gentlemen who are probably Poppy's age and a woman who is probably around Dad's age.

Emma makes the introductions as I take a seat next to my sister, promptly surrendering my hand for her to squeeze the life out of it.

"Jaxon, Jacinta, these are the lawyers for the Count Bucătaru trust. This is Daniel and Winston Hammel and Patricia Caine. This is Jaxon and Jacinta Summers, who we're pretty confident are the biological children of Dragos Bucătaru, therefore the sole known beneficiaries to the count's estate."

When I stand up to shake hands with them, Daniel and Winston are looking at me like they've seen a ghost, but they quickly recover, each giving me a firm shake. Jacinta barely reacts, simply nodding in their direction instead. When I move on to Patricia, both her skepticism and limp handshake are easy to note. She doesn't even make an effort to acknowledge Jacinta, which practically screams her lack of enthusiasm about this whole situation. Is she assuming that we're lying? Or is she unexcited about the idea of the estate being out of the trust's control?

"Well now, *alleged* biological children. There will

need to be extensive tests run to confirm this." Patricia has a slight accent, one I don't recognize. Kind of like a Bond villainess from some sort of Eastern Block country.

"Yes, yes." Winston waves his hand at her. "But it will be merely a formality. Jaxon is the spitting image of a young Count Bucătaru. Even a blind man could see that they are related. He looks exactly like the painting hanging above the entrance to the house!"

"Yes, I almost swallowed my tongue when he walked in," Daniel agrees with his brother, but Patricia only sniffs disdainfully.

"We will see." She stands and lifts up a brief-case. Opening it, she removes two plastic-covered cotton swabs and passes one to me and one to my sister. "If you could just swipe it along the inside of your cheek, we will have them sent off to be tested right away."

Dad's lawyer clears his throat while also opening his briefcase. "We will be sending off our own inde-pendent analysis too." He pulls out his own set of swabs as Jazzy and I do as we are asked before passing them back to Patricia. Forrest then hands us his set, and we repeat the process before handing them over to him. "If you could send over the DNA sample you have on record, we can have them compared as well." Patricia has a distinctly sour look on her face, like she's just been asked to bite into a lemon rather than share a DNA sample with our legal team. Thank god her partners seem to make up for her lack of social skills, softly and quickly agreeing to Forrest's request.

"Okay, shall we go over the terms of the estate?" Daniel looks to me and my sister, and we exchange a quick look before I nod for him to continue. "I'm not sure if you are aware, but I'll give you the backstory as far as we know it. Whatever we share today is a matter of some public record, so please be assured that we are not violating the family's privacy. Count Bucătaru and his son went missing probably twenty-six years ago now. Disappeared without a trace. Though the count's personal vehicle was found in the main parking lot of LAX, it doesn't seem that either of them got on a flight, nor were they ever spotted anywhere else. Now, please remember we were appointed trustees after the fact. Although the count had a will, he had no set lawyer, so we had no personal relationship with the count. After a little bit of investigation, it seems that the elder Count Bucătaru's dealings may not have been completely above board, but it could never be proven." Daniel has a small frown on his face as he says this, not disapproving so much as just disappointed that he has to be saying it.

Winston takes over. "Because it couldn't be proven, none of the assets were seized, and we were appointed to preserve all the assets in case they ever reappeared. After five years, we had them declared legally dead, and the trust was set aside for twenty-five years. If, in that period of time, no legal heirs appeared, it was to be divided up by the people who had been caring for it—which included Ms. Cullen's father, and now her, as well as the three of us in this room." Jacinta and I look to Emma, whose mouth has dropped wide open as if this is the first time she's hearing this. "But now that will no longer be the case, though there is a stipend set aside for Ms. Cullen so that she can find new accommodations."

"Emma can stay for now," Jacinta interrupts, opening her mouth as if she's got more to say. However, I know my sister. Whatever comes out next is likely to be laced with bitterness and as sharp as a knife, so I put a hand on her leg and squeeze, hoping she reins it in for now.

"Yes, we have invited Emma to stay while we sort out everything. The last thing we want to do is stress her out about finding somewhere new to live." As seems to be the general pattern, the two men nod in agreement, while Patricia's scorn is obvious. "We will also have our lawyers take over, though we appreciate everything you and your firm have done in such a difficult situation."

"It's no problem. We were happy to do it, and we're thrilled that a family member has been found. There were always rumors of Dragos' girlfriend being pregnant, but she was incredibly difficult to track down. Not that she could have claimed any of the assets anyway, but she would have had a stipend to support her until the children were of age." Well, that sounds like something Dad—Brad, I mean—would do, so maybe our possible bio-dad is actually the kind of person we've been assured of thus far. There's something about Daniel that just makes me trust him. Plus, I want to believe that my biological father—if that really is Dragos—would be the kind of guy who would make sure his kids and their mother were taken care of.

"How did you come to adopt them?" Patricia asks, eyeing Dad suspiciously, and Winston gasps.

"That is none of our business and extremely unprofessional," he scolds her. "Please ignore our associate." He addresses that comment to Dad, receiving a throat clearing and a nervous hand through the hair in return. Dad's going to go bald at this rate. All that hair ruffling can't be good for a man his age.

"Yes, well, shall we just go over what the inheritance involves? Unfortunately, we have other pressing matters that we need to get through, completely unrelated to this," Dad suggests.

"Yes, of course." Daniel opens the file in front of him. "Count Bucătaru's will initially indicated that his son was to inherit everything, and if for some reason he had outlived his son, it was to go to any remaining blood relative. Should the DNA tests provide confirmation of the relationship, it will split equally between the two twins as we were never able to find any other blood relatives here, or in Transylvania. The count was an only child, and any of his parents' siblings had perished when he was a child. Dragos' mother died in childbirth, so you guys would be the last of the line."

Daniel gives us both sympathetic looks, but it really means nothing to me. These people are names and nothing more. How am I supposed to feel sad about that? I don't know if that makes me cold, or damaged, or something else that would make people look at me aghast, but I can't force myself to feel something that isn't there.

"We will start with the inheritance in Romania and then move on to what is here." Daniel pulls out a picture and passes it to Jacinta and me. On it is a gothic-looking castle surrounded by a dark and imposing forest. "There is a fully furnished estate in the Transylvania region of Romania. It's nestled at the base of the Carpathian mountains, and it has a groundskeeper much like the one across the road." Jazzy meets my gaze with complete shock on her face, but I can see a gleam of interest in her eyes. Good, I'm glad she's not burying her head in the sand about this. I thought she would just wipe her hands of it completely, but this just might be the thing to keep her interested.

"There is also a house on the French Riviera, a vineyard in Tuscany, and a chalet in the Swiss Alps." He hands over three more images as my mouth drops, but he still has more to say. "All properties are fully furnished and have had management companies looking after them for the past twenty-odd years. You will need to decide what to do with each of those."

Winston opens the folder in front of him. "Here in the States, there's the property down the road. All of the exotic animals were donated to zoos throughout the country, and as such are no longer a part of the inheritance. I'm not sure if any of them would still be alive for you to claim anyway. There is a garage full of what I'm assuming are now classic automobiles, but we would have to get a mechanic in to check them over and evaluate them. There's a substantial amount of money in various shares, stocks, and investments, as well as a hefty bank account." His finger trails down the sheet of paper. "There is also a safety deposit box at his nominated bank and two bank accounts in the Cayman Islands, though we only have records of those—no in-depth financial details. Then there's the vault..."

If I wasn't actually studying her at that very moment, I might have missed it, but Patricia stiffens ever so slightly, and her annoyance smooths out to carefully concealed interest.

"We actually have no clue what the inventory of the vault contains, only that it is activated by a biometric scanner. We don't even know where it is, but then we haven't specifically looked for it. We didn't think it was our place to do that. In any case, it's certainly not glaringly obvious, so we assume it's hidden behind a fake wall or a painting. I couldn't even tell you how big it is since it's only referred to as the vault. Apart from taking a general inventory of furniture, the only people that have been in the house are Ms. Cullen and any tradesmen that were needed for any reason, and they were fully supervised while there." Patricia deflates the slightest bit when no more information is given, but nobody else notices the way she stares at the file. Finished with those details, Winston takes back everything he has shown us and puts it into an envelope that he sets aside. "As soon as we have confirmation of DNA, we will pass everything on to your lawyers."

"Do you know anything about this vault, Emma?" Jacinta asks, and Emma shrugs casually.

"I may have an idea or two, but we can discuss that later." She side-eyes Patricia. Well, that's another point in Emma's favor. She's sharp enough to know where she should be looking while everyone else is distracted.

Daniel takes over again. "There is also an estate in Columbia. Rumor has it that he was good friends with Pablo Escobar, which may explain the zoo he housed here. The estate there is managed by a man whose father managed the estate for the count before he went missing. There is actually a Colombian law firm that manages all of those assets, and once we get the DNA results, we will pass on your lawyer's information to them. I'm sure a meeting can be arranged to deal with all of that. All in all, the count's estate is worth close to ten billion dollars."

"Holy fuck!" I can't stop the words from leaving my mouth as my mind runs at a million miles an hour, trying to come to terms with everything I just discovered. Jacinta grabs my hand and squeezes it hard.

"Pinch me, Jax. I'm having a really weird dream. I must have drunk way too much last night. I could have sworn he said ten *billion* dollars." Jazzy sounds incredulous, but I can't blame her. Yes, Dad is wealthy, probably twice over, but ten billion… for just Jacinta and me? That's a level of wealth that blows your mind.

The two men stand up, followed quickly by Patricia. "We know it's a lot to take in. We'll let you be and will be in touch with the results," Daniel says gently. Before they can take their leave, Forrest whips some paperwork out of his briefcase.

"I'm sure you can understand the reluctance that the Summers have in this getting out prematurely. If the three of you could please sign these NDAs, we would appreciate it." Daniel and Winston are quick to comply, and although Patricia seems reluctant, she ultimately has no choice. She sends alarm bells through my systems, but Jazzy distracts me from blurting something out right then and there.

"Holy shit, that was a lot more than I thought it

was going to be." She looks at me with wide eyes, and I chuckle.

"And you told me you wanted nothing to do with it. Well, I'm certainly not dealing with it on my own."

Emma, Forrest, and Declan escort the trust lawyers out, and Dad clears his throat. "Guys, I know it's a lot, and we will come back around to this in a little while, but right now Forrest and I need to move on to the next disaster."

"Oh god!" Jazzy sits up straight. "Harlow! How is she?" She looks at me and so does Dad. I run a frustrated hand through my hair, feeling way too much like Dad, before sighing loudly.

"I think she was alright. She doesn't want me to tell you this, and I'm probably going to get into trouble for it, but I hate seeing her so sad. Maybe keep it between the three of us for now. She got rejection letters from some of the jobs she had applied for. Then she broke down in tears. She doesn't think she'll ever get an internship now."

"Oh no. That was her dream, and now it's shattered because of that petty bitch and small-minded individuals." You can see Jazzy's temper on the rise as she grits her teeth and her hands form fists. She's practically one move away from stamping her foot.

"I'm sure there's one out there who will take her on, especially if they know there would be a rather large donation if they did," Dad murmurs, and I can practically see him scheming. God knows he'll have to think quickly to beat Nana at it. As soon as she finds this out, she'll probably purchase a zoo... or two.

"Actually, I may have an idea regarding that." When she had been muttering about the Tiger King earlier, it had gotten my own mind turning. "What about if we gave her the estate next door? She could turn it into a refuge for exotic animals. You know, rescuing animals from people who had bought them illegally or didn't know how to care for them properly, that sort of thing. Sort of like what the Tiger King did, but legit and above board. There could be an education center too, one we can allow schools to tour and shit. I mean, I haven't really thought it out, and Harlow would need major input, and we'd have to hire a chief veterinarian or something to teach her, but it's an idea at least..." I trail off because Dad and Jacinta once again look like they've been hit over the head by a two by four.

"Yes!" Jazzy shouts, jumping up and throwing her arms around me. "That would be perfect. And then maybe you all could move in with her and play happy family." She does a little jig and leans over for a high five from Dad. Even though he's chuckling, he indulges her, never about to deny his favorite princess.

"Ah, hang on, don't you think you're getting a little bit ahead of the game?" I splutter. Even I can hear the panic in my voice, but happy family? I get up and start to pace back and forth as Dad and

Jazzy look on in amusement. I hadn't thought about us moving with her, if she'd want us to, or if we're even there yet. The estate needs a lot of work to get it up and running, and I'm not sure if my brothers would be open to the idea, but now that Jacinta has put the idea in my mind, I don't completely hate it. I guess I knew, going into this complicated relationship with her and my brothers, it was a long-term thing, that it wasn't going to be just a fling. Or my brothers and I are, at least. Who knows what Harlow is thinking? I stop suddenly, realizing I need to take another leap of faith.

"No matter what, it's worth bringing it up. She may hate the house when we do a tour, but I think it's worth exploring."

Dad gets up and crosses over to us, folding his arms around me. "I am so proud of the man you have become, Jaxon Summers. So very proud. I love you," he murmurs into my ear, and a lump develops in my throat as I choke up with emotion.

"Love you too, Dad." I hug him back, holding on until I feel my sister's arms wrap around us too.

"Aww, I love you guys too."

Dad smiles and pulls away. "Okay, I'm going to go deal with the fallout from Cecelia." He kisses her on the head. "I'll leave you to contemplate your new fortune. God, I may have to ask the two of you for a loan to buy this new airline." He chuckles again as he walks out. "Imagine that, my own kids giving me a loan." He's still laughing as he walks away.

"Come on. Let's join the others in watching a movie, but don't say anything about my idea. When we tour the place, we can see if she likes it. If she does, we can talk about it with the others before we spring it on her. No sense in getting her heart set on an idea if some of the others aren't into it. The way things are going, I think we may be in an all-or-nothing kind of situation."

"Sounds good, big bro." She's all smiles, but I can still see the tension in her body. "I can't deny that I don't feel the same way. I think I'm just going to pretend we didn't hear any of that for the next hour or so anyway."

Chapter Twenty-Two

Harlow

I'm snuggled in between a snoring Holden and a cuddly Oliver when Jaxon and Jacinta find their way into the theater. Jacinta dramatically sniffs and wrinkles her nose, but Jaxon's eyes heat, a smirk crosses his lips, as they each find a comfortable seat nearby. God, my cheeks are practically on fire. I don't really care about Jaxon knowing what we were up to, I mean, the man has been intimately close to my vagina, but I don't want to traumatize my new sister-bestie.

"How did it go?" Oliver quietly asks the twins, and they exchange a glance.

"Can we just not talk about it for the moment?" Jacinta waves a hand as if shooing the topic away. "I'd rather only tell it once at dinner tonight when everyone's around." I can see it takes all of Oliver's self-control not to push, but he reluctantly leaves the two of them alone. I can't say I blame him. Anything to get me out of my own head would be great, but then I guess I wouldn't want to be pushed either.

The day seems to get away from us, and before we know it, it's dinnertime. We've all been called to the formal dining room; Forrest, Molly, and Emma have gone home, but everyone else is here, including Hope.

Her face is drawn in sympathy as she wraps her arms around me in a hug. "How are you doing?" she asks as she pulls away, and I shrug.

"I'm okay. The worst that could have happened has, so nothing else will faze me now." I try to brush off the heartbreak of the rejection letters, but I can tell she knows about them. Jaxon must have said something to Dad despite me asking him not to. I guess I can't be too mad; with Hope being head of PR, they probably thought she might have some creative ideas for fixing my ruined reputation.

Nana pushes Hope gently out of the way and hugs me too. Then I feel another set of arms and smell Poppy's familiar scent. It's enough to have tears pooling in my eyes, and I feel a shudder of emotion run through my body.

"Now, see here, Hally. I will just buy you a freaking zoo if we have to. You've worked so hard for your dream, and no one's prejudices should be able to steal that away from you." Poppy sounds all gruff, but I know it's his way of dealing with everything I know we're both feeling. It's been a rough day for the Summers family, but the most amazing thing is that they've all been a rock of support.

"Thanks, Poppy, but I'm not sure if that will help. I still need someone who will work with me."

"Pfft." Nana waves her hand dismissively, looking every bit like Jacinta did in the theater. "Throw enough money at people, and they will do anything. Do research on anyone you want to work under, and we will get them to teach you. Summers can be *very* persuasive." Nana pulls away and smooths down her clothes before taking a seat at the table while Poppy helps me into a chair on the other side of Jaxon and then takes a seat himself. The table is strewn with pizza boxes, and while the smell is appetizing enough, it's a far cry from the type of homey spread that would normally decorate their table.

Kai sighs, his eyes on the pizza buffet. "Is anyone else missing Mrs. Heyton right about now?" Every single person at the table raises their hands, and laughter breaks out, shedding some of the tension in the atmosphere. For the next few minutes, slices of pizza are passed around and drinks procured from the kitchen and the bar. Finally, after everyone is served and has eaten a little bit, Dad starts talking.

"Okay, we have issued a media statement slamming the inflammatory 'incest' claims and established everyone's relationships—blood or otherwise."

"But that's crap! We shouldn't have to explain anything to anyone," Oliver argues, but Dad just runs a hand across his tired face.

"Yes, Oliver, you're right. We didn't *have* to explain anything; you know what the media is like. They probably won't pay any attention to it, but at least our side of the story is out there. The people who want to believe us will, and we won't be able to change the minds of the people who aren't interested in the truth."

"We also announced that yes, you are in a loving and committed poly relationship. It was made clear that you have the full support of the family and the board, and in no way does your relationship affect the day-to-day running of the businesses," Hope adds in. "We asked that they respect your privacy and to stop the speculation and mudslinging, but how effective that will be is anyone's guess."

"So what happens now?" I ask quietly, not sure what the process is or what else needs to happen.

"Nothing really. You go about your everyday lives as you normally would. If you leave the premises, you may find yourself harassed by the media, but don't let it stop you. And don't let it stop you from being seen with any of the guys, and *most definitely* do not let it stop you from showing each other affection. Soon enough, the media will get used to it and move on. We're going to throw them Ninja Starfish's story this week, which will distract them, then some other celebrity duo will fuck and raise some public outcry. Before you know it, you will be old news."

"Thank you, Hope." Dad smiles at her affectionately. "You are such an asset to our business, not to mention our family."

"Yes, it was a wonderful day for us when Holden dragged you home from college because you had nowhere to go that first Thanksgiving." Nana smiles joyously, and I just love the way they've accepted her into the family. Much the way they accept me now.

"Okay, let's open the table to whatever other news we need to talk about, and then we'll get to the twins," Dad says, looking around the table. "I know quite a lot happened today, so let's catch up."

"I got a phone call from Hank. He was down in New Zealand with the winter team, and Slade Fairchild took a fall and tore his ACL. I've arranged for him to see the best orthopedic surgeon on the West Coast, but that just pushes up his retirement from the team. His contract finishes in a couple of months, and he didn't want to renew it. He has a young family at home and didn't want to be away from them for such long periods of time."

"Make sure you send his wife a bunch of flowers from us all, dear, assuring her we will take care of everything. Make it clear that he will earn out the rest of his contract regardless. The last thing they need to be worrying about is money," Nana instructs Kai, and I smile. She's so sweet. Of course the company will be taking care of everything, but it's the small gestures that count.

"We have excellent insurance policies on all the athletes, Nana. He and his family will be fine," Kai reassures her.

"I guess I'm next," Declan calls out, looking smug. "I put out some feelers to the networks regarding the search for a new member of Ninja Starfish, and even without naming who the band is, I have a bidding war. Especially after today's announcement." His smug smile drops, and he looks at me. "I'm sorry that bitch outed us like that, but I'm not ashamed or embarrassed, and I will not hide our relationship. I'm pretty sure she hoped it would hurt our business, but it had the opposite effect for me. Star Network has picked up both that and the Neighpalm Ink one, so we are looking good for the next twelve to eighteen months."

"I'm happy for you, Dec, but it was a disaster for me." I feel my anger start to rise. Not at Declan, so much, but at the situation. "For all of you guys, any publicity is probably good publicity, but my life and career are much different. Having a 'scandal' like this linked to my name is basically the final nail in my coffin. It was bad enough after the billboard when I got turned away before I even had a chance to interview." I stop, trying to control the tears that want to enter my eyes. On the other side of Jaxon, Jacinta looks so freaking guilty. "That, I probably could have worked around since it was only up briefly and we played it off as an error, but there is no way I'll be able to recover from this one. I got a rejection letter for almost every single job I applied to yesterday. They *never* respond that quickly. The chances of me getting a job now are slim to none."

Did I plan to blurt that out to everyone? No. But if I'm correct about Jaxon already spilling the beans to Dad, and therefore Hope, it was only a very short matter of time before the entire family knew.

Jaxon grabs my hand and squeezes it reassuringly. "Don't stress, Harlow. Between all of us, we will find a solution for you. We're good at that kind of thing. Summers stick together, and if all else fails, our checkbooks have amazing power."

The attitudes of these people still blow my mind. Nothing that money can't fix. I almost giggle a little hysterically, but I manage to push it back down. Jaxon pulls me closer, wrapping an arm around my shoulder, and I lean in, accepting the comfort he provides. You'd think it might be awkward with all of us being here, particularly Nana, Poppy, and Dad, but there's something about accepting this comfort that just feels so natural to me. That warm, homey feeling is lit up in me once more.

Thomas clears his throat, giving Declan a glare

that's definitely a bit cranky. "Yes, I have to agree with Harlow. Unfortunately, it hasn't worked well for me either. That airline we're trying to buy has bumped their dinner up to two days from now. If we still want to be in with a chance to buy it, we need to leave for Europe tomorrow."

"And that's going to be seen as you running away," Hope helpfully points out, causing Thomas to scowl.

"I know, but unless we give up on the company, I'm not sure what else we should do. I hate to think that I might be losing out to the slimy fucking Russian again."

"Who cares what people think? We'll just cut the trip short. In and out, no chance for Harlow's stalker to realize where we've gone. No side trips, just straight to Prague and dinner, wow the sellers, pick us up a new airline, and straight home." Holden's lighthearted attitude lifts a little of the tension that had developed. "RSVP and tell them we are all coming. That should wow the buyer. Who else gets all the Summers at his dinner table?"

"Wow, arrogant much?" Jacinta teases him, and he shrugs.

"Who knows? It might just be what is needed to tip the balance in our direction."

"It's a good idea, actually," Dad muses, "but I think maybe not all of us. I think it would have more impact if you six and Harlow went. It will show a united front and that we're not afraid your relationship is going to damage our business. The media and our business connections need to get used to seeing you guys as a complete package. We don't need someone's business if they're only willing to deal with one Summers at a time so that they can pretend your relationships don't exist. Not to mention it will show that asshole that Clarissa's actions were nothing but an inconvenience."

"But, but, I'm not involved in the relationship," Thomas stammers, sounding surprised and a little confused, but Nana just waves that imperious hand again. I swear, she's got it down to an art form. I think I might need her to teach me. It's like the ultimate power move, stopping these Summers men in their tracks.

"It's all about public perception," she assures him with that devious little glint to her eye and smirk on her mouth.

"Oh yeah, exactly. Plus, I'm sure it will be no hardship to fake it until you make it," Jacinta adds in, looking at me with the same conniving glint in her eye. Damn it, this is payback for lunch the other day. I knew it was coming.

Hope claps her hands and jumps up and down in her seat. "Yes, Brad, yes! That is perfect. It shows they're embracing what they feel for Harlow, and she for them. Normally, I would drop hints to the media, but for Harlow's safety, we won't. Maybe I'll contact someone I trust to take a few photos of you guys boarding the jet or something as you leave Czech Republic."

I can practically see the hamster wheel furiously running in Hope's mind as she makes a few notes on her phone. My eyes move around the table, noting the shared confusion, and I'm glad I'm not the only one. I mean, I know why it would be good for the company, but how does "dating" me help Thomas out?

"For those of you who don't know, the slimy Russian that Tom is referring to is the asshole that Clarissa sold our plans to. He will undoubtedly want to rub it in Thomas' face to make us look bad. He does that kind of dirty backhanded dealing where he'd bring up Tom's personal life to try to sour his chance to make the business connections we need. But if Tom shows up with a beautiful girl on his arm, boldly and bravely claiming his part in an unconventional relationship, well, who's going to listen to anything that bastard has to say?"

Oh, I can see how that riles up the brothers, and I can't help but get angry too. That bitch did significant damage to Thomas' soul, and to have it rubbed in his face has got to hurt. It's not like it will be a hardship to pretend I'm dating him as well. Everyone keeps insisting that he will come around, and even though I'm still not sure about the likelihood of that, I can give it a try for a few days. What's the worst that could happen?

"I'm all in," I announce to the table, and Nana

actually gives a little fist pump. Thomas does a double take and raises a questioning brow. "I hate smug assholes like that... and I guess it *will* distract me for a couple of days. As long as it's okay with Thomas, of course," I quickly finish, a little unsure. Rejection is never fun, even if it would be rejection for a pretend relationship.

For the first time, Thomas looks a little like he doesn't know what to say. He runs his hand through his red hair a couple of times, and by the last swipe, it's standing up more than Oliver's messy style. He heaves a big sigh. "I loathe that fucking Russian and the thought of him winning again. Fuck it! I'm in."

The rest of the table cheers, and I roll my eyes. This family.

"Okay, but now that's settled, I gotta know." Oliver puts his hands together like he's begging. "Please tell us what you guys scored." He looks to Jacinta and Jaxon, and I feel Jax's hand reflexively tighten in mine.

The twins exchange a glance, and Jaxon nods for Jacinta to take the lead.

"Well, there's the place across the road, some vintage cars, stocks, bonds, and investments. There are bank accounts in the Caymans, but we don't know what they contain. Then there are the four different properties in Europe." Everyone around the table is showing various degrees of shock. Not surprisingly though, Nana and Poppy are unfazed.

Jaxon takes over. "Not to mention the estate in

Columbia and the secret vault in the house next door that has no inventory. All in all, it totals about ten billion dollars."

Holy fuck! You could hear a pin drop in the room. My hand goes loose in Jaxon's, but he grabs it like it's a lifeline and won't let go. "Please don't pull away," he whispers.

The table explodes into a riot of noise from the boys and Hope. I can almost visibly see Jaxon and Jacinta shrinking away from all the questions, and I must not be the only one who notices.

"Enough!" Dad shouts, silencing the cacophony. "Leave them alone to deal with it before you ask them a whole heap of questions that they really don't know the answer to. I think it's time to call it a night. You seven need to pack for an overseas trip, including formal wear. By the time you get back, the DNA results will be in, and we can start to deal with all of that then. Does that sound fair to you?" He looks to Jacinta and Jaxon, who agree enthusiastically. They're going with my favorite "ostrich head in the sand" route for the moment, which I *completely* understand. I reach for Jazzy's hand so that I'm holding one from each twin, hoping they can borrow some of my strength for a moment. On one hand, I don't like to see her upset, but on the other, I kind of like to see her ruffled. It proves she really is human.

"Jazzy, could you please find Harlow a dress she can wear? If there's nothing here, have something couriered over to the jet from the office. And make sure you pick someone who won't fuck it up. Maybe young Jace can help. Such a sweet boy, that one, and talented too," Nana enthuses, and a little pink tinges Jacinta's cheeks.

"Of course, Nana. I know just the dress. I'll get in touch with Jace as soon as we're done here."

"Alright, it's all settled. Just be careful, and Harlow, please don't go anywhere alone. Nobody will know that you're going to Europe except the people in this room and the pilots. I'm hoping that means you will be safe, but don't take any chances. Tom still needs to be with you everywhere you go."

"Okay, Dad, I won't take any chances," I promise him, and with that, we effectively get dismissed. Dad starts to pack up, but Thomas stops him.

"We got this. You guys head to bed; it's been a long day." The three of them give their goodnights and disappear. Kai and Declan grab all the empty pizza boxes while Hope and Holden grab the dirty plates and glasses.

"Come on. If we all pitch in, we'll be done in no time," Holden says to Oliver, the latter groaning as he gets out of his seat.

When I try to stand up to help, Declan subtly shakes his head then nods at the twins. Okay, my job is to wrangle them.

"Come on, you two. I know what it's like to be hit over the head with mind-blowing information. I think what we need is one of Holden's joints to calm your minds, and then bed."

Hearing his name, Holden gestures for us to follow him. He leads us through a door I hadn't noticed, into the kitchen, then back out into the main living area. He pulls out a drawer of a nearby side table and grabs an old-fashioned cigarette case and a lighter.

"Here, I'll help them finish cleaning up, then come out and join you. I haven't touched it while I've been on painkillers, but I really think this is what we all need. Good thinking, babe." He gives me a quick kiss before I take the box and nudge the still shellshocked twins outside. I shove them both into chairs and take one myself before opening the box and pulling out a joint.

Putting it to my mouth, I flick the lighter, bringing it up to the end and taking a couple of puffs. The acrid smoke fills my lungs, and I cough a couple of times, sputtering. That seems to knock the twins out of the stupor.

"Smooth," I rasp out, eyes watering. Thankfully, Jacinta giggles, and even though Jaxon shakes his head, he's smiling when he reaches out to grab it next. I pass it over as the smoke starts to work its magic on my body, already making me feel a little bit lighter. Like all the weight that I've been feeling for I don't know how long is just floating away.

I lean back, smiling. "You know, this was a really good idea." Jaxon takes a couple of puffs before passing it to his sister. She's not much smoother than I am, and we both end up giggling madly. The good-natured eye roll from Jaxon lightens the load even more; like our sexscape earlier, this can't fix everything, but the evidence that I'm helping him even a little makes my soul feel a little happier.

It doesn't take long for the rest of them to join us, but we've smoked our way through the first joint, so Holden lights another. I wave it off when he offers it to me, knowing I'm good now—just the right amount of relaxed.

By the time we head up to bed, we're all a little lighter, even if it's just temporary.

Harlow

After a really fucking good night's sleep, we're up bright and early and loaded into the helicopter, making our way to the airport for our flight to the Czech Republic.

Nana, Dad, and Poppy were there to wave us off in the morning, but Jacinta caught the flight with us. Jace was meeting her at the airport with my dress so she could do any quick alterations to make sure it fit properly. Or that was her excuse anyway. I'm pretty sure she just wants to see Jace again, and maybe his roommates if he brings them.

The helicopter is cleared to land near the jet, and as we unload our luggage, Chris and James appear to give us a hand transferring it to the plane. It's the big one that I had first arrived in, which in reality was only a few weeks ago, but it feels like so much longer. Jacinta grabs me by the hand and drags me up the steps, leaving all of the guys to deal with everything.

"Come on. Jace is waiting inside with the dress. You need to try it on while we're both here to fix up any spots that need work."

"Why don't you just come with us? You *and* Jace?" She turns and looks at me with an eyebrow raised.

"Why would you suggest that?" I give her a nudge to keep her walking up the steps, totally unwilling to play this game.

"Don't play coy. I saw how the two of you were on Friday. You're hot for him, and if I'm not mistaken, he feels the same way. You could be building your own little harem there, you know." Again, she stops suddenly.

"Harem? With who?" She won't meet my eyes this time, and her cheeks are pink.

Rolling my eyes, I push past her, claiming my turn to drag her up the steps. "Pfft, with Shane and Alex, of course. Damn, that must be a sexy pile of man meat with the three of them together," I tease, hoping for a reaction, and when her hand just about breaks mine, I know I've hit a nerve.

I chuckle as we reach the top of the steps and enter the plane. "Where to?" I ask her, and she points in the direction of the master bedroom.

Opening the door when we get there, I find Jace lounging on the bed, posing sexily. "Hello there," he drawls with a wink. His shaggy blond hair has that well-fucked tousle, and his different-colored eyes are sparkling behind his black-rimmed glasses. Smiling at my handsome new friend, I jump on the bed, giving him a kiss on the cheek after a good bounce. "Hi. Thanks for coming over so quickly." He gives me a hug, taking care not to linger.

"I feel like a superhero. Solving fashion problems in a flash." He strikes a Superman-style pose, and I giggle.

When he stops being silly, we find Jacinta looking at us, arms crossed and tapping her foot. She's the very picture of annoyance.

"Whoops." I scramble off the bed with as much grace as I can, which is to say not much. "Sorry." I look at Jace. "She's in a hurry, but I told her you guys should just come with us. Maybe you can get some old-world European inspiration. What do you think?"

His eyes light up. Like me, I know he's never left the States before. I turn to Jacinta, hands together, pleading. "Please come with us? You can buy whatever you need over there. I've barely used the card Dad gave me, so it's my treat. Well, his. You and Jace can do some sightseeing while we go buy an airline. It will be fun!" She's frowning, but I can see she's coming over to the idea. "I'm sure Prague is full of that old-world charm which will help a couple of *amazing* fashion designers. You could grab some sketchbooks and call it a work trip."

"I have plenty of design equipment in the conference room of the plane..." Her voice trails off like she's still thinking it over, but I can see that I've won. "Fine, I'll call Lindy and tell her Jace and I will be out of the office this week. Nana can supervise. I do *not* trust Lindy and Rowena to manage my business on their own for a few days."

Jace and I high five, and she rolls her eyes again. "Come on, let's do this dress."

Jace goes over and picks up a garment bag from the desk on the side of the room. Opening the zipper, he pulls out a dress that is an absolute confection of color and fabric. The top part of the dress plunges dramatically in front, and it's dark burgundy in color, though that becomes a light dusty pink at the floor with a slightly full skirt. He passes it to me. "All right, get naked." A soft growl comes from the other woman in the room, practically shocking me. Since when do ice queens make noises like *that*?

"Ah, ok, I'll just step outside." I can't help but laugh as Jace leaves that room faster than I would have thought possible.

"How are you going to cope when he's at fashion week, surrounded by gorgeous women? Not to mention Alex and Shane are also always surrounded by gorgeous women too." Waiting for her to answer, I pull off my yoga pants and top before unclipping my bra. No point in being shy; she's seen it all anyway.

"I guess I don't know where I stand with any of them. Sure, you say they're interested, and they were definitely attentive during our lunch the other day, but the reality of a poly relationship is nothing to sneeze at. Let's see if they're still interested after they see what you and the guys go through."

I pull the dress over my head and turn so she can zip it up and tie the straps around my neck. The plunging neckline makes me gulp, and I'm already thinking about how in the world I can hide any of… *me* from spilling out. "Well, they're already in a poly relationship, the three of them. Adding you to the mix doesn't change anything, not really. Maybe a few more eyes on them, but it will die down eventually. Or that's what I'm hoping."

She zips the dress and spins me around, searching my eyes for the truth. "This hasn't scared you away? You're not going to run because of what happened?" I can see she's really worried about it, so I grab her hands, more worried about Jacinta than the cleavage I'm now rocking.

"Jacinta, I'm happier with your brothers than I've ever been in my whole life. I was apprehensive at the start, worried there would be jealousy, but they've all taken to this relationship like it was meant to be. I feel loved and wanted for the first time ever. Don't get me wrong, Chuck and Melinda were wonderful and still are, but in the back of my mind I always had a worry that it was out of obligation or because they felt responsible for my mom.

With your brothers, it feels like they like me for me. I just want this stalker shit to go away so I can make some more permanent decisions about where I want to live and what I'm going to do. You've all got your own things, and now I need that too. I need to feel a sense of normal again."

She pulls me into her arms and gives me a big hug. "You don't know how happy it makes me to hear that." A moment later, she steps back and wipes at the tears in her eyes before giggling. "Hey, perv, you can come back in."

He pushes the door open and cautiously steps back in. "I'm sorry. I wasn't thinking about asking you to get undressed," he stammers, looking between the two of us. Jacinta blushes this time instead of growling, which is at least a lot less scary for him. It's so funny to see this confident as fuck woman nervous.

"Don't worry about it. I know you meant it professionally." I give them a twirl, loving the flare of the skirt. "But as you can see, the dress is perfect." I smooth my hand over the fabric and marvel at how it really is an exact fit.

"I went in super early and adjusted the couple of things I thought it would need. Glad to know I was right."

"Do you think I can have some tape so that I'm not flashing my nipples at the whole table?" I gesture to my cleavage, and both of their eyes sparkle with amusement.

"Might swing the vote for the sale in your direction." Jace winks, and Jacinta laughs and slaps his arm.

"I'll grab some when we get there," she assures me.

"Jacinta, why don't you show Jace the plane while I get changed? I'm sure we'll be ready for takeoff soon," I suggest as the silence between us becomes a little awkward. Jace's face lights up, and I see Jacinta relax a little now that she has something to do. They wave goodbye and leave me to get undressed.

I'm just pulling the dress over my head when I hear the door open again, and before I can untangle myself from the fabric, a pair of hands are on my waist and a mouth is on my naked nipple. My knees buckle, and I moan when the sucking motion goes straight to my pussy. *Holy fuck.*

The mouth pulls away. "Now, that's what I call a beautiful sight." Kai's hands leave my waist, and I can feel him helping me with the layers of the dress. Finally, we get me untangled, and I toss it onto the bed before throwing myself into his arms, fusing my mouth to his, and kissing him furiously.

He grunts in surprise as he catches me, returning the kiss, my naked chest pressed against his shirt, my nipples rubbing against the soft material.

"We're just about at our runway time, so everyone needs to take a seat and prepare for takeoff." Kai pulls away, groaning in disappointment as James' voice filters through the intercom.

"Damn it, just when things were getting good." I chuckle as I look around for my clothes, quickly pulling them back on.

"I miss you too. How about you take me on a tour of this plane once we get to cruising altitude? I wouldn't mind joining the mile-high club since I didn't get to last time we were on a plane together." His eyes light up, and a grin crosses his handsome face.

"Oh baby, you know how to treat me right," he jokes. "Come on, the guys must be done with the luggage by now. I had snuck away to see if you were done with Jazzy and Jace. Then I passed them on the way in, and she told me you convinced them to come with us." He takes me by the hand as we head back toward the seating area.

We meet the other guys at the top of the entry steps where they're talking with two women, one whom I recognize—unfortunately. Frowning, I take in the two women who are warmly greeting each of the brothers. One of them could be Ruby Rose's twin sister. She's smoking hot, with her dirty blonde hair in a pixie cut, and both her arms are covered in tattoos. She has smoldering blue eyes and plump lips that combine with her sharp cheekbones and pointy chin to make her all the more show-stopping. She's dressed in a uniform of pants and a black tunic-style top with the Neighpalm Airlines logo above her left breast. She's friendly and familiar, but she manages not to cross that line of professionalism.

Turning my eyes to the other one, I almost cringe as Veronica, the hostess from my very first flight, flutters her eyelashes and simpers at each guy as they pass her. Her uniform is the same in color, but she's wearing an inappropriately short skirt, and her top is low cut enough that the tops of her breasts show. I can't imagine what it looks like when she bends over in front of someone. The guys are all polite, smoothly passing her by without engaging overly much. Thomas is the last to enter, looking over his shoulder as he does, and he doesn't see her face light up.

"Tommy!" she squeals, throwing her arms around his neck. Well, okay then. I don't miss Kai's quiet laughter when I accidentally tighten my hand maybe a bit too much.

"Is that a smidge of jealousy you're feeling, babe?" he whispers, but I just huff, ignoring his question as we watch Thomas try to untangle himself from her.

"Jilly," Kai calls, and the unfamiliar woman turns around, her annoyance at her co-worker smoothing out when she spots us.

"Kai! I was wondering where you were. How did you sneak past us? And this must be Harlow! Chris and James have told me so much, and it's a pleasure to meet you." Jilly holds out her hand, and there's not an ounce of insincerity in her face. Phew, another nice one. I was beginning to think that most of the women who worked for Neighpalm were assholes.

"Hi, it's nice to finally meet you. I feel like I know you already; the family has so many nice things to say about you."

"It's me that's lucky. Not everyone gets treated as one of their own. The Summers are a very welcoming family." I raise my eyebrows and snort at the scene behind us, and she shares a frown with me as Veronica is still attached to Thomas like an octopus. For someone who's supposed to have secret agent training, he's not very good at evading capture.

"Yes, maybe a little *too* welcoming." The sarcasm can't be missed, and Jilly tries to hide her smile.

Kai finally takes pity on his brother, or maybe he's taking pity on me—who knows? "Veronica!" he snaps. "What the hell are you doing? That is not appropriate work behavior." She drops her arms, raising an eyebrow at him.

"Oh really, Kai? I seem to remember another incident when you didn't exhibit very work-like behavior on my flight. In fact, it was both of you together." She points between them, and I feel myself stiffen at her insinuation. Fuck! Kai and Thomas look at me, obvious guilt in their eyes, and she smirks, pleased to have gotten the upper hand.

"Veronica, I believe you will be working in the galley for this trip. Jilly will be running." The voice behind me is fully annoyed, and when we spin around to face Chris, he has his arms crossed. "I'm actually not sure why you're even here. I had asked Samantha to do this flight, and Grace had you moved to the public flights."

"She's my roommate, and when she got food poisoning last night, she asked if I would fill in," she tells Chris—rather rudely if you ask me.

"That's not how the process works. She should have called in for a replacement," Jilly points out, and Veronica gives her a dirty glare. "In fact, I could have handled the whole flight myself."

"We can't kick her off now," Kai whispers in my ear. "Not if we want to keep this trip relatively secret." My back stiffens even more, so much so that I could swear my spine has turned to steel. I might be overreacting to a simple situation, but having another of their exes thrown in my face is not something I'm excited about. They're all so fucking catty.

"Shall we just get this flight in the air?" I ask, changing the subject and breezing past the group. When I get to the seating area, Jaxon waves to me. He had taken my backpack when Jacinta dragged me away for the dress fitting, and he's still holding it. I grab my book out of it then put it in the overhead storage before taking a seat between him and Declan. Oliver and Holden are sitting together, as are Jacinta and Jace, and I really don't want to sit next to Kai or Thomas right at this moment.

"Is everything okay?" Declan asks, snuggling closer to give me a kiss on my cheek.

"Not really. It's never pleasant to have exes thrown in your face, but to have her brag about her sexual escapades is especially off putting."

A growl escapes Declan's mouth. "Veronica is a leech, not so much an ex as a convenient hole to stick it in."

"Wow, don't hold back on my account," I tell him, my sarcasm bitingly obvious. There's a small part of me that's almost glad though, knowing that she's the one who gets that description, not me.

He shrugs. "Just telling it how it is, or was. Kai and Thomas made a big mistake there, but up until recently we've all made stupid mistakes like that. Even though Dad has always told us not to mix business and pleasure, we've *all* made that mistake." He gestures to himself and Jaxon. "Well, okay, maybe not all. The only one I know who definitely hasn't is Oliver. He has a strict policy of no sex at work or with any of the artists."

"I don't think Holden has either," Jaxon admits. "He likes to keep his kink to the clubs he frequents. It's less messy that way. People know what to expect, so there are no surprises." That's an interesting point. Between our moment with Oli and this comment, I've really got it pushing at my brain to talk to Holden. I need to learn more about his needs and boundaries. I'm not opposed to trying anything that's important to him, and I don't want him feeling like his needs are being pushed aside or ignored.

"Well, they just became my favorites." Said favorites are not even hiding that they're listening, proven by the grins on their faces. I blow them each a kiss, and they pretend to catch it before high fiving one another.

"I knew that policy would pay off," Oliver crows, and Holden winks at me like he knows what I was thinking. I shiver at the thought of that future conversation and what it might lead us to.

Thomas and Kai quickly come down the aisle and take seats, their walk of shame catching all our attention. Kai looks at me with hurt in his eyes, but I guess now he knows what it feels like. I know it's not his fault she was on the flight, but it *is* his fault for fucking someone who doesn't know how to be discreet.

"Is there any way we can fire Veronica?" I quietly ask Declan. "Without her retaliating with any kind of sexual harassment charges." He looks surprised that I would ask the question, but I shrug.

"I'm not immune to pettiness. I can't stand her, and I don't want to dread getting on a flight, thinking she may be the one working it."

"I'll send Dad a message and get him to look into it. I'm sure she's probably ducked out of her rostered flight to be here. That may be grounds enough."

I feel the big plane start to taxi down the runway as Jilly walks toward us.

"Everyone strapped in?" she asks, smiling, and we all confirm we are. "Great! As usual, James will let you know when you can get up and move around. The flight to Prague is about twelve hours, but we will be going forward in time. We'll arrive in Prague late Sunday afternoon. I suggest you nap at some stage during the flight, but don't sleep the whole time, or you won't want to sleep when we get there. Just double checking, you all have your passports with you?"

I look toward Jacinta and Jace in horror, but he winks and pulls his out of his back pocket. "Alex suggested that I bring it with me just in case. I thought he was being silly, but the guy must be psychic or something."

"And I keep mine in a safe in the conference room. We all do. This is the only plane we use for overseas trips, so it's just easier to store them here," Jacinta explains, and then I have to swallow my annoyance and look at Thomas. Before I can even ask, he's nodding.

"Yours is in there too now," he tells me, his gaze searing into me for the barest of seconds before it becomes neutral again. Kai tries to catch my eye, but I turn away. Damn it, I was looking forward to joining the mile-high club, and Veronica fucking ruined it for me.

Or at least that's what I'm thinking until I have a devious idea. Maybe I can get a bit of my own payback. Show that bitch that she really does mean nothing to them, or Kai at least.

As Jilly disappears to strap in, I plan my revenge, squirming in my seat at the thought of what's to come. I'll make him sweat for a little while since I need to go visit with James and Chris like I promised I would, but then Kai will be making up for his bad choices in the most delicious of ways.

Thomas

I was so busy watching our backs that I wasn't paying attention to my front. So fucking stupid of me. I missed the ambush waiting just inside the plane. Veronica's lips on me feel like a wet fish, and try as I may to untangle her, she's like an octopus. Finally, Kai makes the mistake of coming to my rescue. Yep, that didn't fucking work out like he probably hoped at all. I don't miss the hurt that Harlow tries to hide behind annoyance. Up until now, I don't think she had realized that Kai had dipped his dick in crazy too. We both had fun playing with Veronica a couple of times, but it soon became apparent that she wasn't playing with a full deck. Both of us had to block her number and had requested that she not be on any of our flights, but she's wiggled her way onto this one. I wouldn't put it past her to deliberately poison her roommate so that she could be on this flight.

Thankfully, Chris has perfect timing and puts her in her place, but there's a lingering feeling of guilt sitting in my stomach. I didn't like seeing Harlow hurt, and that's unsettling for me. I mean, I'm not a horrible person, but other people's feelings, people other than my family, don't usually bother me. Harlow is technically family, I guess, but my feelings for her are so confusing.

I'm attracted to her, and that fact is making it hard to stick to my guns about never becoming emotionally involved with a woman again. After Clarissa, I swore I wouldn't catch feelings, but I have. They've slowly crept up on me while I've been quietly observing her with my brothers.

I've been feeling jealous of all the easy affection they share, and isn't that a kick in the balls? Seeing the way they smile at each other, the way it's not a surprise when one of them puts their hand on the small of her back, it actually fills me with longing— something I never thought I'd actually feel again.

I scrub a hand through my hair as Harlow disappears down the aisle, Kai's sorry puppy dog eyes following her every movement.

"Fuck!" he yells, whirling on Veronica. "Stay away from me and my brothers. We are off the market, and if you so much as come near us on this flight, I will make sure you get all the barf bag duties for the next six months." He storms off after Harlow, and Jilly attempts to hide a small smile as Veronica tries her luck with me once more.

"Tommy, how about once we get in the air, you and I meet up in one of the bedrooms? You can do that thing to me that you like so much." She's not even trying to be quiet enough that Chris and Jilly don't hear, nor subtle, as she runs her hand across the front of my pants. My cock almost shrivels in response, which is not the reaction she was looking for if the frown she gets as she looks down is anything to go by.

I remove her hand and step back, bringing out my cold asshole self. "Probably just better if you do your job like you're meant to."

I walk away without a backward glance, not even getting any pleasure out of the scolding I can already hear her getting from Chris and Jilly.

Harlow won't look at either Kai or me, and she's found a seat between Declan and Jaxon. Lucky bastards.

"Fucking hell," Kai quietly growls as I take a seat next to him. "Talk about a cock block. Harlow wanted me to introduce her to the mile-high club, but I guess that's out now," he grumbles as I strap myself in. My cock instantly hardens at Kai's words, doing exactly what Veronica had hoped her words would. The thought of bending Harlow over one of the surfaces in the plane is tantalizing, and I realize I'm in much deeper than I thought I was.

"Don't think I don't see that," Kai whispers, smirking and nodding at the bulge in my pants. "You're as attracted to her as all of us are. Stop allowing Clarissa to win. By shutting Harlow out, that's effectively what you're doing. You are missing out, brother. She is seriously the woman of our dreams, so get your head out of your ass and get on board before you permanently lose and become a cynical, jaded asshole for good."

I think about what he says. Is he right? Is Clarissa winning by closing myself off to love? Fuck! Maybe he is right. By doing that, I'm giving her actions more importance than I should. Sure, we were engaged to be married, and I was devastated when she betrayed me, but it's better that it happened before we moved in together. Or, god forbid, before we had children together or she got half my stake in the company, which is what I had been planning on doing. To be honest, she did me a favor because that would have been messy and disastrous for all involved.

My eyes drift to the beautiful woman sitting between my brothers, and my heart races. I can't remember the last time I had that kind of reaction to a woman, and it's happened from the moment she landed in our lives. So much of what Clarissa did and how she affected me is wrapped up in my life prior to joining the Summers family. Maybe I need to explain all of this to Harlow, maybe then she will understand that if I hand her my heart, she needs to treat it like the fragile piece of glass it actually is. Because if she does something to shatter that, I'm not sure I would be able to put it back together again. As it is, it's already a cracked and battered thing, with some pieces missing thanks to Clarissa, and other pieces permanently darkened from the aftermath of that harpy's betrayal. Maybe it's time to turn my back on the dark part of me... Maybe Harlow is the sun that I need to chase away those shadows.

As the plane starts its trip down the runway and ascends into the sky, my stomach lurches—not just with the motion but with anticipation.

There's nothing I like better than the hunt, and Harlow has just become my prey.

Chapter Twenty-Four

Harlow

Once the seatbelt sign goes off and James announces we can move around, I unstrap and squeeze past Jaxon.

"Where are you going, snookums?" Oliver calls, though his pet name has me turning and raising an eyebrow. The smile on his face tells me he's not entirely surprised by the reaction.

"No? You don't like snookums?" he asks. "I'm just trying out some pet names, and I think that's a good one." The look on everyone else's faces says that they're definitely much more amused by this than I am.

"Sure, puddin'. I don't mind if you don't." He wrinkles his nose, but a smile lights up his face when he shrugs a minute later.

"Sold," he calls after me, and I wave him off. "But seriously, where are you going?"

"Off to visit my first California friends," I call back over my shoulder to a chorus of grumbles.

Holden's words sneak out more clearly than the others'.

"They're just lucky I know they're banging each other."

I roll my eyes and continue on my way to the cockpit, my footsteps slowing as I get to the galley.

"Keep your hands to yourself, Veronica. Didn't you see the news over the weekend? Harlow is in a poly relationship with all the brothers. You may not want to believe it, but you need to respect that they are and keep your filthy hands to yourself." Jilly sounds angry, and it's no wonder. Being in her own poly relationship, she's probably used to people's prejudice and disregard for the seriousness of her relationship simply because it's unconventional.

"Just because you're as big a slut as she is doesn't mean that Thomas is taken with her. There weren't any pictures of her and him in the media." Veronica sneers, the clanking of slamming dishes accompanying her bitchy attitude.

"Watch yourself, Veronica. Neighpalm Airlines is a great company to work for, and if you're not careful, you're going to find yourself out of work. Who knows if they'll even give a reference. Insulting and pissing off all of the heirs might not be the best route to job security." Jilly sounds exasperated, so I open the door to the galley and walk in.

"What are you doing in here?" Veronica spits, looking me up and down. Fuck, I hope I can be the one to tell her she's fired.

"Just passing through. Don't mind me," I tell them both as I head toward the cockpit door.

"Do you want me to take down anything for you to drink when I get the others theirs?" Jilly asks me, a smile plastered on her face, but I can see the worry in her eyes. She knows I would have overheard their conversation, but she wasn't doing anything wrong except warning her co-worker to keep her hands to herself.

"Coffee would be great, thanks, but I'm not sure how long I'll be in there. Maybe you could bring one down when I finish catching up with them?" I ask, and she nods, that easy smile on her face looking more real as the moment goes on.

While Jilly and I talk, Veronica just stares at me, disgust curling her lips up in a mockery of a smile. "What? Not happy with the men you're fucking, so you're going to blow the pilots too?"

"Maybe, and then afterward I might see if Jilly would like to meet me in one of the bedrooms. I can show her why all the Summers brothers are dating me." I blow a kiss in Jilly's direction, adding a wink before I show her my back and knock on the door to the cockpit. I can hear a snort of amusement behind me, and a shriek which quickly cuts off as the cockpit door opens.

"Harlow, hi! Come on in. James was just saying he hoped you'd come by for a visit," Chris says, giving me a quick hug before looking at Jilly.

"Hey, babe, can we get a couple of coffees when you serve the bosses?" He winks at her before closing the door. "We normally keep the door open, but Veronica somehow ended up on this trip again. We love Jilly, but neither of us wants to listen to Veronica for the next twelve hours. Jilly's probably going to kick our asses when we get to Prague."

James stands up too, pulling me in for a hug then gesturing to the spare seat I sat in the last time I was here. Similar to that day, the sky is bright blue and clear around us. James reaches into a nearby storage area and pulls out a pair of sunglasses. "Here, it can get a bit much sometimes." He passes them to me, and the glare disappears the second I slip them on. "So, Harlow, let's talk tea. Give us all the ins and outs of your life, starting from when we landed this plane the first time in California. And don't leave anything out."

"This might take a while. Are you sure?" I ask.

"We're not going anywhere for at least twelve hours," James replies.

Still not sure they know what they're getting into, I start telling the story—from Jaxon's reaction to seeing me that very first day and the backstory behind everything.

It's at least an hour later when there's a knock on the cockpit door again. Thinking it was going to be Jilly, imagine my surprise when Kai pokes his head in. He looks between the three of us before his eyes meet mine. I can see the apology in them, but he really doesn't need to. During my retelling, I came to the conclusion that none of their past actions should be held against them. I can't hold them accountable for anyone else's action. None of them are actually encouraging the behavior; these women have taken it upon themselves to assert some kind of claim even though I'm fairly sure that they all knew from the start that they were just easy sex—except maybe Jaxon's PA. They were in a relationship, but that had been off for a while anyway.

"Hey, guys! Harlow, we're going to put a movie on in the theater. Someone suggested an action movie marathon, so we're watching the *Die Hard* series. Do you want to join us?" I lick my lips as I study him. Kai's wearing sweats that mold to his sexy body, and his hair has grown out over the last few weeks. By this point, it's looking a little shaggy, which adds to the sex appeal. He's the ultimate beach bum, and it really gets my engines revving.

The opportunity to teach Veronica a lesson is within reach.

I jump out of my seat and wave goodbye to James and Chris, handing back the sunglasses. "Happy flying, boys. I am off to watch shit blow up." James waves and starts checking over instrumentation, but Chris picks up his iPad and waves it at me.

"Got myself a crossword to keep me busy." Pulling the door closed behind me, I find both Jilly and Veronica in the galley. Jilly looks like she's busy preparing snacks for the movie if the smell of popcorn is anything to go by, but Veronica doesn't look like she's doing much of anything. Well, not anything useful anyway. I lean against the wall and watch while Kai tries his hardest to ignore Veronica's desperate attempts to engage him in conversation. Because his family instilled him with manners, he answers, but it's kept to short single-word answers. I chuckle to myself but let him suffer for a little while longer. If you're going to dip your dick in crazy, you have to deal with the fallout.

"Isn't there a galley at the other end of the plane as well?" I ask Jilly after a moment, trying to remember my tour with Poppy.

"Yes, but I try not to dirty more than one if I can avoid it unless I have a full staff on to assist. And I get extra exercise walking back and forth, so it's a win win. Otherwise, there's not a lot to do on these kinds of flights. The younger Summers just kick back and chill and are super easy. I'll probably serve snacks and nap for an hour or so while you watch your movie. Lunch is already catered, just needs to be served, and we'll bring that out mid-flight to try to keep you all in line with the timezone we're traveling to." She edges a little closer to me and lowers her voice. "I am *so* sorry about her. She has been banned from this jet, but she… well, as you can see, she has no shame. I was going to send her home, but I didn't have time to contact another girl."

"Don't worry about it. I've learned I'm going to need thick skin to be a Summers, and Veronica is a fly compared to all the shit I've dealt with up until now." She raises her eyebrows.

"Oh?" I can tell she's dying to ask, but she's too well trained to pry.

"Yeah, just ask your boyfriends when you get five. They'll tell you all about it." Her eyebrows jump as I point to the cockpit door.

"You know about our lifestyle?" I snort, unable to contain my amusement.

"Honey, you're the reason that I find myself with five boyfriends of my own. Nana thinks every woman should be living your life. She thinks you're the bee's knees, and everyone listens to Nana."

Her eyes light up. "Grace is a hoot. She always makes me sit down and tell her all about my dates and partners. I was on holiday when they picked you up, and I was sorry to have missed them."

"She missed you too. When we get back, you should come over for dinner and bring Chris and James and whoever else is part of your family. I know everyone would love to have you."

"That would be awesome. I know the family fundraiser is coming up soon, and we always get an invite to that, but it's usually filled with ass kissers hoping the Summers are going to donate to their cause that year. Family dinner sounds like a perfect alternative. In the meantime, ya know, since I've got you here and all, tell me about what's going on with Jacinta. I haven't had a chance to talk to her, but she looks very cozy with that fine tall drink of Southern she brought on board."

Jilly and I gossip a little longer as I tell her about Jacinta and her want-to-be harem. The galley fills with the smell of popcorn, and I finally take pity on Kai. But before I extract him from Veronica's clutches, I ask Jilly for a favor.

"Could you please give us fifteen minutes or so, then send Veronica to deliver the first round of snacks? Oh, and maybe hang back here for a little while longer before following unless you want to catch the show." Her eyes widen with surprise, but she quickly agrees to my request. "And I'm sorry if she ends up in a foul mood for the rest of the trip."

She waves a hand at me. "She's always in a foul mood with me. She doesn't approve of my 'selfish choices' and never fails to make digs. I've learned to tune her out."

I give Jilly a hug. "Thanks, I've had fun talking. When I get sick of action movies, maybe we can talk a little more?"

Her smile is more gentle this time, and she's lost a little of the brittleness she had when talking about Veronica. "I'd love that." Alright, maybe another new friend for me. I can totally nail this whole social thing. But for now… to crush a certain bitchy flight attendant's dreams.

"Come on, Kai. I believe our family is waiting for us." I drag him from Veronica, feeling her filthy stare boring into my back as we walk away, but we don't get very far. I push the door open to the master bedroom and pull Kai into it.

"What?" he stammers, eyes wide as I spin him around and force him against the wall, leaving the door open a good crack.

"Do you want to make up for Veronica rubbing your indiscretions in my face?" I ask him as my hands wander over that chest. I can't help it. I love the feel of his pecs under my fingers, all perky and round and hard. And here he is, looking so delicious and tasty and *mine*. I'm ready to resume our sexual relationship, and now is the perfect time.

Even though he nods, he's still looking a little confused, so I kiss him hard.

"Good! You're going to initiate me into the mile-high club by bending me over that bed and making me scream so loudly that little miss inappropriate hears us when she walks by to take the others their snacks."

The confusion disappears, replaced with an understanding that's quickly followed by hunger. "Yes, ma'am, your wish is my command." Yanking my top over my head and discarding it somewhere behind me, he fuses his mouth to mine as he removes my bra in one quick movement then reverses our positions. His tongue tangles with mine, and before I know it, I'm dry humping his leg and begging for more. I think the open door is doing more for me than I thought it would. The idea that anyone could walk by and see—or even join in—is intoxicating.

My hands scramble to remove my clothes, but before I can start on his, he moves me to the bed, bending me over it, pushing my legs further apart, and trailing little kisses all the way down my spine as I pant in anticipation. His touch moves away, and I'm left waiting and wanting until I feel his hands run up the inside of my thighs and his warm breath blowing across my dripping folds. Not torturing me any longer, he dives in. Unlike our previous encounter, which was unhurried, this is a frenzy of sensation as he devours me, drawing feral sounds from my mouth.

"Fuck yes, Kai, oh fuck," I cry as he feasts on my aching pussy. Thrusting two fingers deep, he leans back, taking that talented tongue away from me.

"God, you're delicious. Your cunt is gripping my fingers so tight. It's going to feel amazing around my dick." Another moan leaves my mouth as his dirty talk makes me squirm. He pulls his fingers out, and when I turn my head to watch him stand up, he thrusts them into his mouth and sucks them clean before slapping my bare ass. A surprised squeal slips out of my mouth, and the grin that takes over his face is almost desperately feral.

Peeling his shirt off, I can't look away as he drags his sweats and underwear down his thick thighs. His cock bobs free, the precum at its tip telling me just how excited he is for this moment. Once his sweats pool at his feet, he fists his thick length and lines up with my aching core. "Don't hold back, Harlow. I want Veronica to hear me giving you pleasure so there's no mistake who our girl is."

And with those words, he slams home, railing into me like nothing he's shared with me before. I couldn't control the sounds coming out of my mouth even if I tried. His hands are going to leave bruises on my hips, but I don't care. Each time I feel that little twinge of soreness, it'll just remind me of this moment between the two of us. How could I be mad about that? His hips continue to snap forward, his thick length hitting all the right spots as I arch my back and lock my knees, meeting each thrust with my own passion. As he continues his punishing pace, my hands fist the bed in front of me. The amount of pleasure he's wringing from me is already so overwhelming. I can barely stand to hold my head up, so I let it drop, moaning loudly enough that Veronica will be ready to claw my eyes out once we leave this room.

"Please, Kai," I plead, my voice a desperate rasp.

His hands unclench from my hips, those strong fingers of his parting my butt cheeks instead, and a finger circles my back entrance, creating another kind of sensation. My knees almost buckle when I feel him drag lubrication back from my leaking pussy.

"Do you like that?" he growls, his thrusts not faulting for a moment. "Do you like my finger in your ass?" He pushes it in a little further. There's a slight sting of pain, but soon I'm begging.

"Please, Kai?"

His finger slips a little more. "Have you been fucked here before, Harlow?" he asks before he leans down and runs his tongue up my spine. The teasing bastard blows on the trail, following his tongue's path, and I'm about ready to lose it. That cool whisper of air makes me shiver, jostling his finger and his cock in the most delicious way.

"Yes, but not for a while," I pant out as I wiggle backward, his finger sliding even deeper with my motion.

"You know what I would like to see? I'd like to see you take my cock in your ass as you ride

Thomas. Would you like that?" As he asks, his other hand slips around to my clit. With that image in my mind and a flick of his finger, I explode, screaming my orgasm so loudly I'm sure James and Chris hear it in the cockpit.

My spasming pussy must be too much for him because he only makes it a few more thrusts before he groans and stills, emptying himself into me.

"Yeah, that's a good girl. Your cunt feels so hot and tight, taking all my cum," he growls into my ear, and my pussy spasms again. Don't get me wrong, I liked the sex we had before, but I *really* like this dirty side of Kai.

Still seated deep inside me, he shuffles us forward, and we slide onto the bed, his body wrapped around mine as he peppers little kisses all over my back and strokes my hair, praising me. My mind floats, overloaded by the intensity of the feelings. I must drift off because I'm woken when Kai drags a wet cloth over me, cleaning me up. There's a smile on my lips as he gives me a gentle kiss. I return it, but before he pulls away, I grab on to him.

"What was that?" I ask, and he looks a little sheepish.

"I guess I got a little carried away. I'm sorry." He won't meet my eyes, so I grab his chin and force him to look at me.

"Don't ever apologize for showing me you care or just how much you enjoy it," I order him before smacking a kiss on his lips. "I bet Veronica didn't miss it either." I smirk before letting him go. He returns the cloth to the ensuite and comes back to snuggle with me.

When Kai and I finally find our clothes, I make the conscious decision to leave my hair a mess, and I won't let Kai straighten his out either. I want Veronica to see the well-fucked look on the both of us and smell it as we walk past her, showing her that she's never going to get that from any of *my* guys again.

The satisfaction I had when I heard her at the door just made my orgasm so much sweeter, which is petty, but fuck, I'm sick of being the one that gives in or gets walked over. I'm going to take Nana's advice from back when we were first on this plane. It's time for me to take life by the balls and squeeze.

It's with a cat-that-got-the-cream smile on my face that I head toward the theater, but when we get to the section where the other bedrooms are, I quickly lose the smile. Veronica has Thomas cornered.

"Please, I just need to talk to you for a moment," she pleads, sounding somewhat desperate.

"Veronica, just stop! I've asked you to leave me be. I'm sorry if you thought what happened meant I wanted more. Especially since I'm pretty sure Kai and I were clear about our expectations. Just do your job and don't make things worse than you already have." He's being firm but kind, and really that makes me respect him even more. He could have easily dismissed her with a sneer and a nasty word.

"Hey, Tom! Are you coming to watch the movie with us?" Kai gives him an opening, and his eyes light up at seeing us.

"Yup, sure am. I was just coming to find the two of you; the others are impatiently waiting." He maneuvers himself out of Veronica's reach and heads toward the theater, Kai and me quickly following behind to block her. When I turn back, she's looking at us, and for a moment I'd almost say she looks sad, but then a calculating glint enters her eye. Shit, what the fuck is that about?

"Harlow, I was wondering if I could sit next to you." Thomas asks as the three of us shuffle into the theater. The back row is empty, with the others sitting further in front, and Thomas gestures to the empty seats.

My pulse quickens at his words, and I find myself quietly thrilled that he's asking. Damn it, it's that damn Ash syndrome kicking me in the vagina again. Gotta have 'em all.

"Sure, I would really like that. I feel like you and I haven't really had a chance to get to know one another like I have everyone else, and now that you're supposed to be my shadow, I'd really like to know more."

His eyes widen, and now I'm certain that he

thought conversation wouldn't be included. If he thought sitting next to me during the movie would mean he didn't need to actually talk to me, he's fat out of luck. I've got him right where I want him now.

Chapter Twenty-Five

Harlow

I slip past him and take a seat in the middle of a double recliner, giving him no choice but to sit in it with me. Smiling, Kai moves a little forward and finds a seat with one of the others. When I look at the screen, John McClane is already shuffling through the air vents of the Nakatomi Towers. The others must not have wanted to wait while Kai and I took our little detour.

Thomas sits down next to me, and I find myself sliding closer to him without a thought. I didn't realize how soft these recliners were, but the deed has been done. I throw my hands up to stop myself from banging my head against his shoulder... or at least that's what I attempt to do.

Instead of placing my palms on the seat

between us, I accidentally slam my hands into his crotch. He flinches, and a huff of air escapes his mouth followed by a groan as I crush his manhood underneath his sweats. *Oh, fuck me. I might want to use that at some point. Just figures I'd break the man's dick before we even get to the good part.*

"Oh my god, I am so sorry." Just as I try to move, the plane lurches to the side. I slide further into him, my body pretty much slamming into his. "Agghh!" I slam my eyes closed as I scream, bracing for some kind of catastrophic crash, but the plane rights itself.

"Yippee ki yay, motherfucker." I hear that idiot Oliver cheer, and I try to control my breathing without much success.

"Sorry about that, folks," James says over the intercom. "It looks like we're flying into a little bit of turbulence. Could you please strap in? We will advise you when it's safe to unstrap again."

"Oh my god." I'm frozen in panic, no longer caring about the way I just cock punched Thomas. In fact, it seems that I've now wrapped myself around him. *Traitorous harlot instincts of mine.* "Harlow, honey," he says gently as he pries my hands from his shirt. "If you just sit back, I'll strap you in. We can stay here and do it. Just in case the plane drops, I don't want you to go flying."

I'm shuddering with fear, so badly there's no way I'm moving. Thomas feels around underneath me, playing some kind of weird twister tetris with my grasping limbs, and then I hear a click. He must have strapped himself in. Carefully, with a touch gentler than I would have expected from him, he rearranges me so that I'm sitting in his lap, then wraps his arms around me. "I guess I can be your seatbelt for now." His voice tickles my ear, which would normally send me into that wonderfully teasing full-body shiver, but I'm still in panic mode. Imminent threat of death > getting turned on right now.

"Everything alright back there?" I hear Kai call, but I can't reply.

"Nothing I can't handle," Thomas calls back before talking to me again. "What can I do to help, Harlow?"

"Talk to me. Distract me," I beg in a rush of words.

"Well, what do you want to know?" he asks, sounding like he's not sure what to talk about. I'll take that as an improvement. When I first met him, I'd thought that Thomas said everything with the undertone of not wanting to talk to me. Now I think he's willing, but he just seems a little lost with how to start a conversation between us.

"Tell me how you came to be with Brad." I feel him stiffen underneath me, his arms tightening around my body.

"It's pretty miserable. Are you sure you want to

hear it?" he asks, his Irish lilt getting a little stronger with his rising nerves.

"Yes, and don't try to hide your accent. It really is lovely," I tell him quietly. He pauses before sighing and relaxing a little.

"Well, as you can tell from the accent, I was born in Ireland. I was the youngest of six children, the only child to be born with red hair. Now, you would think it wouldn't matter in this day and age, but everyone else was black-haired and blue-eyed, so to suddenly find this green-eyed, red-haired child in their family was a great shock. I'm pretty sure my mother had had an affair, but because of my family's devout Catholic status, that would have been a scandal, so they decided that I had been sent by the devil to test them." He stops and lets me absorb the information, but my mind is stuck on those last few words.

There's a bitter twist to that word—*test*—that causes this tangible pang in my heart. Poor Thomas, persecuted from birth because his family prized their religion and reputation over the importance of loving their child. I snuggle my body closer to him, wanting to soothe his broken psyche. No wonder he took Clarissa's betrayal so very hard. He'd found someone he thought would love him unconditionally—and unlike Dad, Nana and Poppy, she was solely his—but she was just using him.

"Nothing I ever did was right, and my siblings learned very quickly to blame it on me when they were naughty. It seemed like no matter what happened, I would get shoved into a cage in the basement for however long they wanted, with only a bucket, some bread, and barely enough water. If I served the punishment, I was absolved, but only until they remembered that I was a walking, talking, and breathing sin simply due to my existence. It was their job, their *divine right* to exact such extreme measures on a creature that was a sign of ungodly offense within their home."

He takes a breath, and this time it's his turn to shiver—though it's not the good kind. "I'm pretty sure they would have tried to drown me, but there was a record of my birth and visits from pediatric nurses to track my development. Not to mention murder is a sin. That scandal would have destroyed them even more thoroughly than the affair. Eventually, I spent more time in the cage than anywhere else, and my teachers actually noticed. Truancy officers paid a visit to the house, and it just so happened to be on the day when my dementia-ridden grandma was home alone. She let them in and gleefully showed them the cage the devil child was kept in. Thank goodness for her addled brain because they promptly took me away. I lived in a few foster homes until one day my guardian angel appeared and brought me home. Since then, I have never looked back."

"Nana?" I ask, and I feel him nod. I haven't been looking at him during his story, and between his quiet voice, our private seat, and the warmth of me on his lap, it feels like we're in our own little world. In this space, it's safe for him to reveal these parts of himself, peeling away the protective layers on the surface to give me a glimpse at the broken heart that his brothers are so determined I can save.

"I'm sorry your family were assholes, and that girl didn't know how lucky she was," I mutter to him as my eyes drift shut, the emotional overload from today finally taking its toll. I pat his chest, and if my touch lingers just a tiny bit too long… Well, that'll be our little secret. "You're a good man, Thomas, and you deserve as much love as the next person. You just have to be receptive to it." My words are a little slurred thanks to my exhaustion, but I still feel the faintest pressure of a kiss on my head with perfect clarity. A moment later, he shuffles me to the side and clicks me into my seat.

"Maybe you're right," I hear him mumble before everything goes dark.

I must have slept a few hours since Thomas eventually wakes me for some lunch. His hands are gentle as I flounder, not quite sure where I am.

"Shh, Harlow, it's okay. You fell asleep, but you need to get up and eat something. Otherwise, jet lag will be a bitch when we get to Prague."

Lunch is served in the big room with the table, and the open space is filled with chatter as we devour the subs and everything else that Jilly has served up. Veronica brings around drinks, and even though she's acting pretty subdued, her eyes are constantly drawn to Thomas as she makes her way around the table.

Once lunch is finished, we return to the movie room for the last couple installments of the *Die Hard* franchise.

"You know what?" Oli asks, shoving popcorn into his mouth despite the amount of food he just ate. "Bruce Willis can do no wrong. Seriously, why isn't he in any of the Marvel movies? He'd make a great crusty commander or aging superhero."

We all jeer at him, but he's not wrong. Bruce Willis *is* awesome; he just ain't stacked up against heartthrobs like Jarred Reed, Chris Hemsworth, or Cayden Storm. Speaking of Cayden, my mind jumps on the reminder of Max.

"What's put that sad look on your face, buttercup?" Oli points to me, and everyone turns in time to watch my shrug.

"I was just thinking about Max. She was cagey and evasive the last time I spoke to her, and I'm worried. She's hiding something."

"Did you want to stop in for a visit on the way back from Prague? I'm sure we can have a quick stopover. I know Oli has something he wants to do on the East Coast," Declan suggests, and my heart leaps before I shake my head.

"Thank you for suggesting it. That's very sweet, but she's still filming in California. I'm hoping she'll come for a visit once she's finished."

"We can also grab some more of your own clothes," Jaxon suggests. "Plus, it could be great to check in on Chuck and Melinda, just make sure everything is okay. We haven't seen them in ages, and I know they'd probably love to catch up." Now that he's brought them up, I'm already swaying toward a yes. Hearing their names brings up a little reminder of the email and the fact that they're already in the stalker's sights. It could do me some good to see them with my own two eyes, not to mention the fact that if I'm there, the stalker might be too focused on me to do anything to them.

"And I wouldn't mind stopping in to check out the horses," Jacinta says. "You know, in all the time we've known them, they've always come to us. We've never been to their place. Isn't that weird?" I feel a little guilty. I'm sure Dad was just avoiding running into my mother. Even if she wasn't working for the Bostons anymore, it still would have been possible for him to see her around town.

"Okay then, let's stop. I'd really like to grab a few more things since I plan on staying longer than I had originally thought."

"Oh, and I need an introduction to your tattoo artist while we're there. I want to give her my card in case she ever wants a job," Oli says around a mouthful of popcorn, and Holden shoves his hand over our boyfriend's mouth.

"Nobody needs to see that, babe," he shushes, and we all laugh.

By the time we land in Prague, everyone is a little twitchy and a lot ready to get our feet on the ground. Customs makes their way through the plane, checking our passports, and we're eventually cleared to leave.

As we make our way off the plane, our luggage is already being offloaded by airport employees. I frown at James when he and Chris come out to wish us goodbye.

"What the hell was that? I thought you were a top gun or something?" I growl at him, and he looks a little sheepish.

"Sorry, sometimes there's nothing we can do, but we got it under control."

"Scared the crap out of me. Remember, I'm not all that seasoned a flyer yet, and it was my first experience with turbulence."

"Don't stress, James," Jace teases as he pushes past me, my garment bag over his shoulder. "Harlow was just fine, all wrapped up in her personal sexy seatbelt." His grin is cheeky, lighting up his entire face, and I can't help but notice his other hand is in Jacinta's as the two of them giggle like school kids as they clatter down the steps to the three waiting vehicles. My frown disappears when I see that, replaced with a pleased smile. All the others say goodbye until it's just Thomas and me still on the plane with the two pilots and Jilly. Veronica is nowhere in sight, thank god.

"This will be a short trip. The dinner is tomorrow night, and then we want to leave first thing Wednesday morning. I've got you booked into the same hotel as us, and we will leave one of the vehicles and drivers for you. Feel free to charge your food to the room if you decide you don't want to go out. If you do, make sure you keep your receipts for reimbursement."

Jilly waves her hand at Thomas. "We know the deal. Don't worry about us."

"Yeah, just go buy us some new planes." James slaps Thomas on the shoulder and winks at me. "All I plan on doing is making the most of room service and the amazing beds at the hotel. I'm exhausted after that flight."

"Me too. But I wouldn't mind doing some sightseeing tomorrow. It's been a while since I've been to Prague." Chris turns his attention to me. "Hey, Harlow, did you know that Prague has an amazing zoo? I know you missed your trip to the one in Hawaii. You should make Thomas take you to it tomorrow morning—you know, to repay you for dragging you all the way out here for a business function."

"Oh yes! Your dinner isn't until late tomorrow evening, so that's a great idea," Jilly chimes in.

I turn hopeful eyes in Thomas' direction, and he rolls his. He may be trying to keep a smile off his face, but I catch a twitch of those sinful lips. "Damn it, Harlow. How am I expected to argue with those eyes?" He huffs out a sigh as I clap my hands together.

"Please, Thomas, I may have to consider coming to Europe to get zoo training, and I'd love to see an example of what's here." I throw in that little bit of a guilt trip, knowing it'll make him soften even more.

"Ok, I give. I'm pretty sure we can arrange it. Nobody knows we're here. We've checked in under aliases, and I can order a car to take us there and back so we aren't on public transport. Between Jacinta and Jace, I'm sure they could rustle up a disguise too. Hell, Jazzy will probably think it's all a great deal of fun."

I squeal in excitement and throw my arms around him, smacking a kiss on his cheek. As I pull away, Veronica finally appears from somewhere.

"Tommy, can I speak to you for a moment?" she pleads, but he shakes his head.

"I can't right now, Veronica. The others are waiting. I'll make some time for you on the flight home though, okay?"

She sags a little in disappointment before quickly agreeing, and we wave our goodbyes and make our way down the stairs.

"Maybe you should stay and speak to her; she

seems kind of desperate." I look back over my shoulder. The others have disappeared, probably finishing off whatever needs to be done on the plane, but she's still standing there staring after us.

"I can't imagine what she has to say. Kai and I have made it perfectly clear that we are not interested in her, and if it's a work thing, that needs to be discussed with airline management. The owner or CEO is not your point of contact if you have a work issue, even if you know them personally."

I have a gut feeling that this is not going to go away, but I'm too excited about being in Prague to worry about it. A shiver goes down my spine as we go down the plane's stairs. Being late afternoon, the sun is lower in the sky and the breeze has a bite to it. I hope our restaurant is heated, otherwise my shoulders are going to freeze in that dress. Maybe I need to ask Jacinta and Jace to find me a wrap somewhere.

Thomas opens the back of one of the limos, and I climb in, finding Jaxon and Declan waiting for us.

"The others went on ahead. Jacinta and Jace need to book a room, and Kai was going to get us all checked in so that Harlow could bypass the front desk. The less we're all seen, especially together, the better," Declan explains as the vehicle starts to smoothly move away.

"At least we aren't as well known in Europe as

we are in the US," Jaxon says, his eyes fixed on the window.

"Well, at least not yet. I'm pretty sure you and Jacinta are going to make a splash once it becomes known that you are the new Count and Countess Bucătaru."

Jaxon's mouth drops open in surprise at Thomas' words. "Is that how it works? Are those kinds of titles hereditary?" He looks at each of us, desperation in his eyes.

"I don't know. Maybe we can google it when we get to the hotel." I shuffle over to sit next to him and take his hand in mine. I don't like seeing this normally confident, sexy man look so unsure. I want to take the panic off his face, so I whisper in his ear to distract him.

"If it turns out you are, I wouldn't mind role playing the count and his chambermaid or something. You can be lord of the manor, and I can see to your *every* whim."

His hand tightens in mine, and the panic disappears from his eyes, replaced with heat.

"I don't know what you just whispered to him, but I would like you to whisper the same thing to me if it deserves that kind of reaction," Declan teases, and I wink at him.

"Oh hush, you," I scold him, and the three of them chuckle before we fall into silence. I turn my body as Jaxon wraps his arms around me to watch the view of Prague slip by through the window.

"Will you call me, sir?" he whispers in my ear, and I feel my cheeks pink up at the possibility. The small nod I give seems to satisfy him, and maybe, just maybe, I might be starting to understand what Holden gets out of his end of the whole Mistress thing. Maybe it'll be kind of fun to give in and just follow someone's orders.

Harlow

When we get to the hotel, we head straight to the elevators and up to our room. The boys and I have a four-bedroom suite with enough space for all of us, while Jacinta and Jace have secured rooms on a lower floor.

"Jacinta and Jace said you need to be showered and ready for hair and makeup by five tomorrow evening. They'll take care of shoes and a wrap for you, so everything will be delivered in time to get ready," Holden relays, leading me into the room they set aside for me. Oliver and Holden are going to share one of the others, while the other four will share the last two. How thoughtful of them to give me my own room, but does that mean that none of them want to share my bed? I don't know how I feel about that. I've gotten used to sleeping next to someone, but maybe this is their way of making sure no one will have to argue about who gets to share my bed tonight. Maybe I'll just let it happen organically. They haven't shared any complaints with me so far, and I've really been just playing it by ear and hoping for the best.

My bags are already in my room, and I can't wait to have a shower. I drop my trusty backpack on the bed and start stripping off my clothes, not caring that Holden has just thrown himself onto my bed and is watching with his hands behind his head. By the time he claims my attention, I'm wearing nothing but underwear.

"Now, *that's* what I call entertainment." His eyes are hungry as they run the length of my body, and his sweats are tented with his arousal.

"You can keep it in your pants, you horndog. I need a shower. I want to wash my hair, and I'd really like to do that alone," I growl playfully, and he pouts, grabbing his package.

"But what am I going to do with this? It would be such a waste," he whines, but I roll my eyes.

"You've got two working arms and a heartbeat. I'm sure you can figure something out," I tell him just as Oliver walks into the room.

"What's he working out?" he asks, his eyes locked to my semi naked body, and I throw up my hands and point to him.

"There you go. Maybe he can help you out.

That way it's not a waste." Oliver takes his eyes off my ass to look questioningly at Holden, but understanding sparks in his eyes when he spots the tent in Holden's pants. He turns quickly and pokes his head out of the door.

"Harlow's having a shower and wants to be left alone," he calls to the others before slamming the door and locking it.

"I most definitely can take care of it. Tag, I'm it." he growls, then stalks to the bed while stripping off his shirt. I snort before hurrying away. If I watch, I'm going to join in, then I'll never get my shower. Holden's shout almost has me turning to join, but I grit my teeth and close the bathroom door. They need some one-on-one time to work out their shit.

Stripping off my underwear, I run the hot water and groan when I climb in, letting the water cascade over my body. All the sexual escapades are wreaking as much havoc on my body as the stalker has, though they are most definitely more rewarding.

I feel a smile spread across my face at the thought of all the sex I've had in the last few days. And honestly, it's not just the sex but the relationships I'm building with each of these unique and wonderful men. Yes, I've had a setback with my professional goals, and yes, I'm devastated about it, but I also don't feel guilty when Poppy offers to throw money at it. I know I deserve those internships, and my personal life should not factor into the decision of who would be best for the job. They should be looking at recommendations from all of my lecturers and local vets that I've worked with—not some tabloid trash that doesn't know what they're talking about.

My anger runs through me as hot as the water flowing over my body, but I shake it off. I haven't actually taken any time off between high school and college, and I've been in college for a long while now. A temporary break is going to be good for me, and I plan on making the most of it. I just wish this stalker wasn't hanging over our heads so that we could spend more time in Europe.

By the time I've finished washing my hair and drying off, I wrap the towel around me and head out to where I left my bags. The view that greets me is breathtaking, literally stopping me in my tracks. Holden has Oliver on his back, and they're chest to chest, arms wrapped around each other. I can see Holden's cock moving in and out of Oliver's ass while Oli's thick length is trapped between their bodies as they kiss each other with so much passion I can feel it from where I'm standing. A noise must have left my mouth because they break apart, Holden offering his hand.

"Would you like to join us?" From the genuine smile on Oli's face, I'm pretty sure they were just waiting for me.

"Are you sure? I don't want to cut into *your* time together."

"Baby, we would never turn you away." Oliver moans as Holden thrusts a little harder, and my pussy starts to drip with desire.

"God, you both suck. How can I refuse an offer like that?" I drop my towel and hurry over to the bed.

"No. How about *you* suck?" Holden suggests, leaning back on his knees, his cock still lodged deep in Oli's ass. He's shifted his upper body back enough that he can tease me with the sight of Oli's ready cock, standing upright like it's being presented just for me. "Climb on and ride his face while I watch you suck his dick."

Oh my god, these guys and their dirty talk. It definitely is one of my triggers. They only have to whisper filthy words to me, and I'm all theirs.

I'm a little shy about just climbing on as he suggests, but Holden pulls me closer and kisses me hard as Oliver grabs my body and helps me straddle his chest, using both his hands to lift me toward his mouth. I pull away from Holden, yelping when my body falls forward, allowing Oli's tongue to swipe through my folds. My yelp quickly turns into a groan as I come face to face with Oli's dick. Wrapping my hand around it, I pump my fist up and down a couple of times, savoring the way he groans into my wet heat. Holden lazily thrusts back and forth, holding my hair out of the way so he can watch.

"Oh yeah, baby, that's it. Lick it." I run my tongue up and down his length a couple of times, getting it wet before engulfing it with my mouth and taking him down deep.

"Oh yeah," Holden groans, and his thrusts speed up. I use my other hand to reach around and play with his sack that's slapping with every one of his thrusts.

Oliver steps up his attention to my clit and shoves two fingers deep inside me, causing my actions to falter as I ride the sensations.

My hands keep working, and I moan around his length, the sound choked by his thrusts into my mouth.

"You guys are a fucking wet dream. Watching the two of you like that is hot as fuck." Holden grips Oli's hips and steps up his pace. "I want you to come all over his face, Harlow, and make sure you swallow him down."

His words are like a detonation switch. All of a sudden, my orgasm explodes, my pussy clamping down on Oliver's fingers and drenching his face in my cum. At the same time, he groans into my pussy as his own cum floods my mouth. It's all a bit too much, so some of it dribbles back out, painting my face.

Holden's eyes are wide as he groans and slams himself deep into Oli's ass, shuddering and joining us over the edge. He leans down and kisses me, licking the dripping cum from my face, and I spasm around Oliver's fingers again.

"Fuck, now that was hot." I turn from Holden's mouth to look at Oli, and he's watching us with heat in his eyes.

A bang on the door has the three of us freezing. "For fuck's sake, we're waiting to order dinner. Hurry up, will you?" Jacinta growls from the other side.

We all still for a moment before bursting into laughter and untangling ourselves. Before I can get far, Holden has me slung over his good shoulder.

"Put me down, you idiot! You don't want to re-injure your shoulder," I demand, pounding on his back.

"Silence, wench." He slaps me on the ass but obeys, sliding me down his body once we reach the bathroom, where Oliver's already running the shower. "We have to clean you off now that we've made you all dirty again."

He leans in and kisses me before passing me over to join Oli in the shower. "It's my favorite way to get dirty and clean." He pushes me up against the wall and kisses me, but as soon as Holden gets in, he pulls me away. They sandwich me between them, and the three of us lazily exchange kisses while we wash each other's bodies before getting out and helping each other dry off. Both boys give me a last round of affection before disappearing to their room for clothes, leaving me to finally get dressed.

Dinner is ordered, and a few drinks are had by all of us. Eventually, Jace and Jacinta disappear back to their rooms, and one by one we all make our way to bed. Somehow, I find myself wrapped up in Declan's arms, my face pushed against the tattoo of Princess on his chest.

Any lingering bits of tension release in a big sigh of contentment. He hasn't tried for sex; he's been content to silently hold me. His hands rub up and down my back in a completely nonsexual way, but it's nice. It feels like we've somehow gotten to the next step. I mean, we've been together for practically five minutes, but this comfort of just being with each other, touching each other with no real expectations, feels like some sort of advanced step. It's actually something I haven't ever had much of before, and it's so refreshing. I squeeze my hands between our bodies, our naked chests sticking together the slightest bit before we pull apart, and I run my hands over his pecs, my finger circling the tattoo over his heart.

"Have you booked the kittens in for their first immunizations yet? And are you going to have them all microchipped before they go to their homes? Have you had anyone interested in giving them homes?" The words flow out of my mouth, and when he stays quiet, my eyes drift up to his. He's smiling down at me with such warmth and affection, its intensity makes me shudder.

"No, but I'm sure my girlfriend who is a vet will be able to make all those things happen for me." He's smiling at his joke, but my mood plummets as well as my gaze. I want to look anywhere but at him, but he sticks his finger under my chin and lifts it so he can look me in the eye.

"What's wrong, Harlow? Did I say something wrong?" I shrug, trying to fight the tears that want to fall.

"I can't officially do anything for the kittens. I can't order vaccinations or chips or anything without a business to create accounts or anything. I guess I could have Chuck send me through my things from home."

"Oh hey, baby." He tugs me close again and rubs my back soothingly. "It's okay. We will work everything out. I promise." The utter conviction in his eyes makes me feel a little better. "Come on, let's not talk about it. There are so many better things to gossip about. I hear my surly brother has had a change of heart. He seems to be pulling out all the stops to show you a good time in our brief visit here. The sly bastard has planned for you to go to the zoo with him tomorrow, even arranging a disguise to make sure you're not at risk." He rolls onto his back, and the sheet slips down to his waist, his washboard stomach on full display as he pushes his hair out of his face. "Talk about an unfair advantage. Using his bodyguard status to take you places the rest of us can't, and then my little brother has also leapt ahead in the stakes as well. Full access to the not-so-abandoned house you're so fascinated with. How's a guy supposed to compete?"

His voice is light, but when he turns his head to look at me, I can see that there's real worry in his eyes. I shuffle closer, and his one arm comes up around my shoulder as I snuggle into his side. "That's the wonderful thing about this relationship; there is no competition. This right here is just as special and important to me as any trip. This is just perfect." I lean over and place a kiss over his Princess tattoo before sliding back down. "Just keep being you, Declan. That's more than enough," I tell him as we both fall into a thoughtful silence that leads to sleep.

The next day starts with a bang as I wake to Declan running his tongue through my pussy. Before we get up, he fucks me like it's our last time together, only giving me a break when breakfast is delivered to our suite. Nobody wanted to risk heading down to the dining room. Jace and Jacinta join us toward the end of the meal, and they both look like they hadn't slept all that much during the night, though when I go to say something, Jacinta shoots me a death glare and shakes her head. Well, okay then. I'll corner her later when she's on her own and interrogate her.

She throws a wig at me, the hair styled in a red bob, a wig cap, and a long fur-trimmed coat with a large hood on it. Then she throws me a pair of leather pants, a skintight black low-cut top, and a pair of knee-high boots with a chunky heel. To top it all off, she hands over a pair of dark glasses before throwing herself on the nearby couch and putting her hand over her eyes.

"You are the deposed Russian countess Olga Romanov, a distant cousin to the famous Romanov family. You have spent many years on the run from your family's enemies, and you're here in the hope of establishing a new family home. Today, you will be sightseeing with your bodyguard Alexei." She waves her hand in the direction of Thomas' room where Jace had disappeared to. When he exits, I jump in fear for a moment, thinking someone had somehow gotten into our room, but I relax once I realize it's Thomas with his hair dyed black. How did they get that done so quickly? When Jace follows him with a spray can in hand, I get my answer. Thomas is wearing a leather jacket, a gun bulge clearly visible, along with leather pants and a black t-shirt. I giggle at the thought of what the two of us are going to look like together.

"Jacinta and I spent most of the evening in a

nearby club and bar, drinking way too much and talking loudly about the Countess Romanov." Jace puts the can on a table and moves over, picking Jacinta up then slumping down on the chair before pulling her onto his lap.

"We are going to find the things you need for tonight, and then we are taking a nap," he announces, his eyes closing as he grimaces in pain. "We drank way too much and partied with the most ridiculously vapid people, but I guarantee you there is a small media presence out front to take pictures of the countess."

Jacinta snuggles into his chest with a satisfied smile on her lips. "Yup, and I promise you they will not be seeing Thomas Summers and his sister Harlow, or Harlow the stalking victim, or Harlow the long-lost Summers heir. You two will wave and hop into a car which will whisk you away, lose any tails, and then take you to the zoo for some peace and quiet."

We're all staring at them in amazement, and it's not until a few moments later when Jace starts snoring that we realize they've both fallen asleep. Kai goes to shake them, but I wave him off. "Let them be until we're ready to leave. They must be exhausted."

I hurry back to my bedroom and get dressed in the provided clothes, which fit perfectly of course, before braiding my hair, stuffing it under the wig cap, and pulling on the red wig. Stepping up to the mirror, I do my makeup, going with a style that's a lot more dramatic than I normally wear, outlining my eyes in black and lengthening the lashes with a number of swipes of mascara. I then use a dramatic red, left over from a costume, to outline my lips, giving them a vampy look before filling in the rest with lipstick. When I step back from the sink and look at myself in the mirror, I think even Max would be hard pressed to recognize me.

A thrill runs through me as I think about the guys' reactions. Maybe I have a little kink because dressing up and role playing really floats my boat. I'm horny just thinking about one of the guys peeling down my leather pants and fucking me while I'm wearing my boots and this wig. I plan on keeping all of this for another time, and when I step out into the living area, I know they're all having the same thoughts.

"Holy fuck." Oliver cups his dick through his sweats before grabbing a cushion and putting it over his crotch, aiming a guilty look at the two sleeping in the chair.

A wolf whistle pierces the air, and Kai's mouth is twisted into a smirk when his fingers pull away from his mouth. "Oh baby, this is a good look on you." Jaxon, Declan, and Holden follow with compliments along the same lines, but it's Thomas who has caught my gaze. I can't tear my eyes away from the heat that's blazing in his eyes.

I'm not sure how long it goes on for, but a

clearing throat has us both startling. "Ah, yes, right. Shall we go then?" he asks, holding his hand in the direction of the door. I grab the sunglasses Jacinta provided and put them on my head before grabbing my backpack. But before I can put it over my shoulder, Declan stops me.

"Oh no, Countess Romanov is *way* too important to carry around a backpack or anything so mundane as money. Her bodyguard takes care of all that. The only thing you can keep is a phone in your hand for selfies."

Everyone chuckles as he reaches in and pulls out my phone, sliding it into the pocket of my long coat.

"Does someone want to wake the 'tired twins'?" Holden asks dryly. "So they can give them a final check over."

Everyone looks to Jaxon, who just rolls his eyes and gives his sister a shove. "Hey, get up! They're leaving."

Jacinta jumps so badly she falls off the chair with Jace sliding off on top of her. We watch as they try to untangle themselves from the heap on the ground, Jace's hand cupping Jacinta's boob before they freeze.

"Oh for fuck's sake," Jaxon groans, hauling his sister out of Jace's tender hold. "I think the two of you better nap first and then shop. Who knows what kind of a wrap you might buy Harlow in the state the two of you are in."

"Ah yeah, you might be onto something, brother dearest." Jacinta bares her teeth in what I think is supposed to be a smile, but it's most definitely a grimace.

"Do you think they might come to us if you throw your weight around?" Jace groans and rests his head on Jacinta's shoulders. Poor guy is forced to move when her head snaps up, almost hitting him.

"Fuck, of course they will. Why didn't I think of that?" Jacinta pulls her phone out of the pocket of her jeans and dials a number before pausing. Someone must pick up because she rattles off a barrage of words in French. The conversation goes on for a few moments, all of us waiting patiently, before she ends the call and throws her arms up triumphantly. "They'll be here this afternoon, which gives us four hours to nap." Even though Jace cheers, there's a bit of a wince on his face. It has nothing on the full force of a Summers man's pout, but it's a cute look nonetheless. Jacinta is screwed.

"Can we go now?" I ask, and she finally takes a proper look at me.

"Holy shit, Harlow, you're fucking hot." She holds out her hand to Jace, and they do some kind of fist bump with an explosion at the end. "We are fucking good, my friend," she congratulates him, and he nods.

"Smoking hot femme fatale. Nothing like normal Harlow at all."

"Hey!" I complain, and all the guys jump to my defense while Jace practically cowers.

"Shit, no, I don't mean that Harlow isn't normally smoking hot. She is!" This gets more disgruntled looks, and even Jacinta crosses her arms. I chuckle at the panic on Jace's face. "No, what I mean is she's gorgeous anyway, but this way she does not look like Harlow and therefore is safe."

I see his sigh of relief as everyone takes their stares off of him. Poor Jace. I decide to give him a break and head for the door, drawing their attention away from him.

"Davay, Alexei. Nash voditel' zhdet. Posmotrim etot zoopark." My Russian is a little rusty, but the accent is flawless, and once again everyone stops and stares at me, mouths dropping open. "What? Max and I used to have fun practicing accents in case she ever needed it for scenes in the movies. Stuntwomen have to speak sometimes, and Russian just happened to be my favorite. Though I do pretty well with a few others too."

"But, but, but," Oli stammers, "you speak it too?"

"Look, I was too tired to party all that much with my college course load, so I chose to stay in more often than not. Learning different accents was a way to keep myself entertained. Then I expanded it to the actual language. I didn't have a lot of friends. I was too busy, and nobody stuck around for long when I kept turning down invites to go out.

Apart from a couple of friends with benefits, I spent a lot of time on my own." The looks of surprise become pitying, but I turn away because I don't want to see it.

"Well, what did you say?" Kai asks, changing the subject, and I spin around to give him a grateful look.

"Come on, Alexei. Our driver is waiting. Let us see this zoo."

"Wow, you really do sound like a Russian princess, and you're more beautiful than one too." Oli is looking at me with a gleam in his eye, and I know he's thinking wicked thoughts. I shake my head at him and move toward the door, unable to indulge no matter how much I want to.

"Hang on, Harlow," Thomas calls, stopping me in my tracks. "The others can't be seen with us, so they're staying up here."

Reluctantly, I wave goodbye, not wanting to see them looking at me like they're lost puppies left behind.

Thomas already has his professional bodyguard face on this morning, but his eyes soften as he takes my arm and leads me to the elevator. "Remember, I'm your bodyguard. It would be normal for you to wait for everything I say. We should be safe enough since we're disguised, but let's just be careful." As we step in, the doors closing behind us, his hand is a hot but comforting weight. "The press will shove, but we have a car waiting. We will get straight in, and it will take off. We'll be at the zoo before you know it, relaxing for the day before the blasted dinner tonight." I look at Thomas in shock. That's the first outward sign I've seen that he isn't as cool and collected as he should be about this deal. He goes to rub his hand through his hair as the elevator moves down, but I grab his arm to stop him.

"I'm not sure if the dye will come off in your hand or not," I explain when he raises an eyebrow. Before I can say anything else, the elevator stops, Thomas walking ahead while I adopt a spoiled, bored expression that I've seen so many of the pampered Hamptons princesses wear over the years.

Harlow

The media is shouting, their cameras flashing as we hustle out to the car. Thankfully, their chaotic calls are silenced once the door closes behind us. Thomas holds my arm and pushes his way through the throng with the help of the hotel security, his grip centering me in a way that little else possibly could. I hadn't intended to truly rely on him, but I can't deny it; there's something about him that makes me feel safe. Between Thomas' safety blanket potential and Declan's bedtime snuggles, these men are pleasantly overwhelming my relationship-starved heart.

The two of us fall into an easy silence for the duration of the drive. Once we get there, we wander around the zoo unmolested for a few hours in some unexpected fulfillment of one of my favorite dreams. The setup is really world class, and I'm thrilled to read about all the success they've had with their breeding programs. So many endangered species have a fighting chance because of programs like this all over the world, and I'm so excited about all of this that I'm struggling to keep my inner geek in check.

Thomas is attentive and protective and generally really good company. Surprisingly good company, actually. He seems happy to stand beside me and observe, having no need to fill the silence with chatter, which suits me fine, while I endeavor to read every bit of information provided. It's not awkward or uncomfortable, and when he does talk, he asks intelligent questions and actually listens to my answers. I know how boring this must be for someone who isn't as obsessed with animals as I am, but he never once tries to hurry me along.

We both have a good time at the sea lion show. I know there are people who object to those kinds of things, but it's a useful way to keep animals active, engaged, and mentally stimulated. He doesn't judge me when I laugh at their tricks, and one of the lightest smiles I've seen yet absolutely transforms his face. From what he told me, he didn't get to have a childhood; now, maybe he's getting a little taste of what it would have been like for him to be carefree, spending a lazy day at the zoo like so many got to when they were young. I'm not glad that he had such a shitty upbringing, but I am glad I'm sharing this with him. I want to see more of those smiles, want to be the cause of those smiles, even if it's indirectly by guilting him into a trip to the zoo.

After the sea lions, we see the hippos, polar bears, big cats, and gorillas before I finally have to call the day done. Even with the chunky heel, my feet are killing me, and I know that Jacinta will shove me into something worse tonight. My poor feet need a break; the thought of convincing one of my dashing Summers men to give me a foot rub is already poking insistently at my brain.

We make our way back to the car, and when Thomas slides into the backseat next to me, I snuggle into his side so that we can talk without the driver overhearing. I don't want him to realize we're not who we're saying we are.

"Thank you so much for that. It was wonderful, and I had so much fun." He smiles down at me, still light, but it's somehow softer than it was before.

"It's the least I can do since you're helping me tonight." I frown a little and pull away just a bit, feeling on edge after that response.

"Is that the only reason you took me? As 'payment' for tonight..." He looks confused for a moment then quickly shakes his head.

"No, no, it wasn't. I'm sorry, Harlow. I didn't mean for it to sound like that. My flirting skills are rusty."

"Look, Thomas, I don't believe in beating around the bush. I was very straight with your brothers, so I think it's time you and I had the same conversation. Is this all just so we look convincing tonight, or are you interested in joining my... harem?" Yes, I've finally admitted to myself that is what I have. It's better than a menagerie or flock, so I'll take it even though I still feel kind of ridiculous when I say it.

His mouth drops open before a burst of laughter explodes from him. I fight the smile that wants to cross my lips because I do actually want to know, but I'm glad I got him to react like that.

He gets himself under control and picks my hand up, pulling me close again. "I would be honored to be a member of your *harem*, and no, this is not about tonight. It's me finally getting my head out of my ass and seeing exactly what is in front of me." His hand cups the back of my neck, slowly drawing me forward until he kisses me. It's not long, only a gentle brushing of lips, but it's enough to let me know his interest. Out of the corner of my eye, I can see the driver watching us.

"Oh, Alexei, you know it is forbidden! We cannot." I drop into the role I'm supposed to be playing, and Thomas' eyes widen before they dart to the front, his lips twitching like they want to curve up, but he controls it.

"But, Olga, you are my one true love." The Irish accent is gone, and in its place is a Russian accent as good as mine. It's my turn for my mouth to drop open, and Thomas doesn't hesitate to take advantage of my surprise. He swoops in and takes my mouth with his, his tongue teasing and caressing the inside before I can recover and give back as good as I'm getting.

The driver really is getting an eyeful this time, and the car swerves enough to break us apart.

"Keep your eyes on the road," Thomas snarls, then pulls back his jacket to expose his gun. The driver pales and follows the order with a nervous gulp. I smother a giggle in Thomas' jacket, and we stay snuggled together until the car gets close to the hotel.

The media are no longer around, so our return to the hotel is a lot more relaxed than our departure. We're both laughing about the driver when we make it back to the room, and Thomas opens the door to a quiet suite with a note on the coffee table. He picks it up and reads it out loud. "Have gone shopping for a few things. We will be back in plenty of time. Love, us." He snorts and puts the note back on the table. "Of course they couldn't stay put for one day."

"I don't blame them; it was bad enough for the flight here. Anyway, I think I'm going to go soak in that amazing bath in the en-suite of my room. It has a huge window in front of it with an amazing view of the Prague Castle. That's as close as I'll get to it this trip, but hopefully I can come back."

Thomas strides over to me and takes my hand. "I come to Europe on business all the time, and if this sale goes through, we'll need to travel back and forth quite a bit over the coming months. I'd love for you to accompany me, maybe we could do a search for abandoned places you would like to visit and make a list of them for when we do."

Holy wow, inner swoon. When he really decides to go all in, he really commits. "I'd love that. Let's see what happens with my job, but I may very well take you up on the offer if I can't get hired anywhere until the media attention dies down." I kiss him on the cheek, thinking about more but not wanting to rush this newfound closeness so soon. "Thank you again for today. Best date ever." I leave him and head for my bedroom, but when I turn back to look at him, I see him fist bumping the air. Wow, this really is a change. Everyone told me he would be different, but I just hadn't expected so much. It's almost like a weight has lifted off of his chest. He catches me looking, his pale skin lighting up with a blush, but I just chuckle and wink before entering my bedroom.

Five hours later, after a bath and a nap and another shower, my boobs are being wrangled into the dress by Jacinta, with tape being applied so that I don't flash the whole table during the meal even though Jace had suggested it may tip the scales in our favor. Both of them are looking much better this afternoon, and they keep exchanging cute looks that are totally not as sly as they may think. I still haven't had a chance to corner Jacinta about what is happening between them, but I will on the flight home. She can't run away from me at fifty thousand feet in the air.

"Alright, those puppies aren't going anywhere," she declares, stepping back to take in her and Jace's handiwork. Hair and makeup have already been done, so all that I need to do now is put my shoes on my feet and grab my wrap.

"Damn, girl, you clean up nice. The boys are going to be the envy of everyone at the table. We did good!" Jace crows, and the two of them exchange a high five.

Rolling my eyes, I slip my feet into the too-high heels and grab the wrap off my bed. "Yes, yes, you're both fashion geniuses. Now hurry up and finish getting yourselves ready."

"Babe, we *are* ready. You can't beat perfection," Jacinta replies, adopting a haughty tone, and Jace mimics her, smoothing down his suit jacket.

"No, it's really not fair for everyone else that we're going to be there. Poor Thomas will miss out on his airline because they're so dazzled by us."

I look back and forth between the two, not sure how to react to all of that, but they can't keep straight faces. They burst into giggles, leaning on each other like they can't stand up straight without the other's help. God, it's nice to see Jacinta like this. Every moment between us now, I'm seeing the real her, I think, the sister that the guys are devoted to and want to protect because she's worthy of their dedication.

"Idiots," I growl on my way out, but there's a smile on my face. I really like their relationship, the way they fit so well together. I hope it develops further. Jacinta needs some fun and friendship in her life, and Jace seems to be giving her that.

When I step out into the living area, I'm struck speechless by the sight before me. The Summers men are already a good-looking bunch on a normal day, but put them all in suits, and holy fuck... They're *deadly*. Even Oliver is wearing one today, and I want to fan my face at the sight of his waistcoated self.

"Fuck me." The reverent whisper comes from the one person I least would have expected it to come from. Declan reaches down and discreetly adjusts himself. "Harlow, you look beautiful."

"Fuck beautiful, she looks smoking hot," Oli says, a cheeky grin on his face. "Why are we going to this dinner again?" I can feel my cheeks heat at his silliness, but I'll totally accept it. What woman doesn't want to sweep her men off their feet with just a single glimpse?

"I just want to drop at her feet and worship her," Holden adds in with a wink.

Thomas and Kai are silent, but I can see the desire in their eyes that speaks loudly enough on its own. Jaxon steps up to me and opens a little box, and he can't quite meet my eyes, like he's nervous for my reaction. Poor guy has taken a few hits over the last few days, and I really want to see confidence coming back to life. "I picked this up for you when we were out shopping. Jacinta may have let me know that the dress was missing some bling." Sparkling inside on a bed of royal blue velvet is a delicate strand of white diamonds that meet in a v. Perfect placement to draw eyes to my breasts.

"Oh my god, Jaxon! It's gorgeous. Thank you." He steps closer and gives me a kiss on the cheek, a surprisingly chaste gesture that's actually very sweet.

"Just like you." He takes the necklace out of the box and places it around my neck, fastening it for me. When he steps in front of me again, he's looking at it, eyes intently focused on where the necklace lays against my chest... I think. "Perfect!" he declares, but now I'm actually thinking his gaze is lower than where the necklace is sitting because he whispers, "Promise me I get to share your bed tonight?" I nod, and he fist bumps the air. Idiot! Why do they all do this? Is it some kind of weird brother thing?

"Alright, you losers, let's get going," Jacinta says to everyone, breaking the emotional tension. The guys gather their jackets and put them on while I wait patiently, ready to walk out the door.

"Hang on." Declan halts us all before we can get far. "We probably should have had this conversation before we got ready, but I guess we all wanted to forget about the drama for the moment. How are we playing this?" He gestures between me and his brothers. We all look at each other, waiting for someone to speak first, so I bite the bullet.

"As far as I'm concerned, it's no one's business, but I have no problem claiming you all. I will officially be Thomas' date for this, but don't hold back from showing me affection. I'm all in, and the sooner people get used to it, the better."

Tears well in Jacinta's eyes, and she hastily dabs them away with her fingers as she nods her approval at me. The rest of the guys look like they're trying to decide if I'm serious or not, and my stomach starts to drop with panic. Maybe that's not what they want? Shit.

"Or we could hide it and deny it. Whatever you all want." I try to backtrack and save face, but if they go with that suggestion, I think I will die. I can't even meet their eyes, so I look down at my feet, suddenly finding my painted toenails incredibly fascinating. I hear a growl just before a pair of black shoes comes into view next to mine. A finger under my chin has me looking up into Kai's fierce gaze.

"Don't ever say that. We are all in too. None of us are ashamed, and we refuse to hide our relationship with you no matter how hard it might be until people move on to the next bit of hot gossip." Five more voices throw in their agreement and promises, and that lump in my stomach melts away.

"Okay then, shall we go buy an airline?" Thomas steps up to me and holds out his arm. Taking it, he escorts me out of the room while the others follow along behind us.

"Listen up," he says, and the others stop talking to hear him. "The only important people at this table tonight are Novak Dobrov and his wife Yalena. They are who we need to impress because they'll make the ultimate decision as to who gets the airline. It was a done deal between us, but his board overruled him and said he needed to consider Urie Sokolov and the RAE as well. Some of them weren't too impressed with the idea of an American coming in and buying the airline. At least Urie is European, or that's the opposition's argument, anyway. So he agreed to this dinner. In the end, if we lose, it really is no skin off my nose, outside of losing to that Russian asshole. We don't need the airline in order for our business to be successful, so let's go down there, be polite, and enjoy a lovely dinner with our girlfriend, sister, and friend. If by tomorrow we have another airline, great. If not, then we've had a nice trip to Prague." Thomas sounds like the consummate confident businessman, but I can feel how tense he is under his jacket. I don't know if it'll work, but I have to at least try to help him feel better.

"Now, don't let him get to you. He's going to try to provoke you into reacting badly, but you *cannot* fall for it. He means nothing, and she means less than nothing. If he brings her up, you can say how much you were hurt because loyalty is everything to your family, but that is it," I whisper, coaching him as best I can. "You have got this. You made sure she paid for his treachery, and one day he will get his. Don't you worry, karma always bites people in the ass. Look at my mom."

The elevator arrives, and we step in, moving to the back so all the others can join us. I feel him press a kiss to the top of my head, surprising me with his willingness to offer even that little display of affection while the others can see. "Thank you, honey," he says quietly. With that, the elevator doors slide shut.

Thomas

Holy hell, Harlow's dress looks amazing on her, and her beautiful eye-catching tattoos are on display. They're usually covered by her clothes, but thanks to the halter dress, her sleeve is now very visible. The splashes of colored butterflies are bright against the grayscale of the flowers. The tattoo on her torso peeks out from the plunging neckline of her dress, and although it's hard to make out all the details right now, I know it's a collage in honor of her love of zoo animals. I also know that there's a tattoo of mythical creatures, as well as a merman wearing my brother's face, under that dress. She looks incredible, and my pants feel a lot tighter than they were before.

On the walk down to the dinner, I'm a ball of

nerves. For the longest time, I never allowed myself to feel—real happiness, hope, or those "weaker" emotions like the anxiety rioting in my stomach right now—and it has nothing to do with winning or losing this airline or the fact that the Russian asshole is going to be there. What's truly driving my system wild is that today I went on a date with a beautiful woman, who not only declared herself all in with all of us, but she spent the elevator ride trying to coach me on how to deal with this situation. She was *worried* about me. That was her focus. Not the fancy dress or the jewels that Jaxon had given her or the fact that we were going to eat in one of the fanciest restaurants in Prague or that there were going to be a number of wealthy people at this dinner. Nope, she simply cared about how I felt and wanted to make sure I knew she was there for me.

You know, even though I was with Clarissa for over two years, I don't actually remember her ever asking me how my day was or showing any interest in anything I did, let alone concerning herself with my feelings. Now that I look back, everything was always about her, twenty-four-seven. Here I thought I was in a relationship with mutual equality, but it turns out it was as far from equal as you could get. I gave, and she *always* took.

I gave her my heart, soul, and everything she asked for, and she took it with her grabby hands while giving me nothing in return except for a pretty ornament on my arm and an occasional dead fish in the sack. I felt more from my and Harlow's brief kiss in the car than I felt the entire time I was with Clarissa. I don't understand how I could have been so blind. Apparently I needed a taste of something real to shine a light on just how artificial my ex was.

I actually feel like a million bucks with this woman on my arm despite knowing that I will share her with my brothers. Harlow has more than proven she has enough time and love to share with all of us. Honestly, I'm kind of amazed at how well my brothers are doing with this arrangement so far. I haven't heard an ugly word exchanged by anyone during this initial courtship, nor do I expect to hear any. Sure, we will have our arguments and will piss one another off, but having others in the relationship to vent to is only going to be a benefit, not a hindrance. And, well, after only a brief taste of her, I can't wait to see what make-up sex is like. That little sample is addictive, and I can see why my brothers' eyes do not stray even a bit.

A tug on my arm reminds me of where we are, and I realize we're at the entrance to the private dining room.

"Are you okay? Just say the word, and we will bust this joint if it's too much," Harlow fiercely whispers in my ear. I smile like an idiot. I can admit it. Besides the Summers, no one has wanted to stand up for me or protect me as much as this beautiful woman by my side. Now I just need to show her that I can keep this bullshit from breaking me, show her that I'm deserving of the care she wants to give me.

"Oh, baby, don't you worry about me. For the first time in a long time, I'm ready to play this game." I wink and then push the door open.

A host leads us over to the large table in the middle of the room that's fit for a royal banquet—one of the reasons this hotel was chosen. It's long enough to fit fifty people, but right now most of the arrivals are standing around, waiting for the signal to sit. I don't bother looking around to see who else is here; my focus is on the one person I am here to see.

Novak Dobrov, the owner of the airline I want, is an older gentleman who is ready to retire, but he and his wife were never able to have children, so they don't have anyone to pass his legacy on to. Instead of leaving the company to be run by a board, he's made the decision to sell it all so he and his wife can enjoy everything that the money they get for it will buy.

I spot them standing off to the side while the members of their board do their rounds, chatting up the various attendees. I know there are one or two other companies here to show their interest in the company, but none of them are on the level of Neighpalm Airlines or RAE.

I beeline straight to them with Harlow still

wrapped up next to me, and Novak's eyes light up when he sees us. His wife looks between me and Harlow with a slight lift of her eyebrows before she hides her reaction. It's not something I can't just shrug off, so it's no big deal. We knew we would get some kind of reaction, and considering what could have happened, that was mild.

"Mr. and Mrs. Dobrov, it's so lovely to see you again. Thank you for inviting us to dinner. May I introduce you to Harlow?"

"Thomas, my boy." Mr Dobrov's heavily accented English is jovial in tone. "None of this Mr. and Mrs. Please, it's Novak and Yalena, and it is so good to see you. It is us that are so very pleased that you could come on such short notice. I know we had planned to meet later in the week, but I'm afraid the board insisted." He shakes my hand before turning to Harlow. "And what a pleasure to meet you, Harlow." He shakes her hand with equal enthusiasm before letting the two women greet one another. Yalena is not as enthusiastic but still seems genuinely polite, which is a better reception than Harlow's gotten from most of the women we've forced her to spend time with. Now that that's settled, I introduce them to my siblings and Jace. "Thank you for allowing my family to attend this dinner. Dad sends his apologies, but he just couldn't get away at the moment." They all exchange pleasantries until Novak turns back to me with a frown.

"Yes, I was sorry to hear that Brad could not

make it, not to mention how the American media is dragging you through the mud over some ridiculous story." Before I can reply, Russian asshole number one steps up with a smug smile on his face and a blonde bimbo under his arm. He's a large man, not quite fat but not all muscle either, and he has a ruddy complexion. I always wondered what Clarissa had seen in him over me. The blonde on his arm looks bored, chewing away on her gum like it's the only thing keeping her from falling asleep. She looks like she may be twenty, tops. I guess Clarissa taking the fall and being incarcerated for crimes against the US wasn't enough for him to stay loyal to her.

"Surely those stories cannot be true. She is your sister, yes? But then I did not see her in a photo with you, so maybe it is only your brothers she prefers. *Shlyukha, kak ni kruti.*"

Yalena and Novak both gasp at the bold rudeness of his comment, and I feel Harlow stiffen next to me. Not that I really would've expected any differently, but their reactions confirm that whatever he said was far from polite. I may have the accent down, but I could never wrap my head around the language. I clench my fist, ready to punch this fucker out, but Harlow calmly puts her hand on my arm.

"I got this, babe," she tells me before turning to Urie. "*Ya luchshe budu shlyukhoy, chem trusom, pozvolyu zhenshchine rasplachivat'sya za svoi prestupleniya.*" She turns to his companion. *"Razve ty ne predpochel by imet' shest' krasivykh bogatykh muzhchin s bol'shimi chlenami?"*

The blonde looks us up and down, then shrugs her shoulders and nods. "Da."

The slimy Russian growls at this, his face filled with fury, and drags her away as Novak and Yalena laugh. "Oh, Harlow, I do like you. Come, let us eat." He gestures to the table, and we make our way over to it, Harlow and I being directed to sit across from our hosts.

Oli claims a seat on the other side of Harlow, and I hear him whisper to her, "What did you say?" I listen in, also curious to know.

She takes her napkin and places it in her lap, creating the picture of politeness that completely contrasts the words that come out of her mouth. "I said to him 'I would rather be a whore than a coward, letting a woman pay for his crimes.'"

"And what did you say to his companion that he got so upset about?" he pushes, and she blushes prettily, grabbing my hand and giving it a squeeze.

"It doesn't matter. I didn't mean how it sounded."

"But I want to know. Come on, Harlow. We won't be upset," Oli pleads, and she sighs.

"I said to her, 'Wouldn't you rather have six handsome rich men with big cocks?'." Oli is silent for a solid minute before he bursts out laughing.

"And she said yes. That's the limit of my Russian, but even I understood that." He turns to whisper in Holden's ear, and Harlow looks up at me, biting her lip with worry.

"You know I didn't mean it," she says quietly.

"So you don't think I'm handsome or that I have a big cock? I mean, I'm willing to take one for the team and show you if you would like." Her eyes widen in surprise, and I bring her hand up to my mouth, placing a kiss on it. "Yes, Harlow, I know you're not with us for the money, don't you worry." She sighs with relief before a smirk teases her lips.

"Maybe we could revisit the proof of the other thing later though." I groan as said cock hardens, pushing against the zipper of my pants. I turn to scold her, but of course I get a view of that cleavage that I had been trying to avoid looking at all evening. Now there's no chance of my dick ever going down. That creamy expanse of skin, the dress cupping those perfect breasts like I want my hands to be cupping them. I just want to nuzzle my nose against those erect nipples that the fabric of the dress does nothing to hide before taking them into my mouth and seeing if they taste like raspberries.

Her throat clearing has me looking up into the beautiful green eyes that are sparkling with amusement.

"How about we buy a company and then you can spend the night spouting odes to my breasts?" she says quietly.

"I said that out loud?" Wow, she really has got me rattled. I'm usually a vault.

"Yes, you did, and your accent gets thicker the hornier you are. Not gonna lie, that's sexy as fuck too." She squirms in the chair next to me.

Right. Let's buy an airline and get the fuck out of here.

The evening goes very smoothly, and when we all arrive back at the suite, we are the proud owners of a new airline. I think that asshole blew it from the moment he called Harlow a whore. Novak and Yalena loved her and were enthralled by her love of animals and abandoned houses. She so thoroughly charmed them both that she extracted a promise for them to come visit once they started traveling. She promised that she would show them how she teaches a stunt horse to rear on command.

It's late, and we only have a few hours before we need to check out and get to the plane, so we all say our goodnights and go our separate ways. Jaxon had already claimed dibs on sharing Harlow's bed, and I don't think either of us are quite there yet anyway. Okay, so maybe that's a lie. I'm totally there, but I need to learn to play fair with my brothers so I don't fight for it. With them being ahead in the game, so to speak, I'm the one who feels a tiny bit like an interloper, taking more of her attention away. So I'll let Jaxon have it without being a pouty brat about the situation. God knows he's going through an identity crisis right now, and if Harlow makes my little brother feel better, I won't deny him that TLC.

We're a weary bunch when we board the plane in the morning, bidding the crew hello. Jilly is bright and cheerful despite the early hour and informs us that she has breakfast ready for us once we hit cruising altitude. Nobody hangs around chatting. We're all ready to get home, so we quickly take our seats. Before we know it, we're in the air.

Once breakfast has been served and enjoyed by all of us, Jace and Jacinta disappear down to the back bedrooms. They had drunk entirely too much again last night, celebrating our win, and are both suffering their second morning of hangovers in a row. The rest of us hang out, chatting until I need to get up to use the bathroom. I head forward to the master suite and use the bathroom there, but when I finish up, wash my hands, and make my way back out, Veronica is sitting on the bed. She looks up at me with hope in her eyes, an emotion that's entirely misplaced if I have anything to say about it.

"Look, Veronica, I'm not sure how many times I have to tell you this, but it was a one-time thing. We told you then, and I'm reiterating it now. *Again.* If you have a work problem, then you need to take it up with your supervisors. You can't keep cornering me," I say, no longer giving a single fuck about whether or not I'm coming off as a little—or maybe more than a little bit—cold.

There's a flash of anger in her eyes as she stands up, hands on hips, and opens her mouth to say words that have my stomach sinking to my feet.

"I'm pregnant, and either you or Kai is the father."

Chuck

I'd had a rough day; Luke hadn't appeared for work this morning, and with Peter still gone, it left me with a lot of horses to deal with on my own. Thank god for Brad's stable manager Josh. He's been a godsend.

After learning Luke had disappeared the previous afternoon, with only Josh's mention of a mysterious phone call as some kind of evidence, I'd decided then and there that I was done with him and Peter. I was putting a job advertisement in the classifieds as soon as I got home that evening. But as Melinda and I sat down to dinner together, she suggested that maybe it was time for us to sell up and move west. The horses were almost always needed over there for movies, and Max was booking alot of stunt work with them, not to mention

Harlow's biological father living there and our bonus daughter's relationship with Brad's boys.

What incentive did we have left to stay on the East Coast? Especially considering this bullshit with the stalker situation, it was killing me to be so far away from my girls. Getting Harlow's messages and learning that we were also being watched wouldn't deter me from trying to be there for Harlow. Let the bastard, whoever he was, keep an eye on us in California.

We talked out the pros and cons and finally came to a decision: we were heading west. I still had to inform my parents of the impending move, but I was going to put that off as long as possible. By the time I went to bed, I was feeling good about our decision, so much lighter because I had one less thing to worry about.

When the phone rings, I'm dead to the world, so the sound of it has my heart racing like it always does when you have adult children and you get a call at an hour when they should be tucked up safe and sound in bed.

"Hello?" My cell phone illuminates the room, making the worry on Melinda's face all too clear.

"Mr. Boston, it's Detective Brown." Shit, that's the detective who gave us the news about Diane. I reach out for Melinda's hand and hold on tight, not ready to hear whatever he has to say. Did they learn something about her death? Has there been some kind of new threat against Harlow? Fuck, I need to actually listen to what he's saying.

I tune back in just in time to hear him ask, "Do you have a Luke West working for you?"

"Yes, I do, but he never showed up today." My pulse settles a little now that I know this isn't about either of the girls, but there's still a lingering sense of confusion. Sure, I'm Luke's boss, but what could he have done that would require them to call *me*?

"I'm sorry to have to tell you this, but a body washed up on the banks of the Connecticut River this morning. It had Luke West's ID in the wallet. We can't find any relatives, and your place is listed as his primary residence, so I was wondering if you could come in and identify him for us."

A wave of sadness washes over me. Luke was a strange and secretive kid, but I never thought he was suicidal. I say as much to the detective before agreeing to come in, feeling much too unsettled for comfort.

"I'm sorry for the confusion, but there is no doubt in my mind that this wasn't suicide," the detective tells me.

"Oh, why would you say that?" I ask him. It's not that I don't believe the man or trust his credentials, but to have someone you saw almost daily just disappear without warning—and reappear in circumstances you would have never expected—well, it feels a bit unreal.

The detective clears his throat, taking a pause that's both heavy and awkward at the same time.

"Well, Mr. Boston, the undeniable 9mm bullet hole in the middle of his forehead."

The end!!!!!

Thank you for reading!
I hope you enjoyed the book. It would be super awesome if you could leave a review wherever you bought it, because I love to hear what you thought of the story.

Want more of Harlow and the gang?
Pre order Book Five
Cherished Girl
On Amazon now

Want to keep up to date with new books coming soon? Sign up to my newsletter here
Newsletter

Another way to do that is to join me Facebook group. I drop teasers and giveaways in there all the time. Here's the link
Lexie's Ladygarden

Visit my webpage and check out reading orders and what else I've written.
www.lexiewinston.com

Acknowledgments

Thank you to all the normal crew this book wouldn't be possible without you all.

Michelle for your invaluable editing.

Emma for all the late night and early morning chats.

Infinity Book Designs for the cover

My beta team for being super awesome as usual.

Grace and Hope for being my rocks, long live the throuple.

Lastly to you the readers. The love that people have given the Neighpalm Industries Collective has absolutely blown my mind. Never in my wildest

dreams would I have thought that it would get the reception it has. So thank you to each and every one of you for taking a chance. Thank you to everyone who reviews and recommends it and thank you to all of you who take the chance and preorder the next one as soon as you've finished the last. You guys are the reason I can keep writing this story.
Until next time. Happy Reading
Xoxo

Lexie

Check out something else by me. A Sci-Fi reverse harem romance.
Apprentice
Galaxy Circus 1

Chapter One

"Miss Jenson, did you hear what I just said to you?" Mr. Ryding, the weaselly-looking lawyer, says to me from behind the large walnut desk. He's fidgeting with the papers in front of him, stacking them, picking them up, tapping them, and then placing them back on the desk in front of himself. While I sit there, waiting for him to say more, he straightens the pens in the holder to the right of him. Given he's done this all at least half a dozen times, it seems like he's doing everything in his power to avoid making eye contact with my very confused self.

"I'm sorry. I'm not sure I understand you. I received a letter from your office saying I have been bequeathed something. I was told that I must present myself in person to sign some papers in order to receive it. Now, you are *also* telling me it was from a grandfather I didn't even know existed, one who obviously didn't want me, as I spent the first eighteen years of my life in foster homes."

He looks up, briefly pausing his fidgeting. "Yes, that's correct. Though it's grandfathers. Plural."

Plural? I puzzle internally. *Never mind, I'll come back to that.*

"John, William, and Eric Adams are your paternal grandfathers, and it wasn't that they didn't want you." His shifty eyes soften briefly before he continues. "They weren't able to find you. Your parents were estranged from them, and they were not notified at the time of your parents' accident. When you were placed in foster care, they weren't in the States, making it even harder for word to come down the appropriate channels." He shuffles his papers again. "When they did eventually find out, John rushed back. Unfortunately, you'd been placed in the system and had your name changed, as per a request in your parents' will, by then. You'd disappeared and were well hidden. Due to the nature of their business, they decided that maybe you were better off. Their job required constant traveling, never settling in one place for very long. It was no place to raise a child, or so they thought. They believed you were safe and loved."

I scoff out loud at that one, hitting my limit of holding my tongue. Though I have to give the man credit. Despite his obvious nerves and my apparent skepticism, he soldiers on. "Otherwise, they would have claimed you immediately," he assures me.

"So, why am I finding out about this now? I'm assuming they're all dead, so why leave our estrangement until I had no chance of getting to know them?" I'm trying my best to keep my tone under control, but I'm honestly at a loss. There isn't a part of me that can reconcile these strangers leaving their granddaughter at the mercy of the system, name change or not. There had to be something terribly wrong with them, or maybe they thought there was something terribly wrong with me, if they'd chosen to stay away until we lost the chance to ever have a relationship.

The shifty look in his eyes is back, and the fidgeting obviously isn't cutting it since he gets up from his desk and starts to pace behind it. He marches back and forth in front of the big picture window which holds the view of the river his office backs onto. He stops, takes a deep breath, and turns to look at me.

"Well, actually, that's not quite true. Misters Adams have not passed on. They've decided to retire, and the family business may only pass down to a family member. You're the one that was chosen, so they contracted our firm to find you. It has taken quite a while, I can assure you."

"Excuse me?" I gasp. "Are you saying my grandfathers are alive and want to meet me?" As a little girl, I would have dreams of a relative swooping in to rescue me from the never-ending cycle of foster homes. I had finally given up around the age of thirteen. I wasn't one of those kids who were beaten or abused in care; I just never seemed to fit in. I was never really included or felt like I was one of the family. It would've been nice to know there was someone out there who wanted me.

Of course, my very skeptical nature decides this is too good to be true, turning my surprise into anger.

"Why the fuck am I dealing with a lawyer and not them directly? Can they not even be bothered, or are they too fucking chicken to face me themselves?" I can practically feel the steam escaping from my ears. It takes a lot to get me mad, but when I get there, you better watch out. Mr. Ryding swallows nervously and brings a finger up, trying to loosen his collar.

"Ah… but… They're…" he stammers. The man must be good at his job if he was able to track me down, which was apparently quite the feat, but he's horribly unprepared to deal with a woman's anger.

Taking a deep breath, I try to calm down. *Don't take it out on the lawyer, Lila. He's just the messenger.*

"Why me? I'm assuming there are other family members they could turn to?" I rub my eyes, already feeling a headache brewing. They've steadily been getting more frequent, and this meeting is not doing me any favors.

"Yes, well, no. There *are* other family members, but you are their only grandchild, and they've decided that it's time you join the family legacy. You are to be given the opportunity first. All the details are in the package." He sits back down at the desk and gestures to the stack of papers he'd been fidgeting with. "You're required to spend twelve months within the business, learning all the ins and outs. If, at the end of the twelve-month period, you're unwilling to continue, the business and the role of CEO and all it entails will pass on to the next eligible family member. You will carry on with life as if the previous twelve months had never really happened."

I stare at the package like it's a snake that's going to bite me. I just don't know what to think. Do I ignore it, sign it over now, and wash my hands of the whole debacle? Or do I take a leap of faith and at least meet the men that could be the best *or* the worst thing to happen to me?

"Can I have some time to think about this?" I ask. "It's quite a decision I need to make."

Mr. Ryding shakes his head. "I'm sorry, but this

decision needs to be made as soon as possible. Our firm has been looking for you for a while, and I'm afraid we're out of time. You need to be on a plane to London in two days' time. We're going to need an answer now."

It's my turn to start pacing. Jumping out of the chair I've been sitting in, I start stalking back and forth across the room. The pounding behind my eyes has intensified, and I rub my temples in an attempt to alleviate it. What to do? It's not like I have anything keeping me here. I don't really have friends, mainly acquaintances. My best friend and roomie is head over heels in love with her partner, so she'd be ok if I left. I have a dead-end job in a bar that pays crappy but keeps me busy. Looking at the facts of my life, as totally unimpressive as they are, I guess there's nothing specifically stopping me from going. I've always dreamed of adventures, feeling sure that there must be something better in store than the life I've been living.

"All right," I tell him, making the decision, "I'm in. Show me where to sign."

He goes to the stack of papers on the table and pulls some out. "You need to sign here, here, and here. One of them is a non-disclosure form. No matter what happens, from here on, you are bound by a confidentiality clause. Even if at the end of twelve months you change your mind, everything you see and do will be confidential, and there are some very harsh consequences if you break the clause. A plane ticket is also in the pack, in your name, with the details of your flight. You'll be met at the airport by a driver who will take you to where you need to be. For your peace of mind, you can tell people where you are going and why, but there is to be no sharing of any other details. It's actually a good thing that you don't have a huge circle of friends." I'm torn between surprise that he knows that fact and being insulted by the comment despite its truth.

"We've been looking for you for so long I wouldn't hesitate to say we know everything about you," he replies to my look, a little more defensively than I expected the nervous guy to manage.

"Yeah, ok, because that's not creepy or rude," I reply sarcastically.

I busy myself with signing papers, and by the time I'm finished, my hand aches and my head throbs incessantly. Gathering my copies of every-thing, I shove them in my hand bag; I'll read it all when I get home. "So what business have I just signed my life away to?" I ask Mr. Ryding, thinking this is probably something I should have asked *before* signing. Fuck, I'm an idiot. Why didn't I ask that first? I mentally slap my impulsive self.

"Have you heard of the Galaxy Circus?" he asks, slightly distracted with gathering all his copies of the paperwork.

I nod enthusiastically, feeling more upbeat than I have this entire meeting. "Oh yes, isn't that the circus that claims it has aliens as its performers? It pops up throughout the globe and is always sold out even though the schedule is too random for anyone to know where they'll be next. People have been trying to debunk them for years. I remember reading that PETA was trying to gain access to prove that their animals are mistreated." I laugh loudly, remembering how that particular situation worked out. Apparently, the circus claimed their animals were really shifters, a clever gimmick that allowed them some special dispensation and gave PETA no ground to stand on. Hey, if people were gullible enough to believe it, then that was their problem.

He looks at me, a strange glint in his eye. "Are they gullible or just looking to be entertained?" he questions, his words coming oddly close to the thought I hadn't spoken aloud. "Well, whether they're gullible or not is besides the point. It still attracts huge crowds when it does tour. It is one of the most popular circuses around, even outselling Cirque du Soleil despite having less shows each year."

My heart starts to beat rapidly as Mr. Ryding looks at me with an oily-looking grin, possibly the first time I've seen him smile since I walked in the door. "Miss Jenson, with the papers you signed, you just joined the circus."